The Wish Club

"Why would a ser⋯⋯⋯ng
with a bowl of wat⋯⋯⋯e.

"Why, if ye⋯⋯⋯as
about an important⋯⋯⋯,"
she told him, gigglin⋯⋯

Max studied her face. He had never kissed her. He'd wanted to often enough, but her innocence and her trust in him gave him the strength to resist—so far.

Her gaze didn't waver from his, but she lifted her right hand, the tips of her thumb and forefinger touching, and blew sofly until a bubble trembled between them. Sunlight stroked its rainbow colors. Her generous mouth remained pushed out in a soft "ooh."

He felt his own lips part.

"Make a wish," she whispered. "Go on, Max, make a wish and blow t'bubble away."

❦

DISCOVER THE PLEASURES OF STELLA CAMERON . . . IN BOOK AFTER BOOK

"Spellbinding. . . . Once again, Stella Cameron
has given us a unique, creative,
sensuous romance."
—*Rendezvous* on *Wait for Me*

"Will appeal to those who devour Amanda
Quick's romances as well as a reader who simply
enjoys a bit of a dark, ancient secret blended with
passion, witty dialogue, and humor."
—Kathe Robin, *Romantic Times*, on
Dear Stranger

"One of the best books you will read all year.
Great book from start to finish . . . outstanding!
5 Bells!!!"
—*Bell, Book, and Candle* on *Dear Stranger*

"Cameron leaves you breathless, satisfied . . . and
hungry for more."
—Elizabeth Lowell

"Her plots and subplots are wonderfully dark and
devious with a bleak atmosphere that heightens
all tensions and dangers to the shrieking point."
—*Affaire de Coeur* on *Bride*

"A marvelously talented historical author."
—*Romantic Times*

Books by Stella Cameron

Only By Your Touch

His Magic Touch

Fascination

Charmed

Bride

Beloved

Breathless

Pure Delights

Sheer Pleasures

True Bliss

Dear Stranger

Wait For Me

Stella Cameron
The Wish Club

WARNER BOOKS EDITION

Copyright © 1998 by Stella Cameron
All rights reserved.

Cover design by Diane Luger
Cover illustration by Michael Deas

Warner Books, Inc.

A Time Warner Company

WARNER BOOKS

A Time Warner Company

WARNER BOOKS EDITION

Cover design by Diane Luger
Cover illustration by Michael Racz

Warner Books, Inc.
1271 Avenue of the Americas
New York, NY 10020

Visit our Web site at
http://warnerbooks.com

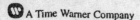 A Time Warner Company

Printed in the United States of America

First Printing: June, 1998

10 9 8 7 6 5 4 3 2 1

For Jerry, Matthew, Clement, Claire, Kirsten, and Bryan.
You remind me that life is here, and now, and full of joy.

The Wish Club

Scotland, Spring 1834. On Kirkcaldy land.

Max was the only name he knew was truly his. Just Max. Nothing more. He'd become Max Rossmara because a good man had rescued a desperate boy destined for a London workhouse, or worse, and given him a family name to call his own. He was nobody, not really, yet he'd been made part of a great family tradition, and he was expected to bear its standard high.

Did he really want to call that standard his own?

If he took it up with his entire heart and bore it with the weight of all it meant, might he pay for the shelter of its privilege with his soul?

Yes.

Would he do so anyway?

Answering yes again would likely cost him what he loved most.

He scanned the wild countryside he'd come to love so well. Overshadowing the surrounding landscape, Castle Kirkcaldy rose atop its mound, a massive, many-towered, and castellated bastion, harsh against a crystal blue spring sky.

Presently the home of his father's older brother, Arran, Marquess of Stonehaven, Kirkcaldy had been held by the noble family of Rossmara for generations.

And Max, the boy who had once picked pockets in London's Covent Garden, had been given the right to move about that castle with as much freedom as if he had been born there.

In its sharp, gorse-scented snap, the air bore the memory of winter. The breeze tossed his hair and stung his eyes. He turned his back on Kirkcaldy's hill to regard instead the simple croft where Robert and Gael Mercer lived with their children, Kirsty and Niall. She was inside—Kirsty was inside. He knew because he always knew when she was near. And she would feel his presence soon enough, if she hadn't already.

Robert Mercer was also near, watching from the chicken coop, while pretending not to watch, and worrying about his beloved daughter and what he perceived as the danger of her being hurt by a man above her station.

Max could never hurt his sweet Kirsty, not if there was a choice. And the choice was his unless he allowed that choice to be taken from him.

His boots making no sound, he entered the croft.

The flood of feeling surging into every part of him grew stronger each time he saw her, and he was not fool enough to pretend that those feelings were entirely of the higher nature he'd have sworn to as a boy.

The boy had become a man.

With her back to him, Kirsty bent over the table in what served as the Mercers' rude kitchen. She hummed and plunged her hands into a bowl of water.

Max walked softly across the earthen floor of the croft until he stood behind her.

Sunlight through the open door made a halo of the fair hair she wore in long braids pinned on top of her head. Curls sprang at the nape of her thin neck. The soft, vulnerable skin there brought Max another rush of emotion, and need.

The stuff of her blue-and-white-checked dress was cheap, but on Kirsty it looked fresh and pretty. Slightly made, she was neither tall nor short, and although she didn't have her mother's red-gold hair, there was much about Kirsty that reflected her pretty, fragile mother's aura of sensitive inner strength.

He could not give her up.

Max stopped. He couldn't loosen the fists he'd made, or fight down the swell of tenderness that mixed with anger in his breast.

"Master Max," Robert Mercer had said not ten minutes earlier, doffing his battered woolen bonnet and winding it in work-scarred hands. *"It's no' my place t'say as much, but ye'd be doin' me a favor if ye left my lassie alone the now. Ye're no' a laddie anymore, a laddie who wants t'play bairns' games. Ye're a gentleman. A gentleman, and kin t'the lairds o' this great estate. My lassie's—my lassie's no' for the likes o' ye."*

What Robert Mercer had meant was that he feared Max would use his daughter as other men of means sometimes used humble young females. He also meant he'd guessed that a childhood friendship had grown into something more, something so much more, and that he didn't approve any more than Max's own father would approve. Well, what he and Kirsty shared was more than a childhood friendship, but less than Max longed for it to be.

A gentleman? He was a bastard. He was Struan Rossmara, Viscount Hunsingore's adopted son.

"I feel ye sneakin', Max Rossmara," Kirsty said without looking at him. "And I feel ye standin' there, starin' at me."

Of course she did. They had often confided how they felt

close even when they were actually far apart. He hadn't told Kirsty how he sometimes reached for her in the night, and awoke expecting to find her in his arms.

"Ye're troubled." She held her soapy hands out of the water and twisted to see him.

He smiled, easy enough to do when he looked into her startlingly blue eyes. "Not a bit of it, Miss Mercer. Not troubled at all. Only puzzled. Why would a sensible girl of sixteen be playing with a bowl of water for no reason at all?"

She grew a little pink and used a forearm to push strands of hair away from her face. "There's a reason for everythin', Mr. Rossmara. Why, if ye'd eyes t'see, ye'd know I was about an important creation."

Her voice, a trifle husky, sounded as if laughter couldn't be far away. "I would, would I?" he said, going to her side and bending low over the water. "Are there kelpies in there? Are you bathing kelpies?"

"Noo," she told him, giggling. "I'm makin' bubbles. An' dinna laugh, or ye'll have me cryin'."

Max straightened slowly and studied her face. Intelligence shone there, and how well he knew it. He was the older by years, yet she'd badgered him to teach her to read well, to learn her numbers, to study whatever he studied— and between the two of them she'd often been the quicker to comprehend. She'd attended the village school but never been satisfied with what little there was to be learned there.

He had never kissed her. He'd wanted to often enough, but her innocence and her trust in him gave him the strength to resist—so far. Would they never kiss? Never know even that small intimacy?

"Whist?" she said, frowning a little. "Ye're thinkin' if ye'll laugh at me?"

He inclined his head and allowed himself the pleasure of staring at each of her features. "I'll never laugh at you," he said. He looked at her mouth and knew he must not kiss her, for if he did he'd surely lose all power to make the decisions, take the actions he must pursue for both of them.

Her gaze didn't waver from his, but she lifted her right hand, the tips of her thumb and first finger touching, and blew softly until a bubble trembled between them. Sunlight stroked its rainbow colors.

Her generous mouth remained pushed out in a soft, "ooh."

He felt his own lips part.

"Make a wish," she whispered. "Go on, Max, make a wish and blow t'bubble away."

"A wish?"

"Aye. We should always have somethin' t'wish for. Haste ye, before it pops."

He closed his eyes and blew, and felt minute droplets scatter his face.

"What did ye wish for?"

"I thought you weren't supposed to tell."

Her smile wobbled a little. "Mayhap it'd be all right for the two o' us t'know? If we kept t'secret between us, d'ye think?"

He thought that being twenty-two and in love with sixteen-year-old Kirsty was the sweetest, yet the most painful thing in the world. "I think it would be all right."

"Tell me, then." The top of her head reached his chin. She'd inherited her mother's light skin and freckles. The end of her nose tipped up just a little. "*Tell* me," she begged.

"I wished for time to stand still. Right now. I wished to be standing here with you—looking at you—forever."

Her smile fled, and her throat jerked as she swallowed. "I see."

She knew.

"Ye've come t'say ye're leavin' again."

"For a few months. My father and Uncle Arran want me

to study crop rotation on the Yorkshire properties. The yields are higher there, and we want to improve them here."

"Yes." Nodding, she bowed until he couldn't see her face anymore.

He ought to say something about it being time for them to see less of each other, about how she should think about looking for a husband, but he said, "You'll read those books I brought for you? So that we can talk about them when I get back?" And he thought he would die if he ever had to see her with another man and know that man was her husband.

"I'll read them," she said.

He heard tears in her voice now, and said, "Will you make a wish before I go?"

Silently she dipped her hand into the water again, swished it around, and raised her joined finger and thumb to blow. Then she closed her eyes tightly, and he saw her lips move.

The bubble separated from her fingers and floated toward the roof.

"And what did you wish for, Kirsty?"

Her arms fell to her sides. She pressed her lips tightly together and stood quite still. Her eyes glittered.

"Oh, Kirsty." Not caring who might come, who might see—or that he must find a way to let her go—Max enfolded her in his arms and held her close. "My Kirsty. Please don't cry."

She shuddered, but slowly returned his hug. "I wished for t'same as ye. I want too t'stay here like this. I never want it t'end."

"Sounds as if we've one mind, then," he told her. "We ought to form a club for people who think alike."

"Aye, a club o' two." She nudged her sharp chin into his chest. "A club for wishin'."

His smile, the smile she couldn't see, was bitter. A man and a girl could have their wishes, couldn't they? At least they could keep those.

Max said, "A wish club."

Chapter One

Scotland, Summer, 1842.

W hat manner of man conspired to be daily in the company of a woman he wanted, but should not, could not, *would* not have?

Max Rossmara. He was just such a man—a man who loved without hope, had loved without hope for more than eight years.

And the damnable part of it all was that, although she'd learned to guard her feelings well, he was almost certain she loved him, too.

Kirkcaldy lands were beautiful in summer. He'd all but forgotten just how beautiful. Or perhaps, since he'd been denied Kirsty's company, he'd stopped seeing them as they were. He noticed them again now, now as he waited to see her. Beyond the windows of his spacious study in the castle's Eve Tower, the undulating hills were soft green-gold, dusted with wildflowers, the precise fields separated by hedgerows where bright vines entwined with scrubby bushes. He didn't have to walk through the grass to smell its warm fragrance, or lift his face to the sky to feel the late-afternoon sun's warmth. He had only to remember walking just so, and lifting his face just so, as he had with Kirsty when they'd wandered those hills too long ago—yet not so long that the poignant memories failed to stab at his heart.

In the name of opportunity—hers—he would try to bring Kirsty Mercer here, to his very side, to install her at Kirkcaldy permanently. That was his motive, wasn't it? To better

Kirsty Mercer's position by exposing her to a situation where she might once more use her excellent mind? It had to be the motive. After all, there could be no benefit to himself.

She would be here, in this study, every day, in this study and close to him rather than engaged as an underling to the young Stonehavens' tutor.

She would sleep within the castle walls at night, rather than trudge home to sleep beneath her father's poor roof.

And she would advance herself considerably.

These were chances she would be foolish to refuse. Kirsty wouldn't refuse them because she was levelheaded and would see how . . .

Damn it all, but he could at least be honest within the secrecy of his own conscience, couldn't he? Hah, but the question of how honest he could be with himself was a thorny one, and no doubt one that festered at the root of all that plagued him in the dark hours of his too-private nights.

He knew what was said of him, how there were those who feared his temper and avoided him. And he knew his own family worried about him, but at least they had the wit to leave him be when he was unfit company. A man had a right to his anger, and the manner in which he dealt with that anger.

Even in summer the rooms within the castle were cold. A fire crackled in the fireplace. Max vaguely acknowledged the sound but found no comfort in it.

The anger was evil, and he knew as much. It had not always been so, this blackness that descended. *Rage.* That was the name of his affliction. He raged within himself, and, on blessedly rare occasions, without. That was when he knew he must keep his own company.

Anger was his affliction. Deprivation had infected him with such an ill, being deprived of the love of the only woman he would ever truly desire.

Forgetting her had proven impossible. Years of following his father's instructions to avoid her had only led him to malignant desperation. If he could do nothing more than look upon her as often as he might, then so be it. That much he would grab for a salve to his pathetic soul, the soul he had not the courage to heed because to do so could mean severance from everything else that was part of the life that had become his.

A thousand glimpses of her had not helped put her from his mind. True, she was almost always at some distance and engrossed in her work. But there had been those moments when their eyes had met. No, his feelings for her had not dimmed. In those minute visual exchanges there were fleeting messages which burned inside him: *Only think of what might have been. Think of what we have lost. I hold your heart within me, Kirsty.* And in her eyes he imagined he read: *You turned away from what we had. You promised you would come for me, but when you came, you ignored me. Now we must be as strangers.*

At this very moment she was on her way to see him. Timing the delivery of his message with care, he'd made sure she would be preparing to depart the castle for the day when she received his summons. Currently the tutor and her pupils were away, would be away for some weeks, and Kirsty would be filling her days with mending and other tasks set by for such times. With the exception of his uncle, Arran, the family was visiting relations in Cornwall. They'd gone together with Max's own parents and his brother and sister by adoption. His father, Struan, would make sure everyone was settled at Franchot Castle, home of their old friends, the Duke and Duchess of Franchot; then he would also return to Kirkcaldy, where he and Max's mother made their home a few miles from the castle, in the extraordinary, whimsical building that had once been the hunting lodge. Arran would go to Cornwall to bring the women and children back. Max was to have made the journey south with the rest but had excused himself, pleading the need to tend to pressing estate matters.

He'd lied.

Arran knew as much, and Max suspected his father had guessed, too. The onus of proving there was nothing for anyone to fear from his plan for Kirsty would be on his own head. Father thought her an exemplary young woman—as long as she lived within her station. Arran was very fond of the Mercers, but Max didn't know how his uncle viewed any prospect of a friendship between his nephew and a crofter's daughter.

Shaking his head, resting an elbow on a high windowsill and massaging the back of his neck, Max congratulated himself on the ability to laugh at himself, even if that laugh was derisive. The truth was that he'd finally given in to his own weakness. The rest of the truth, that which he would continue to fight, was that he needed more from Kirsty Mercer than to look at her, to hear her voice, perhaps to feel the accidental brush of her hand against his.

The devil take him, for he was a bounder.

There was already no drawing back from the course he'd taken today, not unless he wished to confuse her even more than he had already confused her.

There had never been any hope for them.

Max let his head bow deeply. Convention was pathetic, yet convention bound him, bound them both. In the name of convention he'd been persuaded that to pursue Kirsty would be cruel, cruel to her, and disastrous for himself.

Lucky Max. Max, the man who, as a wild ragamuffin boy, had been rescued from the gutter and presented with a silver spoon to which he had no right. And now that silver spoon was choking him.

A tap sounded at the door, and the elderly butler came in. "Miss Mercer's here, sir," Shanks said, sniffing, his thin, beaked nose elevated. "I've brought her in as you said." His bald skull glistened. Apart from becoming even thinner, somewhat more stooped, and increasingly disapproving of almost everything, he seemed unchanged from when Max had first come to Kirkcaldy as a lad.

"Thank you, Shanks," Max said automatically. "Please make sure we aren't disturbed."

The man lowered his eyes and stood aside to admit Kirsty.

Once the door closed Max was certain he'd made a horrible mistake. He should have kept to his promise of some years earlier and made sure he and Kirsty were never alone together in the same space again.

Composed, her head held high, she regarded him with suitable deference, suitable but for the trace of bright question in her eyes.

He looked back, but could not summon a smile. To stand just so seemed a painful pleasure. Each second, each word from now on would take them from this point where neither harm nor good had been done, to . . . Where would they go from here—if anywhere?

Words crowded forward. All the wrong words. *You are as much a part of these beautiful hills as you ever were, Kirsty Mercer. I have tried not to see you, to really see you. And while I would not look at you, I could not look at the hills. Take off your bonnet so I may see your blond hair closely. May I touch your hair? Your eyes are unchanged. Beautifully clear and the most brilliant blue I ever saw. Once I wondered if I should ever kiss your mouth. I still wonder. So soft. And your skin—the freckles are there, a sprinkling— and a faint glimmer as if a bloom of silver were dusted over your cheeks.*

He drew in a great breath and settled his features in an austere mode. If she had touched him, he could not feel her more acutely. His own skin, his body, felt open, exposed, raw in the way that wounded tissue felt raw.

A curtsy, her curtsy, caught him unawares, and he flinched. She bobbed a curtsy and dipped her head.

Natural grace.

Max cleared his throat and walked around his desk to pull a small leather wing chair forward. "Sit down, please, Kirsty," he said formally. "I'm glad you could come."

"Thank ye." She sat with ease enough, and folded her thin, pale hands in her lap. Her simple, gray cotton dress was unrelieved but for a high, white-lace collar and matching cuffs. With none of the usual feminine fluffing or smoothing of skirts, she settled and looked at him direct.

A club for two. A club for wishin'. Long ago. Only a memory.

She hadn't changed, not really. Devoid of any paint, her face glowed from the fresh air. The bonnet she wore was of straw, of unremarkable style, and lacking in adornment.

Kirsty Mercer needed no adornment.

"Ye asked me t'come," she said, her eyes steady, but no longer showing anything of what she might feel.

Max pushed back his coat and shoved his hands into his pockets. Already his rehearsed speech sounded ridiculous in his mind. "How are you?"

"Well, thank ye. And yoursel'?"

"I'm very well, thank you very much."

She nodded, and took a deep breath that raised her small breasts inside the stiffened bodice of her dress. Her waist was tiny. How thin she'd been as a child, and a girl. Then, before his eyes, the coltishness had softened to slender, gracefully gentle curves.

"Ye sent for me, sir."

Sir. The urge to remind her that he'd been "Max" wasn't easily quelled.

"Mr. Shanks said ye were insistent. Ye sounded angry, so he said. I hope I've no' failed in my duties."

"Shanks is a fool," Max replied. "If the marquess weren't

so wedded to tolerance, he'd have let the man go years ago. Of course you haven't failed in your duties. How could you?"

"I dinna know, sir. I just thought—"

"Well, you thought wrong. And I'm surprised at your faulty reasoning. You were always sharp of mind, Kirsty— too sharp—" *Stop, you fool.* He threw up his hands and sighed, and went to sit on the edge of his desk. "Forgive me. I'm troubled. I shouldn't allow those troubles to shorten my temper. Not with you. Never with you." His tongue would give him away yet.

Her expression became intent, so intent he felt an unaccustomed discomfort before her scrutiny. A slight movement brought his attention to her hands. No longer carefully relaxed in her lap, the fingers were curled into her skirts.

This was going badly.

"It's been a long time since you and I were children together, Kirsty." What was there to lose by being direct? "The time seems to have flown. But then, childhood does fly, doesn't it?"

That shimmer on her skin—so familiar—like dew on flowers. And her full lips were as pink as ever, her chin as pointed, her nose as charmingly tilted. Her pale brows winged upward slightly.

"It's no' so long ago," Kirsty said quietly. "There's moments when it seems no more than an hour past."

"Our childhood?" he pressed, unwisely, he knew.

"Childhood," she said tersely.

Max swallowed, then cleared his throat. "This was beautiful country to grow up in."

"It's beautiful no matter when, sir. The most beautiful place in the world." She rolled her r's softly. Now she did not look into his face.

"Hm." His lauded way with words had deserted him. All he wanted was to move nearer to her, to observe her more minutely. "Your family?" he asked, pushing upright from the desk and leaning over her.

"They're all verra fine, thank ye," Kirsty said. "They'll be wonderin' where I am soon enough."

"Your routine never varies, then? The hours when you come and go? That must become tedious to one with so free a spirit."

She inclined her head and looked up at him, and he saw his Kirsty in the firm set of her mouth, the quizzical pulling together of her brows. "Routine's no' a bad thing. For the likes o' us it can be a comfort."

"The likes of you?"

"Simple folk of no particular importance."

The urge to argue was automatic, but he was wasting time. If he wasn't careful, Arran might arrive for his daily consultation. Most men in his uncle's position would expect Max to wait upon him. A musical composer, and an intensely private man, Arran preferred to come to Max, and to come when he was ready.

"Take off your bonnet." Instantly aghast both at what he'd said and the abruptness of it, he smiled and hoped he tempered his inappropriate behavior.

Kirsty said, "I'm ready t'away home, sir."

"Presently you're with me. I have matters to discuss with you, and I should like you to be comfortable."

"I'm comfortable enough," she said, and got up so abruptly that she startled him.

Edging past him to do so, she went to the window and stood on tiptoe to look out through leaded panes bowed with age. She held the stone sill.

The gray dress might as well be blue and white. The sight of her took him immediately back to that day in her parents' croft. He had hugged her, and she had returned that hug. And they had never touched again.

Max opened his mouth to breathe.

In most ways she was no different from the sixteen-year-old he'd left at her mother's kitchen table that day. Her straight back was as narrow, her air still that magical mixture of fragility and lissome strength. Kirsty was magical.

"I've no' seen the land from here before," she said. "I wonder ye'd choose t'work here."

Mesmerized, he walked behind her, but rather than look through the window, he looked down at the curls that escaped her bonnet at the nape of her neck. No, she was hardly changed at all.

"I'd have chosen a different place meself," she told him.

"You don't like it here?"

"Och, aye, I do, o' course I do. It's verra fair. But I've a notion I'd no' do my work, I'd be moonin' t'be out there."

Max raised a hand, but stopped himself from touching her. His fingertips hovered so close he felt the warmth of her. He closed his fist and flyaway hairs floated free of her curls to greet his knuckles. His skin stung with the need to put his hands on her, to feel her against him.

A salve to his soul? He barely contained a bark of laughter. More likely she would become as salt in a million open wounds he bore, yet he would take the pain gladly.

"I see you, y'know, Kirsty," he said, when he could speak again. "Often."

She stood quite still.

"I mean, I've noticed you about the castle from time to time."

Her fingers whitened where they gripped the windowsill. "Aye, sir, and I've noticed ye from time t'time, too. It's no' so big a place that a body can disappear."

"Oh, I think a body could very well disappear if he or she chose. My uncle is only seen when he chooses."

"Your Uncle Arran—the marquess, that is—is a wonderful man. His music's so beautiful it fair breaks my heart t'hear it."

"Of course—"

"My mother and father think him the best there is. An' there's never been a better husband and father than t'marquess."

"True," Max said, smiling a little. He'd forgotten how the Mercers worshiped Arran, who was a champion to his tenants. "Arran and Grace are—"

"They care about everyone, and if they think themselves better than any, then they hide it well. There's none who'll tell ye otherwise."

"I'm sure—"

"O' course some say the more a body's sure o' himself, the less he takes himself away from the common folk, and puts on airs and thinks himself great in the eyes of God and man."

Max sensed a tightening in her slight body. He felt she had chastised him for what she perceived as his arrogance. He wanted to say, *I've hurt you. I've gone on and on hurting you. But I've hurt myself, too, and it has all been because I feared for you, Kirsty Mercer. True, I wanted to do what would please my father, but even more I didn't want to subject you to a life you were never meant to lead.*

"I'd really best be on my way." She dropped from her toes and turned away from the window.

When she turned, she confronted his chest. She gasped and stepped sideways. "They'll worry about me."

"The children are old enough not to need a nursemaid," Max remarked, and silently cursed himself for his awkwardness. "I refer to the Stonehaven children. Lady Elizabeth is eighteen, older than you were when we . . ." So much for prepared speeches. "She's a young woman, and Niall's only two years younger."

Kirsty threaded her fingers together at her waist, and said, "The marquess and marchioness feel strongly that their children not be sent away t'school too early."

"The marchioness feels strongly. And the marquess—well—Niall will go to Edinburgh in the autumn. He must. Elizabeth should have made her season this year. She will do so next year."

"There's still Master James," Kirsty said. "He'll no' be away so verra quickly."

Max clasped his hands behind his back and paced to the fireplace. The room smelled of old leather books, and polish, the scuttle of coals on the hearth, and brass polish. And it smelled faintly of the sweet woodruff that was Kirsty's own scent.

"The marchioness will not want her bairn t'leave her yet. She'll have him stay at least as long as she's had the young viscount with her."

He had already said too much on that subject. Rather than lead her to be open to what he intended to suggest, he was managing to frighten her into thinking she might be about to lose her place because she wasn't needed.

"Do you still read?" he asked her suddenly, swinging to face her, and pacing back across the room. "And take interest in worldly matters?"

She blinked, the tips of her gold lashes catching a shimmer from the sun's lowering rays. "O'course I still read," she said, frowning. "How would a body ever learn to read and then not read?"

"Some do."

"Then they dinna know what they waste."

"And the worldly matters? Do you follow what happens?"

"Yes." A worried shadow entered her eyes. "I only deal with the simplest of areas of instruction, sir. But I know I'm competent in my tasks."

"Naturally. I taught you a great deal myself, remember."

She became quite pink. "Indeed. And I thanked ye for it

often enough. Or I did when there were times when I could speak t'ye. I thank ye again now."

"I don't want your thanks," he told her shortly. Why could he not control such sharp rejoinders? "How about your numbers? Have you had reason to use them?"

"Oh, yes. Miss Lamenter prefers that I instruct the young masters in that subject while she's about Lady Elizabeth's watercolors and the like. And I teach them . . ." Her voice faded.

"It's all right, Kirsty. I shan't chastise Miss Lamenter, or mention that you've been doing her work. In her position I should have done the same thing."

"May I go now, please?"

"No."

"Thank you . . . No?"

"No. No, I think you shall stay exactly where you are, miss. I have a good deal to discuss with you about the plans I've made for you."

An even deeper shade of pink washed her cheeks. "There is talk about your—" She stared at him. "Ye never used t'be so sharp o' tongue."

"Talk about my what, Kirsty?" He contrived to appear only vaguely interested.

"I . . . Oh, I dinna know."

"Don't you?" He did, but he wouldn't press her. Rather he would set about proving his detractors wrong—if he could manage to change himself. "Kindly take a seat again and be comfortable." Surely with Kirsty near he would become his old self.

"My family—"

"I took the liberty of arranging for a message to be taken to them."

"Did ye now?" The words were tart, but weakly delivered. "It might have been nice if ye'd told me as much when I arrived."

He bowed. "You're right. Forgive me, please. We might as well be frank. This is no easier an interview for me than for you. Neither of us forgets that we were once . . . We were childhood friends and companions."

The corners of her mouth turned down in a sardonic smile. "Another age. I remember o'course, but I've too much t'do to think o' foolish things."

They both knew they were dealing with deep discomfort. He refused to believe she considered their years of being inseparable allies as "foolish." "Come then," he said, standing by the wing chair. "Let us continue."

Soft skirts swishing, she did as he asked.

"You do agree that your duties with the young Stonehavens are growing less demanding?"

"Aye." She looked up at him, and he saw concern in her eyes.

He could bend over her and kiss her. He could kneel beside her and take her in his arms.

And she could shriek and rush from the room.

Max crossed his arms and returned to sit on the edge of his desk. The fire hissed. The flames sent a sheen over the leather bindings of books that crowded the walls in untidy disarray.

He glanced at the portrait of his sister, Ella, above the mantel and wished she were here to advise him in person. By letter she'd told him she applauded his decision to approach Kirsty, but since Ella was in the very late stages of her third pregnancy, she could not travel.

"Ella's well?" Kirsty asked, startling Max. "And Saber, and the wee ones?"

"Oh, yes." Ella was his biological sister. They'd had the same mother but had never been certain as to the identity of their father.

"You think I'm—" Kirsty paused for breath "—I'm likely

to be let go here? If ye know, I'd appreciate knowin', too. We're no' poor, o'course, but what I earn does help, and—"

"That's not why I asked you to come." Damn his insensitive, bombastic bumbling. "I want you to work for me."

Her hands stilled in her lap. The pink drained from her cheeks.

"You have a most competent mind, Kirsty, and I have need of a competent mind to assist me in the complicated task of running this estate."

She stared at him so long he wondered if she understood at all. Then she looked around the room. "Runnin' the estate? I'm no' qualified t'help wi' any such thing, and ye know it well."

"I know that you learn more quickly than any man or woman I know. You learn more quickly than I do."

"Your assistant?"

"Yes. I would instruct you in your duties, and you'd soon become indispensable to me. I should particularly appreciate your taking over the task of running the estate office, dispensing wages, documenting needs and complaints."

"A woman in such a job?" she said, obviously to herself rather than to Max. "There's never been such a thing."

"It's past time there was."

Her eyes snapped into focus. "Why me? Why would you choose me?"

Because I want you with me. I want an excuse to see you every day. And he wanted more, but that could never be, so he would take what he could get.

"I'm choosing you because I consider you the best candidate."

"There are men who have worked for you, and for Caleb Murray before you, who are more than capable."

"But not nearly as capable as you, nor as deserving as you of the chance to better yourself."

"To better myself," she said quietly. "Now ye care about my betterin' myself?"

"I've always considered your welfare, Kirsty."

"Have ye?"

She did resent his abandonment of her. That should probably annoy him, but instead it brought him a sense of triumph. He was a shallower man than he'd ever dreamed.

"Her ladyship would no' be pleased if I left her service and her not thinkin' of relieving me o' my duties yet."

Max had anticipated this argument. "I shall speak to Grace myself. She will be understanding. She always wants the best for her people."

"Miss Lamenter—"

"Miss Lamenter will have to become accustomed to executing her own duties."

Kirsty popped to her feet again. "I'd as soon remain in my present position. But I thank ye for the fine offer."

"You will accept my offer."

"If ye'll excuse me."

"I won't excuse you. I need you."

"The children still need me."

"You're afraid of me."

"I—" She pulled absently on her bonnet ribbons, pulled them undone, and the bonnet slipped sideways. "—I am no' afraid o' ye. I'm afraid o' no man."

Her agitation brought him far more satisfaction than it ought. "Then you're afraid of yourself."

She took the bonnet all the way off. "What can ye mean? I'm no' afraid o' doin' the work. I could do it well enough, better'n most, but it'd no' be seemly."

"Explain."

Her hair was as fair as ever, and as shiny. He'd once promised himself the pleasure of running his fingers through that hair. That could never be, but he would not deprive himself of the pleasure of considering such an experience.

"Explain yourself, Kirsty," he insisted. "I don't recall *seemly* as a word you would have been likely to use."

"I'm surprised ye remember aught about me, Mr. Rossmara. And I'll not explain myself further, if ye don't mind. It willna do. That's that."

"And I say it will do, and that it *shall* do. I have decided you are to become my assistant."

"Ye dinna own me, sir!"

She had always had the power to silence him.

"Ye may have the reputation as the hardest man in the land, and the man wi' the meanest temper, but I'll no' be frightened by ye."

His throat turned dry. Blood pounded at his temples. "What do you know of my temper? Have I ever been less than civil to you?"

She shook her head.

Feeling his hands tremble, he made fists. "Tell me exactly what you've heard—what lies?"

"I should have held my tongue."

"*Tell* me."

"Verra well!" She blinked rapidly. "If ye insist. Ye've a roarin' temper, Max Rossmara. It never used t'be so, but it only gets worse they say. They say ye're violent wi' it now. There, I've told ye."

A slow, deep breath didn't calm him. Sweat broke out on his brow. "I won't argue the point. But I will tell you that you have no need to concern yourself with my humors. All you have to do is what I tell you to do, and we'll manage remarkably well."

Kirsty's mouth fell open. She closed it, swallowed loudly, and said, "Och, there's a great deal I could say t'ye, but I'll no' say more. The arrogance o' men of certain stations fair takes a woman's breath away."

He smiled. He couldn't help but smile. Her ire stiffened her back and straightened her shoulders. Her eyes flashed, and he didn't have to look at her feet to know they were firmly planted.

"As you've said, I don't own you, Kirsty Mercer." *More's the pity.* "But I admire you. I admire your spirit, and I admire your potential. If I lose my temper, it's because I'm oppressed. Will you have mercy on a man in need and help me? Will you save me from the crushing responsibilities of a position grown so huge and so far-reaching in its implications? Many families depend upon this estate for their livelihoods. The Rossmaras have always been committed to serving their people in kind. That is, in giving back a measure of what their people give them. We owe safety and a good living to every man, woman, and child on our estates. Arran's is the final responsibility. My task is to be his eyes and ears. But now I need eyes and ears to work on my behalf, and only the very best will do. Yours. What do you say?"

She said nothing. But she frowned mightily, and Max decided she was the only person alive in whom a frown could be considered charming.

"Mr. McWallop—"

"Mr. McWallop is steward to the marquess," Max said quickly. "He has his own duties and no time—nor would it be *seemly*—for my demands."

"Your assistant?"

"Yes. You'd be a woman ahead of your time. You'd learn a great deal about running an estate. Shouldn't you enjoy that?"

The bonnet fell to the floor, and she retrieved it. "It sounds verra interestin'. Yes. Yes, I'd like the work, I think."

Max's mood soared. "Good. It's done then. And you'll start tomorrow."

"Oh, I dinna—"

"What is there to stop you? The children are away. If it's mending and the like that you think you have to do, well then, we'll give the work to someone else."

"I'll have to ask my father," she said quietly, but with no hint of apology or embarrassment.

He should have expected that. "Of course. Please talk to your parents and tell them I'll ride over to see them this evening because I need you to start at once. I know Robert and Gael well enough to anticipate that they'll be anxious to have you be of service to me."

"No doubt," she said, even more quietly. "No doubt at all."

The Mercers were loyal tenants and Kirsty was right, they wouldn't interfere with her working for him. But Robert was no man's fool, and he'd suspect that Max had other than the stated reasons for seeking out Kirsty's help. And Robert and Gael would worry about their daughter's honor. "I'll reassure your parents," Max said. He went to Kirsty, took hold of her hands, and pulled her to her feet. "I know what worries you, but there is nothing to be concerned about, I assure you. You will be absolutely safe with me."

"Will I?"

Max looked down into her clear, blue eyes. His skin on hers, their joined hands—how could something so trivial become so desperately important? The moment was too long, or was it too short? They faced each other, each with their own thoughts, each speculating on the thoughts of the other, each aware that their shared past could not help but shadow the future—any future they shared in any manner at all.

"I will never do you harm, Kirsty. Or allow any other to harm you."

Very deliberately, she took her hands from his. "If my father agrees, then I shall accept your flatterin' offer. Aye, I'll gladly work for ye. And I'll do my verra best to make your lot a lighter one."

Work for him. "I'm glad." He wished with all his heart that they could have quite a different relationship, and he cursed fate for making that impossible. "You'll tell your parents I'll visit, then?"

"Aye," she said simply, and replaced her bonnet. "I'd best away."

"Since you will no longer be part of the regular household staff, I'll arrange for you to have quarters here in the Eve Tower."

"Quarters? But—"

"You will have to maintain a certain distance from the servants. It'll be necessary for you to be conscious of your position. That will require that you exact their respect. Naturally I will not expect you to abandon friendships, but these things do change somewhat." He was talking too fast, and preparing for her protests as he did so. "I'm sure I don't have to explain that I will be taking you into my confidence on many matters, and I'll expect you to keep your own counsel on those matters."

"I've never lived anywhere but wi' my family. They rely on me."

He slapped his brow. "Oh, how foolish of me. I did know that, didn't I?" He had once considered himself quite the thespian. His current performance suggested his talents had dimmed. "Don't concern yourself with such small details, though. When I come to speak to your parents, I'll explain the necessity for you to be close to your work—and me—at all times."

"Y'mean I'd have t'live here?" Her brow puckered, and she looked around the study.

"Not *exactly* here," he told her. "You shall help me decide on suitable rooms for you."

"Rooms?"

Max felt a shaft of pure pleasure and smiled. "Your duties won't be easy. It will be essential for you to have comfortable quarters when you are at leisure." She had never had even a room of her own. The prospect of having not just one, but two or more had finally occurred to Kirsty, and, unless he was mistaken, the idea wasn't without appeal—a great deal of appeal.

"Here in Eve?" she murmured. *"Rooms."*

"They will be our first priority." The lifting of his heart was something he hadn't felt in too long. "In the morning. And then you shall get settled before we begin work. Perhaps we'll put a second desk in this room. It's certainly more than adequate in size."

"I'll live here." Her gaze snapped into focus, focus that rested squarely upon Max. "Ye live here, too? In the Eve Tower?"

Best make exceeding light of that. "Oh, yes. Have for years. I'm particularly fond of the aspect of the countryside." Until today he hadn't as much as considered the countryside in years—other than as part of his responsibilities. "I hope you'll be as comfortable as I am."

Kirsty watched him with far too narrow a gaze. Surely she didn't fear that he would be less than a gentleman!

Hmm. If she doesn't at least consider the possibility, she is a foolish girl.

"Ye're sure ye want this, sir?" Kirsty said.

"Absolutely sure. We've decided, remember?"

"Aye." A softness, the old, remembered softness entered her voice. "We've decided. I'll do my best for ye, sir."

"Kirsty, you don't have to call me . . ."

A small, sad smile tugged the corners of her mouth down. "Oh, but I certainly do, sir. Mr. Rossmara. Times have changed now."

Slowly he smiled back at her. "You're right, of course. Always the levelheaded one, weren't you?"

"Not always," she said.

"You used to tell me I was a dreamer," he told her.

"Ye were."

He looked away, and back. "Only with you. You and your

imagination—and your—" Stillness had settled between them, and he scarce dared continue speaking for fear of shattering what he felt in that moment.

"You told such stories," Kirsty said, her smile wider. "You were a bad one wi' your tales. And ye'd make folks believe ye, too."

"But you were the one with the gentle dreams," he reminded her. "The wishes." As soon as he'd said the words, he held his breath. Since the day of his departure from her parents' house, since the years of avoiding the promise he'd made to her, there had never been mention of what had once been between them.

Kirsty nodded. "Childish things. I'll tell my father and mother ye'll be along then, shall I?"

He let his breath go. "Yes, do that. Thank you, Kirsty. I look forward to our association."

"It's I who should thank ye for the opportunity."

The opportunity indeed. He offered her his hand, and she took it. "We ought to shake on the agreement. Here's to a long and fruitful alliance."

She took some time to respond. Finally she wetted her lips, and said, "A long and fruitful alliance."

Max looked at her hand in his and lifted it. "I'm sure it will be," he told her softly, and kissed the backs of her fingers.

He'd intended the lightest brushing of his mouth on her skin but with the touch, his eyes closed. He heard her sigh, felt heat gather in his own body—placed another kiss on her hand, and another kiss.

A clattering beyond the door startled him. Opening his eyes, he was in time to view the entrance of Lady Hermoine Rashly and her aunt, Countess Grabham, the latter of The Hallows, a large and somewhat flamboyant mansion on a modestly-sized estate that marched with Kirkcaldy to the east.

In the women's wake came a man Max had not seen before. Of average height, and robust figure, flaxen curls frothed unfashionably about his collar. His pouting red lips—over which he repeatedly darted a pointed tongue—and protuberant blue eyes gave him a greedy, too-eager air.

"We are come," Lady Hermoine announced, her beautiful face radiant. Jiggling on her toes, she set the skirts of her green-and-gold-striped gown swaying. Hermoine's eyes were as gold as those stripes, and her luxuriant hair the color of honey dropped from a spoon. Everything about the lady was luxuriant . . . everything.

Max muttered, "I see you are come," but felt removed from this woman whom he had met on only a few occasions.

"Oh, Max," she continued, "I cannot believe such fortune. Now of all times, now when I so need family around me. Well, you will never credit it, but my cousin Horace has returned. The Honorable Horace Hubble. Isn't that wonderful? Am I not the most fortunate of women? Dear Aunt Grabham never complains, of course, but I know I must be quite a burden on occasion. But dear Horace absolutely insists—he will *not* take *no* for an answer—he absolutely insists that he will take my dear, departed papa's place in my life at a time when strong male influence—and guidance and wisdom, of course—are essential."

"Good of him," Max said. Kirsty remained where she was, standing before him with her eyes lowered.

"Horace Hubble at your service, sir," the blond popinjay announced, flinging wide an arm and revealing an affected red-and-silver waistcoat tightly buttoned over a bulging stomach. "Hermoine speaks very highly of you, very highly. Aunt Grabham, too. Highly, very highly."

The countess, who towered over both her niece and nephew, contrived to pinch her narrow nostrils even more tightly than usual. Dressed entirely in jet-studded black taffeta, as was her habit, her little black eyes skewered Max from the shadow of a black veil, which she also made a practice of wearing at all times.

Kirsty cleared her throat.

"Good of you all to come," Max said, more heartily than he intended. "Can't think what Shanks is thinking of, letting you show yourselves in."

"Oh, the poor man is quite ancient, so we told him he need not put himself out, isn't that so, dearest Horace?" Hermoine caroled, her charming smile showing off dimples in smooth cheeks.

"Quite so," Horace agreed. "Oh, yes, quite so, quite so."

Max's back teeth began to ache. He flexed his jaw. The man was frightful.

"Good of you," he said. "Allow me to introduce my new assistant, Miss Kirsty Mercer."

She raised her face and looked at him with pure, agonized embarrassment in her eyes.

"Really?" Horace said. "A female assistant? Really?"

"Yes, really," Max said. "And a very able one she'll be."

"I best be off, then," Kirsty said.

Only then did she realize he still held her hand. "Do remember to tell your family that I shall visit them later this evening."

"Aye," she said, wrestling to resettle her bonnet and tie the ribbons. "I'll do that."

"Max is a very forward-thinking man," Lady Hermoine remarked. "Who else but Max would retain a woman as his assistant."

"As you say," Horace agreed, "who else, who else, indeed?"

"Where were you last employed, Miss Mercer?" Hermoine asked.

Kirsty curtsied to Hermoine. "I've been employed here."

"I've been employed here, *my lady*," Hermoine said. "I am Lady Hermoine Rashly."

"Aye, m'lady," Kirsty said.

The countess spoke for the first time. "Here, child? Employed here? Surely you misunderstood the question. Mr. Rossmara said he's just retained you."

"Aye, but I've been employed wi' the children. Helpin' Miss Lamenter, the tutor."

"A household servant?" Hermoine said, raising her perfectly arched golden brows. "What a very unusual choice, Max. But then, you are a very unusual man." She came to his side and threaded her hands around his elbow. "You will always be innovative in everything you do. Fascinatingly so in some respects, I'm sure. In fact, I can hardly wait to find out just how innovative you really are."

Max glanced from her perfect face, to the tops of her large white breasts, much on display at the low neckline of her gown. She all but swung on his arm.

Kirsty backed away.

"I'm pleased to have met you, Miss Mercer," Hermoine said. "Mr. Rossmara works far too hard. Don't I often tell you as much, Max?"

He couldn't respond. He could, in fact, do nothing other than watch Kirsty. From tomorrow onward she would be with him every day. His heart lifted.

"Perhaps now you'll feel you can leave these lovely, but dreary walls behind for a month of so. Leave matters in Miss Mercer's capable hands, that is."

"Leave?" Kirsty said. She had begun to open the door. "Why would he leave?"

Max looked at the ceiling.

"Why," Hermoine said, "because we're to be married, of course. And we must plan our wedding journey."

Chapter Two

"**W**ell?" Mairi, the marchioness's plump maid, grabbed Kirsty as she hurried from the corridor that led to Max's study. "Oh, don't ye gi' me that closed face o' yours, Kirsty Mercer. I'm fair burstin' t'know what Mr. Rossmara wanted o' ye."

Mairi had become the marchioness's maid when that lady had arrived at Kirkcaldy shortly before her marriage to the marquess. Plagued by sickness and headaches wherever she traveled, rather than accompany the family on their journeys, Mairi remained at Kirkcaldy and busied herself with the care and mending of her mistress's wardrobe—and with voracious gossiping.

"Our Niall will be waitin'," Kirsty said. Her brother and the young viscount, heir to Kirkcaldy, had the same name. "I'm verra late." And she was desperate to escape into the fresh air and to find a place where she could be alone with the unhappiness that weighed her down.

Max was lost to her. She must finally accept that loss.

"But ye canna leave without tellin' me *something*'." Widowed some years earlier after a brief marriage to a groom, Mairi had shown neither grief at her loss nor the inclination to marry again. Nevertheless, she thrived on chatter about romances in the household, and if there was no real romance in progress, she invented one. "I've no' forgot how close the two o' you were. Runnin' free and wild on the moors. Together all the time. And I'd have t'be blind not t'see how he looks at ye now. And I've seen him watch ye, miss. He's always watched ye."

"Ye do blather, Mairi."

"I know," Mairi said happily. "Always have. Ye should hear what me father says about me blatherin'. Happiest day in his life when my dear mistress took me on here, and I didna go home for more'n visits anymore. He reckoned I made him deaf wi' all me blatherin', but that was just his excuse for pretendin' he couldn't hear what I said. And that was his excuse not t'answer me."

Patience came naturally to Kirsty, but she had to get away. "We'll talk tomorrow, Mairi. I promise ye. But Niall will be—"

"He's no' the same gentle one ye played with. Master Max—Mr. Rossmara. Ye know it, don't ye, Kirsty?"

"Tomorrow we'll talk," Kirsty said firmly, but her heart thumped harder.

"Ye'd do well t'think about it. I don't know what went on between the two o'ye in there, but ye were together—alone—a long time. Did he kiss ye?"

"Mairi!"

Mairi's light blue eyes shone with innocence. "A harmless enough question if he didna. But I'd be bound to wonder, particularly with that kind o' reaction from ye. So, he did kiss ye. And did he hold ye tight?"

"Mairi! No, in either case. I wouldna allow it—even if he weren't a gentleman and unlikely to behave so badly. But he is a gentleman and treated me wi' deference."

"What did he want wi' ye then?"

"Tomorrow," Kirsty said firmly. "Good night to ye, Mairi. And angels watch over ye while ye sleep."

"They will. They always do." But Mairi was not to be diverted so easily. "I'd best go and see if he wants anythin'. I know he sits in that study alone until all hours. I'll see if he'd like a wee bite. Shanks forgets things these days."

So Mairi hadn't seen the visitors arrive. "I think Max—that is, Mr. Rossmara—would prefer to be left alone."

Mairi smiled naughtily. "Left alone to think about ye, ye mean? Och, I'm sure. Did ye speak o' old times?"

It occurred to Kirsty that since Mairi was at the center of the household comings and goings, she might know more about Lady Hermoine. Just thinking the woman's name clenched a body's stomach.

"Kirsty?" Mairi prodded.

What had she expected when she'd been told to go to Max? That he would apologize? That he would tell her he'd made a terrible mistake in not renewing their friendship years earlier and that he now wanted them to be friends again?

He'd become a strapping man. So tall and broad, with shoulders that spoke of his frequent forays into the fields to work beside tenant and laborer. The years had made his dark red hair even darker, and his eyes . . . Well, his deep green eyes were deeper yet, if that could be so. They glittered, and there was a band of black around the iris. His brows flared, and his cheekbones were sharply hewn. But when he smiled, oh, yes, when Max smiled a woman's heart might forget to beat entirely. His mouth was wide and firm and expressive. And a dimple settled in each of his lean cheeks. And his teeth were straight and white, and there was a dent in the middle of his chin.

Kirsty sighed. She'd like to touch each feature—first with her fingers, then with her mouth. Horrified that she should think such brazen things, she gasped and covered her own mouth.

"What is it?" Mairi asked, frowning. "What ails ye? Did he hurt ye? Is that why ye're so quiet. Was it one of his terrible turns he had?"

"Terrible turns?" Kirsty shivered, but not from fear. "What can ye mean, Mairi? Your imagination is unruly."

"It's nothing' t'do wi' my imagination, ye puddin' brain. If ye'd not your head in the clouds, ye'd know he's a black one wi' his temper."

Kirsty had heard about Max's temper. She didn't understand the rumors. He'd been a gentle lad and a gentle young man.

"Do ye not know how he goes away on his own? Shuts himself up, and they say they hear things break. There's some as say he drinks when he's alone and in one o' his moods, too."

"Max wouldn't do any such thing!" Kirsty turned raging hot. "And I'll no' listen t'such nastiness about him. So there."

"Ye love him."

"I—" Kirsty moved her lips but wasn't sure what to say. "Ye've been readin' silly romantical novels, Mairi. It's ashamed I am o'ye."

"*Silly romantical novels* is it? And what are the books I see your nose in a' t'time?"

"Mr. Dickens doesna write romantical novels."

"What does he write about, then?"

"*Life,*" Kirsty declared. "The way it really is for some who don't have our blessings. Poor little lads in London Town, and in orphanages."

Mairi sniffed. "Ye're tryin' t'change t'subject."

She would change the subject quickly enough, Kirsty decided. "Do you know Lady Hermoine Rashly?"

"Countess Grabham's niece?" Mairi pulled a face. "Her as comes t'call on Mr. Rossmara? I know how sometimes when she comes he tells Shanks t'say he's no' at home."

"But they've been acquainted a long time?"

"I wouldn't know about that. I would know that there's a good deal said about The Hallows. The countess's home. Grumpy says it's a hell's kitchen. That's what she calls it, hell's kitchen where all manner o' evil takes place. Carriages comin' and goin' by night. And wildness, wi' laughter and drinkin'." Her eyebrows rose, and her eyes became very round. "An' who knows what else they're up to over there. It's gentlemen they say comes by the carriages at night. Sometime a lady or two. But they're always gone by t'mornin'."

Kirsty realized her mouth was open and snapped it shut. "At *Countess Grabham's*? She's a most correct lady. And in mournin' by the looks o' it."

"Aye, well mayhap. No' countin' Lady Hermoine, she's three permanent houseguests. Surely ye know all this? Surely ye've seen Dahlia, Zinnia, and Wisteria?"

"Ye're talkin' riddles, Mairi."

"I'm tellin' ye there's Dahlia, Zinnia, and Wisteria livin' at The Hallows and they're all dressed in gowns that must cost enough to clothe every man, woman, and bairn on this estate. And their faces are painted. And they show a great deal too much o' themselves, not that they're seen about too much. Only when they're in their carriage goin' t'Edinburgh. On their way to spend more money, no doubt. They say what goes on in that house of a night would turn a body's stomach." For a woman considering an upset stomach, Mairi smiled a good deal too eagerly.

"Good night t'ye, Mairi," Kirsty said. "I'll speak with ye tomorrow."

"I'll tell ye more about The Hallows," Mairi promised. "Rituals, that's what they have over there. No virgin should be abroad at night, they say, so ye watch yoursel'."

Kirsty shook her head and went belowstairs to gather her shawl. If Niall hadn't given up on her and headed home, he'd be in a rare mood, she thought glumly. Just what she needed when her mind was so troubled.

She was startled to see the housekeeper, Mrs. Moggach— Grumpy to the staff—sitting in her chair by the stove. The woman had gained considerable bulk in her long service at

Kirkcaldy. She and Shanks were of an age. Sometimes they showed each other great deference. Sometimes they argued bitterly. But they always supported each other against the rest of the staff. Tonight Grumpy pored over a small, well-worn book in her lap.

"Good evenin' t'ye, Mrs. Moggach," Kirsty said, speeding across the big kitchen toward the corridor that led to the back door. "I hope it's a good book ye're readin'."

Grumpy slapped the book shut and thrust it into a big pocket in her voluminous apron. "Sneakin' around," she said. "Always sneakin' up on a body. Puttin' your nose where ye've no right t'put your nose. What I read's no affair o'yours, miss, and don't ye forget it."

"I'll not forget it," Kirsty said, unmoved by the onslaught. "Was the travelin' library in Kirkcaldy this week? I didna want t'miss it again."

"Well, ye have missed it. It'll not be back for two weeks, so ye'll have t'make do wi' fillin' your time wi' work. And good it'll do ye. Idle hours on your hands, that's the trouble wi' ye, Kirsty Mercer. Idle hours and ideas beyond your station."

Kirsty mumbled nothing in particular, escaped to the corridor, and dashed past the meat and fish larder, and the dairy scullery, to the door that led into the kitchen gardens.

Niall had obviously given up on her and gone away. He was younger than Kirsty but behaved as if she were his sole responsibility. She would have a good deal of tongue-lashing to listen to when she saw him. He'd want to know why she'd been so late.

The explanation wouldn't be an easy one to give.

She had a goodly distance to tramp to reach the little settlement of crofts where she'd lived all her life.

Rooms in the castle. *Rooms.* Her own place, where she'd be alone when she had a mind to be alone.

And a desk in Max's study. To her he would always be

Max, just as he always had been. She was to have a desk with him—where she'd see him often, maybe every day even.

She stood still, abruptly overcome by that which she must accept and incorporate into the way of things. Max was betrothed and would marry beautiful Lady Hermoine Rashly.

They had to plan their wedding trip, that lady had informed her while Kirsty still reeled from the shock of hearing that Max was to marry. Throughout all the years while she'd grieved for the loss of him—and she still grieved— she had not allowed herself to think of him with someone else. Well, she would have to think of it now because she would have to see him with his wife.

A small sound broke from her burning throat.

A silly dreamer. That's what she was. He was a gentleman, and she was the daughter of a poor crofter. But she was about to get a most wonderful opportunity to better herself, and it was Max who would give her that opportunity.

In the gathering gloom a shape emerged from behind a bush. "Kirsty!" Niall said. "What kept ye?"

She gave a little shriek, clutched her heart, and staggered about.

"Oh, stop your playactin' wi' me," he said. "It'll not distract me, I can tell ye."

"You've given me apoplexy," Kirsty gasped, letting each knee sag almost to the ground in a manner she'd learned from Max's boyhood antics. "Fetch a sawbones. I'll not recover from this, but at least try for our mother's and father's sakes. Oh, it's my heart, I tell ye. I feel it leapin' out o' my chest."

An explosive sound came from Niall, who could never hang on to a bad mood for long. "Look at ye, ye daft hapeth. Another minute o' that and ye'll trip on your skirts and really kill yourself. Stop it now, Kirsty."

She coughed, and took deep, noisy breaths, and pretended

to mop her brow. "Oh, I think I'm recoverin'. I may yet live. As long as ye don't press me more, Niall. I need t'be quiet. If I'd a sawbones here, he'd tell ye as much."

"Ye worried me," Niall said. He was as dark as Kirsty was fair, a fact that was remarked upon since their father was fair and their mother a pale redhead. But Niall had eyes as brilliantly blue as his sister's.

"I'm sorry," Kirsty said. "I know a message was sent home t'let Mother and Father know I'd been kept back, so they'll not be worryin', except about you, mayhap."

He scoffed. "They dinna worry about a great strong man like me. Why did they keep ye back? There's little t'do at the castle, so ye told me."

Niall was a finely built young man and he drew every female eye in his direction, a fact that made Kirsty very protective of her brother. "I had to have some discussions," she told him evasively.

"What kind o' discussions would that be?"

"About things I could do—things I've particular skills t'do. I'm glad t'have the opportunity."

"Why? I thought ye were happy wi' what ye're already doin'."

Kirsty slipped her arm under her brother's and they half ran down the castle mound. Birds swooped, swift black shadows against a darkening sky, and the scents were of approaching night. She hadn't realized just how long she'd remained at the castle.

"Well," Niall said. "Aren't ye happy wi' your duties?"

"Very happy. Or most of the time I'm happy. But I get bored when there's nothing different to do. And the young Stonehavens will have no need of me soon enough."

He took hold of her hand and broke into a run, and Kirsty had to struggle to keep up without falling. "Slow down, ye great lug. Ye'll kill your own sister at this rate."

Niall stopped running at once, but kept a hold on her

hand. From the day when he'd realized he was bigger than she was he'd decided she was his to protect. He looked over his shoulder and put an arm around Kirsty.

She struggled, and said, "What is it?"

"There," he said in a triumphant whisper. "It's him. The man on the great horse. Father's seen him passin', too. Now you will."

Kirsty managed to turn around. Some distance above them, where the dusk sky met the hill, a man on a big horse stood in stark silhouette.

"See him?" Niall asked.

Kirsty clutched her brother. "I see him." She recalled Mairi's warnings. "Why did ye no' tell me about him before?"

"Father forbade it. Until he saw for himself, he said I saw the man because Mother said she did, and we were not to fright ye wi' our stories. I've seen him three times now, and Ross McCreavie's seen him as often."

"He's away," Kirsty said. "Gone behind the hill. Who can he be?"

"I dinna know. But I'd like to. Don't say anythin' t'Father."

"I wouldna. Come on. Hurry now." She pulled him along.

"Wait," Niall said. "This new position at the castle. Will they pay ye more?"

Kirsty bit her lip. "I didna ask."

"So who's the great lug now? They'll gi' ye more t'do. That means more duties. But ye don't know if they mean t'pay ye more."

The sooner she was honest about what was to happen, the better. "Niall," she pulled him to another halt where they looked down upon dwellings huddled into a fold of the hills. Dogs barked, and children screeched with laughter that carried on the air.

"What is it?" He'd picked up on her anxiety and mirrored it in his own voice. "What's wrong?"

"Nothin's wrong. I want ye t'be happy for me. D'ye understand?"

He grew very still, and she was afraid to look into his face. He said, "How do I know if I understand if I don't know what it is ye're happy about?"

"I'm goin' t'love livin' at the castle," she told him in a rush, clutching the ends of her shawl and keeping her face turned from him.

He didn't answer.

"It'll be good for all o' us. There'll be more room at home, and more money I'm sure. I'll still bring my wages home, but I'll have my keep up there."

"Good for all o' us?" he asked softly. "Kirsty, ye canna leave. Ye canna."

"O'course I can." She did look at him then, and she made herself laugh. "We both have t'grow up and make a life for ourselves, Niall. You'll do the same one day."

"I'll not so."

"Ye *will*. When ye take a wife o' your own ye'll not be livin' wi' Mother and Father."

"Why d'ye have to live there?" He sounded stubborn as only Niall could sound stubborn. "Why can ye no' take on more duties and still live wi' your family where ye belong?"

"I'll be needed at Kirkcaldy. I'll have important duties that'll mean I must be able t'be reached if there's an emergency. And I'll work much longer hours."

"I don't like the idea of ye bein' alone in one o' those servants' rooms. It's one thing for us t'make our livin' from the Stonehavens the way we always have. It's another for ye t'be servin' them and beholden t'them even for your bed."

Kirsty took hold of his arm again and urged him to walk faster. They continued downhill towards the crofts, where lanternlight showed through doors left open to welcome the cooled air of evening.

"Ye must tell them ye don't want t'stay there."

"I've already said I will." Somehow she would explain exactly what she would be doing. "Tomorrow I'm t'take my things and move in."

"Tomorrow? Oh, Kirsty, no. Mother'll cry, y'know she will."

"I'll just be at the castle. I'm never going to be far away, and I'll see ye all every day." She would make sure she did.

"There's tales about that place."

Tales, always tales, Kirsty thought. "They aren't true. If ye spent as much time there as I do, ye'd know it. It isn't haunted."

"There's plenty to say it is. But it's the livin' I'm no' happy about ye encounterin', no' the dead."

She'd been afraid of this. "I'm going t'be very safe."

"Ye always said ye loved our family more than anythin'."

"I do."

Niall pulled her to a halt and turned her to face him. "Then why d'ye want t'leave us?"

"I don't. And I won't—not really. I'll just be on the hill, that's all."

He shook her gently until she looked into his face. "Ye've never forgotten him, have ye?"

"I don't know what ye're talkin' about." She could never get away with trying to fool Niall.

"And everything about ye says ye do. It's t'be near him that ye're wantin' to go, isn't it?"

She was a poor liar, but she couldn't admit the truth. "I'm goin' because I've a chance t'better mysel' and t'help my family."

"Mayhap," Niall said. "I'll pray ye don't ruin our family. But I've the sight on me, and I don't like what I see. If ye leave us t'go there, ye surely will ruin us all."

Chapter Three

If ye leave us t'go there ye surely will ruin us all.

For the rest of their journey together Niall didn't speak at all. Kirsty smothered the temptation to plead with him to support her decision. She wanted to be a mistress of her own fate, her own decisions. In turn she must allow Niall his own decisions.

They drew closer to home, and she saw her father's slight but unmistakable form in the doorway. He raised a hand and waved, and called out, "There ye are. Ye must both be starvin'. And your mother's no' pleased t'have her dinner ruined."

Father couldn't sound angry even when he tried. "Sorry," Kirsty called back. "We'll eat it cold, won't we, Niall? As punishment, although it'll still melt in our mouths anyway."

"Ye wee flatterer," their mother said, appearing beside her husband and wiping her hands on her apron. "Ye think ye can flatter your way out o' anythin'."

"Can't I?" Kirsty asked, and laughed.

"Och, get away wi' ye," Gael Mercer said. "I've kept it hot. Now wash your hands and get inside, the pair o' ye. Robert and I have both waited for ye, and your father needs his dinner when it's time, so don't keep him waitin' again."

She was too old to be ordered so. Startled at the thought, Kirsty obediently washed her hands in the trough outside the front door and dried them on the rough, wind- and sun-dried cloth her mother gave her.

Inside they sat at the same wooden table where they'd sat

as long as Kirsty remembered, and watched their mother ladle barley broth into enameled tin bowls. Their spoons were wooden, carved by their father, and scoured diligently after every meal.

The broth was hearty, and, despite her apprehension, Kirsty found herself hungry. As was their custom, they ate in silence, mopping up the broth with oatcakes.

Each time Kirsty looked up she found Niall watching her. He was waiting for her to tell her parents her news. Her mouth grew dry, and suddenly she was no longer hungry. She pushed her bowl away.

"Whist?" Mother said. "There's plenty. Ye're too thin, my girl."

Kirsty smiled. "A puff of a breeze would toss you from this hill," she told her mother. "It's a marvel ye've all the energy that goes into your day."

"I've reason to have plenty o' energy. I've the finest husband in the land, and we've the finest children. Lookin' forward to seein' ye at the table of an evenin's enough to keep a body strong."

Once more Kirsty met Niall's eyes.

"We're to have a visitor this evening," Kirsty said, stumbling over the words. "Mr. Rossmara asked me t'tell ye he'll be comin' for a few words wi' ye."

Father stopped eating and set his spoon down slowly. "I didna know ye were on friendly terms wi' Max Rossmara, Kirsty."

"I'm no' on friendly terms or otherwise," she said. "He's responsible for the runnin' o' this estate, and he asked me t'bring ye a message. Was that wrong?"

"Of course it wasn't wrong," Mother said, patting Father's hand. "We'll be glad to entertain Mr. Rossmara won't we, Robert. His uncle thinks verra highly o' him, and that means we think verra highly o' him, too."

Father made a grumbling sound.

"I knew there was something you weren't telling me," Niall said. He pushed back from the table and stood up forcefully. "It is somethin' t'do wi' him, isn't it? How could ye be so stupid?"

"Niall!" Mother said, her hand at her throat. "Don't speak t'your sister so."

"What's afoot here?" Father asked. "Out wi' it, miss. Out wi' it now."

"Let's be sensible," Mother said. "Sensible and calm. I'm sure Kirsty will tell us if there's something we ought to know."

"Oh, there's somethin' ye ought t'know, isn't there, Kirsty?" Niall's expression was thunderous.

"I'll thank ye t'let me speak for myself," Kirsty told her brother. "There's nothing afoot that's cause for unhappiness. I've been asked t'take on more duties at the castle, that's all. It'll be good for me. An advancement. I know ye'll be glad for me."

"*Tell* them," Niall pressed.

Kirsty frowned at him, but said, "I'll be living at the castle, so I can be readily to hand when I'm needed."

"Oh, Kirsty," her mother said softly, dropping her hands into her lap and lowering her eyes.

Niall threw open the door and stood with the dusky sky painting a backdrop for his big body. Anger etched every line of that body. "Ye've ruined it all," he said without looking back. "See what ye've done to Mother?"

Kirsty looked from her mother to her father. "It's a wonderful opportunity," she told them. "I'll learn more things, and in time it'll make a difference to all o' us. Please be happy for me."

"Your place is here with us," her father said gruffly. "Your mother needs you."

"Leave her be," Mother said. "She's a life o' her own

t'make, and if this is what she wants, well then, I'm happy for her."

"And I'll be home all the time, I promise I will."

"When it suits ye," Father said.

Niall stiffened in the doorway. "I think our company's coming—unless one o' our neighbors managed to get himself a great Thoroughbred."

Kirsty's heart flipped, but she made sure no sign of her excitement showed on her face.

A horse's trotting hoofs sounded on the hard-packed earth outside, and, very shortly, Max appeared in the doorway. Niall didn't budge or greet the visitor.

"Niall," Father said, his usually cheerful voice flat. "Welcome our visitor properly, if ye please."

Niall's response was to step back into the room and withdraw to a shadowy corner.

"Good evening to you, Mr. and Mrs. Mercer," Max said, ducking his head to enter the croft. "I expect Kirsty told you I'd be calling."

"She did that," Father said.

Mother got up and quickly cleared the table. "Will ye have something with us, Mr. Rossmara? A wee dram?"

"No, thank you, Mrs. Mercer. But you're very kind. I came to make sure you fully understand my proposal for Kirsty's future. Understand and approve. Kirsty would always want your blessings for anything she undertakes."

Niall made a choking noise in his corner, but Kirsty wouldn't look at him.

Max's hair was ruffled from his ride, and color showed in his face. His vibrancy overpowered the shabby little dwelling, something she'd never felt as strongly as now. He didn't belong in a place like this. His manner and bearing, his forcefulness, were of another world—the world of privilege.

"Kirsty tells us she's to live at the castle," her father said.

"I'm surprised ye bother yoursel' with such minor domestic arrangements."

"This is a domestic arrangement that affects me deeply," Max said, looking at Kirsty rather than her father. "She is very important to me."

She flushed instantly and didn't trust herself to check her family's reaction to Max's statement.

"Did you explain what the manner of your new duties are to be?" he asked her.

She shook her head.

"Well," Max continued, "you'll remember how I told you that Kirsty was a most capable student. I taught her a great deal when she was growing up. Anything I learned, she wanted to learn, and she did so more than ably. Your daughter is a highly intelligent woman, and I want her to have an opportunity to put a very fine mind to work."

"It's no' a woman's place to flaunt learnin'," Father said. "Her place is in the home. We've been happy enough with her helpin' out Miss Lamenter with the children since it'll be good experience for when she has children o' her own."

Kirsty bowed her head to hide her face. Father didn't sound at all himself.

A silence followed until Max said, "But Kirsty has explained that she has accepted a position with me?"

The sound of a sharp movement brought Kirsty's head up. Niall stepped out of his shadow, and said, "What kind o' position would that be? A position wi' ye?"

"As my assistant," Max said calmly. "She will do an admirable job and make my own life so much the better."

"An interestin' manner o' expressin' yoursel'," Father said, and his voice shook.

Kirsty looked at him and filled her hands with her skirt. He was angry, more angry than she'd ever seen him. His face was red, and he made fists at his sides. Niall moved beside his father and the two of them glowered at Max.

"Leave this t'me, Father," Niall said. "Mr. Rossmara can deal wi' me. And if he thinks the likes o' us are too stupid t'understand his wiles, he'll wake soon enough. We'll settle this as men."

Mother felt her way to a chair and sat down with a thump. "Stop him, Robert," she said. "He'll be hurt."

"I'll not be the one—"

"Enough, Niall," his father said. "We must hear Mr. Rossmara out."

"Thank you," Max said. "I intend to train Kirsty into my ways. I trust her implicitly. I know she will serve me well."

"Where will she work?" her father asked. "When she's servin' you?"

"In my own study."

"Wi' ye? In your study? Alone?"

After a brief pause Max said, "No one will question the arrangement, I assure you."

"Because my daughter's a peasant and of no account?"

"Because she is my choice and *I* am of some account. And I'm surprised you speak of Kirsty in such a manner."

"We're simple people, Mr. Rossmara," Father said. "But we know our place. And, in case ye thought otherwise, the children o' the poor are as important t'them as the children of the rich. Mayhap more so. We keep our children with us from choice. We'd no' like t'be sendin' them away t'the fancy schools when they're little more'n bairns."

"You've known me since I was a boy, sir, and you've known my father much longer. Your hostility shocks me. I'd thought you'd be pleased to see your daughter have a chance to better herself."

"My daughter has never given me any reason t'feel ashamed o' her."

Max stared at Kirsty. She felt his eyes upon her and eventually had to look at him. "It wasn't my intention to make trouble for you," he said quietly.

Her family shamed her. They were not rational. "I know that," she told him. "They haven't had time to get used to the idea yet."

Mother shifted in her chair. "I've no' seen the inside o' the castle, ye understand. But I've heard enough o' it. A great place. Kirsty's no' used t'the likes o' such a place."

"I've worked at the castle for several years," Kirsty said, her embarrassment deepening. She wasn't a child to be treated so by her parents. "I know Kirkcaldy well, and a fine place it is. Mr. Rossmara is giving me the kind o' opportunity ye should be glad of for me."

"And her quarters," Father said. "In some warren o' little places where all the servants sleep. Alone, and wi' no one o' her own t'turn to."

Max approached her father until the latter was forced to look up to see the other's face. "I've known Kirsty since she was a child and myself little older. I think of her in a very special way. Her rooms will not be in the servants' quarters, and she will not be alone unless she chooses to be alone. She can always come and go as she pleases. And if she needs someone to turn to at the castle, it shall be to me."

"Kind o' ye," Niall said. "If she's no' t'sleep among the servants, then where is she t'sleep?"

"Kirsty will have rooms in Eve—Eve Tower. And most comfortable they will be. Whatever she desires for her pleasure there, she shall have."

She looked from face to face among her family and felt she did not know them. They had closed out what Max was telling them. Their hostility formed a wall between them, and any chance of reason.

"Eve Tower," her father said. "Is that where some o' the staff lives?"

Max narrowed his eyes, and his face tightened. In a quiet, harsh voice he said, "That is not where members of the staff live."

Father fidgeted, running his scarred fingertips along the edge of the table. "I thought the marquess and his family lived in—Revelation, is it?"

"It is. And Adam Tower is where guests are usually housed."

Niall took a step toward Max, but Father grabbed his sleeve, and said, "Hold ye, Niall. So will my girl be alone in that great big tower, Mr. Rossmara?"

Max's jaw worked. A nerve twitched at the corner of his left eye. "My rooms are also in the Eve Tower, Robert."

Kirsty felt sick and weak—but determined. The men in her family were suggesting Max was about other than the stated business with her. They were degrading her in front of him by presenting such foolish ideas.

"I came here this evening because Kirsty wanted—as is only proper—for me to obtain your approval for the arrangement I presented. If I don't have your approval, then I shall, of course, withdraw the offer."

All feeling fled Kirsty's legs. She trembled, then realized she trembled not from fear or any emotion she had ever felt before, but from fury that her future could be manipulated by others. She was a mature woman and could make up her own mind about her future.

"Mr. Rossmara is to be married," she announced, and took a sharp breath at the loudness of her own voice. "He is to marry Lady Hermoine Rashly, who is the niece of Countess Grabham."

"Is that so?" Father said.

"It is so," Kirsty said. "Isn't it so, sir?"

"Sir," Niall muttered. "Now she has to call the whelp she played with, 'sir.' And he'll house her where she's no one t'turn to but him."

"He's to be married, I tell you."

"And then what will ye be?" Niall asked. "Somethin' worse than ye'll be before he's wed if ye stay in that place and continue behavin' as he's clearly got a mind for ye t'be-have."

Max pressed his lips together, then said, "And how is that exactly, Niall?"

"Doin' your biddin'. We may be simple folk, but we can well imagine how easy it would be for such a man as ye t'have your way wi' an innocent like my sister."

Mother cried out, and Kirsty covered her own mouth.

Niall continued, his voice low, "And when ye've ruined her and she's nowhere else t'go, what then? If ye choose t'keep her for your own purposes, she'll be nothing but a ladybird, a kept woman in the same house as her keeper's wife. It's a foul plan, and well ye know it. Only ye've not reckoned wi' me."

"Say no more!" his father stepped forward, and said to Niall, "Ye're no' t'speak o' such things in front o' your mother."

"And you, Robert? What do you think my motives are where Kirsty's concerned?" Max asked, mildly enough to send terror toward Kirsty's heart.

"I think we both know. There's no call to repeat what's already been said. Ye've always had a liking for Kirsty, we'll no' deny that, will we?"

"We certainly won't," Max responded.

"But she's no' good enough for ye. If she had been, ye'd no' have been so willin' t'leave her behind ye when ye'd given her reason to hope for more."

An urge to run away all but sent Kirsty from the house. This was the most terrible moment of her life, yet she was helpless to stop what was happening.

"Have a care," Max said. "You are concerned for your wife's feelings. I suggest you have a care for your daughter's."

"It's my daughter who has all o' my concern the now. I

must guide her, for she canna guide hersel' where she's no experience."

"And your experience," Max said, "is all gleaned from the gossip of others, from idle chatter around the tables of men with no experience at all in such areas. I would never hurt Kirsty."

"You'll not get the chance," Niall said. "Kirsty willna be goin' back t'Kirkcaldy. Not for any reason. So ye can get back on that fancy horse o'yours and away wi' ye."

"Is that your decision, Mr. and Mrs. Mercer?"

Mother continued to cry softly.

Father raised his chin, and said, "I'll speak wi' your uncle about this."

"My uncle already knows," Max said.

A great rising up of emotion all but overwhelmed Kirsty. It had always been so. Men decided the fate of women, and women were supposed to say nothing while they allowed themselves to be placed as men chose to place them.

"I've accepted Mr. Rossmara's offer," she said, breaking the silence. "And I'm a woman o' my word. I'm honored t'be asked t'serve him. I'm honored he thinks me capable of filling such a responsible position."

"As his trollop?" Niall demanded. "I'll kill him before he uses you so."

"Niall," she said, "hold your foolish tongue. He's t'be married. I'm t'be his assistant. What can ye be thinkin' of?"

"I'm thinkin' that it'll be convenient for him t'take a wife suitable t'his station while he has the woman he'd rather bed right where he can bed her at will. Men o'his class always have other women. It means nothin' t'him. And it'll mean nothin' t'his lady since she'll be amusin' hersel' elsewhere as soon as he's got her wi' a bairn."

Kirsty's horror turned her cold. That her own brother should suggest such monstrous things was beyond belief.

And that her father should make no attempt to stop his son must mean he agreed with him.

"I'll be moving t'the castle tomorrow," she told them all. "Mr. Rossmara and I made that arrangement, and I'll be keepin' to it. I'd hoped ye'd be happy for me, but if ye won't, then I must do as I see fit. I'm no' a wee bairn for ye to order around. Thank ye for comin', sir. I'm sorry it wasna a more pleasant visit. I'm sure my family will come t'understand that this isn't a personal business."

"Kirsty," her father said, leaving his place close to Mother's side and coming to stand in front of his daughter. "Ye're goin' no matter if we say we dinna want ye to?"

Her eyes were too dry for tears. She whispered, "Yes, Father, I'm goin'. Ye aren't thinkin' what you're sayin' or what ye really believe. Ye've known Mr. Rossmara since he was a wee thing. Ye know he's a good man, just as he was a good boy. That's by the by now, but ye ought t'know ye can trust his honor as I do."

"I'll not say what's on my mind, then," Father told her. "Except that ye've been an unhappy girl these past years, and someone made ye so."

Kirsty felt her face flame. "My mind's made up." She turned to Max. "I'll come t'ye in the mornin' and start my duties."

"Kirsty—"

"Enough, Niall," his father said, as Niall started forward. "There'll be no more discussion. Good-bye t'ye then, Kirsty Mercer."

She stared at him.

"Nooo, Robert," her mother wailed. "Dinna say what canna be mended."

"Dinna, Father," Niall echoed.

Father's throat jerked. "Ye'll go now, my girl. Ye've made your choice, and it's for him, not your family. I won't have ye makin' your mother's sufferin' the longer by bein' here another moment." He gave Max a long look. "Ye've torn a strong family asunder, but ye'll come t'your own reckonin'. It's not up t'me t'take such things into my own hands."

"Father, I'm not leavin' for good, only—"

He waved her to silence. "Go now. And God go with ye."

"Father, please—"

"Out. *Now.* Go with the one ye've chosen even though he'll do ye no good. Forget us. We'll forget ye. Ye have no father. And I have no daughter."

Chapter Four

Twenty years. Twenty years she had waited for her due. An eternity. But it was finally over. The time for justice had arrived, and she, Gertrude Grabham, was ready to grasp it with both hands. How unfortunate that her so-called allies, her emissaries, her pawns, were fools to a woman—and man.

She sighed, and removed the veil of which she grew so tired. Nevertheless she would wear it religiously. (Hah, an amusing word for one such as she whose religion was singular: her own gratification, in all things.) She would wear the veil whenever there was need for extra care in the matter of her identity.

The sound of her bedroom door opening caused her to pull the veil hastily over her head and face again.

Horace Hubble slipped into the room and closed the door behind him. "You don't need that with me, Gert. You know who I am, and I know who you are. Make yourself comfy. I'll get us a little something to warm the cockles."

She eyed him with distaste, but retired to her chaise nevertheless. Horace's presence was an unspeakable complication. He must be carefully handled if she was not to run the risk of his interference proving disastrous. His unheralded arrival in Scotland that very day—when she'd been certain he was dead in France—had struck panic to her bones. If he could not be dead, why could he not at least have remained far away?

"Still the same, is it, Gertie?" he asked. "Whiskey and water?"

Gertrude sniffed. "I think I should prefer you to address me formally, Hubble."

He'd changed into a green-velvet dressing gown the color of new spring leaves, and had brushed his luxuriant blond curls to bubble where they touched his shoulders. "Am I really to call you Countess? My dearest friend? My *oldest* friend?"

She would not allow him to rouse her temper. "Yes, Countess."

Hubble spread a hand over his paunch, and bowed. "Very well, Countess. We shall enjoy a glass of whiskey and water together."

"I have given up water," she said, examining the diamond rings she wore on top of black-satin gloves. "One never knows what manner of nastiness may be in water."

Hubble grunted and set about pouring drinks. He had been a nuisance to her for far too long, but since he'd dropped from sight almost a year earlier she'd had reason to hope he might never return. "Why did you decide to come to Scotland?" she asked. Really, the disappointments a patient woman was called upon to endure.

Hubble swung around, slopping whiskey from each of the glasses he held. "You aren't glad to see me? Why, I'm crushed, *Countess*."

The glass he held out to her spread drips over the front of her gown. "I asked why you are here," she said irritably.

Without the slightest indication from herself that she wished him to do so, he sat beside her on the chaise, wiggling his scrawny nether regions to make room for himself.

"Hubble? Answer me."

"I went to Europe on a little mission for a friend, and you packed up, and closed the London house, and tried to disappear."

Gertrude smiled to herself. He had assessed her actions with perfect accuracy. "You were lining your pockets with gold you have not seen fit to share with me. Why should I concern myself with you?"

"Not so." He shook his head until his curls flew. "The entire undertaking was a disaster. Some French farmer went to the authorities and accused me of stealing his daughter for *immoral* purposes. Can you imagine? Ungrateful dog. He'd been paid well enough, and I already had a most suitable buyer for the girl. Instead, it cost me everything I had to get out of the country alive."

"You were always a bumbler," Gertrude said. She sipped her whiskey, closed her eyes, and breathed deeply of the delicious fire.

"So unkind," Hubble said. "You acquired this beautiful house and made yourself and your friends comfortable, and you didn't invite me to join the party." He pushed his red lips out in a pout.

"Exactly."

"So, naturally, as soon as I discovered you had come north, I set out with all haste to find out what you are up to. In other words, dearest lady, I'm here to protect my own interests and to make certain I get my share of whatever it is you are intent upon securing."

Ooh, she detested him. "My affairs are no affair of yours. But there is nothing afoot here that should concern you. We have been in Scotland a year. The climate agrees with me, and I am pleased with a more gentle pace of life. I may never return to London."

"Pah." Pausing, he drank deeply and wiped his mouth with the back of a sleeve. "London is the stuff of your very life, dear lady. No, no, you will have to devise a better excuse than that. All this posturing and bowing to the Rossmara fella. That's what it's about, isn't it? And our little Hermoine posing as the blushing virgin—priceless. Trembling with anticipation at the thought of becoming his bride. That's rich. A few words from yours truly and—"

"Enough." Just as she'd thought, the wretch was intent on making trouble, but he should not be allowed to do so. "Not another word, do you understand?"

"I hardly think you're in the position—"

"French virgins," she said succinctly, looking into her glass. "I've a Frenchie friend or two who might be interested in a man who thought he'd the right to trade in little French girls."

Hubble sputtered. "You wouldn't."

"Wouldn't I?"

"Well—" His lower lip trembled. "All right then, wound a man, but give him a chance to be of very considerable use to you. I wasn't going to do this—at least not this way—but I've no alternative. The chap who let on as to where you were told me an interesting little story."

"What man?" She wouldn't be easily hoodwinked.

"Oh, his name doesn't matter really, except that it appears in a certain place where he wishes it didn't appear, and he's having discussions with a number of others in the same position."

Gertrude choked on her whiskey.

Hubble smiled sweetly. "Got your attention, have I?"

She coughed, and sputtered. "I have no idea what you can be saying."

"I'm not really saying anything except that I know what you're after, and how you intend to get it—or try to get it."

Her heart beat faster. He couldn't know. He couldn't. "You bore me, Hubble." She yawned. "Stay a day or two if you must, then off with you. Run along and find someone else to pay your bills."

"H.R.H.," Hubble announced, attempting an offhand manner.

Gertrude sat forward. "What about the queen?"

"Oh, not the queen. Quite another H.R.H., I assure you. A royal personage who is no longer with us but who was famous for his excesses, particularly when he was the Regent. But you know this. However, the gentleman who mentioned that personage is, or was married to a certain Lady Caroline Lamb. William Lamb, Lord Melbourne. Rich circles, my love—in many ways. And he is certainly still with us. According to him a good many men in high places could have cause to shake in their boots if you're successful in your quest. What do you intend to do if you manage to get what you want? Threaten to publish the thing? Offer to remove the names of those prepared to pay handsomely?"

Gertrude all but shrieked, but she was a woman of great resourcefulness and she took a drink instead. How had he guessed? Did he really know exactly what she sought in Scotland, and how she intended to acquire it?

"You'll have to silence those girls of yours, you know. Delectable they may be, and a great boon in the matter of keeping your coffers filled by deep-pocketed gentlemen visitors, but at least one of them is talking too much." He grinned. "Not that I'm not extremely grateful she did. My, my, if one of those lovely ladies hadn't mentioned a certain journal to one—I'll call him Viscount M for now—I might never have guessed what you were about."

"You haven't guessed," she snapped. "Now, go away."

"The Rossmara fella's the key, isn't he?"

"Not another word, Hubble."

"That's why you're here. What's his connection to the old scene? Did someone give him the journal?"

"I don't know what you're talking about." Gertrude felt her confidence slide. Max Rossmara must not guess the true reason why she and Hermoine had pursued him so assiduously.

"He sent us away this evenin' y'know," Hubble said fatuously. "Not exactly the way one expects an eager man to treat a woman he wants to marry, would you say?"

"Max was tired. He said as much."

"Hah. He had other matters in mind. Or should I say there was someone else that mattered more than my luscious cousin. Once the little peasant left he scarce heard a word any of us said. Then he as good as told us to leave. And I'd wager that the instant we were gone he went in search of her."

"Not at all," Gertrude blustered. "I should hope Mr. Rossmara would feel comfortable enough with us to be honest, and he does. He runs a great estate, the greatest estate in all Scotland."

Yawning, Hubble rose. "The little peasant has a certain appeal. A freshness. He's an eye for her, I tell you. Probably feels a kinship. After all, they're both of low birth."

"*Hubble*. Hold your tongue. Max Rossmara is the adopted son of Struan, Viscount Hunsingore. The Marquess of Stonehaven is his uncle. And Max is the marquess's right hand."

"Max is also a bastard who ran the streets of London before the viscount took the notion to rescue him—and his lovely sister, of course. One does wonder about that, doesn't one? But that doesn't concern me. Guiding Hermoine does. She needs me—*you* need me to take charge. I shall make certain your very clever scheme doesn't go awry, dearest one. I shall make certain we gain possession of the journal you seek, then we shall all become very, very rich."

If the truth of what she planned should reach the wrong ears, everything she'd worked for could be ruined. "How much do you want?"

Horace Hubble set down his glass and gifted her with a haughty stare. "*How much?* Oh, you wound me again, Gertie. Do you imagine that I came here for *money?* Do you think so little of me that you believe I can be dispatched with a little blunt?"

She tossed down the rest of her whiskey and said, "Yes."

His laughter disconcerted her. He laughed, thumped his chest, and coughed. "Well, you're wrong. I have a great deal at stake here, don't y'know. And I intend to collect all of it. After all, you cannot have forgotten that I can stop your plan entirely." He bent over and grasped his knees. "But I probably won't. Instead I shall take command. Unless I misjudge the fella, Rossmara will not be easily broken. He won't talk unless he wants to—or has to."

"We can get what we want without his ever being able to prove we were involved. He must have a secret place he guards well, and we shall find it."

"Aha!" Hubble pointed a short, blunt finger at her. "So you admit there's something. It's a journal, isn't it? With a very surprising list of names? Secretly compiled for the very reason for which you intend to use it. Men are mentioned who would be ruined if the details in that journal were connected to them and made public. A chronicle of *daring* acts, so I understand. Ah, but I can imagine what titillatin' reading it will make."

"You're guessing." She might faint at any moment.

"Am I?" He behaved like a man in a hurry. "You know I'm not. And I know Max Rossmara will be best brought down if he doesn't see his downfall approaching. Then, when he's felled, it'll be too late for him to save himself."

Chapter Five

The man at her side was a stranger.

How could that be?

Once, once not so many years before, he'd been as familiar to her as she was to herself. Tonight he was a tall, silent, dark form who didn't as much as glance at her.

The rush of foolish tears to her eyes shamed her—not that Max would see them.

He walked at a slow, almost a leisurely pace, leading his mount by the rein. Kirsty trudged beside him, carrying the small bundle of her possessions that had been hastily collected.

She was leaving her home with this stranger, going with him to his home as if she was an orphan in need of charity.

"I shall understand if you feel you should return to your family," Max said quietly. "I would never try to force you to go against their wishes."

And what about our wishes? We made wishes, remember?

"I'm old enough to make my own decisions. I intend to become a very good assistant to ye."

"I'm sure you will. But I'm equally sure you won't be happy if you don't have your parents' blessing—and Niall's."

The night was still and warm, and heather-scented. And despite the absence of human souls upon the long hill they climbed, that night seethed as if a crowd gathered about them.

"I'll take you back, Kirsty. Come, let's get you home now before there's more hard feeing."

"Ye want me t'go back?" She hadn't intended to ask him such a thing. "I'm sorry. Ye're being thoughtful."

He halted and turned away from her. Gripping his horse's saddle, he stared toward the sky. "I don't want you to go back."

Kirsty pressed a fist against her breast and gulped air. "Why don't ye?"

"Because I don't, dammit!" He whirled toward her. "Why don't you understand? Why must I explain myself? I thought you had a brain worth cultivating. Was I wrong? Are you a fool?"

Shaking her head, she shrank from him.

"*Fools.*" He snatched away her pathetic bundle and dropped it at his feet. "I'm surrounded by fools who know nothing about me and care less. I should have taken your arrogant brother at his word and faced him as a man. Perhaps if you'd seen me thrash him to silence, you'd have believed I want you to do the job I've asked you to do."

Kirsty stepped backward. "Why did you offer to take me back home then?"

"Because I'm supposed to be a bloody gentleman. I'm condemned to live my life in gratitude for all that I have, all that has been gifted to me. And for that I must not disappoint them. I *owe* them the satisfaction of seeing their experiment succeed, and I am their experiment. *Damn it all,*" he raged to the skies. "I am a man. A *man.* Do you hear me? And I want my needs to be met. Could I not have my way without question for once?" He shot out a hand and grabbed her wrist. "Why must I always consider the feelings and needs of others? What about *my* needs? Answer me. What about *my* needs?"

Scarce able to take a breath, Kirsty forced herself to stand tall before him. "Tell me your needs, and I'll do my best to fulfil them. I want t'help ye. I will serve ye, sir. I promise ye I'll do my best t'lighten your load. I've already told ye as much."

"Have you?" He bent over her, bent her backward and tightened his grip on her wrist. His eyes and his bared teeth glittered. "I've told you what I want. I want you to work with me. At my side. I want to teach you again as I taught you before. I want to see you make the best of yourself. You're too special to waste."

Had she not clutched his coat she would have fallen. "Ye aren't yoursel' " she told him, gasping. "Hush now. Hush."

"I'm not myself?" He laughed, a loud, short laugh. "What is my sin that God makes me suffer so? Why am I doomed to appease the will of others, and deny my own?"

"Max."

"Let me speak from my soul, from my heart," he thundered. "Be silent, and *listen* to me. Can you hear me? Have you any idea what is inside me?"

She whispered, "No," but she knew the blackness others spoke of was upon him, the rage, and it frightened her.

"No? *No?* You, of all people don't *feel* what beats within me?" He shook her. "You were the other half of my heart, Kirsty Mercer. We shared more than most will ever share, yet you no longer know what it is that drives me close to madness?"

My heart is maimed without yours. I will never love anyone but you, Max. Her heart was still only half a heart without his to make it whole, but she could never tell him.

He shook her again. "You don't know what drives me to all but lose my mind?"

She knew what she wished it might be, but if she told him, then she would run the risk of embarrassing them both. And if she thought he might be pining for love of her, then she was the fool he accused her of being.

Abruptly he straightened, his grip on her wrist growing gentle. "I hate what I am," he murmured.

And she could not comfort him. The warm wind plucked at them, tossing his hair, flipping her skirts. Familiar things that were somehow foreign tonight.

"Have I hurt you, Kirsty?"

"No," she lied. "Of course not. And since I willna go back, should we no' carry on? The night's growin' older, and we'd best be on our way t'our beds or we'll not be ready for the morrow."

"You want to come with me? A man who loses his temper as I do? You want to let me drive you hard until you are as capable as any man I could train?"

"I'm no' afraid o' ye. And you'll no' have t'drive me any harder than any man ye might choose for t'job. Mayhap it'll be easier for me."

He laughed again, this time a kinder sound. "You were always an audacious wench. But rightfully so in this case. I'll warrant you could put most men to shame if your wits were pitted against theirs." Bending, he retrieved her bundle and brushed at it. "Up on my horse with you, Miss Mercer. I want you fresh for the morning when we start work."

"I'll walk, thank ye verra much." She'd never learned to ride and didn't want to try now. "A walk is an invigoratin' thing. And I'll carry my own things, too."

At that he slung her possessions over his shoulder, caught up the beast's reins, and strode onward once more.

First Kirsty tried lengthening her stride, but she fell rapidly behind. Then she broke into a trot.

Max stopped and glanced back, and waited until she caught up, at which point he proceeded at a saunter that made her task easy.

He didn't speak.

Kirsty's mind scurried, and struggled with disjointed

thoughts. The silence unnerved her, yet she could not think of a suitable comment to make.

The hill grew steeper, and she had to work harder to climb upward.

Her companion's long, strong limbs made simple work of the task. His strength seemed to cloak him, and to touch her. Just his presence at her side made her tingle. He was at one with the night, and she was drawn to that night with both joy and terror, as if it were too desirable to resist, and too dangerous to embrace.

She had never tasted strong liquor, but she was certain the very strongest could not intoxicate her as this man intoxicated her.

An owl hooted.

In the long grass a small creature skittered.

"Predators everywhere," Max said.

She leaned into the hill, surprised at how her legs ached. This day had been long. "Aye," she said, "but they dinna always get what they want. A wee, weak thing can defy the biggest foe if it's the mind t'do so."

Max paused, and Kirsty also stopped walking. "Catch your breath," he told her. "Why will you not ride? You must be tired."

Falsehoods were good for only one thing—wearing a body out with trying to keep them up. "I canna ride. If ye'll remember, Mr. Rossmara, my family doesna own cattle for transportation so I'm never likely t'learn."

"Of course you'll learn."

"I willna," she said firmly. "I shouldna care to."

"You will learn to ride because you will ride with me when we've business to accomplish, miss. How do you imagine I'll take you with me on estate affairs? Shall I lead you behind me on a rope."

"That's no' amusin'," she told him. "I'm no' sure I can learn such a thing now. I'm too old for such tricks."

"You are five-and-twenty," he said, his smile in his voice. "A trifle ancient, it's true, but we'll do our best anyway."

Kirsty hid her own smile and walked on. "If ye're rested," she said over her shoulder, "then we'd best be on wi' it."

"If *I'm* rested? You were always an impudent girl, and you haven't changed."

Oh, but she'd changed more than he could know, or would ever know now.

The castle rose against the sky, a vast black silhouette painted on shades of gray. Her new home. She didn't know how, but despite the sadness that weighed upon her at her family's anger with her, she was excited by what lay ahead.

"They'll come around," Max said.

Kirsty jumped. "How did ye know what I was thinkin' about?"

"What else would you be thinking about but your family. Robert and Gael Mercer are fine people. And Niall is a fine young man. They're hurt that their lives are changing, but they'll be glad for you in time."

"Mayhap." She hoped he was right. Tomorrow, after her day's work, she would go to them and ask them to discuss matters with her.

When they approached the stables, running footsteps sounded in the yard and a groom rushed to take Max's mount. Max thanked the boy and stood back to usher Kirsty ahead of him toward a path that led across lawns toward the base of Eve Tower.

With the disturbing sensation that some would question why a single woman—alone—would feel it appropriate to accompany a man in such a manner, she moved swiftly to the door at the base of the tower.

Once inside, Max rested a hand lightly at her waist and guided her with purpose to the stairs. "I've a mind to suggest you use the rooms that used to be Ella's when she stayed here—before she was married, and when we used to come here to visit Arran and Grace."

"Anywhere would do," she said, breathless with anticipation. "I dinna need anythin' fine. Ye know what my life is, my means; it'd no' be seemly for me t'have a better place than the other servants."

"Another flight," he told her when they'd climbed two. "We won't discuss what is or is not seemly. You may make your own choice of where you would like to live. Your rooms will be your home, and you shall be happy and comfortable there. I insist upon it."

"Oh, but I couldna choose anythin' mysel'." She halted and looked down at him behind her on the stairs—and grew weak with wanting to rest a hand on his upturned face. He was the most handsome man in the world, the dearest man in the world. "I couldna," she repeated, mumbling.

He was betrothed, and she had no right to look at him the way a female looked at a man she'd like to hold. Oh, she was bad. She was a bad, evil thing without discipline. But she'd improve. She'd become the very best that anyone could be as an assistant to an estate commissioner, and be so busy making his load lighter that she'd never think about him as a man at all.

And just as likely, kelpies cleaned the flowers with dew while humans slept.

Och, she was daft, and getting dafter as she got older—if that was possible.

Max smiled at her. "You were always pretty, but you're even prettier now. I've had precious little time to really notice that."

Confused, and shamed by the rush of blood to her cheeks, she muttered, "Thank ye," and rushed up the third flight of stairs.

"To the left," Max said from behind her.

See, she told herself, *he's just being polite, the way he'd be polite to anyone because he's a kind soul.*

"I'll show you Ella's old rooms first, then we'll look at what else is available and ready to be used, and you can make up your mind."

Not trusting herself to speak, she let him lead her along a wide corridor with worn, but beautiful gold carpets on uneven wooden floors turned black with age. Rather than the expected portraits of family members, paintings of the fields around the castle hung here. The fields and hills. A stone wall covered with flowers. The little church in the village. The occasional likeness of some family dog or horse. Kirsty found she liked the plainness of it all.

"Here we are," Max said, reaching past her to throw open a door. He stepped around her and lighted a lamp on a painted table just inside a small sitting room. Then he set about lighting more lamps and passed through another door to light even more.

She couldn't possibly stay here. They were rooms meant for a lady.

"What do you think?" Max asked, returning. "The rosy rooms, Ella called them. They have a warm appearance so she's told me. Not that a man can be expected to understand the working of a woman's mind in these matters."

Kirsty couldn't speak at all.

"You don't like them," he said, frowning. "At least look at the bedroom before we eliminate them."

With a sense that her tongue had been frozen, she went obediently into the bedroom and was even more overpowered. The bed was hung with rose pink draperies, the four-poster frame elaborately decorated with gold scrolls. And the mattress was so high and soft in appearance that she was instantly even more tired. A dressing table had a frothy skirt of the same rose-colored silk as the bed draperies. On the dressing table lay a profusion of silver things. Brushes, combs, buttonhooks, a shoehorn, crystal perfume bottles with silver tops. The lamps beside the bed had rose-colored chimneys, and their light turned the whole room pale pink.

"Think about it," Max said from the doorway. "Perhaps you don't care for the color. If that's all, it can be changed. My uncle agrees that you should have whatever pleases you."

Bemused, Kirsty wandered back into the sitting room. A chaise and several small upholstered chairs were elegantly placed, and tables made of patterned wood held exquisite porcelain pieces, and an enameled clock commanded the mantel above a fireplace tiled in rose and white with a painted blossom on each tile.

And on one of the tables was Ella's marvelous Parcheesi set, the one with the pieces shaped like wee silver ladies in ball gowns from different times. Oh, she shouldn't be here among such things.

Max waited in the doorway to the corridor. Kirsty looked about her with longing, but joined him and started toward doors on the opposite side.

"My own quarters are at the far end," he told her. "I sleep lightly. You would only have to call, and I should hear you, not that there is anything to fear here. But you've been accustomed to your family being around you and could be a little nervous of solitude at first."

"I think I shall like solitude," she told him.

He didn't move, not at all, only looked into her face. "You're tired, my girl, even if you don't think you are. We must find somewhere that pleases you and get you settled."

Without any idea of what made her so bold, Kirsty said, "If I must choose, then I choose the rosy rooms," and covered her mouth.

Jutting his chin, Max frowned and smiled at the same time. "What? What troubles you?"

"I'm forward. Tellin' ye what I'd like."

"I *asked* you what you'd like, but you showed no sign of wanting those rooms. Don't accept them just to save effort, please."

"Och, they're beautiful. I never thought I'd sleep in the like o' such rooms."

"Wonderful!" Pleasure shone on his features. "Come along then, and we'll see that you have everything you need. Then I'll let the appropriate staff know where you'll be, so you're well taken care of."

He strode back into the lovely rooms and set about drawing heavy draperies over the windows. "I expect you'd like your breakfast in bed? If you'd care to tell me what you prefer to eat in the morning, and at what time, I'll tell them belowstairs."

Tell them belowstairs. Kirsty winced. "I'll eat in the kitchens, but thank ye."

"You will not eat in the kitchens, and I never want to hear such a suggestion again. If you prefer to rise before eating, you will eat in the breakfast room where I eat. It's across from my study. Go there whenever you're ready."

"Verra well." She rubbed her hands together and looked around. Her ragtag bundle was on a chair. "I'll not need anythin' else, then. Except water for washin', and I'll go see t'it."

"I'll see to it," he said very firmly, and went to his knees before the fireplace. In moments flames spun up in the chimney, and he stood again. "Now, relax. Someone will bring you water. How about food?"

She sighed. "I had supper wi' my family."

"Yes, of course." He sounded uncomfortable. "Good night to you, then."

"Good night," Kirsty said, but he didn't leave.

"You're sure you wouldn't like a little something more to eat?"

"Quite sure, thank ye."

He moved a chair closer to the fire. "Warm yourself. It's always cold in this great stone place."

"I will. Thank ye."

"Hmm." He went to a wardrobe and opened the doors, and the drawers in a central bank inside. "Ella left all these things. She doesn't want any of them. They'll do for you until we can arrange clothes to your taste."

"Oh, I couldna," she said, genuinely horrified. "I've a few things wi' me, and I'll get more."

"I shall want you well dressed, Kirsty. Simple clothes, of course, because they suit you, but of excellent cut and quality."

Her face flamed yet again. "I'm afraid my own things are no verra special."

"You always look lovely, but your wardrobe will be part of your remuneration. A modiste will be arranged. She'll come to you. In the meantime, please find suitable garments among these. Ella's tastes are for pretty but simple gowns." He frowned. "She is somewhat taller than you, of course, but I'm sure you will use your ingenuity to accomplish something serviceable."

"I've a little money put by," she told him. "I'll go into the village and see Mrs. Mackay—the dressmaker. She'll make me—"

"Did you hear what I said?" His voice had hardened, and the angry light returned to his eyes. "You will use Ella's things until I can get a modiste here to the castle. Are my wishes understood?"

Kirsty nodded yes.

"Good."

With that he turned and left, closing the door hard behind him.

It took so very little to annoy him. When they'd been children, Max was the carefree one who smiled and joked his way through whatever came, and welcomed challenge. Now he changed like the wind on the moors, blowing one way, then the other, and so often fierce.

Kirsty looked around. What would she do with so much space, and with time on her hands?

She shouldn't be here at all. And she certainly shouldn't use Miss Ella—no, Ella was Lady Avenall now. She shouldn't use Lady Avenall's things.

Best go to bed and try to make sense of all that had happened to her so quickly. She undid her own things and extracted the plain, white-cotton nightgown she'd brought.

Mother had made the gown. No, she wouldn't cry. Tears didn't make things different, or better, or even worse for that matter. Surely her family wouldn't turn their backs on her for long. They loved her, and wanted her with them, but they would come to accept that this was a chance she would be foolish to turn down.

It would probably be Mairi who'd come with the water. Kirsty felt very warm again, obviously at the thought of Mairi coming to her like a maid waiting on a lady. Well, Kirsty would put an end to any such notions and make sure Mairi understood that in future Kirsty would be attending to herself.

She was tired. Bone tired, and with a brain that wasn't making sense anymore.

In the bedroom she slipped out of her dusty clothing and put on the nightgown. She took her hair down, brushed it rapidly, and made a single braid that hung past her shoulder blades. She'd wash her face and hands and climb into the tall, soft-looking bed, and say her prayers. The good Lord watched over honest people in their times of trouble, and she was troubled.

"Kirsty?" Max's voice called out. "May I come in, please?"

She looked down at the nightgown. A very demure nightgown. And since there wasn't a great deal of her to be concerned about anyway, she looked respectable enough.

"Aye," she said, peeking into the sitting room and watching him come in, carrying a water jug and a bowl with great care lest he should spill some of the water.

He looked up, saw her, and immediately looked away. "I couldn't find anyone to help, drat them all. I shall have something to say about that tomorrow. It's Arran's fault. He's too soft on all of them when Grace is away. Where shall I put this?"

"I'll take it into the bedroom," she told him, too aware of her thin gown now.

Keeping his eyes lowered, he advanced. "It's too heavy. I'll set it down for you." And he passed her to cross the bedroom and place his burden on the marble-topped washstand.

"Thank you very much," she said, hugging her middle. "I'll be sure to be ready for my duties by six."

"Then you'll be ready alone," he said. "I breakfast at seven, and like to be in my study by eight or so. You may make your own time."

"I'll be there when you arrive," she told him, feeling very vulnerable. Her bare feet didn't help her dignity. "Good night to you, sir, and thank you again."

"I don't like you calling me . . ." his voice trailed away, and he looked at her. His hands dropped to his sides. "Doesn't it seem strange to call me sir?"

"Strange or no', it's only right."

"Yes, I suppose so." He started for the door. "Yes, that would be true. Are you going to be comfortable?"

Kirsty shivered.

"What am I thinking of," he said. "You need a fire in here, too."

"I can light it myself."

"In that flimsy thing you're wearing. You'll catch yourself on fire."

Flimsy thing?

He lighted the fire, not quite so effortlessly this time, but light it at last he did. "There. Are there plenty of covers on that bed?" Before she could respond, he went to the bed and threw back the embroidered counterpane. Then, to her amazement, he counted the coverlets aloud and frowned deeply as if calculating. "Enough I suppose. But there should have been a warming pan. I'll get one at once."

"No! No, thank you. Once I'm in bed I'll warm up soon enough."

Max looked at her with dark speculation. He said, "Will you, indeed?"

"Yes."

"Then you'd best get into the bed at once. You look very cold to me."

"I'll do that."

She stood, waiting for him to leave.

Max stood—exactly where he was.

Kirsty considered and rejected the idea of going to the washstand and pouring water. She glanced down and saw the outline of her limbs through her gown. She pressed her thighs tightly together and wished she could be somewhere far away.

"The bed is high," Max said.

"Yes."

"The step appears to be missing."

"I'll stand on the siderails to get in."

"That would hurt your feet."

"My feet are tough."

"Not that tough."

Oh mortification. "Then I shall use a chair. Please don't concern yourself. You've already been far too kind."

"You speak as if we were strangers."

Kirsty didn't respond. If she had spoken, it would have been to remind him that they had become strangers.

Without warning, he closed the space between them and swept her up into his arms. Her shock was so great that she clung to his neck.

Four strides and he was able to deposit her atop the mattress. "There," was all he said.

"Yes," was all Kirsty could say. She supported herself with her braced arms and took deep breaths to calm her thundering heart.

"Good night to you, then," Max said, backing away.

Kirsty said, "Yes. Good night."

He reached the door, said, "White becomes you," and left.

The door to the corridor slammed, and the sound of his boots retreated rapidly down the corridor.

Chapter Six

Surely the air had left the night. He could scarce breathe, and his linen stuck to his back.

What did he think he was about?

God help him, but he'd made a pretty mess of the disaster that had already been his life.

Max stopped at the door to his rooms. He'd told her he slept lightly, that she need only call out if she needed him.

He spread his arms and braced his weight against the doorjamb. For her own sake she'd best never decide to call for him—for her own sake, and for his. If he went to comfort her, he'd not make himself leave again. The wonder was that he'd had the restraint to leave her tonight.

He slept lightly? With the image of her in her childish nightgown—that hid precious little—burned into his brain, how would he ever sleep again? An innocent. His eyes stung. Passion smote its victims in mysterious ways. He could rant his frustration at wanting Kirsty Mercer to the silent skies. And he could have had her. She could be his this moment if he'd been prepared to turn his back on the man who had given him a life worth living.

Tonight, when Kirsty had made up her mind to come with him rather than remain with her family, she'd had more courage than he'd managed to summon when his father told him to keep his distance from her. *You're a gentleman's son, a viscount's son. Kirsty's a good girl, but she's the daughter of tenant stock. The two cannot mix, Max. I've never asked you to do other than that which I considered for your best interests. Heed me if you please. Now, that's an end of it, then. It will not be mentioned again.*

He could go to Arran and beg advice. With Grace in Cornwall, the marquess would be in his music room far into the night, playing and composing. Arran understood. He'd held his opinions to himself rather than go against his brother, but Max had seen his uncle shake his head when father told Max he must marry "appropriately." And Arran had supported Max's plan to employ Kirsty as his assistant—an unprecedented idea, and one that his father was likely to attempt to scuttle on his return.

Arran could help the cause considerably if he chose. Max considered the possibility. If he were completely honest, he'd admit that although Arran hadn't opposed the idea of Kirsty coming to the castle—and he'd said she should be made comfortable if she did come, he hadn't exactly endorsed the idea.

Would she go away with him if he asked her?

He could support them well enough. He was a man of simple tastes and had put goodly sums away, and invested well. And his father had made handsome provision for him.

And how would she survive if he took her from this land

where she'd grown like a perfect flower, and where she thrived on the love of her family—who would surely relent in time—and the certainty of her place in the order of things? She'd never complain, but she'd suffer, and in time they would both regret what they'd done.

Bringing her here had been wrong, but he would not turn back.

He went into the dark anteroom to his chambers and restrained himself from slamming the door. The rage simmered, but it was still deep, where there was a chance he could contain it. He'd shouted at Kirsty, and shaken her. "My God! What is to become of me?" he asked himself aloud. A man capable of taking out his anger on a slip of a girl.

Confess that you intend to make her your mistress. At least confess it to yourself.

He stood still and listened. There was an atmosphere here—in his rooms. He'd swear he wasn't alone.

Cold climbed his spine, and he looked toward the dim light that spilled from his library. He walked forward cautiously until he could see into the book-lined room. Before he could contain his surprise, an exclamation burst from his lips.

"Are you angry, Max?" Lady Hermoine rose from the chair behind his desk, but made no attempt to approach him. "Please say you are not angry, that you are glad to see me. I know I have shocked you, but do be gentle with me. I am desperate and I need your assistance." She played with a honey gold curl and swayed her skirts.

"My assistance?" He could not make himself go to her. From the moment they'd met and it became obvious that the meeting was arranged by his parents and the countess, he'd tried—without success—to respond to Lady Hermoine.

She lowered her thick lashes and trailed her fingertips over the desktop. Her low-cut lavender-colored gown displayed her fine figure provocatively. "Not assistance exactly. Oh, this is embarrassing. I know that ours is not a match of the heart. Not *your* heart. But I long for it to be so and pray that in time you will come to love me."

"How did you get in here?"

She shrugged and kept her bare shoulders raised. "It was simple." Her gown clung precariously to her breasts and covered far too little for comfort. "I will not be other than honest with you. I bribed the coachman at The Hallows to bring me back. Then I hid in the gardens. I waited until I saw the butler leave, and let myself in. He doesn't lock the doors when he takes his outings. I knew your rooms were somewhere in this tower, so I searched. As soon as I entered here, I knew I had found you—or found the place you have made your own. I felt you here."

Max smothered the urge to be harsh with her. "Shanks left? You say he takes evening outings?"

"Every evening. Sometimes with the housekeeper. They take a book and stroll out into the gardens."

"Extraordinary," Max said. "I shall escort you home at once."

"No!" She hurried around the desk and threw herself at him. She wrapped her arms around him and pressed her face to his chest. "Do not send me away. I am despondent."

The woman was a stranger to him and would remain so. "You should not have come here." He didn't hold her.

"I am to be your wife. Very soon if our families have their way. Yet I feel I do not know you at all, and I am afraid." She trembled and ran her hands up and down his back. "Make me feel unafraid, Max. Make me your wife tonight and show me that you care for me."

Surely he misunderstood her. "You are overwrought. This is always a difficult time for a young woman, or so I'm told."

"You mean the time when they are betrothed and anticipating the changes which must occur—the happy changes—when they are married?"

Did he mean that? Was he actually accepting that he would take this woman as his wife? "I must repeat that you should not have come here. Had you been seen, your reputation would be ruined."

"I was not seen," she said, keeping her eyes downcast. "Please do not send me away. Let me stay with you. If you'd prefer, I will sit by your bed. But only let me be with you. You make me brave."

"You hardly know me." *And will never know me better.*

"I am a woman of intuition. I have often been told so. Your goodness and understanding are things I feel in here." She spread her right hand over her all-but-bared left breast and looked beseechingly up into his face.

He could not help but note that her nipples were visible. Large, pink nipples and sumptuous breasts no man could fail to find arousing.

"You want me," she whispered. "I feel it."

"I want you to leave," he told her, in a voice that cracked enough to put the doubt to his words.

Hermoine rose to her toes, put her arms around his neck, and kissed him.

Surprise unbalanced Max. His hands went to her waist to steady them both. Surprise became shock as she thrust her tongue into his mouth and rubbed her body against his. She took one of his hands from her waist and thrust it inside her bodice and over a breast that overflowed his fingers.

She whimpered, and his rod swelled hard.

The force of her ardor drove him back a pace, but she only pushed her tongue farther into his mouth. Her fingers, delving past his groin, brought a groan to his lips. Her arousal broke into a fever. She probed him, and squeezed, and struggled to raise her skirts until she could spread her legs around his.

Sweat ran from his brow into his eyes. No woman had ever assaulted him, yet that was what Lady Hermoine did—she assaulted him in a blatant quest for sexual satisfaction.

A high-class whore.

Not possible.

"Stop." He captured her wrists and held them behind her back while she struggled. "You cannot know what you are about."

Her bright, impassioned eyes and flushed cheeks spoke to the height of her excitement. "I have never felt so," she told him, panting. "It is most inappropriate, I'm sure, but you make me feel what I have never felt before. I want you to make me yours. Oh, please, Max. *Please.*"

He would be forgiven for accepting her offer. "Calm yourself," he said. "Think what you're about, I beg you. I'm sure you will regret one more moment of this, and it is my duty to make sure that nothing more occurs."

"*No.*" She struggled, and her breasts were completely bared. "I see how you look at me. You want me, too. We should not deny ourselves such ecstasy. And we can hasten the marriage, Max. But I cannot leave you tonight without learning all there is about a man and a woman, together, alone."

He could lose himself in her. Her body could make him forget what he truly wanted, *who* he truly wanted.

Hermoine turned around. "Unfasten my gown, please."

All so easy for the taking.

She looked back at him, revealing how her flesh balanced, creamy and overflowing, atop the boned gown. "Please, Max. Do help me."

He took a step backward, and another, and finally walked behind his desk to slump into the chair. "Why must I be tempted so?"

"Tempted? *Tempted.* Soon we shall be man and wife and together like this whenever we please. I shall not have to search you out to assuage my need. And, Max, I do need you. You have awakened me as a woman, and I am glad."

He shook his head and grasped the arms of his chair, and noted that a drawer in his desk was open. No drawer was ever left open. In fact, they were locked.

"Hermoine," he said quietly. "How long have you been here?"

"Oh," she gasped. "How can you be so calm when I am beside myself? I told you I came into the castle when Shanks left. That was at least an hour or more ago."

Had she heard him arrive with Kirsty? And if so, why had she not come to investigate—and seen them? And if she saw them, then why no questions?

He opened the drawer and found the contents shifted. A less organized man might not notice. The rest of his life might be in ruins, but his attention to business detail never wavered, and that attention extended to the manner in which he maintained his papers.

The next drawer also slid open, and the next, and all had been tampered with.

"What is it?" Hermoine asked, facing him.

Max found it all but impossible to avoid staring at her.

"*Max,* I asked you what's the matter. You look so strange. Do you not want me?"

"How did you unlock my desk?"

Her mouth fell open.

"When I arrived you were sitting here. And, very obviously, my desk drawers have been searched."

"Oh, how could you accuse me of such a thing? Why would I want to search your desk? What would I want to find there?"

He stared at her and said, very quietly, "Why don't you tell me? Perhaps your interest was only idle. That I might accept. But then there would be the question of where you obtained a key. The desk is always locked."

"I did not touch it," she said, her eyes wild. "Why, that you should think me capable of such an invasion undoes me. You must have something to hide, or you would not suspect such a monstrous thing. Oh, I am beside myself. Why would I do such a thing to the man I love?"

His need for privacy was not something he would discuss with Lady Hermoine. "There is only one key, and I have it. Where did you get what you needed to accomplish this invasion of my privacy?"

"Oh." Her breasts rose and fell with magnificent insult. "I hold you in the highest esteem and had hoped you at least respected me. If I invaded your desk, what was I looking for, if you please? And did I find it? And where is the key or whatever, that would be required for me to commit such a crime?"

Max wasn't moved by her dramatic performance.

"Search me," she said spreading her arms. "Come, search me. If I have appropriated something of yours, find it, for I would have no place to hide it but about my person."

If he told her there was nothing in the desk that could not be replaced, he would appear foolish for his zealous care. "We will speak no more of it. But I should like you to remember that I am a very private man who prefers to protect that privacy. I always will."

Unmoved by his speech, Hermoine tore at her gown and contrived to push it down and step out of it.

"Stop!" Max got to his feet, but knew better than to approach the lady.

She set about untying her petticoats and persevered until she stood in drawers, stays, and the tattered remnants of a chemise. The stays were superfluous except to hold her breasts high, and thrust them out as much as possible.

Once again she spread her arms. "Come. Search me at once. Find what I have stolen from you." She began to cry, and, when she could speak, sobbed, "Oh, Max, I am undone."

The day and night had been entirely too long, too gruelling. "Undone?" he sputtered. Much, much too long. He began to laugh, and despite his best efforts could not contain his laughter. "I—I—I should say you're undone. Almost entirely undone."

She stopped crying. Her trembling mouth grew hard. "You *dare* to laugh at me? Why, I've a good mind to summon help. I've a good mind to summon Shanks and ask him to go for help because you have molested me."

"Mo—molested you?" His laughter burst forth anew. "You tear off your clothes, you handle me in a most intimate and, I might add, unexpected manner, and it is *I* who molested *you*?"

"*Cruel, cruel.* How can you treat me so? I came to give myself to you, and you have embarrassed me beyond all."

"I suggest you dress and go home. I'll have a carriage brought around."

"Just like that? Dress and go home? Oh, Max, I am to be your wife."

So everyone assumed. "I think we should forget this event ever occurred." She was not a stupid woman. He should assume that if she had made the opportunity to examine his affairs, she would be unlikely to leave evidence that she had done so. At that moment he rather doubted that she had been the culprit. Which left him with the question of just who *had* gone through his desk.

Hermoine had picked up her petticoats, and these she wrapped about her. And she blushed, actually blushed.

"Why did you come to me like this?" Max asked.

"Why, to invade your privacy, of course. To go through your papers."

He played with the silver top of his inkwell. "If we decide that you didn't come for that purpose, then what? Explain why you felt you must come at all. We both know your visit—and your behavior—are unsuitable."

"You all but turned me away earlier. When I came with the dear countess and my cousin. Horace is confused by your behavior. I would not be fair to anyone if I didn't tell you as much. He . . . he said you did not appear to be a man who was joyful at the prospect of his approaching nuptials."

Astute of the fop. "And that was a reason to all but force entry into my uncle's home?"

Tears streamed suddenly down her cheeks. She wailed, her wails scaling higher and higher until they were a continuous thin shriek.

"Lady Hermoine," Max said, getting up, afraid she would be heard by Kirsty. "Please collect yourself. There is no need for such an outburst."

"Bu-but I am shamed before all. The dear countess has informed anyone who *is* anyone of my coming marriage to the son of Viscount Hunsingore, to the nephew of the Marquess of Stonehaven."

"But not," Max remarked cynically, "to Max Rossmara, very much a man in his own right."

"Oh," she flapped a hand. "You know how these things are. The foolishness of the generation before ours. I have no time for it, but neither can I change it."

He almost liked her for her directness. "Indeed. You are correct."

"Give a thought to my unhappy position. I have been considered without prospects because I have no money and would not accept a dowry from the dear countess. These past weeks here have been so joyful. Your family seemed not to mind at all that I'm penniless. Your dear papa even offered to buy me an entire trousseau. I turned him down, of course."

"Of course." And if the lady intended to treat every garment with the willful disregard with which she'd treated her gown this evening, well then, any money spent in such a manner would be wasted.

"But Horace, darling cousin Horace, has arrived and persuaded me that it will be his greatest joy to stand beside me during this time before the marriage, and during the ceremony. And he will hear of nothing but that he be allowed to provide me with a most handsome dowry. He wishes to speak to you about this, but I have put him off because I have been unable to tell what your attitude toward me is."

"The countess acted for you," he said, more shortly than he'd intended. "She and my father made the necessary agreement." And he had gone along, keeping silent, never mentioning his own feelings, because after so many years of reaping the rewards of the viscount's overwhelming kindness, Max could not bring himself to go against him in this when it seemed so important to the man.

"You would not understand," Lady Hermoine said, "but it is so hard to be without means. My parents died some years ago, in the Greek Isles. They traveled constantly and spent without restraint. I was left with almost nothing—except my dearest aunt, and Horace. But Horace is a wanderer himself and has not until recently been aware of my pecuniary situation. Now he is determined to rectify the situation."

"Admirable," Max said, unable to reconcile such fine feelings with the self-involved man he had met just that afternoon.

"I have felt that you are less than keen on casting your lot with mine, sir."

His thoughts returned again, and again, to Kirsty. Alone in a room like none she'd ever slept in before, and thinking of how her beloved family were angered with her—and perhaps wondering about him. They did not fool each other. There was love between them, love that had grown from when she was a scrawny-legged child and he a callow young fellow trying to pretend he was a man of the world.

"Max?"

"Yes." He looked at her and saw a woman who was the antithesis of his Kirsty. *His* Kirsty who had never considered that womanly wiles were of the slightest use. Lady Hermoine had been trained to use her physical assets, trained in the art of capturing a man. Max smiled at her. "Perhaps we should proceed a little more slowly, my lady. After all, there is no rush, is there? We would not want to make a mistake with which we should have to live for the rest of our lives."

Tears spurted again. Surrounded by the tangle of petticoats, she sank onto an ottoman before a rather worn green tapestry chair. "You do not want me," she wailed, and he did not miss the fact that her undergarments no longer entirely covered her breasts. "If you wanted me, you would be unable to wait a moment longer than necessary to call me your own."

To please his father and mother, and to also please himself, that was his impossible task. "You are a delightful young woman," he said, the words drying his throat. "And I am very concerned for your reputation. Will you please allow me to escort you home? Then, very soon, when I have dealt with some pressing estate matters, I will meet with your kind cousin, Horace Horrid, was it?"

"Horace Hubble."

"Yes, yes, Horace Hubble. I shall meet with him to discuss how to proceed." And meanwhile he'd consider what manner of relationship he should have with Kirsty Mercer. Could he crush down his own desires and revel in what he knew he could make of her in a professional capacity? Oh, there would be much grumbling about "a slip of a girl" doing a man's job, but she would do it so well that in time they would all come around, and she would be both respected and their pet. He knew the people of Kirkcaldy, and a more generous lot never walked the face of the earth.

"Will you kiss me?" Lady Hermoine asked with downcast eyes. "Just once?"

He swallowed. "I think you should dress, madam."

"You don't find me alluring."

"I find you exceedingly alluring. So much so that the more of you that is displayed, the more difficult I find it to control my male urges. Not, of course, that you would understand such things." From what he had observed of her behavior, the lady was hardly the blushing innocent she pretended to be.

She simpered and twittered at his comments and made much of turning her back while she struggled into her clothing. "Dear Max," she said, "you are a gentleman through and through. I'm sure there are many men who would have taken advantage of a green girl such as I."

Green indeed, Max thought.

"Max," she said when she was more or less clothed, "do you think we could set a date for our nuptials? And puff them off in the *Times*, perhaps?"

He felt the net descending about him. "My father will return to Kirkcaldy soon. I think it best to await his arrival. I know he and my mother have thoughts on the matter. And, of course, they will want to discuss them with the countess and your cousin."

"Oh." A pout did not suit Lady Hermoine. "Are you sure?"

"Very sure."

"Oh. Well, if your mind is made up. Kiss me before you call for the carriage."

She closed her eyes and raised her face.

Max studied her face, and saw Kirsty in his mind. He brushed his lips over Hermoine's brow and took her purposefully by the arm. Walking much more quickly than could have been easy for her, he took her to the lower regions of the tower and rang for a servant.

Evidently Shanks was still on his jaunt, doing whatever a man of Shanks's age did on a jaunt, for a young fellow Max didn't recognize rushed from belowstairs, straightening a powdered wig as he came.

"Yes, sir, yes, sir," he babbled, bobbing up and down from the waist.

"See if you can summon Lady Hermoine's coach, if you please."

Still mumbling, the man dashed away, and within blessedly few minutes the crunch of wheels sounded on the gravel driveway outside.

"Your conveyance," Max said, and realized that Hermoine was staring with horrified fascination at a very old and treasured Stonehaven artifact—the upper portions of a polar bear holding a preserved, but rather green fish between its dead paws.

"Magnificent, isn't it?" Max said.

"Why, it's horrid."

Max recalled that his aunt, the Marchioness of Stonehaven, often recounted her own less than joyous first acquaintance with the polar bear—of which she was now quite fond.

"Oh," Max said, unaccountably overtaken by an old urge to shock, "you mean because there's only half a bear."

Hermoine gave a small scream.

"I thought so," Max said. "You see the long knives crossed on the wall? Well, there used to be a whole bear, but a fastening came loose, and . . ." He let the rest of the sentence trail away and raised his palms.

"The knives are so sharp?"

"Oh, yes, and unfortunately the stuffed bear was neither the only, nor the most tragic victim of a little slip in this hall, so to speak." He shook his head and rubbed his eyes. "There was a charming young woman who came to visit and she stood—well, just about where you are."

Lady Hermoine spun around and looked up at a claymore on the wall, its double-edged blade glittering. Her hands flew to her mouth. "You mean?"

"I'm afraid so." He made a whacking motion against the back of his neck, and indicated how a severed head would have rolled. "And her life was filled with so much promise. Such a pretty thing—before, well—*before*."

Aghast, Lady Hermoine threw herself into his arms, and said, "Save me."

He patted her back and smiled over her head. Ella would have been furious with him for resorting to old and bad habits.

"My dear," he said, leading Hermoine to the front door and flinging it wide, "you have been through far too much for one day. I blame myself for that. You are clearly too delicate for so much excitement. Please, don't think you must come to me. I shall come to you."

"Egads," he said, when the carriage rolled away. "I am beside myself. What in God's name am I to do?"

"If I were you, I'd put my foot down, m'boy."

He swung around to see his tall, darkly handsome uncle, Arran Rossmara, Marquess of Stonehaven, approach.

"If you imagine your only problem is that dreadful young woman, you are much mistaken. Come here."

Max joined his uncle on the front steps and took the sheet of paper the older man offered. He read a few words, then looked at the signature. "Great-grandmama?"

"Yes," Arran said. "Your great-grandmama, the Dowager Duchess of Franchot, herself. And her companion, the extraordinarily annoying Blanche Wren Bastible—*my* mother-in-law."

"Egads," Max said again, more quietly. "And coming here. Because Great-grandmama has decided there's something afoot with me that is being kept from her."

"No one will ever stop that woman from interfering,"

Arran remarked. He wore his curly dark hair tied in an un-fashionable tail at the nape of his neck. So many females stared longingly at Arran and remarked on how they "adored" that tail, that Max had once considered growing one himself. He had changed his mind when Kirsty told him she liked his hair as it was.

Arran continued, "The dowager must be a hundred years old if she's a day, yet she continues to wield her cane like a pike and reduce all around her to cowering, gibbering idiots."

The comment was kindly made, and Max smiled. "But we all love her, don't we?"

Arran sighed. "We do indeed. But it has been so nice to spend time alone with my music. Something tells me all that is about to come to an end."

Max looked at the toes of his boots.

"Max," Arran said, "do you have something on your mind?"

"Nothing you need concern yourself with."

"Why don't I like the sound of that, I wonder?"

Because his uncle had been exposed to a few of Max's scrapes in the past. "Do you think Great-grandmama will side with Papa on Lady Hermoine?"

Arran considered. "If your father considers her suitable, and he certainly seems to, then the dowager duchess will lean in his direction."

"Do you remember that I spoke to you about Kirsty Mercer."

"Mmm."

Max glanced at him, at the speculative light in his dark eyes. A big, solid man, who adored his wife, his son, and his daughter, Arran was a man with music rather than blood in his veins.

"I asked you about Kirsty Mercer," Max pressed.

"You spoke of the possibility of hiring her as your assistant. You reminded me of her fine mind—which I had not forgotten."

"Yes, well, you said you didn't disapprove, and I've hired her."

"I see." Arran sank very straight teeth into his bottom lip. "I wonder what the dowager will make of that."

"Kirsty's family doesn't like it."

"They're old-fashioned. They believe people have their place and should not overstep their station. I'll speak to them about it."

Max grinned. "I was hoping you'd say that. You can do no wrong in their eyes."

"We go a long way back. I had the honor of delivering young Niall."

"Kirsty told me as much. She said you saved her mother's life."

"I doubt it," Arran said. "She'd have been well enough without me."

Max didn't pursue the topic. His uncle wasn't a man who sought accolades. "I'd very much appreciate your speaking to the Mercers. They're special people, and Kirsty loves them very much. I hate to see her so troubled."

"Do you?" Arran looked at him very directly. "You've never answered my questions on your feelings for Kirsty."

"We spent time together as children, nothing more," Max said, and knew he'd spoken too rapidly. "She's a remarkable young woman with a sharp intelligence. She will be very useful to me. Perhaps you can impress upon her family that I respect her ability."

"I can do that," Arran said. "Is that all?"

"Um, yes, more or less."

"More or less?"

"You said you considered Lady Hermoine a dreadful young woman."

Arran paused before saying, "Did I? A careless comment. After all, I scarcely know her."

"Why did you say it, then?"

"Because I know her type. She will bore you. In fact, she is very probably entirely wrong for you, but that is not for me to decide."

"Kirsty Mercer's in the rosy rooms."

Arran stared, then frowned. "She's what?"

"In the rosy rooms. You know, the rooms that used to be—"

"Ella's. Yes, I know. But what in goodness name is Kirsty doing there?"

"Her job as my assistant will be grueling, and I will want her ready to hand."

Arran looked at him sharply. "*Ready to hand?* An odd expression, wouldn't you say?"

"Not at all," Max shot back, but knew he was blustering. "It will be easier on Kirsty if she doesn't have to travel up from her father's home very day."

"Ah, I see," Arran said softly. "But, of course, it wouldn't be easier for you?"

Max whistled lightly before admitting, "Yes, for me also."

"And aren't the rosy rooms in the Eve Tower?"

"You know they are."

"And aren't your rooms in the Eve Tower?"

There was nothing for it but to meet his uncle's direct gaze. "You also know that is true."

"Isn't there a saying about trying to have one's haggis and eating it, too?"

"I thought cake was the edible in question."

"Cake, then," Arran said. "Could you be thinking in such terms?"

"You'll have to be clearer," Max said, heat inflaming every inch of him.

"Fair enough," Arran said. "I think you and I should go inside and discuss what's likely to occur as a result of your actions."

He'd hoped for more sympathy than this.

"I'll ask you one question direct, though, young friend. And now. Are you ready for that?"

Max doubted he was, but he raised his chin and said, "I'm ready for whatever comes my way."

"Anything but the loss of the chance to be with Kirsty Mercer."

There was no answer to that.

"Struck you dumb, I see," Arran told him. "Let me put it this way. You want to do your mother and father's will—and that will require marrying Lady Hermoine because they see her as the best possible match to cement your position as the gentleman son of a viscount."

"I'm an adopted bastard," Max murmured.

"You're a fine man," Arran said. "And it's time you stopped dwelling on the other. Let me finish, then we'll discuss more in private. You intend to go through with a sham of a marriage, correct?"

"I do not want to disappoint my parents."

"Quite so. But you have brought Kirsty Mercer to live under the very roof—and in close proximity—to the place where you live."

"I have," Max said, aware of how stubborn he sounded.

"Your intention, Max Rossmara, is to marry Lady Hermoine to please your parents. To get her with child, then give your blessing to whatever *diversions* she cares to entertain."

"You're remarkably direct."

"But accurate?"

Max looked skyward. "Perhaps."

"Don't mistake me for a fool, young friend. I have been in this world long enough to know the ways of men—especially desperate men, and men deeply in love. I should say you will definitely not concern yourself with Lady Hermoine's intrigues after you marry her. Because Kirsty Mercer is, even now, sleeping in the rosy rooms, and as soon as you can, and with little concern for what it will mean to her, you intend to make her your mistress."

Chapter Seven

Horace made a very thorough search of Hermoine's wardrobe and moved on to her dressing table. The little opportunist had certainly not been wasting her time—or her charms—since last they'd been together.

He examined the finest of silk stockings, each a masterpiece of embroidery right down to the tiny seed pearls sewn where they would not be sewn if they were meant to be seen when the lady was dressed.

And the jewels! Well, she had been a very busy girl. Much of what was in her jewelry box was worth comparatively little, but the single strand of black pearls was very nice. Even nicer were the diamond-and-ruby pendant and matching earrings, and a magnificent emerald ring. Oh, but there was a great deal for them to discuss.

"Mr. Horace, sir?" The door opened without his having heard a knock, and one of Gertie's girls came in. He knew this was Dahlia, Zinnia, or Wisteria, but despite their different coloring found the three well-endowed and willing creatures indistinguishable one from the other—especially in the dark.

He said, "Yes," but kept any hint of welcome out of his voice. He had more important matters to attend this night.

"I thought as how I might come and see how you were doing," the woman said. "It's a lonely life for a gentleman without a woman in these parts. I wanted you to know that, being as how you're related to the countess and Lady Hermoine, I'll be more than glad to cheer you up at any time. Just call for Zinnia, and I'll come at once, no matter what I'm doing."

Willing Zinnia wore a white-satin dressing gown trimmed with swansdown, and loosely belted. In her thick black hair were more white feathers, and her face was painted as if retiring for the night were the last thing she had in mind.

"You're very kind," he told her. No point in insulting the inmates of Gertie's cozy nest. "I'll remember your offer."

Smiling broadly, she loosened the belt on her robe to reveal a skimpy garment, also white, this apparently made of silk, which she clearly wore with nothing underneath. Her stockings were topped with a ridiculous band of swansdown to match that on her robe. Obviously no expense was spared on fripperies.

"I was thinking of going to bed," he told her.

"Why, what a coincidence," Zinnia said coyly. "So was I. Why don't we go together?"

"I find I'm rather tired this evening, or I'd be delighted to take you up on your generous offer." He couldn't deny to himself that his rod had risen to the challenge with remarkable alacrity. It now pressed, almost painfully, against his trousers.

"Oh, I understand. You're waiting for you, er, *cousin*."

"How do you know that?"

She smiled, and dipped, and wiggled her derriere. "This *is* her room, isn't it? And she is out at the moment?"

He felt annoyed at his own stupidity. "True, true. I wasn't

thinking. My cousin and I have a great deal of catching up to do. We haven't seen each other in months."

"How nice. I do agree with strong family feelings. I've got them myself. I'll leave you then. After I wish you sweet dreams."

She swished across the floor, feathers floating, the long open robe trailing behind her. Before he guessed her intent, she spread her legs and sat astride his thighs on Hermoine's dressing table stool. Wrapping her arms around his neck, she kissed him deeply. When she drew back, her mouth was moist, and her eyes sparkled. "You're a rare one," she said. "Wasted unless I miss my mark."

"You're a rare one yourself," Horace said, pulsing with need.

Promptly Zinnia slipped undone two little buttons that held the straps of her shift in place. The garment fell to her waist and Horace was confronted with two perfect, gold-tipped breasts. He wriggled on his seat, and the girl reached down to squeeze him.

"Just a little kiss good night," she said. "Or two or three. Here." With happy abandon, she cupped her breasts and offered them to him.

"Look," he said, eyeing the irresistible flesh, then the door, "it would be difficult if Hermoine were to, well, you know."

"Well, then, the quicker you have a little taste, the quicker I'll be gone. I'll be gone, and you can think about the next time I come to kiss you good night, can't you?"

She jerked back and forth on his thighs, and he felt warm moisture penetrate the cloth of his trousers.

"Oh, all right, just one, then," she told him, lifting one breast, and hauling his head down until his mouth met her nipple. "There you are. It'll make you feel ever so much better."

Better? He fought temptation for a second before opening

his mouth and drawing in as much of her as possible inside. She squealed with delight, and began to bounce up and down on his thighs, and to croon.

He grasped her other breast and pinched it until she forced him to switch his mouth there. Groping, he delved between her legs and found things as he'd assumed. She wore nothing beneath the scant shift, and she was wet, and hot.

Dimly, Horace heard the door opening.

"Bloody hell! In *my* rooms."

Dazed, he raised his face and looked into Hermoine's flashing golden eyes.

"Oops," Zinnia said, standing up. "Caught! Night, all." Holding her clothing together, she made a wide circle around Hermoine and ran, laughing loudly, from the room.

"Zinnia," Horace said. "Don't go too far away."

"What are you doing here?" Hermoine demanded, glaring, and slamming the door behind Zinnia. "What gives you the right to be here with that whore?"

"You're too harsh," Horace said, his heart slowing only the slightest bit. He was still aroused. "She came to comfort me, is all. We didn't do anything."

"Oh, I can see that." Looking pointedly at the bulge in his trousers, she tossed her reticule on the bed and went to the dressing table, where open drawers were proof that he'd been searching her possessions. "Find anything of interest?"

"Lots, dear cousin." He took advantage of the opportunity to look down the front of her dress. "More and more of interest. You always did have the best pair I ever saw."

She slapped his face hard but he caught her wrist and twisted it. "I shouldn't advise you to try that again. Not unless you want me to really hurt you. And you know I can. *And* you know I'm not speaking of hurting you physically. I can ruin your little plot."

"Go away," she told him. "I don't know what you're

doing here in Scotland. And neither does the countess. We thought you'd died in France."

"And you're both extremely disappointed. Can you imagine how that makes a man feel."

She found her diamond-and-ruby necklace and earrings and sighed with evident relief.

"Oh, Hermoine, dearest, I'm so wounded. You didn't think I'd *take* anything from you, did you? Why, all I've ever wanted was to give you things." With that he thrust his hand beneath her skirts and found the way inside her drawers to stroke the curls between her legs.

She struggled to evade him, but he took a firm hold on rapidly moistening hair, and held tight.

"You're a beast! A sick beast. Unhand me at once."

Rather than do as she asked, he put a hand around her waist and pushed several fingers into her heated channel. He restrained her and worked up and down until she cried out and panted and sagged against him.

"Still want me to unhand you?"

"This is wrong, and you know it."

"I don't know it. That little harlot served to get me in the mood for a real lady. You are a real lady, Hermoine, and your sex cries out for me. And, after all, what are relatives for if not to aid each other in times of need?"

Her sudden twist away caught him by surprise. She freed herself from him and backed across the room to take refuge on the far side of her bed. "What do you want, Horace?" she said.

"To be your champion," he said easily. "You said it so well earlier. I am going to be the support you need at such a time. Your needs will be met, I'll see to it. I shall stand beside you in all things?"

"And then what? What do you intend to do once I am married to Max Rossmara?"

He spread his hands. "I have been giving that some

thought. But after all, darling, I'm not at all sure you intend to marry the man."

The draining of blood from her face gave him all the assurance he needed that he had come to the right assumption.

"I don't know what you're saying," she said. "Of course I will marry him."

"Will you?"

She glared at him. "Yes, I will, and if you try to get in my way, I'll kill you."

He knew a cold moment of fear. She might just hate him enough to do what she threatened.

"I wouldn't get in the way of the good of all, my little bird. Oh, no, I will help the cause, you may depend on that. Did you have a chance to, er, do any reconnaissance tonight?"

Her frown let him know that Gertie hadn't revealed his knowledge of the plot at hand.

"I do know about the journal, my lovely."

"What journal?"

"Oh, don't take that tone with me. The Journal of the League of Jolly Gentlemen. What else?"

She grew even paler. "Who told you?" she whispered.

"A certain gentleman who knows of my connection to you and Gertie. He sent for me. Quite the moment that was, I can tell you. After all, we've all heard a great deal about him. Finest general this country has ever known, perhaps the world has ever known. And he sent for me and talked to me like an old friend."

"You mean Welling—"

"*Don't* speak his name aloud, not ever, do you understand?"

"Yes," she whispered. "But why did he want to talk to you about—well—about it?"

"Because his name's there. The esteemed gentleman who

compiled the journal in the first place—a man of the *highest* rank—wrote down the names of all who took part in his little *experiments* as he liked to call them. Their names and some enlightening diagrams."

"I know," Hermoine said. "But it was another gentleman who came to the countess. How many more of them can there be? Rich and famous ones, I mean?"

Horace got to his feet and approached the bed. "Quite a number, I gather. Quite a number with good reason to want that book out of harm's way. And if what I was offered by the person we've discussed is anything to go by, we're going to be set for life."

"If we can get our hands on the journal," she reminded him.

"We will. Stolen by a scrawny red-haired pickpocket in Covent Garden. Why, the royal gentleman himself told the story about how the boy leaped into his coach and made off with a valuable fob watch and the journal. The boy was never seen in the area again. And that was the night when Viscount Hunsingore took a little criminal into his home and called him his own son. A little, red-haired, green-eyed bastard whose sister the viscount had already rescued from a brothel. Can't be two of them, can there?"

Hermoine's smile pleased him. She was a fighter, and she wouldn't miss an opportunity like this. "Ella," she said. "I'm told she's married to a Lord Avenall and leads a life above reproach. And Max Rossmara is her brother. Their early lives were hideous. You're right, clever Horace, there cannot be two such brothers and sisters connected to the Rossmaras, *and* connected to the situation we know of in Covent Garden."

"Well," he said. "So the time has come to find out exactly what our pigeon did with that journal. He's got it about him somewhere. You can be sure of that. He's waiting for a moment when he thinks it's worth the most—only you're going to get it for us first."

"What if the journal is just that, a list of names? Who would care about that?"

Horace laughed. "I know different." He gathered a handful of ribbons from the dressing table. "The royal gentleman considered himself quite the artist. As I said, he liked to draw certain diagrams, as it were, of certain activities. I insisted that at least a few were described to me, so I'd know when I had the right volume."

"Really?" Hermoine said.

"Really, cousin. Of course, I'm going to have to make sure you'll recognize them, too." He rushed her, backed her into a corner beside the bed. "It's been too long since you and I had a little fun, and this is in the name of commerce."

She pressed herself into the corner.

"You're limber, my love. I remember that, too." At moments like this he wished his belly didn't overhang his greater glory. "Of course, you'll have to remember that the Jolly Gentlemen shared and shared alike. All for one and one for all, as it were."

"You're frightening me, Horace. I shall scream."

"Come back in here, Zinnia, my love dove," he called. "Come in and close the door."

"No," Hermoine cried. "I don't want her here. She's nothing but a leech. Send her away."

Zinnia, her face flushed, entered the room and obediently closed the door.

"Hermoine and I are going to perform an experiment," he told her. "An experiment guaranteed to silence Hermoine's strident tongue and bring her to heel very nicely. Are you strong, Zinnia?"

She ran her tongue over her lips. "Oh, very strong. There's some who say Zinnia's got the strongest legs in the land."

"Stop it at once, Horace," Hermoine demanded. "Otherwise, I shall summon the countess."

"By the time you are able to do so, it will be too late. We are going to study one of that elevated personage's diagrams and follow his instructions—as they were explained to me. Get on the bed, please, Hermoine."

She let out a howl and crossed her arms.

"Now, if you please." He had to break her if he was going to make her his willing emissary.

"Nooo." She slid down the wall and huddled on the floor.

"Very well. Zinnia, kindly assist me. I shall take Lady Hermoine's ankles, you shall take her wrists. She will try to strike you. Can you manage?"

A look of pure delight entered Zinnia's eyes. "Oh, I can indeed, sir. She'll be no match for me."

"Good. Since she abhors the bed, kindly help me carry her to the center of the floor. Oh, you might want to lock the door first."

Zinnia rushed to do his bidding and returned, standing like a fighter with her arms and legs spread and her tongue held between her teeth.

"Now," Horace said, and managed to capture Hermoine's flailing feet.

With only slightly more difficulty, Zinnia pinned Hermoine's wrists, and they carried her between them across the room.

"Put down my skirts," Hermoine shrieked. Horace hoped that wasn't a hint of laughter he heard in her voice. "At once. How dare you treat me like this. You'll suffer, see if you don't."

Horace met Zinnia's excited stare and shook his head. "Help me get her clothes off."

Hermoine screamed afresh, and Zinnia cackled. She put Hermoine's wrists on the floor above her head and knelt on them, then set about leaning over her victim to tear at the lilac gown.

"I shall kill you for this," Hermoine said through her teeth. "The countess will have you thrown out."

"You will never say a word, will she, Zinnia? After all, how could a woman of any respect explain what she will take part in tonight. Especially when we both speak of the entire affair having been her idea."

"Let me go!"

Her bodice parted, torn asunder, and Horace dealt with the skirts and petticoats. In short order Hermoine lay dressed only in stays and drawers. Her chemise was a tattered thing that was quickly disposed of.

"Look at those tits," Horace said.

Zinnia promptly pulled her flimsy white garment over her head and, completely nude, resumed her position on Hermoine's wrists. "She doesn't have anything I don't have," Zinnia said petulantly.

"Of course she doesn't," Horace said. "But there are variations in all things." He'd forgotten how sumptuous the fair Hermoine's body was, how shapely her legs and curved her hips below a tiny waist, and her breasts, ah, yes, such breasts.

He struggled to free himself of his trousers.

"You wouldn't," Hermoine gasped, and this time Horace was certain she was trying not to laugh. "Not in front of *her*."

"Not exactly." He hauled her to her feet. Quite the little actress was Hermoine. "Lie down, Zinnia, if you please."

"Now, look 'ere, I—"

"Lie down. I assure you this will be an occasion to remember."

Moving far too slowly for his liking, she began to stretch herself on her back.

"On your face," he snapped.

"I don't know what you're about," Zinnia complained.

He made a circle with a forefinger to encourage her co-operation and said, "But you're going to find out." Containing Hermoine's struggling body became more of a chore, but a rather pleasant chore.

Zinnia did as she was told, and without ceremony Horace pushed Hermoine down so that she lay back-to-back with the other girl, who lay facedown. Sitting astride them both, he appropriated the long sash from Zinnia's robe to lash the pair together. Casting about, he located a piece of ribbon and joined their wrists. Anything they might choose to do with their legs could only make the process more interesting.

"I'm puffed," Zinnia said, sounding weak. "She's 'eavy."

"I most certainly am not."

"You'll soon be transported, both of you. Pain will be a small price to pay for such a prize."

"Let me up," Hermoine beseeched. "I don't like this."

"Don't you?" Horace said, standing to remove his trousers and smallclothes. "Just tell yourself you're going to feel the ecstasy all the way to your vitals." He was erect and ready, and he must be fast. "And remember how deliciously wicked this is—under the circumstances. A reenactment of an historic event, as it were."

He gave them no more time to protest, but fell upon Hermoine and parted her drawers to admit his engorged rod. He grunted, and she panted. With something close to transportation, he fastened his mouth on a nipple and suckled while he pumped. For an instant he thought he'd not have the restraint to stop in time, but in the second it took to move to her other breast, he withdrew his penis, and helped himself to quite another part of the woman beneath her.

Zinnia howled, then laughed, a long, deep, gurgling laugh. And all the time he sucked and nipped at Hermoine's magnificent breasts.

"Horace!" Her face was puce. "Oh, Horace, I do believe you . . . Well, this is beyond all. This was in the book?"

"Hush, my love," he said, raising his face but unable to bring hers clearly into focus.

She jerked her hips up and down. "Finish it, Horace. Please. You can't leave me like this."

"We're on our way," he said, and sweat fell from his brow onto her white flesh. He rose up and contrived with great effort to turn the two over.

Zinnia shrieked with laughter again. "Wait till I tell Wisteria and Dahlia. They'll both want a turn."

"Tell them nothing," Horace said, while deciding he'd have to make sure they got their "turn."

"Get off me," Hermoine said. "At once, do you hear? I'm becoming impatient." Unconcerned with Hermoine's patience, Horace set about plunging himself into Zinnia's weeping center. She jerked her hips up and down to meet him and grinned, passing her tongue around her lips. He licked her nipples, and that's when the last of his control failed.

He poured forth into her, to the accompaniment of her uproarious giggling. "I won," she hiccuped. "Nothing for *Lady* Hermoine. Everything for poor, common little Zinnia. But who can blame you Horace, love. How could you resist me?"

"You're disgusting," Hermoine growled from beneath her adversary. "Let me up at once. I must bathe. Ooh, disgusting."

Horace joined Zinnia's laughter, but he quickly untied their wrists and separated their bodies. Before Hermoine could recover enough to fly at Zinnia, he grabbed the latter's clothes and pushed her into the corridor with them.

He locked the door behind her and turned to Hermoine. "Don't tell me you didn't find that interesting."

She glowered at him, her breasts heaving wonderfully. He began to grow hard again.

"You're going to pay for what you did to me tonight," she said.

Horace went to her, hauled her from her feet, and

wrapped her legs around his waist. "Have you forgotten how strong I am?" he asked.

"Leave me alone."

"But you haven't had what you want, what you deserve."

"I'm going to the countess."

He impaled her, and bounced her up and down, alternating his attention between the exquisite satisfaction on her face, and her jouncing breasts. Within seconds it was all over and she rested her head on his shoulder.

Horace carried her to the bed, stretched her out, and arranged himself beside her, where he could continue his play.

"I don't understand you," she said sleepily.

"You do if you think about it."

She opened her eyes.

"Max Rossmara has the journal we need. Do you think he hasn't studied every page?"

"Mmm. What does it matter as long as we get the book?"

"We both saw today that he's got a little friend he's rather fond of."

"A peasant," Hermoine said with disdain, "a nobody."

"Not to him."

"He's going to marry me, and I won't stand for any peccadilloes."

"Coming from you, that's rich." He snickered. "I wonder how many women have made themselves that promise."

She turned her face away.

"All I need is for you to listen, my lovely one," he said. "This evening's exercise has been my insurance. Try to cheat me of my fair share and the fair Zinnia will come forward to tell Mr. Rossmara all about how you've been at his private possessions and how you've put some interesting ideas into practice."

"What if he's hidden the journal? He'll know I couldn't have found it."

"Well, he'll go to check on it, won't he? And I'll be ready to follow him."

"He may not look for it at all," Hermoine pointed out.

Horace buried his face in her belly and smiled. "Then I'll have to implement my second plan and borrow his little friend."

"He won't care," she snapped. "Once he's got me, he'll forget her."

"Mr. Rossmara will not abandon the girl. He'll be told how she's going to be used, and he'll come after her."

"And then you'll have Max Rossmara and the peasant. What a nuisance and a bore."

"Hardly," Horace said. He rolled Hermoine over and slapped her bottom until she reared up and fought. He liked his women to fight. Once he'd restrained her, he said, "With your help—and after all, you're practiced now—we'll give Mr. Rossmara a demonstration. How far we get with the demonstration will depend upon how quickly he agrees to give us the journal."

"He'll call in the law."

"Dead men can't call the law."

Chapter Eight

*B*lack.

Max hesitated in the doorway to the breakfast room and studied Kirsty's back. She wore a black gown of heavy serge. An apparently huge gown, and entirely unsuitable to the occasion, and to the season. She had overcome the problem of the garment being too long by pulling the waist as close to the level of her own as possible and tying a brown velvet ribbon about it. If the front looked even mildly as bad as the back, then she had accomplished a truly frightful outfit in which to make her first appearance as his assistant.

And this was the day on which he intended her to encounter people he wished her to impress.

"Good morning, Kirsty," he said.

With a terrible clatter, she dropped the cup and saucer she was carrying to the table, and whirled around.

The front of the gown wasn't *as* bad as the back: it was worse. A fichu of dull purple lace covered the place where the bodice probably gaped. Max managed to cover his anger with a smile, and to go to his knees to retrieve the broken pieces of china. A servant had already appeared, and took over the task of cleaning up the mess.

"Sit down, sit down," Max said with false cheer, trying not to look at her ensemble. "I'm sorry I surprised you. Tea was it?"

She subsided into a chair, gripped the edge of the table, and nodded.

"Good. I'll join you." He poured for both of them and carried the cups safely to the table. "Now, will you have toast, perhaps?"

She shook her head.

"Eggs? Kidneys? Kippers?"

At each suggestion she shook her head and became more pallid. Too afraid to be hungry, he decided, and brought her a piece of toast and a pot of marmalade. "At least eat a little," he said quietly. "I'm sure you're nervous, but an empty stomach will not help."

She smiled at that, and his heart lifted. Kirsty Mercer was a survivor, and she would survive this.

At that moment Arran entered, surprising Max since his uncle made a habit of dining alone in Revelation when Grace and their children weren't at home. "Good morning,"

Arran said. "And good morning to you, too, Kirsty Mercer. What a charming start to a morning to find you at our table."

Max saw her relax a little. She looked at Arran with complete trust. "Good morning, your lordship. I hope I'm no' in t'way here."

"Not a bit of it," Arran said heartily. "Max has told me how you're going to help him get organized. Long overdue, I can tell you. The rascal is a clever one though. He knows potential when he sees it, and he's seen yours."

She lowered her eyes and blushed.

"I'm off to take a look at things myself today," Arran said. "I'll be stopping in on your parents. Can I given them a message from you?"

Gratitude all but overwhelmed Max.

Kirsty said, "I'm no' sure," very quietly. "Would ye mind sayin' I love them? And that I'll be vistin' after my work's done this day, perhaps?"

"Of course I don't mind. Glad to do it."

Arran poured himself some coffee and emptied his cup in a swallow. "Well, I'd best be off. Look after her, Max. It'll be an intimidating thing to face down some of our fine, but old-fashioned men. But if anyone is up to the task, you are, Kirsty. Welcome to you, my girl, welcome. I look forward to having you as a member of our team." With that, and one of the grins Max understood were so irresistible to women, his uncle left.

"He's a braw man," Kirsty said, her voice still nothing more than a whisper. "We're all verra lucky t'be his tenants."

"You're no longer his tenant," Max said. "You're a member of this household, a very valued member."

She didn't respond.

She didn't drink tea.

She didn't eat toast and marmalade.

Max glanced at the servant who stood, eyes straight

ahead, at one end of the sideboard. Young, with sandy-colored hair and a narrow, ruddy-complexioned face, his pale stare was anything but disinterested in what unfolded around him. "That'll be all, thank you, Wilkie," he said. "Kindly close the door as you leave and make it known in the kitchens that we will not need further attention."

A deferential bow, and Wilkie removed himself.

Max studied Kirsty, and then he began to pace.

That she was here at all was his doing—entirely his doing.

He'd plucked her from familiar surroundings and planted her in a foreign place.

He paused to look at her. She laced her fingers tightly together in her lap and kept her eyes directed at them.

Whatever he did, he must not lose his temper with her. The decisions he'd made, his inability to give up everything for the love of her, were not her fault.

"You didn't find that gown in the closet, did you?"

She raised her troubled eyes, and shook her head.

"Answer me when I speak to you."

"No, sir."

"Damn it all. You were never a mousy creature. Don't turn into a mouse on me now. I'll not have it. Do you understand?"

She flushed bright red. "Yes, sir."

A feeling he knew too well began to overcome him. "Where did that monstrosity come from?" He'd do well to leave her, to come back when he could be calm.

"I'll no' get someone in trouble for tryin' t'help me."

"Mairi, I suppose. She's not in trouble. You must have asked her for it, so why should she be in trouble?"

"Aye, ye're right. She's a bonnie one. Kind."

"Why didn't you do as I told you to do?"

He saw her swallow, and saw how hard it was to do so. He opened and closed his fingers. She should be his wife.

They should be married, with a child or two, and living a quiet, loving life. He need only have returned as he'd promised, and gone to her, and she would have accepted whatever he had to offer. But his parents would have been devastated, and he and Kirsty wouldn't have belonged anywhere but among strangers.

"I asked you a question." Why couldn't he stop himself from berating her?

Kirsty inclined her head. "Lady Avenall's gowns are verra beautiful—"

"I told you she doesn't want or need them anymore." He went to stand over her. "They are gowns from when she was younger. She has probably forgotten they even exist. That is not the point. I have employed you, and I told you to choose one of those gowns, not that ridiculous thing you have pinned and tied upon you."

"It's no' my fault!" She stood up and all but knocked over her chair. She caught it and set it steadily on its legs again. "How can ye think I should go about as your assistant dressed in silks and satins, with pearls and feathers on me? What impression would I make wi' all that lady's finery? Am I t'learn about the estate with satin slippers on my feet? Ye're no' thinkin', Max Rossmara. And your temper needs attention. It's the talk o' the land. Your black moods they call them."

Max's head pounded. "You're angry with me."

"*I'm* angry?" she said, hitching at her skirts.

"Yes, you're angry because I didn't keep a silly promise made when we were children."

"Oh." She took a backward step and put her hands on the table behind her.

"Yes," Max said. "Oh. If you'll think about it, you'll know I'm right." He didn't seem to have any control over his tongue.

"If ye're talkin' about promises we made when ye were

twenty-two and I was sixteen, well then, we weren't children, were we? Not that I'm wantin' to discuss such things—things gone by—but dinna try to make your conscience clean by pretendin' things were other than they were."

"You never overcame that low mode of speech. You'll have to work on it. I'll hire an elocution teacher for you."

She raised her head. "Ye can hire an elocution teacher, sir, but no' for me. I speak t'way my people have always spoken. Is it ugly?"

It was his turn to swallow. "No. But it's not educated." He had always delighted in her soft speech.

"Am I educated?"

"Yes, you are. Very educated."

"Then the manner o' my speech doesna matter, does it? After all, I've no' got t'impress anyone wi' it. I'm no' a fine lady. I'm not the woman at your side who has to entertain the highborn, am I? I'm goin' t'be your assistant. Your servant. It'll stand me in better stead if I'm one o' the folk I'll be dealin' with. Once they accept me, that is."

The fury overflowed. "That's what this is all about, isn't it?"

She shook her head slowly, but didn't move away from him.

"It's because you've never forgiven me for not throwing everything up to marry you."

"No!"

"*Don't argue with me.* The sooner we get this into the open and get rid of it, the better."

"There's nothin' t'get into the open. I'd be grateful t'get t'work, sir."

"We'll get to work when I say we'll get to work." Breathing hard, he went around the heavy, richly polished mahogany table and poured himself some coffee. And into the coffee he splashed a generous measure of brandy. "There are things you must understand. The past must be forgotten. The things of childhood are the things of childhood. They have no place in the adult world."

"No, they don't."

"That black shambles of a thing makes you ridiculous."

"No doubt, it does. It's far too big, but I didna have time t'work on it."

Her audacity inflamed him. "Silk and satin and feathers would have been fine for today, miss. And you should have worn them because I told you to. A modiste will be here by evening."

"I'm t'visit my family this evenin'."

Never a crack in her determination. "Then the modiste will await your return if necessary."

"I'm sorry I've made ye angry," Kirsty said. "But ye're unreasonable."

"*Don't* presume to tell me I am unreasonable." He took a drink. The brandy warmed him.

"This is no' the time o' day for strong liquor," Kirsty said.

He stared at her, amazed. "What did you say?"

"It's too early t'be drinkin' strong liquor. Ye're an angry man who's tryin' t'drive away his demons. Ye'll no' do it that way, sir. My father had to speak to Mungo Dunn—"

"Damn you. Damn your nerve." He tossed off the rest of the laced coffee. "*Mungo Dunn?* A drunken sot laborer. What has he to do with me? When I want your advice, I'll ask for it. Get back to your rooms and change. *Now*."

She started for the door.

"I saw a blue taffeta dress in the wardrobe. Put it on. It will suit you—match your eyes."

Kirsty turned back and said, "I must make sure ye understand somethin'. I'm here because I want to advance myself. I'm grateful for the opportunity, sir."

"Good."

"I'm no' pinin' for love o' ye. As ye said, the blatherin' o' children is just that. Blatherin'. And best forgotten."

He snorted. "A different story from the one you told a few minutes ago when you reminded me of our age when we made those promises."

She raised her pointed chin. Her hair was as flaxen and fine as ever. "I wasna thinkin' how it would sound—just settin' matters to rights. After all, we decided we were t'have a club, too, didn't we? A wish club." Her laugh didn't convince him. "Well, then, we must have been children to make up such silly things. I don't pine for ye, sir. I've no intention of marryin'. I've no intention of marryin' anyone unless I meet a man who'll treat me as his equal, and always be kind t'me as I'll be kind t'him. And mayhap I'll meet such a man. He was never meant t'be ye. So don't trouble yoursel' more about the subject."

Kirsty left the room.

Max poured more brandy into his cup. He didn't bother with coffee.

Arran drew back into an alcove until Kirsty passed and ran up the staircase. He looked at her straight back. She made no sound, but he'd swear there were tears in her eyes.

If this was any man's business but Max's, then it was Struan's. God knew there had already been too many times when Arran had clashed with his brother. Theirs was a strong bond, but a fiery one, and he had no wish to bring about another battle.

Struan wasn't at Kirkcaldy. Arran was. And he'd just heard Max shouting at Kirsty Mercer as no rational man should. Arran waited until he was certain Kirsty was well away, tried again to persuade himself to leave well enough alone, failed, and went into the breakfast room.

"I put an envelope down on the sideboard," he said, giving Max the briefest of glances. "Or I thought I did."

Max didn't answer.

"There it is."

Max grunted. Arran looked at him, then and cursed himself for not having walked away. "What is it?" he asked. "What's wrong with you?"

"Nothing," Max mumbled. He sat at the table looking into his cup.

"Don't lie to me. And look at me when I speak to you." Arran kept his voice low and even. "In case you've forgotten, you may be my nephew, but you do work for me."

"And I work for you bloody well," Max snapped back. "I give you all the hours of the day—and a good many of the night. Every day. What more do you want?"

"Civility would be a pleasant addition."

Max rose and went to a row of decanters on a trolley. He poured cognac into the cup.

"Why not use a glass?" Arran said, but fear curled in his belly. So the rumors were true. Max's evil tempers did coincide with bouts of drinking.

"You've got your envelope," Max said, resuming his seat. "Don't let me detain you."

"I want to call in a doctor," Arran said. "You aren't yourself. You haven't been yourself this past year or more, and you're getting worse."

"There's nothing wrong with me," Max said through his teeth. "Nothing wrong that wouldn't be cured by being left alone to decide what's best for me. But thank you for your concern."

"How long have you been drinking in the morning?"

"I—" Max pushed the cup away. "It makes me feel better. Or it did."

"That's not an answer to my question."

"It's the only answer you'll get. I'll deal with my own affairs."

Arran looked about the beautiful room. Since he preferred

his quarters in Revelation, he'd spent little time here, but he saw its appeal. "Are you unhappy here?"

"No."

"Too fast with your answer," Arran said. "Why were you shouting at Kirsty Mercer?"

Max raised tormented eyes to Arran. "I . . . She made me angry."

"Why?"

"I'd asked her to use some of Ella's old gowns. Kirsty has very little, of course, and I want her properly dressed. She defied me."

"*Defied* you? Surely you're harsh, Max."

"What would you know about how I feel . . . I'm beset. I apologize for my foul humor. There's unrest in the land. But you know that."

Arran shook his head. "I know it, but that's not what angers you. The man I heard wasn't the man I know. The man I know wouldn't frighten an innocent girl."

"No, no!" There was pain in Max's denial. "She has spirit. She wasn't afraid of me. Never that."

"You're in love with her, aren't you?" Arran said. "You as good as admitted it to me on more than one occasion. You're still in love with her."

"Leave me be."

"You denied your love of her to satisfy your father. It's a noble thing to honor your father, but a man has to stand by what matters most to him."

Max fell back in his chair and gripped the arms. "I am not in love with her. She's nothing to me but a good mind worth putting into service. I'm to marry Lady Hermoine Rashly. Or had you forgotten?"

"To please your father."

"How many wellborn women, titled women in their own right, do you think would be prepared to marry an adopted bastard? I bring very little to the match."

The boy could be a hardheaded fool. "Very little but money, of which the lady in question appears to have all but none. Ask your father why he married Justine."

"I already know. He adores her. He has from the moment they met."

"Well, then? An interesting thought to ponder, don't you think?"

"Nothing at all to ponder," Max said, his nostrils flared. "It doesn't change the duty I owe my father. Love cannot be for me, Uncle."

Arran regarded him a few seconds more, then nodded and left the room.

Kirsty reached the hall and curtsied, but his lordship, who had clearly just left the breakfast room, had already walked past, a thunderous expression pulling down his brows. She glanced toward the corridor from which he'd come and guessed he'd just left Max, and that harsh words had been spoken. She looked at the flagstones and blinked, and gathered her courage. Living in fear of someone, even if he did consider himself your master, was no way to live at all, and she wouldn't do it.

All the fine, strong words in her head didn't make the steps to that breakfast room easier, nor did they take the sweat from her palm as she opened the door and went in.

"I'd a good look at mysel' in that black thing, and ye were right," she said lightly. "A terrible fright I was. But mayhap ye miscalculated. I could have frighted all your people into respectin' me."

Max sat at the table where, Kirsty noted, there seemed a considerable muddle of china and silver, and a puddle of whatever had spilled from an overturned cup.

Then he looked at her, really looked at her. Their eyes met and she saw, with a clarity that twisted her stomach, the old

Max. Naked to his heart, the heart she'd only guessed he'd been hiding these past years. She guessed no longer.

He broke the moment by lowering his gaze to her dress, and she felt the wrench of his pulling away from her again. Next time he'd be more careful not to let her see that he had any gentle feelings for her, if there were ever to be a next time.

His sudden bark of laughter made her flinch. He pushed to his feet and planted his hands on his hips. "Contrary miss," he said, still laughing. "I should have known taming you would take more than a day or two."

"I assure ye I'm quite tame, sir," she told him, struggling not to smile.

He approached, pointing at her dress. "That doesn't look like blue taffeta to me."

"I agreed t'change. I didna agree t'wear any blue taffeta."

"So you thought you'd aggravate an already troubled man by putting your own dress back on."

Trusting his changed mood would be foolish, but she would make certain he knew he couldn't break her will with his roaring. "I'll wear what fits. And what shouldna displease anyone. And what pleases me."

"So I see." He reached her, settled a hand on the back of her neck, and steered her from the room. "And, as I've already acknowledged, I should have known taming you wouldn't be easy. But tame you, I will, my girl."

Chapter Nine

Noon, and she'd done nothing more interesting than sit at a beautiful, but much too small desk for practical purposes, and write regrets in response to invitations addressed to Max.

Well, she had done something more interesting—she'd looked at Max whenever she dared, and that was whenever she could tell he was too engrossed to catch her eye.

A discreet tap came at the door, and Shanks entered. With his head thrust forward in a manner that reminded Kirsty of a strutting chicken, he approached Max's desk with a silver tray in hand.

Max continued to write, to frown, and to write more. From time to time he referred to cumbersome ledgers, and to estate maps.

Shanks didn't honor Kirsty with as much as a glance. Finally he cleared his throat, and Max raised his face.

"Luncheon is served, sir," Shanks said. "I wouldn't normally disturb you, but then, you wouldn't normally be late, would you?"

Max pushed back from the desk. "I'll ignore your very thinly disguised rudeness, Shanks. I don't have time for lunch. Kindly have a cold plate sent in for me. Will a cold plate suit you, Kirsty? Or should you prefer to go to the dining room?"

"I'll eat at my desk if ye please," she said.

Shanks sniffed so ferociously she wondered he didn't topple backward. He said, "If that's what you require, sir."

"It is. Thank you." Max looked at the tray. "Is that something for me?"

"Just delivered, sir." The tray was extended, and Max removed an envelope. "Thank you, Shanks. That will be all." He took up a paper knife and slitted open the envelope.

Shanks stood absolutely still.

Max removed a sheet of paper and flattened it on the desk.

Shanks slowly leaned toward Max, his chin even farther

forward on his neck, obviously attempting to read the letter upside down.

"Yes?" Max said, looking up sharply.

Shanks jumped and backed rapidly out of the room.

Kirsty took up her pen again and looked at the next invitation, this one to a ball at The Hallows. "I expect I'm to accept this one for ye," she said.

"Decline them all," Max said vaguely.

"It's from The Hallows. A ball. In honor o' the presence o' the countess's nephew, the Honorable Horace Hubble."

"*Decline.*"

The snarl was back in his voice. Kirsty took a refreshing breath, and said, "D'ye not think ye should accept an invitation from your betrothed's aunt?"

"I damn well . . ." Rocking back in his chair, he ran both hands through his thick hair and clasped his fingers behind his head. "I'm a bad-tempered devil, aren't I?"

"Aye, ye are."

"Hmm. You aren't supposed to agree with me. Do you know what this is?" He indicated the letter on his desk. "It's from my father. He's on his way back here. Even as we speak. And he's not alone. My sainted great-grandmother— Mama's grandmother—and her insufferable companion are with him."

"The viscount's a wonderful man."

"That dress has to go."

"We're talkin' about your father. He's lovely. Kind and generous. And your mother is beautiful inside and out—and a saint t'have put up wi' ye."

Max rocked forward and rested his elbows on the desk. "I'll allow that piece of impertinence to pass." He tented his fingers. "You do remember Great-grandmama?"

"I do indeed. A wonderful old lady."

"A sly, demanding, determined harridan."

"Och, Max! What ever can be the matter with ye, speakin'

so o' the dowager? Age deserves reverence, so my parents taught me. Age and the wisdom it brings."

He smiled, and for the second time in one day she saw the old Max. Devilish and proud of it. "A harridan. And Blanche Bastible in attendance. The troops are gathering, my girl."

"For what purpose?"

He regarded her steadily, and for much longer than was comfortable. "Never mind. Decline the invitation to The Hallows."

"Are ye certain?"

His raised hand silenced her protest. "I have no time to devote to such foolishness. Great changes are afoot in Scotland. If we don't stand firm, before long the order of things will be very different for all. We at Kirkcaldy have done well to protect the old ways for as long as we have."

Kirsty's heart beat faster. "Ye mean it could happen here, too?"

There was no need to ask her what she meant by "it." "No family will be put from Kirkcaldy lands to make way for sheep or anything else. The clearings have been a tragedy— so many innocent people driven from their houses by greedy lairds. But that isn't all of it. Nothing stays the same. We shall care for our own, but the task will only become more troublesome."

"Aye." She thought of her mother and father, and of Niall, Niall who had a lifetime ahead of him and who had never known any other way of things but living and working on Kirkcaldy land—any more than she had. "I thought ye were to have me dealin' wi' estate matters."

"All in good time. First we must be very accustomed to working together. We must develop a . . . *rapport*. That's French for—"

"I know what it's French for, thank ye. We used to understand each other well enough."

"And we will again, but we do need to spend considerable

time together to be completely comfortable. Ideally you should be able to catch my meaning from no more than a look. We'll be dealing with some very sensitive issues."

They were already dealing with a very sensitive issue. Kirsty twiddled her pen and chastised herself for errant thoughts. How would the future unfold? How would it be to watch him with his wife and share what he termed a close *rapport* with him, to read his mind without his having to speak it?

Oh, she'd like to leave this study now and walk upon the hills with Max at her side. She'd like to forget the truth of it all and pretend they were as they'd once been. Beyond the windows streaks of grubby clouds hustled their way over their puffy white brothers and sisters, bringing the promise of rain to come. Sunlight glowed along the ragged edges of a hole to the sky as if its heat had burned a path through the demanding clouds.

Trees bent before a wind. On the moors that wind would grab her skirt and hair, and toss Max's dark red curls about. And the higher they climbed, the stronger the blow.

Only the time of Hermoine's arrival surprised Max. She burst into his study when the hour approached six. He'd sent a servant to The Hallows with his response to the invitation immediately after lunch. But since he knew Hermoine was in the habit of resting at that hour he had not expected to hear from her before the following day—or at worst, much later that evening.

"Max, you must get rid of this person," Hermoine said, casting angry looks in Kirsty's direction. "She is a jealous opportunist." With that she tossed his response to the countess's invitation onto his desk.

"Perhaps ye'd like me t'leave?" Kirsty said.

Max said, "Not a bit of it. Stay where you are, if you

please. Finish your work. Now, Hermoine, what's all this about?"

Gold eyes flashing, she leaned across the desk and for one rather dreadful moment he feared her breasts might spill entirely free of her bodice. As if she knew his thought, she wriggled a little to bring his fears as close as possible to fruition. "Send her away," she whispered ferociously. "I wish to be alone with you."

"Oh, you can feel free to speak in front of Kirsty," he told her in hearty tones. "The soul of discretion, I assure you. I'd trust her with my life."

"She's doing things behind your back, I tell you. She's not to be trusted."

"Rubbish. Honest as the day is long." My God, how would he tolerate this woman as his wife?

Hermoine's dress was pink, overly frilly, and unsuited to her mature figure. Ostrich plumes bobbled above her satin bonnet, and pink roses clustered beneath its brim. "Very well," she said, straightening and turning so that Kirsty could also see her face. "This devious creature interfered with your acceptance of my dear aunt's invitation. She wrote that your *declined*."

Kirsty looked at him directly, and there was a challenge in that look, an "I told you so," challenge.

"And so I did. With regret. I wouldn't dream of troubling your pretty head with the very serious matters presently facing me as commissioner of this estate. Sufficient to say that I have no time for frivolities. I'm sure you understand."

Hermoine's blank expression assured him that she did not understand.

"For that reason," he continued, "I shall not attend the *dear* countess's ball in your cousin's honor."

"Not attend my *ball*?" Lady Hermoine said faintly. "When my aunt intends to announce our betrothal, and you should have concern for nothing other than myself?"

He would not become angry with this foolish creature. She was to be his cross, and he would bear her with as much grace as possible. His eyes met Kirsty's. Heaven help him stand not being able to have her.

Hermoine's voice rose to a shrill tone, "Did you hear what I told you?"

"Indeed," he said quietly, holding Kirsty's gaze. "But the ball in question is in honor of your cousin. There will be no announcement of any betrothal that includes me until I say it shall be so. Is that understood?"

"Oh!" Hermoine staggered back a step. "How can you be so cruel? And in front of a stranger."

"Not a stranger," Max said. "But no matter. I am not cruel, merely factual. No formal negotiations have been completed on the matter of any betrothal. Those will not be dealt with unless my parents are present. I'm sure you understand this. Please tell your aunt that I appreciate her kind intentions, but that I cannot, at present, accept them."

"I am wounded,'" Hermoine said. "That you should find it necessary to place such calculated restrictions on a matter of the heart is crushing to a woman such as myself, a woman of strong passions who puts those passions ahead of such distasteful matters as *money*."

Max found that Hermoine had a strange effect on him. He listened to her and became numbed by boredom. "Yes," he said vaguely.

She turned to Kirsty. "Where are you from, girl? I assume you must have special training to be able to take such a position as this. Not that I was aware that females ever did so. Speak up. Where did you come from? Edinburgh?"

"Och, no!" Kirsty appeared shocked at the suggestion. "I've never been to that city. I'm from here."

Hermoine's eyes narrowed. "*Here?* What can you mean, here?"

"I was born on Kirkcaldy land, and I've lived here all my life."

"Who are your people?"

Max decided he could not do a better job of dealing with this than Kirsty could.

"My people? Ye mean, my mother and father? Why, they're Robert and Gael Mercer."

"Mercer?" Hermoine shook her head. "I don't believe I know anyone by the name of Mercer."

"Och, ye wouldna know us," Kirsty said. "I should ha' said we've been tenants here for many a year. My father's father before him, too. We count ourselves verra lucky."

Hermoine clapped a hand to her breast. "A tenant's daughter? Here at the castle? And you say she is your right hand? What can you be thinking of, Max? Why she's nothing more than an ignorant peasant."

"I'll thank you to—"

"I've been assistant to the tutor for the marquess's children," Kirsty said rapidly, breaking off his outburst. "I'm book learned and verra capable; otherwise, Mr. Rossmara would no' have hired me."

"Max?" Hermoine held her free hand pleadingly toward him. "If this becomes known, I shall be a laughingstock. Please do not do this to me."

"What are you saying?" he asked her.

"A nursery maid—a peasant—masquerading as your assistant. Why, you know perfectly well what everyone will think. And they'll be right, won't they?"

"Hermoine," he said, standing, "I do think it's time you returned to The Hallows. Before your aunt and cousin become concerned for you. And you are wrong in your assumptions."

"But—"

"Good-bye, my dear."

"Max, I insist that you listen to—"

"'You will discover that I am a man who does not react well to unnecessary upsets. Kirsty, would you please ring for Shanks and have him see Lady Hermoine out."

"Why, o'course."

But before Kirsty could go to the bell cord, Hermoine tossed her head, flipped her skirts about, and swept from the room, affording a view of an exaggerated bustle topped with yet more pink roses.

Arran passed Hermoine in the doorway and turned to watch her stomp away. He raised his brows to Max, came in, and plopped down in a chair. Stretching his long, strong legs before him, he said, "A man knows he's not as young as he once was when he can't be in the saddle for ten hours without dreaming of a hot bath."

"You're as strong as an ox," Max said. "We all know you're the only man for miles around who can lift a wagon while its wheel is replaced."

Arran "hmphed," but appeared pleased.

"Well," Kirsty said to Max, "if ye'll excuse the interruption, I'd best be off to my mother and father. That is if ye don't need me further today, sir."

"Well, I suppose it'll be all right. But don't forget the modiste."

She sighed. "Aye, I'll no' forget, but I'd as well go home while the light's strong."

"I saw your parents today," Arran said.

Max grew alert. He stared at his uncle until the other met that stare.

Kirsty smiled. "I've never spent a night away from home before. I feel I've been gone a long time. I'm anxious t'be off."

"Wait, please," Arran said, still looking at Max. "Your father asked me to tell you this wouldn't be a good night for you to visit."

Max closed his eyes and sat down.

"No' a good night?" Kirsty laughed nervously. "But it's my home. There's no' a bad night for me to go t'my own home."

"Kirsty," Arran said, "I promised Robert you'd get his message, and I've given it to you. Be patient with them, my dear. This is a big change in their lives. They'd rather you did not go to them this evening."

Reluctantly Max glanced at Kirsty—and wished he hadn't. She stood with her arms hanging loose at her sides. Her face was white.

"Niall came back with me," Arran said. "I asked him to come in, but he preferred to wait outside. He wanted to talk to you. He's waiting near the stables."

Without a word, Kirsty ran from behind her desk, and from the room. Her footsteps pounded along the corridor and gradually faded.

"She didn't think they'd really turn their backs on her," Max said quietly. "Neither did I."

"You took a bold step when you brought her here," Arran said. "You've a more complicated time ahead than you planned."

Max longed to follow Kirsty. "What do you mean?"

"You won't need me to explain. It'll soon become clear."

"A hint? Could I perhaps have the benefit of a hint?"

Arran let his head rest against the back of the chair. "Like it or not, my boy, from now on you're responsible for the welfare of Kirsty Mercer."

"I've told you I'm more than glad to have her here. She'll lighten my load a good deal. I can already tell it."

"You're not listening to me," Arran said. "Or you're not understanding what I'm saying. Thanks to what you did yesterday—taking Kirsty from her parents against their wishes—she is no longer welcome in their home. Robert says he never wants to lay eyes on her again."

*   *   *

Kirsty sped into the kitchen and collided with Fergus Wilkie, who laughed and held her fast, his narrow face flushed with anticipation.

"Let me go," she said. "I'm in a hurry, can't ye see?"

"Not too much o' a hurry to gi' a laddie a little kiss?" he said.

Kirsty drew back. The scullery maid and a girl who worked in the laundry huddled together before the stove and giggled. Between them they held a small book they'd been looking at. For now Kirsty and Fergus had their avid attention.

"Ye'd better be careful, Fergus," the scullery maid said. "Ye'll be in trouble if ye meddle wi' Miss High-and-Mighty. She's connections in important places, y'know."

Fergus looked abashed, but thoughtful. "Mayhap ye're right. She's savin' hersel' for other lips—and other things, too."

Kirsty dodged around him and made a break for the kitchen garden. Relief exploded within her when she emerged into the open air and ran along the path to the gate.

Fergus Wilkie had never treated her so before. Nor any of the other members of the castle staff. But she'd other things on her mind now. Her mother and father telling her not to come home. How could they still be angry with her when they knew she loved them so, and she knew they loved her, too?

Beyond the kitchen garden lay a stretch of rough ground surrounding the stables. Niall shrugged away from the wall there and hurried to draw her into a bear hug.

She clung to him and couldn't stop her tears.

"There, there," he said, his voice rough and breaking, "it's all right, Kirsty. It'll pass if we do what we must do now."

She rested her brow on his chest and kept her arms wrapped around him.

"Come along wi' me. We must talk, and I'd rather not do it so close t'this place."

"The marquess told me what Father said. I canna believe it."

Niall gently pulled her arms free and took hold of her hand to lead her along the homeward path. "They didna think ye'd do it, Kirsty. Leave like that when they'd told ye not to go."

"I'm no' a wee girl anymore," she said, sniffing. "They canna expect me t'do their biddin' as if I were."

"They want what's best for ye."

"It's best for me to advance mysel', and I'm doin' that. I'm t'learn about the estate, and manage the wages, and keep accounts, and write letters, and—"

"And Father doesna like it. And neither do I. And if ye were thinkin' beyond your longin' t'be wi' Max Rossmara, ye'd know it was a wrong thing ye're doin'."

"It's no' wrong. How can ye say it is?"

"How can ye say it's not? D'ye think we're all green things because we've not spent time inside the walls o' that place?"

"That place gives ye your livin'. It's given us our livin' all our lives, and I canna believe ye could forget it."

"We're no' slaves. And we're no' ripe for the pickin' o' those who think they've a right t'anythin' they want from us."

Kirsty pulled to a halt and leaned against Niall's urging tugs. "Ye're makin' no sense," she told him. "We've had nothin' but kindness from the people in *that place* as ye call it. Ye were brought into the world by the marquess when our mother couldna birth ye alone."

Niall said nothing to that.

"I'd best go back," she said. "I'm t'meet wi' a dress-maker."

"What for?" Niall asked. He ceased his tugging and stepped closer to her.

"Because I need more suitable clothes for my job."

"What's wrong with the clothes ye already have?"

She sighed. "Nothing to me. But Mr. Rossmara wants me to appear more suitable, whatever that means."

Niall muttered something Kirsty couldn't understand. She didn't ask him to repeat himself.

"Come home with me now," he said. "Please. Come home, and we'll mend things somehow."

"*Mend?* What have I broken? I've done nothin' wrong except follow my own desires. And we'll all be the better for it."

"Ye dinna belong here, I tell ye." There was desperation in his voice now. "Come away wi' me."

"I will not. Please go to Father and tell him I love him, and I'm hurt that he's so angry wi' me for tryin' to help us all."

"Ye don't think we understand, do ye? Ye think we're too simple to understand."

The wind she'd seen bending the trees from the windows of Max's study was wild out here. It whipped her hair from its looped braids and flung it across her face. She pushed it back. "I'm the one who doesna understand. What have I done t'make my dear ones angry wi' me? So very angry wi' me?"

"I'm no' angry wi' ye," Niall said, quietly now. "I never could be. I just want ye back wi' us. And I don't want Father and Mother t'be angry wi' ye. Father says ye've shamed them."

She clapped her hands to her cheeks. "*Shamed* them? Niall, how could I have shamed them?"

"It's the talk o' everyone. That wee, nasty laddie, Wilkie, talked t'some o' the men about ye. He said ye were wi' Max Rossmara the whole day."

"I was. I'm working for him."

Niall looked down the hill. "He said ye've rooms in the Eve Tower."

"Yes. They're called the rosy rooms, and they're the loveliest things ye've ever seen. I want t'show them t'Mother."

"She won't come. Is it true that Max Rossmara lives in that tower, too?"

Kirsty swallowed. "Yes."

"But there's nobody else there at night?"

"There isn't," Kirsty said in little more than a whisper, and that all but stolen by the heather-scented wind.

"And ye think that's right?"

"Yes, it's right. I've my own place, I tell ye."

"And where is his place?"

Kirsty's chest was so tight she couldn't take a breath. "At the other end o' the corridor."

"And ye wonder why our parents feel shamed. People are sayin' ye're no better than ye ought to be." Suddenly he clutched her to him again and hugged her so hard she cried out. "I love ye, Kirsty. Ye're my only sister. I know ye wouldna do anythin' wrong. But people are mean in their spirits. They're glad to point at ye and tell Mother and Father how sorry it is that they're bein' brought so low."

"No," Kirsty said, her head pounding. "Tell them it's not true. Max is honorable. And he'd engaged t'be married. Lady Hermoine was there just this afternoon."

"I'll do my best. But will ye no' come and do it yoursel'?"

Kirsty warred within herself. If she went home, they'd try to persuade her to stay. Mayhap that would be best.

She'd leave Max. They wouldn't work together in his study anymore. She wouldn't have to watch him with Lady Hermoine and feel jealous.

Even the crumbs of his attention were better than nothing at all. "No, Niall. They've told me not t'come. Ye go and smooth the way for me, if ye'd be so kind. If they'll see me, I'll go tomorrow. I'm tired now, anyway."

He released her. "I'll not argue further. I'll go to them and say what ye've asked me t'say. But they dinna believe ye're Max's assistant."

"But I *am*. He told them so himself."

"And they don't believe him either."

"What then? What do they believe?"

He looked at the ground and shuffled his worn boots. "They may not believe it. I know it's no' the truth. But everyone's tellin Mother and Father that Max Rossmara wouldna take a pretty bit o' a girl like ye into that private tower o' his as anythin' but somethin' to warm his bed."

Chapter Ten

A day, two at the most, and his father would return with his great-grandmama and Blanche Bastible. He would confront his father and tell him that any alliance with Lady Hermoine was out of the question.

From a window high in the Eve Tower he watched for Kirsty. She'd struck out for home with her brother, and now he could not bear that she was gone and might not return.

If she did return, and did so quickly, it would mean her parents had turned her away. He followed the flight of a bird too distant to identify, noted the way it dipped and struggled upward again as it fought the wind. The possibility of Kirsty's family permanently turning against her had never occurred to her—or to him. Such a loss would pain her beyond endurance, and it would be his fault—one more wound he'd inflicted upon the one he loved.

He was a man torn. If he asked her to join her life with his and she accepted, he'd have to leave all this, the family that had become so much a part of him. At first he would be blissful because he was with her. But would a time come when he'd have to hide regret—or when she'd become unhappy for want of her own folk?

Arran had told him to give himself more time, and to lay his hand bare for his father and mother to see.

They had done so much for him. He owed them obedience, at least in the matter of following the path they had secured for him in the administration of the estate.

A small, bowed figure in gray toiled into view at the top of the castle mound.

"Damn." Max thumped his fists on the high stone sill. "Damn the cruelty of all small-minded people." They had denied her.

He waited until she passed from sight into the lower regions of the castle and took the stairs downward, two at a time.

Before his great-grandmama arrived he must have a plan, or she would be sending for his mother and creating all manner of difficulties that could only make Kirsty's plight—and his own—worse. Doubtless Arran would do his best to influence his mother-in-law, Blanche Bastible, for the better, but he had never had much good fortune in that area.

Max reached the balcony overlooking the entrance hall and stopped. What excuse could he give if he met her when she was on her way to her rooms? Simple enough. He was going out to make a visit.

She must be desolate and in need of comfort, comfort he dare not offer.

Polite conversation should be easy enough to make. Perhaps he could tell her he needed her to write a letter. Or reckon the week's wages for those employees he paid direct.

He should take himself off and allow her the dignity of dealing with her own trouble.

She came from the stairs leading down to the kitchens.

Her thin cotton dress could not have been warm enough out there on that windy hill.

Her hair had fallen free of its usual braids and streamed, curling and shiny around her shoulders. In the center of the hall she stopped, and he saw her indecision. She couldn't decide where to go, and turned first in one direction, then in another.

No place to call home anymore. No place of her own. Just as had once been his own lot. And he had brought her to this pass.

Kirsty looked upward and saw him.

Max nodded and carried on down to the hall. "A chilly evening by the look of it," he said. "You shouldn't be out without a coat."

"It isna so verra cold." Her eyes sought a place to settle, anyplace but where they would meet his gaze.

Be polite and go on your way. "I'm sorry your parents are displeased with you." *Fool. You will not follow your head and leave well enough alone.*

The wetness that filmed her eyes made him a desperate and awkward man. "I had intended to ask if you were too tired to go over some accounts with me before the modiste arrives."

"If it's necessary, sir."

"Perhaps you're too tired?"

She fumbled and produced a handkerchief. "Excuse me, sir, but I've somethin' in my eye. No doubt the wind blew it there. Gi' me a few minutes and I'll be at my desk."

He took several steps toward the study, turned about, and paced back. "Yes, yes, of course. Take care of what you must. And take as much time as you must." *But hurry back to me, sweet Kirsty.*

With a small sound she plucked her skirts above her slim ankles and ran up the stairs.

The slightest movement, more the impression that there

had been a movement, caused Max to look about—just in time to see the servant, Wilkie, draw back behind the staircase. Max thought to call the man before him but heard the soft fall of feet on the stairs to the kitchens.

That there was bound to be gossip among the servants about Kirsty's presence had occurred to him. No doubt her rooms, where she was alone and within a short distance of his own living quarters, were of particular interest to some. Of course they were. Even her parents, who didn't live at the castle, had drawn conclusions that were false.

He would not be dictated to by servants. With grim resolution, he made his way to the study and added coals to the fire. Kirsty's present situation was his responsibility. He would make sure she knew she was secure here.

Half an hour passed before she appeared, her hair plaited once more, but hanging in a single braid rather than wound at the sides of her head. She went at once to her desk, sat down, and took up her pen.

Max closed the door, leaned against it, and crossed his arms. "I see you're ready."

"I am that, sir."

"What exactly are you ready for?"

She kept her face hidden and said, "Whatever ye'd like me t'do for ye."

"I should like you to put down your pen and come here."

She raised her face slowly. Her fine brows drew together in a frown, but she put down the pen.

"Come along," he said, aware that he was choosing to react rather than to think. "Come here now."

"Yes, sir." She got up, stood very straight, and walked to stand before him.

Max put his hands in his pockets. Better there than where he longed to put them—around Kirsty Mercer. "I find myself in quite a pickle," he said, and he forced himself to smile at her. "You will recall that I have had a tendency to place myself in awkward situations."

Inclining her head, her expression suggested she was trying to gauge his mood.

"You do remember that, don't you, Kirsty?"

"Ye certainly had a rare talent for trouble, sir. When ye were a laddie, that is, o'course."

"Well, I'm still talented in that direction, only the trouble I get myself into has become more dramatic—and more important in nature."

"Is that right? I'm sorry t'hear it, sir. I wouldna like t' think o' ye sufferin'."

Despite his best intentions, his hands were out of his pockets and fastened on her shoulders before he could restrain them. "Don't you know what I'm talking about?"

"I wish I did. I'd help ye if I could."

"You'd help me? That's rich. I turn your life upside down. Cause your family to put you out of your home, and *you* want to help *me*?"

"It wasna my intention t'sound presumptuous. I'd not thought ye were referrin' t'my own situation."

"Damn you for being so reasonable. Damn you for being so—so—so impossibly dear and gentle."

Predictably, her face flushed.

Predictably, he felt drawn to embrace her.

The struggle against his instincts was fierce.

"My family will come t'understand they're mistaken in judging me so," she said. "Until then I must just bear it, and I will. I'm verra strong. Ye know I am, sir."

Sir, sir, sir. "I shall go to them myself tomorrow. I've been unwise—made unwise decisions. I'll tell them I've decided it would be best if you lived at home."

"I'd rather ye didna do that, if ye please."

Max glanced from her wide blue eyes, to her soft, slightly parted lips, to the gentle rise of her breasts beneath cheap cotton. Tenderness assailed him, and arousal—a dangerous concoction for a man struggling to do the right thing.

"I don't understand you, Kirsty. I saw your tears when you returned a little while ago. You're very close to your own people. This must pain you greatly."

"It does. And I'm sure I'm a bad creature, but it would pain me more if I had t'leave ye. I mean, if I had t'leave my position when I know I can make a grand success o' it. And t'make the verra best o' it I should be near my work."

Doom hovered inches from him, and he found it an intoxicating lure. "Are you telling me you will be happier here than at your home? If you have to choose one or the other?"

Tears filmed her eyes again. "Aye. I'd rather not choose, but, aye, I'm tellin' ye that."

"Thank you."

She frowned again.

"Thank you for wanting to be here. God forgive me for being grateful, but I am. There's so much I want to tell you, so much I ought to tell you, but later we'd both regret the telling."

Kirsty smoothed her hair and ran a finger beneath each eye. "Mayhap we should get t'work."

"There's no work to be done this evening."

"But ye said—"

"I know what I said. I was searching for an excuse to explain why I was watching for you to return. I made one up."

"Oh." She nodded, looked at the toes of her worn ankle boots. "No doubt ye were concerned because of what His Lordship said. Ye've no reason t'worry. It'll be all right in time. People—some people have a spiteful way wi' 'em. They like t'find bad when they should be lookin' for good. My father and mother are shamed because there are those who have made . . . well, they've told lies about me. But later it'll come right because I've right on my side. I do regret that your good name has been sullied. I'll find that harder to forgive."

Max flexed his fingers. With his palms he made circles on her shoulders, then chafed her arms. "I won't be the one to suffer. You know that perfectly well." He would not suffer because of idle talk. "Those who spread gossip are cowards. They victimize the weak."

"I'm no' weak," Kirsty said. "I've made up my mind that I'm no' bendin' before their wicked tongues. Ye've given me an opportunity I'll not give up lightly."

God help his irresolute spirit. He said, "You told me it would pain you to leave me. Because of the advantage you will have from working for me?"

A bleak light entered her eyes. "Yes," she said quietly.

"Nothing more?"

"What more would there be?"

"That you . . . It couldn't be that some of the closeness we shared as children remains for you?"

She sank her teeth into her lower lip, but still it trembled.

"Kirsty," he said. "Could that be?"

"Could it be for ye?" she countered.

Closing his eyes, he rested his brow on hers—and felt her shudder, and his answering shudder. "It could be," he muttered. "I have absolutely no right to ask such questions of you, or to tell you that I feel anything for you but respect for your intelligence. But I do."

"So do I."

Very carefully, he enfolded her in his arms. He stroked the back of her head, and the soft skin on her neck. After hesitating, she rested her hands at his waist, beneath his jacket. She shook steadily, and he held her more tightly, murmuring senseless words against her temples.

"I do understand why it was that there could never be anythin' more between us once we were both grown," she said.

"It wouldna do. We're from different worlds. Ye're a gentleman. I'm nothin', not really."

"Kirsty—"

"Hush," she said. "Let me speak t'ye while I can. I don't mean I've no respect for mysel'. I mean I'm o' peasant stock. Proud o' my family, but wi'out false notions as t'my place in t'world. It's fine. Please believe that. All except for the fact that I've loved ye. I willna lie, I've loved ye so."

He had to open his mouth to find enough air.

"But now I'm grown. I'm a mature woman and I know what can and canna be. I know what I can never have. I can never have ye and I have to find peace wi' it. I'll serve ye well, and take pride in your accomplishments, and if I can help ye, well then, I'll find my happiness there."

Suddenly, convulsively, he clutched her so tightly, she cried out. "Well, I can't find my happiness in such a manner," he said, hating the harsh sound of his voice. "It isn't enough for me to have you push a pen at a little desk in the corner of this room while we watch our lives pass without the passion we might share."

For an instant he felt her begin to slip toward the floor. He thrust his arms beneath hers and supported her. "Forgive me. This is all too much, but believe me that it is too much for me as well as for you."

"They willna let us be more t'each other than we are, Max."

At the sound of his name on her lips, he squeezed his eyes shut again. "They can't stop us from what we choose to do in private."

"In time ye'd no' be happy. I canna bear to think o' bein' the cause o' that. I love ye too much."

She told him she loved him. Simply, with conviction and no embarrassment, she opened her heart to him. And, at the same time, she tried to take all responsibility for what happened between them.

"Look at me, please," he said, barely able to speak at all. When she did as he asked, he framed her face with his hands and kissed her mouth. Softly, holding back his ardor for fear of frightening her, he kissed her inexperienced lips and tasted her sweetness. She didn't try to draw away. Nor did she encourage him to do more than kiss her. Her mouth moved inexpertly beneath his, but he felt her willingness, and breathed in her breath, marveling at the potent power of that joining, the joining of their breath, to make him feel one with her.

He raised his face and looked down into her eyes. Such trust. He kissed the smooth place between her brows, and her eyelids, and her jaw. He stroked her face, and her hair, and rested his hands loosely around her neck while he placed another kiss on the tip of her nose.

"I have wanted to do this for so long," he said. How deeply he felt the heaviness of responsibility upon him, his responsibility for this darling creature. "I have often stayed away from Kirkcaldy for fear of seeing you and being unable to control my longing for you."

"What does it mean?" she asked. Her fingers, stroking his jaw, his neck, and passing down the front of his shirt, caused muscles in his back and thighs to stiffen. "Does it mean we mustna be together? Does it mean I must go away from ye?"

"It means," he told her, "that I will never allow you to go away from me. If you ever tried, I should track you down and bring you back."

Confusion sent disparate expressions flitting over her features. "But ye're to be married. We canna—"

"Don't tell me what we can't do. And my supposed marriage is not a topic for discussion."

"You were always a lordly laddie, Max Rossmara," she said with a faint smile. "Under the circumstances, I'll have t'defy ye. I thank ye for your kisses, and I'll take the memory o' them with me wherever I go. But I'll no' be able to stay."

He swallowed. "And where would you go?"

Her eyes shifted away. "I dinna know, but I'll be fine."

"You'll be fine because you will remain here. In the rosy rooms you love so much."

"Stay? Stay and look at ye, and think o' this night when ye kissed me and made me feel the way I've never felt before? Like it's a beginning o' something that's much more? Stay and watch ye with Lady Hermoine and know ye're holdin' her like ye've held me t'night? Then go alone t'the rosy rooms while ye're only a few doors away from me? I'm just a woman, sir. I'm no' a magical bein'."

"Yes, you are a magical being. But it's not going to be the way you think it is. I love you, Kirsty. I've loved you since . . . I loved you before I had any right to love you because you were too young. Once I thought having you would be an easy thing. It won't. But I will have you. I'm nowhere near ready to let you go."

"Ye must. I'm ready to go t'my bed. Will ye please have the modiste sent away? It's been a long day wi' many a new thing t'learn. And many new things to accept. We'll forget about all this. You've been worried about me, and I thank ye. I'll no' cause ye further concern."

His mind raced. Tonight was a night for making decisions and he would do so—and the devil take the consequences. "I'd thought that I would not marry Lady Hermoine."

"But your mother and father think it a good match, don't they?"

"A suitable match. One that will ally me with a titled woman and be good for my standing in their circles."

Her repeated blinking was the sign of how hard she fought against more tears. "Well then, ye should marry her. Your parents wouldn't want it for ye unless they thought it good."

How sensible she was, this woman he knew he could not live without. "Perhaps I will." He judged her reaction but she had assumed her smooth expression. "Marry her and attend those functions where I should be seen with a suitable wife."

"It's wise," she told him, her throat jerking. "We canna always have what we'd like."

"I think we can have a good deal of what we'd like. She doesn't love me any more than I love her."

"Oh, but she wants ye," Kirsty protested. "She's verra possessive. I saw that wi' my own eyes. She'll make ye a good and attentive wife."

"She'll make me an irritating, demanding wife, but that will mean my lot will be much easier." He hauled Kirsty to him and kissed her again, with force this time, pressing his tongue past her lips and ignoring her shocked intake of breath. He kept on kissing her just so until she tentatively touched the tip of her tongue to his lips.

Max felt his own legs weaken. He was, after all, only a man.

They pulled back from each other, but he didn't release her.

"Why would it be easier if Lady Hermoine should be an irritating, demanding wife?"

"She will take other lovers, and I shall not care," he said, searching for the words to say exactly what he wanted to say.

"Oh, but that would be dreadful," she said. "I'm a bad one t'be kissin' ye so, but at least ye're no' married. Not yet, anyway. I'm sure ye're wrong about the lady. She's mad for ye. She'll never stray."

"She's mad for the money that my family will settle on us," he said without compunction. "I don't want to heap bad words upon her, or question her motives and her nature, but I see no sign of affection for me in her."

"I see." Kirsty was subdued now. "Aye, I see. The ways o' the rich have always been a puzzle t'me, but it's no' my business. If she can help ye because o' who she is, and that's enough for ye, then I wish ye happiness in her."

"I'll find no happiness there, Kirsty. Surely you guess what I'm saying to you."

She shook her head slowly. "No. But I'll comfort ye as I can, for as long as ye need me. And ye'll find comfort in your bairns when they come. I'll make sure Lady Hermoine comes t'trust me, and she'll never have t'know about tonight. After all, ye're only tryin' t'comfort an old friend. And I thank ye. And I bid ye good night."

"Do you think the way we just kissed is the way a man comforts an old friend?"

"Och, ye'll embarrass me," she said, flattening both hands on his chest.

"Well, do you?"

"I'm not goin' t'answer ye. Ye're tormentin' me."

"And you're tormenting me. You seem to like touching me, miss."

For an instant she withdrew her hands as if they burned, then she returned to smoothing his shirtfront, to pressing and feeling his chest beneath. "I do like touchin' ye. Ye're no longer a boy. Ye've a fine, strong body." She gave attention to his shoulders. "Wonderful strong. And ye're much too handsome for a woman's good."

"I'm glad I please you as much as you please me—although perhaps I presume too much."

"Ye please me greatly."

"Your body is supple, Kirsty. Supple and very female. All soft curves and a gentle way of moving that draws attention to your womanhood without being overtly provocative."

"Hush now," she said, bowing her head.

"You have a little waist." He gripped it. "And hips that sway, just the tiniest bit, when you walk." He smoothed her simple skirt over rounded flesh. "And your breasts are perfect. Just the right size and shape to drive me mad." Expecting her to push him away, he covered her breasts, rubbed them lightly, and looked deeply into her eyes.

She didn't push him, but she removed his hands gently, and held them. "I'm glad I please ye."

"You do. And I want you. And I'm going to have you."

The sad shadows were in her eyes again. "Ye know ye're only dreamin'. Ye've just said ye'll do your parents' biddin' and marry the woman they've chosen for ye."

"Perhaps I will. And very soon my lack of passion will bore her, and she'll go elsewhere for her pleasure."

"So ye say."

"So I do say," Max told her, gathering his courage. "But I won't care because I'll have you."

Her frown showed she had no idea what he was suggesting.

"You will be my assistant in my work, and my companion when we both need comfort. Kirsty, I'm asking you to become my mistress."

Chapter Eleven

"I'm a good girl," Kirsty whispered to herself. "That I am. A *good* girl, a good girl. But Lordy, I dinna want t'be good anymore."

The hour grew late. She didn't know how long she'd sat in her sitting room before a fire that had burned down to no more than embers. The curtains were still open at the casement, and the sky had finally turned navy blue and violet with the approach of deep night.

She hadn't lighted any lamps, afraid that if she did Max might pass by, see the light, and try to talk to her. If she looked at him again tonight, she might not hold fast to her resolve.

He'd asked her to become a fallen woman—his woman in every way but through marriage before the Lord.

And she'd been frightened by his asking, but she'd wanted to say yes.

She was a good girl.

If Lady Hermoine's cousin hadn't arrived to see Max, would it have been so easy to leave him in his study with a quiet, "That willna be possible, sir. Good night, t'ye."

No doubt the Honorable Mr. Horace Hubble had come to talk about the wedding. Kirsty didn't think Max liked the man overmuch, probably because Mr. Hubble made poses and dressed in a fancy way so unlike Max's own simple manner of dress.

She hadn't heard Max come upstairs. He was probably angry with her and gone to find entertainment elsewhere. Kirsty pressed her cheeks. Even to think of such things was wrong. She didn't know what Max was about at this time of night, and she should never judge him harshly.

To pretend was to delude. He had spoken the truth when he'd said he wanted her—and it had been that wanting that had driven him to retain her for a position unsuited to a woman, particularly a woman of her background. He had retained her, though, and she was capable of being a credit in the position. Unless he told her he'd changed his mind, she'd apply herself to the work and try not to think of the other. And if he did change his mind, well then . . . Well, then she'd have to pray she'd find happiness elsewhere.

She was strong. Her mother and father had taught her to be strong, and she had a good mind.

But to leave this place . . .

To leave her family and Max . . .

Oh, his kisses. And he'd said lovely things—and touched her. Her body had never felt such feelings. She felt them again now and blushed from the power of it all.

Her throat ached so. If she started to cry, she might never stop.

He wanted to lie with her.

He wanted to do what men and women did together— make the passion he'd spoken of. If she gave him his way, she'd be no better than Fergus Wilkie and the others said she was.

Did she care what they said, care enough to deny herself the wonder of having as much of Max Rossmara as he'd be able to give her?

The truth was that there was no hope of peace. She couldn't go back, and she would never truly belong here. If she stayed, the future would be one of grasping moments of happiness just from the looking at him, the listening to him. The rest would be watching him with Lady Hermoine, who would surely not be the callous creature he expected. No, not at all. She would love him, and they would be happy. How could any woman not love him?

Kirsty got to her feet and went to the bedroom. Once undressed and beneath covers that smelled of soap, she curled into a tight ball.

The sobs came, dry and unbidden, but impossible to suppress any longer. She turned her face into the pillow to muffle the noise and prayed for morning.

Brandy was misunderstood. It was a wonderful drug, a cure-all, a sure way of banishing the misery visited upon innocent men by uncaring women.

Max climbed the stairs, holding tight to the banister with one hand, and gripping the neck of his all-but-empty decanter with the other. The lovely brandy had served him quite well this evening. He'd drunk a few glasses with the Hubble chap and tempered the man's demanding mood, finally sending him on his way satisfied to wait a while to announce the bloody betrothal.

The warmth in Max's veins had begun to cool. The sooner he got to his rooms, the sooner he could remedy that with another draft of the amber fire.

"That willna be possible, sir. Good night t'ye."

She had turned him down, turned down Max Rossmara, a man who could find a woman to fawn upon him whenever he pleased. Well, if she hoped he'd beg, she was mistaken. The time had come to put any feelings for her behind him.

He paused, leaned against the balusters, and rubbed his eyes. He was foxed, but not as foxed as he'd been many times before. Kirsty didn't approve of his drinking. If he had her at his side, he wouldn't need the bottle.

Damn her anyway, who did she think she was? He didn't need her and her prissy notions.

He carried on, walking more steadily. Deep within him the seeds of fury sprouted. When he reached her door, he stopped. No light showed. She'd have gone to bed, to bed to wrap herself in righteousness. If he went to her, she wouldn't turn him away. Who was master here, anyway? He'd retained her to do his bidding and do his bidding she should.

He raised a fist to beat on the door.

He wasn't himself. Forcing himself on women was not his way, and to force himself on Kirsty was unthinkable.

Stumbling a little, he dropped his arm and carried on to his rooms. He'd never retained a valet, preferring to tend to himself. It was more than enough that his every need was taken care of without his having to as much as mention his desires. Some servant had already dealt with the lamps in his library, and built up the fire.

Papers everywhere.

Screwing up his eyes to see more clearly, he looked about the room. Papers and books. Some bastard had entered where he had no right to enter and pulled every volume from the walls of shelves. The books were strewn about the floor. Most were open, their leather spines bent. Max set down the decanter and stooped to pick up a copy of a favorite philosophy text. Clearly it had been quickly looked at and tossed down, as had many other treasured tomes.

And the drawers in his desk sagged open, spilling papers.

Searching. Someone had searched, and must have known what to look for. He remembered finding Hermoine there, but still didn't believe she had been interested in the contents of the room. Had she been so, she'd hardly have allowed him to find her sitting there.

A single volume rested on the top of the desk. Open. Apparently the intruder had taken more time with this one and had probably sat to peruse its pages.

Max leaned to turn the book toward him. Evidently a volume he'd inherited among many that had already been here when he moved into the Eve Tower. He'd never seen it before. Crudely drawn pictures of copulation in various unlikely positions. He slapped the thing shut. A night when he was about to go, unwillingly, to an empty bed was not a good time to study graphic erotic instruction manuals.

Stepping over books as best he could, he made his way to the bedchamber. The furnishings were from the Orient, shipped back from his visits to those parts, and they pleased him. Heavily carved of ebony, and inlaid with brass and mother-of-pearl, deep green velvet draped the massive bed that rose to a soaring canopy. The rest of the furniture was simple, but also heavy and dark, as dark as the ancient wooden floors. On those age-blackened boards rested silk carpets in rich hues that shone softly in the lamplight.

The boy from Covent Garden had been blessed with great

good fortune, and he must not forget to whom he owed his gratitude.

The cur who had entered his rooms unasked had been in here, too. Chest doors stood open, as did the wardrobe, and a fine shambles littered the floor.

To hell with it all. He would sleep and forget that he couldn't have what he really wanted. Tomorrow he'd start the business of learning not to want at all.

He went about the rooms extinguishing the lamps while he stripped off his coat and cravat, and unbuttoned his collar. All energy left him. He snuffed out the last light beside the bed and lay, fully clothed, atop the mattress.

Of course she'd refused him. He'd insulted her. Resting a forearm over his eyes, he cursed himself for turning a sweet and precious moment into something tawdry. A gentle, well-brought-up girl, a God-fearing girl, and he'd asked her to become his mistress. He deserved to be flayed, not that he wasn't already suffering more bitterly than he would at the wrong end of a cat-o'-nine-tails.

Tomorrow he'd apologize and tell her he'd momentarily forgotten himself.

He felt the atmosphere in the room change and lowered his arm.

Shadows coalesced, and shifted. He strained to see. It must be the brandy that made him see things that could not be there.

He heard the sound of breathing not his own.

Max remained very still. The truth of what had happened rushed upon him. He'd arrived in his rooms and cut the intruder off from escape. He longed to feel a weapon in his hand, but his pistol was in a pocket in the bed draperies, and he'd never reach it in time.

The breathing grew loud, a choking sound, almost a repeated, rasping cry. And the shadows took form. He made to roll from the bed, but a heavy body landed on top of him and blows rained on his head and torso.

"Damn you!" Max yelled. "I'll kill you."

The other didn't answer. Instead he sat astride Max's belly and a flash split the darkness. Max curled upward, against the man, but not in time to completely evade the descending knife. The blade glanced across his shoulder like a white-hot torch.

Max went for the other's face. He missed, and found hair instead. He filled his hands and tore, and jerked until the man swore, and again the knife blade glittered.

"Bastard," Max hissed. "Cowardly bastard." With all the force in his body, he threw his assailant off and smiled with grim satisfaction at the yell when the man hit the floor.

Aching to get his hands on the pistol, Max did all that he could do. He fell upon the scrambling figure and grasped the knife-wielding wrist. They rolled over, and rolled again. Max kicked out, contacted shinbone, and enjoyed the scream that followed. His success was short-lived. His spine smashed into the open door of the wardrobe, and he lost his grip on the man's wrist. Pain stole his breath. Sweat bathed his body.

"Now!" the other man yelled.

Max went to his hands and knees and crawled, keeping low. Spread-eagled like some great bird, the attacker launched himself, arms spread wide, and crashed on top of Max, enveloping him in a suffocating, iron embrace. He squirmed to his back and fought to throw off his burden.

An attempt to jerk a knee into the other's groin failed. The man was heavy, and driven by a fury Max felt to his core. They rolled, and rolled, collided with the legs of a table and brought china and glass to shattering impact with the floor. Shards sprayed the back of Max's neck. Force drove the needle-sharp glass into his skin, and he tried to brush it off.

Somehow he got to his feet, gasping, bent double, and

staggered toward the door. Once more he was flattened beneath the weight of the stranger. Max tensed, expecting the knife to penetrate his body. Reaching over his shoulder, he captured one of the man's ears and twisted. He twisted and pulled until the other screamed. Max made it to his knees again and lunged forward, with the heavy creature draped over his back.

The man brought a fist down behind Max's waist and the pain that burst upon him tore the last of the air from his lungs. He coughed and slumped down. Sensing his advantage, the intruder struck again and again. Max managed to turn, faceup, and was rewarded with a boot in his gut. With all the strength that remained to him, he grabbed the booted ankle and held on, and saw why he wasn't already dead of a knife wound. Moon through the window shone on the blade. Its owner had lost his grip on the weapon and it had slid away and beneath the bed.

Max fixed his concentration on the shining thing. Managing to cling to the jerking, booted ankle, he wrenched, and wrenched again, and brought the fellow sprawling down beside him. Max broke free and crawled for the glittering weapon beneath the bed.

He had the knife hilt in his hand when the bedroom door flew open and a familiar voice said, "I heard the bangin' and came. Are ye ill? I canna see ye, Max. Are ye sick?"

She was silhouetted in the doorway. He opened his mouth to yell for her to leave, and in that instant, sobbing and swarming over him, his would-be assassin brought a bootheel down on Max's hand with shattering, sickening force. Max cried out and released the knife—and found the strength to yell, "Kirsty, get away. Get away or you'll cause the death of us both."

"Unhand him," she cried. "Unhand Max this minute, ye brigand." And, rather than do as he'd told her, little Kirsty Mercer rushed into the bedchamber, whatever she wore flying about her and shining an eerie blue-white in the moonlight.

Instantly, the crushing weight lifted from Max's body.

"I see ye," Kirsty shouted. "Ye come t'me, ye cowardly creature. I'll box your ears, and ye'll wish ye'd stayed away from honest men. Come on."

A burst of movement, and rather than presenting himself to get his ears boxed, a man who had come here intent upon murder, fled, pushing Kirsty aside, knocking her to the floor as he made his escape.

"Oh," she said, gasping. "I told ye this was a coward. Pushin' women about. He'll never amount t'anythin', ye'll see. The likes o' him never come t'anythin'. Wait till I find out his name, and I've another chance t'get my hands on him. He'll wish he'd stayed and taken his punishment now. Ooh, the likes o' him need more t'do wi' their time. It's all this modern notion of givin' everyone time t'relax, as they put it. Gives louts like that too much time t'get into trouble. No direction. That's the problem."

Suddenly exhausted, Max dropped his head to his crossed arms and lay still on the floor. "You're right," he said weakly. "He'll never come to anything."

Chapter Twelve

"Do get rid of them, darling," Hermoine said of Zinnia, Wisteria, and Dahlia. "They have absolutely no breeding, and they talk too much. Horace told me that when he was with Zinnia last night all she wanted to do was talk about the journal."

The countess lowered her lorgnette. Seated on the Chinese daybed in the parlor she favored, she frowned and fidgeted, and muttered under her breath. She said, "Unfortunate that one of our gentlemen thought he might get information from her. That's the only way she could have learned about the journal in the first place—by being asked leading questions."

"I did warn you a long time ago that I thought it was a mistake to insist on continuing with business while we had such high stakes to deal with here in Scotland," Hermoine said.

"And I told you, as I'll tell you now, that I absolutely forbid you to make suggestions that would lead anyone to believe the girls are anything other than my protogées, daughters of a dear friend who died, and whom I promised that I should be certain to guide. Of their kind they are high-class, Hermoine. And they assist me in keeping certain very agitated gentlemen entertained rather than berating me because we don't yet have the wretched journal."

"You shouldn't have contacted any of them until the journal was in our possession, and we *had* something to sell."

"You seem"—Gertie said with pomp—"to have forgotten that it was the duke who approached me because that naughty Prinny mentioned me by name in his letter. And if anyone is to be blamed it is Prinny for failing to make sure his correspondence would be delivered in a timely manner after his death. Years, it took years for the duke to know of the journal's existence and my supposed connections to the Covent Garden pickpockets." She sighed hugely. "One of his wretched spies told him I was kept—I mean that I was, for a very short time, the close friend of the man who controlled those horrid, dishonest children."

"If Prinny hadn't mentioned you, we shouldn't be by way of making a marvelous fortune." Hermoine sniffed. "And one can hardly blame the dead if their solicitors take years to administer their affairs. After all, we all know these men of the law charge by the hour. Like people in a rather less respected profession. But Horace should have been able to find what we need this evening. He had plenty of time alone in Max's rooms. I made sure of that." She hadn't, in fact, given Horace a great deal of time, but she would not tell the countess that.

"Well, he didn't find it, and that's that."

Hermoine adjusted herself inside the heavily boned bodice of her gown. "I wish you hadn't involved Horace at all. He's a nuisance—well, most of the time he's a nuisance although he is still as entertaining as ever from time to time. And now he's probably sleeping peacefully and expecting *us* to do everything as usual. Well, if we are not able to get at the journal in any other manner, I shall just have to go through with a marriage to that man." She shrugged. For Gertie to discover that Rossmara was less than enthusiastic about the match would be a disaster. "A complication, but it will be diverting, I'm sure. And you may be sure that once I have the run of his rooms, and anywhere else he may have used as a hiding place, I shall get my hands on what we need very quickly."

Gertrude puffed at her veil and settled herself more comfortably. "I seem to recall that you were to accomplish the necessary quite easily because Rossmara would want you within his reach at all times. Doesn't appear to be quite the case to me, my girl. No doubt he's prepared to go along with his parents' desire to secure him a suitable wife and has decided you will do, but you'd do well not to get too high an opinion of yourself. Remember, I know all about you. One false step, and I should be forced to punish you."

"And what would that accomplish, since I should be forced to retaliate? *You* remember that we succeed or fail together in this."

Without so much as a single knock, Horace came into the

room. His face was redder and more shiny than was customary, a sign of even greater excess than usual. "There you are," he said to Hermoine. "Thanks to you I had a damnable night. First rushin' about looking for what we *must* have. Then panderin' to that trumped-up street urchin and having to smile and agree with him. We don't have time to wait for his pleasure. We need you in that house now."

"Tell him not to speak to me in that tone, Countess," Hermoine said. She settled herself at one end of a red-and-gold couch, struggled with her bustle and horsehair petticoats, and managed to pull her feet onto the seat. "I assumed you'd already taken to your bed, cousin."

Horace laughed that infuriating laugh of his. "Oh, very graceful, I must say, m'dear." He sauntered close and sat by her feet. "Charmin' bit of lace on those drawers."

She ignored him until he made a sudden lunge, thrusting his head beneath her skirts and managing to get both his face and his hands inside the garment in question.

Gertie laughed, actually laughed while Hermoine batted at him and squealed. "Stop that, Horace. Stop it at once. What if a servant comes in?"

His muffled response was indecipherable.

"Oh," she cried, as his tongue found its target.

"That boy," the countess crowed. "Insatiable, he is. Just like his father before him. I miss his father. This has always been such a *close* family."

Hermoine grunted, and panted, and parted her limbs. There were times when one might just as well lie back and enjoy small diversions that came one's way. Tension mounted, and she pressed her hips upward.

"Well, this is certainly an entertainment," Gertie said. "We can always rely on Horace to brighten up a dull evening. Give it your all, Horace, my boy."

Give it his all. Hermoine decided she should protest a little more and attempted to clamp her knees together. "Stop it,

Horace. Stop it at once. Oh, Horace!" She fell back and gave herself up to the inevitable. "Oh, oh, oh, *Horace!*"

She was still in the throes, so to speak, when his now-purple face emerged, and he grinned at her and hoisted himself astride her hips.

"Oho," Gertie chortled. "One good turn deserves another, I imagine, Horace. What do you say?"

Horace didn't waste time on conversation, he simply extracted his own satisfaction from Hermoine's lips, then wedged himself beside her, bared her breasts, and languidly nuzzled his face.

"Hmph," Gertie said. "Well, if you've both had your little fun, I suggest we put our minds to the matter in hand."

Horace laughed and busied his hand with the matter closest to him.

Hermoine smacked him away, but she giggled. "Concentrate, Horace, do. I understand we've houseguests at present."

"We do indeed," Gertie said. "And if anyone in these parts realized the elevated nature of those guests, they'd be crowding our doors to catch glimpses of them."

"They're only here because they're frightened out of their britches," Horace mumbled.

Reaching for a glass of port, Gertie said, "I imagine they're all without their britches at this very moment, and fear has nothing to do with that little development."

Hermoine laughed aloud. "I doubt they'd appreciate references to *little* developments. Melbourne and Brougham beneath our roof at the same time." She played with Horace's blond curls. "Who could have imagined such fortune as will be ours. We are in an enviable position, my loves. We shall be in the way of emptying some deep pockets before long."

"So you say," Gertie said, dipping a finger into her port and sucking the drops slowly. "Horace, have you told Hermoine about our conversation when you returned from Kirk-caldy?"

"My dear *cousin* hasn't told me anything," Hermoine said, pushing Horace hard enough to land him on the carpet. "Tell me now."

"You've hurt me," Horace said, rubbing his rump.

"You've a rival, my girl," Gertie said.

"The little peasant? Hardly a rival. What does it matter to me if Rossmara is titillated by a game or two in his study?"

"You weren't there this evening," Horace said. "I tried to get the man to agree to an early betrothal. He absolutely refused. Oh, his excuses were fine enough. Wants his family here, and so on, but I've a notion there's something else holding him back."

"Don't speak in riddles," Hermoine told him pettishly. "Say what you mean."

"Very well. When I arrived he was alone with the peasant. And they'd obviously been engaged in what you term a tit-illatin' game."

Hermoine shifted irritably.

"She left when I got there," Horace continued. "And Rossmara couldn't keep his eyes from the door—as if he expected her to return—or as if he could think of nothing else but her once she'd left."

"Foolishness," Hermoine said. "You always had a girlish imagination."

Without hesitation, Horace turned and slapped Hermoine's face. He slapped her so hard that tears streamed down her cheeks. "Now," he said, while she held her cheek and sobbed, "perhaps you'll consider your words more carefully. There's nothing of a girl in me, madam. We have a great deal almost in our grasp, but we could lose it all, I tell you. If we lose entry to that castle, we'll have no more than the demanding company of famous men. You may find that entertaining, but we have bigger plans, and the Mercer creature could prove a great nuisance. Rossmara waited until he thought I had left, then went directly upstairs. They are much closer than you think, ladies."

Hermoine struggled to her feet. She kicked Horace soundly and skittered out of his reach. "She will be no nuisance at all," she said. "I've learned that the viscount is on his way home."

"Learned?" The countess sat up straight. "From whom? Who is your informant?"

"That is my affair. I have made a useful friend. We will leave it at that. But Rossmara will soon have no excuse to put off our alliance, and if he doesn't come to heel very quickly, I know exactly how to force his hand."

Chapter Thirteen

There were times when common sense and necessity must replace other considerations. This was one of those times. Kirsty had lighted a lamp in Max's bedchamber. She pointed to the bed.

He followed the direction of her forefinger. "What?"

"Lie down," she said shortly. "Take off your shirt first, if ye please."

"I don't need a nurse."

"Ye're a bad-tempered man, and ye drink too much liquor."

"*Blast* you, woman, leave me be, will . . ." He gritted his teeth, turned his face from her.

Her legs trembled, but she would not allow him to bully

her. "A black mood ye're in," she said quietly. "Ye're no yoursel', Max, and I'm sad for it."

"Kindly remember who is the master here."

"Take off your shirt and lie down, *Master*. If ye'd been more in command o' yoursel', ye'd probably no' have a scratch on your shoulder."

"A *scratch*! I've a painful wound, and you call it a scratch!" He grumbled on but removed his shirt anyway, and sat on the edge of the monstrously large and ugly thing he chose to sleep in. "You'll find water over there."

"Ye're pale," she said, putting a hand to his clammy brow. "Lie down, if ye please, *Master*."

"Oh, all right, all right. I'm sorry I was overbearing. I'd prefer you not to call me master, if you don't mind."

"Verra well, sir."

He stretched out. "In fact, I see no reason why you can't use my first name as you used to."

"Ye know I canna do any such thing. Now be silent. Ye need your strength, and talkin' will only sap it."

Kirsty adjusted a pillow beneath his head, then examined a long wound on his shoulder. She pressed the flesh on either side.

"Ouch!" He arched his back. "Have a care."

She planted a hand in the middle of his chest and pushed him flat again. "Hmm. Ye've a lovely body, sir. Ye were a bit o' a puny laddie, but ye're no' puny now."

"Dammit all, miss. Do you intend to stand there examining what you've no right to examine, or to clean a man's serious wound?"

She glanced from his wide, well-muscled shoulders to his strong chest with its mat of dark hair. The hair continued in a slender line past his navel and beneath his trousers. A shiver of delicious curiosity warmed a number of places in Kirsty.

"Well?" he asked. "No doubt you're about to give some other opinion about my person."

Smiling at him, she gave all of her attention to his face. "Ye're verra bonnie, sir. Just lookin' at ye makes me want to cry. Not from bein' sad, but just from the pleasure ye gi' me. Some o' the paintings in this castle have brought tears t'my eyes. But the pictures have given me nothin' compared t'the sight o' ye." Whirling away, she picked up his discarded and ruined shirt and ripped out the sleeve that was already torn.

"Kirsty," he said softly behind her.

"Hush. I'll have ye tended to soon enough."

"You are the most beautiful creature I've ever known. I love your face. And your body. But I love that unruly tongue of yours the most. You're overly direct, but you are the sweetest girl."

She glowed, but she'd not let him see how his flattery could please her. The mischief her mother had accused her of housing came tumbling out. Max had brought his decanter of brandy from his study. Precious little remained, but it would be enough. Quickly, she soaked the fine cotton sleeve and turned to press it to Max's wound.

He howled.

"Och, hush yoursel'," she admonished. "I've told ye to save your strength."

"Hard-hearted little wench." He grappled to tear away the cloth. "What did you use?"

"If ye'd your wits about ye, that's a question ye'd no' have t'ask. Brandy. A powerful good thing to clean a wound."

"It burns," he snapped. "I told you there was water."

Kirsty took her opportunity to slap the cloth over the cut again. "Water's no' as good as this. Now behave yoursel'."

He fell back, hissing through his teeth. "Cruel, cruel," he said.

"If it burns your flesh so, think o' what it does t'your insides."

"Don't—lecture—me."

"It's nothing," she said.

"It's damnably painful, you heartless hussy."

"No, I'm no' speakin' o' the sting. I mean the wound's nothing. Just a wee, shallow thing that'll cause ye no trouble now it's clean." She noted blood on his neck. "Turn on your face, if ye please."

Max squinted at her. "It's a deep wound. And turning on my face won't please me. God knows what manner of torture you've got up your sleeve."

She raised her arms, letting her sleeves fall back. "I'm hidin' nothin."

He looked at her, at the parts of her that no gentleman should openly peruse, and said, "How right you are. You're hiding nothing."

Blushing was a waste of energy, but she blushed anyway and attempted to gather her robe more firmly about her. "I'd be grateful if ye'd turn over so I can look at your neck, sir. It's got blood on it, too."

He clamped the brandy-soaked sleeve to his shoulder, winced dramatically, and rolled to his stomach. "Water this time," he mumbled into the pillow.

Kirsty brushed his hair aside and looked closely at his neck. A mass of small punctures was responsible for the bleeding. "Ye've glass in ye. I'll have to take it out. I'll be as gentle as I can."

He mumbled some more and she set about carefully extracting small pieces of glass and dropping them on a chest beside the bed. Her back began to ache and she straightened. "A minute, if ye please. It's awkward."

Max's back was long, wide at the shoulder, the muscles thick and well used, and tapering to his slim waist. Just above his trousers there was another patch of hair, just a sprinkling, a fine patch, but Kirsty's limbs felt funny from looking at him there. Below the waist he was very finely made indeed, all firm flesh and long, strong limbs. His trousers, she decided, were blessed.

"What are you doing?" he said.

"Lookin' at ye." She clapped a hand over her mouth.

He groaned and pressed his head into the pillow again. "And what are you thinking now?"

She shouldn't answer him. "I'm thinking that it's a shame ye ever wear a coat. Ye should never cover up any o' ye."

He laughed.

Kirsty picked up the almost empty decanter and drizzled the last of its contents over the punctures in Max's neck.

For her efforts, he roared, and leaped to kneel on the mattress. "What d'you think you're doing?" His lips drew back from his teeth. "Trying to shock me to death?"

"I'm done now, sir," she told him. "Ye'll no' be the worse for what that wicked creature did. Now we've to get the constable from the village and have him track the villain down."

"McCrackit?" Max's pained expression dissolved into one of amazement. "You think I'm going to ask that fuddle brain to come and poke around here? Oh, no, Miss Mercer, I'll be doing my own hunting, thank you. I'll deal with this alone and in my own way, and the villain, as you call him, will get swift punishment."

"But the constable—"

"There will be no constable called in. Do I make myself clear?"

"Yes," she said meekly, remembering once more that she was scarcely covered at all. "If ye'll excuse me now, sir, I'd best return to my rooms. I would ask ye to lock your door, though. I'll sleep better that way."

His hand shot out so quickly she had no time to avoid it. "*You'll* sleep better knowing *my* door is locked?" He pulled her closer, grinning like a fisherman reeling in a succulent catch. "If the door's locked and we're not on the same side of that door I might understand your feeling a certain type of safety. But I assure you I have no intention of allowing you to be alone and unprotected until I bring our intruder to justice. Why, Kirsty, you might not even make it safely back to your rooms."

Unless she exerted herself, she would find herself sharing his big, ugly bed. "I may have little experience in some matters," she told him, "but I'm not a silly thing. If ye'd be so kind, I'd appreciate ye walkin' back to my rooms wi' me, and makin' sure it's safe for me to lock mysel' in."

"You want a wounded man to leave his bed?"

She started for the door to the ransacked library.

"All right, all right," he said. "I'll come. Of course I will. And you're correct, my wounds are blessedly minor. Thank you for attending to them for me."

"It was my pleasure."

"I'm sure it was. You certainly aren't shy about taking advantage of opportunities to study a naked man."

They picked their way over the library floor.

"Ye aren't naked," Kirsty said. "Ye've your trousers on. They're verra nicely cut trousers, too."

"Let's get you to your rooms," he said, laughter barely restrained in his voice. "Speaking of well-cut clothes. Mrs. Moggach wasn't pleased to have to find a room for the modiste when she arrived and you were otherwise engaged, but it was accomplished. In the morning you'll meet with her. No more argument on the subject. And no dull colors please. If you must, be conservative with your styles, but I cannot bear the sight of black on you. It's all wrong on one so young and fair."

They emerged into the corridor. Kirsty decided not to comment on the modiste. This had been an exhausting night. The morning would be soon enough to deal with that matter.

"How d'ye think that creature came here?" she asked,

peering along the corridor toward the stairs. "I suppose he'd plenty o' opportunity once he was in the castle. There's few enough as come this way—bein' as how there's just ye and me livin' here." She wasn't careful enough with her manner of explaining herself. Reminding him that they were alone together wasn't a good idea.

Max settled an arm over her shoulders in far too familiar a manner. "You didn't see anyone when you came upstairs?"

"No. Nor heard anyone, either."

"I'd wager he was already in my rooms when you came upstairs—not a happy thought."

Kirsty wasn't overfond of it, either. "Was he waitin' for ye? Or did he come t'ye afterward?"

"Waiting, I think. Now, let's make sure there's no ghoulie behind your door, or under your bed."

Max put Kirsty behind him and went into her sitting room. She heard his oath and hurried to join him. "Well, I never!" She marched about the room, surveying disorder created in such a hurry that there had been no attempt to spare damage. "He left ye, and came straight here. A brave one, I'll gi' him that. What if I'd come back direct?"

"Evidently the gentleman didn't expect you to return direct—if at all."

Kirsty didn't give Max the pleasure of a response to his suggestion. "Och, he's broken the wee, painted table. What will your sister say? I knew I shouldna be usin' her rooms."

"They are *not* Ella's rooms."

The sharpness of his tone silenced Kirsty. She looked at his cold face and saw again the man they said was possessed of a great temper.

"These are your rooms now and will remain so. Kindly do not move." While she remained beside the shattered remnants of the delicate table and surveyed the strewn contents of every cupboard and drawer in the room, Max made a thorough search of anyplace where a man might hide.

At last he returned to her. He shut and locked the door, stirred embers in the grate, and started a fresh fire.

"Thank ye," she said, when flames sprang up the chimney. "D'ye not think it would be best t'call in McCrackit, now?"

"Absolutely not. Kindly don't mention the man's name again. I will take care of what has occurred here."

"What *is* occurring," she said, knowing she was bold, but also knowing that blustering achieved less than plain deduction.

"I'll thank you not to correct me," Max said, prowling about, apparently unconcerned by his inappropriate manner of dress—or undress. "Someone is searching for something."

Kirsty choked down a laugh.

"What amuses you?" Max snapped.

"Um, well, I suppose I thought we might no' have to say the obvious, as it were. What we need t'consider is *what* they're searchin' for."

"Some of us are in the habit of thinking aloud occasionally," he said. "The greatest puzzle is why someone looking for an item of mine—as they obviously are—should come here to your rooms."

"Because they used to belong to Lady Avenall, d'ye think? Could there be a connection?"

Max gave her a long look. "Quite possibly."

"We ought to see if there's somethin' missin'."

"How would we know?"

"Ye'd know in your own rooms, would ye not?"

He nodded. "Probably. But I'd have no idea here."

She started straightening furniture, piling up items pulled from drawers, fluffing cushions. "The Parcheesi board," she said. "It was on that table wi' the patterns in the wood."

"Marquetry," Max said automatically. "Are you sure?"

"Aye, I'm sure. Ye taught me t'play Parcheesi when we

were bairns. It's a beautiful board. Heavy. They've taken it and thrown down the pieces." Shaped like ladies in ball gowns, the pieces were made of silver.

"Hardly worth stealing, I should think," Max said.

Kirsty had a horrid notion. "It won't be supposed that I'd do such a thing, will it?"

"Steal a game board? You? Good heavens, no. Put that from your mind. I think it was taken to divert us. There are knickknacks all over these rooms that are of far more value."

"Bravery can leave ye just when ye need it most," Kirsty said. Her hands had begun to shake. "If ye don't mind, I think I'd best lie down the while."

He was at her side immediately. "You're frightened?"

"I dinna say so. Only that I'm no' as brave as I try t'be sometimes. That man wanted t'kill ye, Max. I heard ye call out and went t'ye. And I knew it then—that he intended t'leave ye dead, but I'd no' the time t'panic."

"So you aren't angry with me anymore?"

"I was never angry wi' ye." Her head felt light. "Will ye excuse me, please?"

She went to the bedroom, extinguished the lamp Max had lighted, and climbed beneath the covers once more.

Max came slowly into the doorway and leaned there. "I can't leave you, Kirsty. Not until I'm sure we're secure here, and it's too late to mount a full investigation tonight."

"He'll no' come back so soon," she said, too aware of the intimacy between them. "He'll be off somewhere lickin' his own wounds and recoverin' his strength."

"We can't be sure of that. I'm going to make myself comfortable on the chaise in the sitting room. Don't give me another thought—except to know I'm there and you're safe."

Safe? "I canna let ye do that. Please go t'your bed. Ye've had a shock and ye need your rest."

"I'd never rest knowing you were here alone."

"And I'll no' rest if I know ye're on that chaise." Och, but her mouth ran away with her. She coughed and added, "It wasna made for a big man."

Rather than leave, he shrugged upright and approached the bed until he stood over her, looking down.

She couldn't see his face.

"Have you considered that I may need comfort, too?" he asked.

"That ye're afraid, ye mean?"

He made a soft, whistling sound. "We all feel fear, of one kind or another. But that's not what I meant. I meant that I need comfort."

Kirsty closed her eyes. He was asking her again. Again he was suggesting she become something she could not countenance in good conscience. "I'd like to gi' ye comfort. Deep in my heart ye're still my friend, the one who walked beside me over those moors and hills, and found pleasure in small things. I love ye." She swallowed and felt him waiting. "I love ye the way I always did, as a dear friend." And she lied, but only because she must.

"Only as a dear friend?" he asked softly. "Remember that you have already told me otherwise. But very well, then. I'm glad of it. I will not leave you tonight, Kirsty."

"I canna be what ye've asked me t'be. But I am flattered that ye'd want me."

"Any man who looks at you must want you. It's for me to apologize for making such a suggestion. I'll be on the chaise."

She reached out and caught his hand. "Ye've no' shirt. Ye'll be cold. I've more than enough covers. Take one o' mine."

"I'll move the chaise by the fire."

Kirsty turned onto her back. She didn't release his hand,

and his fingers tightened on hers. "D'ye know what a bundlin' board is?"

He laughed, and she saw his teeth flash.

"Funny, is it? I thought mayhap ye could lie on top o' the sheet, and mysel' beneath it. Then, wi the rest o' the covers, ye'd be warm and we'd both sleep well."

Max laughed again.

"I'm wounded by ye," she told him.

"Don't be. You're wonderful, and I accept." He went around the bed, turned back the quilt and blankets, carefully smoothed the sheet that covered her, and stretched out on top of it. He pulled the covers over himself and rested on his back.

The door to the sitting room stood partially open, and firelight painted the walls with moving pictures. Kirsty watched the rise and fall of flame shadows and tried not to feel the warmth of the man beside her.

He breathed quietly.

Kirsty held her breath.

He breathed more and more slowly, more regularly.

Asleep already, she decided. If they were attacked, she'd be the one to defend the pair of them.

I love ye as an old friend.

She loved him as a woman loves a man, and the power of it all but tore her asunder. That fulsome, overdressed, pettish Lady Hermoine wasn't good enough for him. She'd make him miserable with her demands. She'd be forever wanting more of those terrible, fancy clothes she favored, covered with silly flowers and feathers and the like. And she'd probably nothing more in her head than what gossip she'd most lately heard. Why, she'd bore Max in no time.

It was wrong to judge someone you didn't know. And it was wrong to do so because you were jealous and wanted something you couldn't have.

Max turned on his side.

The side facing Kirsty.

He put an arm over her middle! She opened her mouth to say something, but what would be the point? The man was asleep and didn't know what he'd done. His arm was heavy and very, very warm.

His fingers curled around her waist . . .

Kirsty held quite still. Then, cautiously, she turned her face toward him. His head wasn't squarely in the middle of the next pillow as it should be, but just about on hers. She could see his closed eyes, his thick, curly lashes, the hard, but irresistible lines of his mouth, and the shadows beneath his cheekbones.

He nestled his head even closer, and his fingers trailed up and down her side.

Och, but she was in a pickle.

She was so warm she feared her hot skin would wake him.

He'd had a fearsome experience, and he didn't know what he was doing—not that he was doing anything so very terrible. In fact, it wasn't terrible at all.

She was a good girl. Squeezing her eyelids together she repeated over and over again inside her head, *I'm a good girl. I'm a good girl. I'll no' give in t'temptation.*

Max's face settled beside hers on her pillow, and she felt his soft breath on her ear.

I'm a good girl, she told herself.

He moaned a little and nuzzled her neck, and pulled her closer.

Desperate, she turned away, turned her back to him, and promptly found herself brought against him, his body curled to make a place—a most unsuitable place—for her bottom, and his thighs beneath her thighs.

His strong arm curled about her—just beneath her breasts.

His lips rested against the back of her neck.

And she'd thought a sheet would be an adequate bundling board! No wonder he'd laughed.

Kirsty narrowed her eyes in the darkness.

He'd laughed, but he'd followed her suggestion. Now look what he was doing with himself—and her.

His lips moved.

Very, very softly, he kissed the nape of her neck, then he lifted his head just a little to allow himself to kiss the side of her neck, then to nip at the lobe of her ear.

So, he'd decided she was a foolish wench to be toyed with. Well, one thing she was sure of: Max Rossmara wouldn't go farther than she allowed him to go.

His Part had grown hard against her bottom. Did the silly man think she'd not notice a thing of such proportions? She'd lived on the land too long to not know what it meant. Very well, she would also sleep and be unaccountable for her actions.

Wiggling, she settled her bottom more firmly against him, and smiled to herself at his indrawn breath.

Kirsty breathed deeply and quite loudly.

Heaven help her, but he pulled down the sheet, pulled up her nightgown, and rubbed her thighs. Taking advantage of a sleeping woman. He wasn't the gentleman she'd considered him to be.

He stroked her belly and moved upward to her breasts! One by one he tweaked her nipples! Such feelings. Such wild things she wanted without even being able to name them.

This must stop at once.

He took a nipple between finger and thumb and pinched lightly, then used a fingernail on the very end. She squirmed, and he murmured against her ear. And he pushed his other arm beneath her so that he could hold her fast while he put a hand between her legs.

She'd grown wet.

The next blast of heat upon her skin made her pant.

He probed beneath the soft folds down there, wetted his fingers with her moisture, and found a place that made her forget she was asleep. "Max! Max, what are ye doin'?"

"Sleeping," he said in a rumbly voice against her shoulder. "Like you. Don't be afraid of me, dearest. I won't do anything that could harm you. But I'd like to bring you pleasure."

Oh, she wanted to press harder against his hand, and she didn't want him to stop playing with her breasts.

She reached behind her and found his Part, held it and squeezed. It swelled even more and jerked—answered her!

"Kirsty," Max murmured. "I don't think you should do that until we've had more time to discuss the future."

"You're not goin' t'stop, are ye?" she said, thrashing, turning onto her back and pulling her nightgown up beneath her armpits. "I'm on fire, Max, and I dinna want it t'go out."

"I'm not being fair."

"Oh, but ye are. Oh, I'd not known there were such wonderful feelings. I've no' had time for the laddies who've wanted t'get to know me better. I've no' wanted to."

Max grew still, but held her more tightly.

"What is it?" she asked him.

"Other men tried to *know* you?"

She frowned and rolled toward him. "Only men I already knew a little."

"How little?"

"Och, I grew up wi' 'em. Y'know what I mean."

"Do I?"

He thought . . . "*Max* Rossmara! If ye're suggestin' I was ever together wi' one o' them like this, then I'm insulted."

Rather than respond, he thrust his head under the covers and fastened his mouth on a nipple.

Kirsty's lips parted, but no sound came. The sensation in her breast, where he sucked, and the feeling between her legs, where he rubbed, seemed joined, the one making the other more intense. Her hips rose off the bed.

She pulled his face up, put her arms around his neck and kissed him. Turning her head just so, she managed to make their noses fit quite nicely.

Max didn't stop rubbing.

"Och! It's a magical thing. Why . . . Och, Max! How does it happen? It's like, och, it's . . ." Her legs shot down straight and she crossed her ankles, trapping his hand. Burning waves flashed through skin and flesh and seemed to enter her bone. "It's wonderful," she told him, gasping, not wanting it to stop.

Never mind his warnings; she wanted to see if she could bring him great satisfaction, too. His Part would give her the answer. Pushing her face beneath the covers, she kissed his belly until he drove his fingers into her hair and made sounds that suggested he was feeling pleasure himself.

A little lower, she kissed him, and a little lower. Then, so quickly he'd not time to stop her, she took the Part in her hands and kissed him. He grappled for her hands, but she only held on tighter.

"Kirsty Mercer," he said, diving beneath the covers and curling over her. "Unhand me, you forward wench. Or you'll be sorry."

"I'll not unhand ye. If I do, *ye'll* be sorry."

He moaned, and his hips jutted. He took one of her breasts in each of his hands. "Sweetness, please don't. Please stop. You don't understand. You were right when you told me we shouldn't . . . Well, you know."

"I wasna right. But that was because I didn't know what I'd be missin'. Ye're talkin' too much."

"My God!"

"Dinna take the Lord's name in vain."

"I will be strong," he said. "What I asked earlier was wrong. Aah! I know that now. Aah!"

Why, if she opened her mouth wide she could take a goodly amount of him deep inside. And he liked it. Och, yes, he liked it verra much. He moaned and groaned and clutched at her, and clutched at sheets, and squeezed her breasts, and sweated. He really liked it.

Tangled together, the sheets and quilt over their heads, they paused in their writhing.

"Kirsty," Max said, covering her as if to hold as much of her as possible and easing her mouth from him, "say you'll never leave me."

A great swell of sadness rose in her chest. "I canna think o' not bein' wi' ye."

"No matter what, you'll stay with me?"

He asked so much. "I hope I can."

"I want us to be lovers, but I know I'm wrong to take you."

And she was wrong to want him to take her, but she did. "We'll have t'think hard, Max. But there's no goin' back, is there?"

"No, no going back."

"Perhaps it would be better if I did leave. I—" She stopped and listened.

"I won't let you leave," Max said, kissing her shoulder.

"Hush," she whispered. "Listen."

"Say you won't try to go away."

"*Listen.*"

"Say it!"

"I'll try not t'go away. Now listen, ye foolish laddie."

At last he did as he was told. A tap-tap-tapping sounded from the sitting room. Max made a move to pull the covers from his head but Kirsty stopped him. "Lie still, will ye? These are my rooms, remember. Ye're no' supposed t'be here."

Tap—tap—tap.

"What the hell is it?"

"Ye swear too much. Hush."

She peeked from beneath the sheets and grew utterly still. The door to the sitting room swung slowly wide open. Framed there was a tiny figure in dark silhouette.

Kirsty held her breath.

"You are not asleep," a cracking, imperious voice announced. "You were too busy to respond to my knock, but I heard you talking just now. Are you talking to yourself, Kirsty Mercer?"

Max grew heavy. Kirsty heard him mutter, "Great-grandmama," and groan.

"Speak up! What did you say? Don't try to pretend I'm too deaf to hear. I may not walk as well as I did, but I hear perfectly well."

The Dowager Duchess of Franchot! What could she be doing here? With the exception of the marquess and Max, the family had gathered at Franchot Castle in Cornwall.

"Speak up at once, Kirsty Mercer."

"Your Grace," Kirsty said. "I was sleepin'. Dreamin'." Och, she was a poor liar.

"Really. Would you be so good as to explain why these rooms are in such disorder."

"Ahem. Difficult events, Your Grace. We seem to have had an intruder."

"An intruder? And you go to bed and dream?"

"It was late when I discovered the situation."

Max held her tightly, his fingertips digging into her.

"I see. Am I right in my understanding that my great-grandson has retained you as his assistant?"

"Quite right," Kirsty said, feeling increasingly miserable.

"Hmm. Highly unusual. Would you happen to know where I might find that young man? Despite the late hour, I insisted upon finishing our journey tonight. We are only recently arrived, and I am quite tired. But I should like a word with Max before I try to sleep."

"Ye, er, ye came here to Eve alone?" Kirsty asked tentatively. She had no wish to confront the viscount. She had no wish to confront anyone while she was in a predicament.

The old lady—no one seemed certain just how old she was—used her stick to help her make progress to the side of the bed.

Kirsty bundled the covers around her, slid to sit up and attempted to make the bed look as if it was in particular disarray.

The lamp beside the bed burst to life, casting light over the scene.

"Good evening to you, Kirsty Mercer," the dowager said. Her thin white hair was scraped severely back beneath a black, beribboned cap. She held the ivory handle of her ebony cane with both hands and leaned heavily. She appeared almost transparent, but her eyes flashed bright and canny.

"Good evening," Kirsty said.

"I trust your family is well?" responded the dowager.

"Verra well, thank ye."

"Seems you've not slept peacefully this night." Those bright eyes surveyed the bed. She lifted her cane and brought it down hard on a particularly noticeable bump.

Max yelled.

"Out with you," the dowager demanded. "Enough of this foolishness. I'm not blind. Out with you at once, young man. As usual, my instincts were correct. My presence is far more necessary here than in Cornwall. Present yourself, I say."

Kirsty throbbed, horrified.

Slowly, Max emerged, holding the bedclothes to his chin.

The dowager turned the lamplight higher. "Did I not hear that you were to be betrothed to one Lady Hermoine Rashly?"

"You may have heard that," Max said.

"But this is Kirsty Mercer? Daughter of a respectable family that has occupied land at Kirkcaldy for more than two generations? Didn't my granddaughter, your mother, tell me that?"

"Correct, Great-grandmama. It's been a difficult evening. With the intruder and so on."

"He didna want t'leave me on my own," Kirsty added.

"Thoughtful boy," the dowager said. "It's probably as well that I persuaded your father to wait until morning to see you. Your uncle Arran made too much of telling us how hard you're working and how much you need your sleep. I just knew he was trying to make sure we didn't come here unexpected." She presented her hawklike profile and fell into deep thought.

"Great-grandmama, Kirsty has a lot to learn. You probably misunderstand—"

"Not a bit of it. I'm sure you've a great deal to teach Kirsty."

"It's not the way it—"

"Oh, but it certainly is. There's much to learn about the new ways of farming, and Kirsty will have to learn them, won't she?"

Kirsty closed her eyes.

"She will," Max said.

"And you, my errant young man, have a good deal to learn about a great many things. Such as the danger of meddling with young women who are members of families beloved to the Rossmaras. And, I may add, what affects the Rossmaras, affects my granddaughter, my dear Justine— and, by extension, myself. Then there is my grandson, Calum, your mother's brother, lest you have forgotten the elevated family of which you are a member. The Duke of Franchot is also affected by whatever affects the Rossmaras. Arran may have some foolish, romantic notion about there being a way to bring the two of you together. You and this

young woman. Arran was always a soft-hearted nincom-
poop. I must take matters into my own hands."

"Great-grandmama—"

"Enough. I've seen all I need to see. You will present
yourself to me in the Green Salon at ten in the morning.
Bring Kirsty with you."

Max groaned afresh.

"You may well be concerned, Max Rossmara." She
reached the door and turned back, and pointed her cane at
Kirsty. "Seems too thin for you, m'boy. Not at all your customary, full-figured type. But you certainly seemed to be
finding considerable pleasure in her when I arrived."

This was the worst moment of her life, Kirsty decided.

"You had best hope," the dowager continued, "that you
have not found so much pleasure in her as to bring about a
situation that would make our dilemma any more difficult.
Or far-reaching."

Chapter Fourteen

"There you are, Max."

At the sound of his father's voice, Max rose to his feet
from the books he'd been stacking on the floor of his library.

"Good morning to you, Father. Welcome back to Scotland."

Struan, Viscount Hunsingore, was a lean, dark-eyed,
dark-haired, wickedly handsome man who had once been
set to enter the priesthood. He liked to say that it was his
lovely wife, Lady Justine, who stole him from the church,
but his family knew he'd changed his mind on that score by
the time the two met.

This morning, at the ungodly hour of six, Struan was dressed in his customary black, with black cravat and stark white linen—and an expression that would shock cows into birthing.

Max smiled at him and carried another armload of books to the shelves.

"What in God's name is going on here?" his father asked. "Why aren't you properly dressed?"

He wasn't properly dressed because after leaving Kirsty he'd spent the rest of the night roaming the floor in his bedchamber. At least he'd put on a fresh shirt, even if its tails did trail loose.

"Max," Struan snapped. "I asked you a question."

"An intruder," Max responded shortly. "He entered while I was down in my study last night. I have no idea what he hoped to find, or if he found and took anything at all. To the latter, I tend to say no."

"To hell with intruders. You and Arran must deal with castle affairs. Your great-grandmother came to see you last night, didn't she?"

Max's pulse beat harder, faster. "Yes, she did."

Another pair of boots sounded in the corridor, and Arran entered, the scent of the outdoors coming with him. What few silver hairs flecked the dark, unruly hair he wore tied back in a tail only served to make him more distinguished. Arran and Struan were commanding brothers, and, despite frequent disagreements, wedded to supporting each other. With their friend Calum, Duke of Franchot, they were known throughout Scotland and England as a trio to be feared as enemies and treasured as friends.

At least Arran smiled, even if somewhat sheepishly.

"I suppose you've come to tell me how to deal with my own son," Struan said, his nostrils flaring. "Always to be relied upon for unwanted advice, that's my brother."

"I've not said a word," Arran remarked mildly.

Struan waggled a long forefinger. "Not because you haven't thought a word, I'll wager. You're just getting ready to tell me I'm overreacting."

"Are you?"

Struan glowered. "Am I what?"

"Overreacting," Arran said in the calm tone he adopted when baiting his younger brother.

"Have you condoned behavior on my son's part that would not have been acceptable to me?"

Arran smiled at Max. "I rest my case. Not a scrap of evidence to go on, yet he accuses me of some sort of crime against his judgment."

"Very well." Struan marched over fallen volumes, all but losing his balance on his way to drop into an armchair. "Enough of this shilly-shallying. You, my boy"—he pointed at Max—"waited until I was out of the way and installed Kirsty Mercer right here. *Right here.* Here in this tower where you are the only inhabitant. You are the only inhabitant because you perform the most important task to this estate—to this family—and your wish for privacy has been respected by us all."

"Masterful, he is," Arran said. "Best thing that ever happened to us, Max is. I give thanks for him every day."

Struan drummed his fingers on the arms of the chair. "He knows his mother and I have certain ambitions for him."

"Wouldn't be natural if you weren't ambitious for your children," Arran said. He picked up books and began shelving them. "Grace and I have ambitions for ours, I can tell you."

"No doubt," the viscount said. "And I don't suppose affairs with peasants are among them, eh?"

"Very important to get along well with everyone, old boy," Arran said, checking titles. "A successful estate commissioner takes care of the affairs of every man, woman, and child, and feels responsible for their happiness."

"That's it," Struan thundered. "You are in an impossible mood, Arran, and I refuse to waste my time on you."

"I say." Arran planted his big hands on his hips. "Overly aggressive this morning, aren't we? You know full well that I prefer my own company at this hour of the day. I came to join you out of filial affection."

"Stop it!" Blood pulsed at Max's temples. "Stop it, I tell you, or I'll not be responsible for my actions."

Father smacked the arms of his chair. "Don't take that tone—"

"I said, *stop* it," Max said, and kicked a heap of books with enough force to send several into the air. Arran took one against his thigh. Another knocked a Staffordshire dog to the floor, where it broke into many pieces.

Struan leaped to his feet. "In God's name, Max! Control yourself. You're a man, not a boy—to lose your temper so."

"I'm a man," Max shouted, rubbing his brow. "A man. My decisions are my own to make. I'll damn well do—"

"Max," Arran said loudly, "it's all right, old chap. Your father's tired from the journey."

Struan pounded a fist on Max's desk, and said, "Don't make excuses for me," to Arran. "And don't take his side against me. I'd have thought you of all people would be concerned for little Kirsty Mercer. We're not the kind of men to use those who rely upon us not only for their living, but for moral guidance."

"Damn righteousness," Max growled. "You've tried me for some sin and found me guilty. Now what? The sentence?"

"My darling Justine will be devastated."

"Why?" Max flexed his fingers. They shook, and curling them into fists didn't stop them from shaking. "Mother has no reason to be devastated by anything to do with me. I serve you all well."

"You speak as if what you do is only to our advantage," Arran said. His arched brows rose.

"Not so," Max responded. "You know what my work means to me. You know how dedicated I am to this estate, to you, the family—all of it. This has become my life."

"What do you think will happen if unrest breaks out among the tenants?" Struan turned cold eyes on Max. "Have you considered that? We have maintained the best of relationships between ourselves and those who live on our lands. Those relationships are responsible for our success during times when other great estates have struggled. We could have chosen to become part of the clearings. We could have driven people away in favor of sheep, but we curse those lairds who have committed such crimes against humanity. And we have drawn strength, and we have prospered for this. But our people are proud. They will react to any suggestion that we have ceased to respect them and theirs."

"There is no unrest," Max told him. "And there will be no unrest. Not because of any fault of mine."

"Use an innocent girl who is loved and respected by many, and you'll eat those words. We'll all eat them with you."

"You, of course, never bedded a woman until you married Mama," Max said. He saw Arran tense but would not stop now even if he could. "When you found my sister in a brothel—a happy night for her, and for me—but when you found her, you were not there to save souls, were you? Were you perhaps partaking in what it is that those places offer?"

"Max," Arran said quietly, "that's enough, boy."

"Oh, no," Struan said, a jeering note in his voice. "Let him say what he really thinks of me."

Max swallowed. He held his father's eyes as long as he could before having to look away. "I think you're the best of men," he muttered. "You saved my sister, and you saved me, and you owed neither of us anything. You are good to your very core, and I regret causing you concern."

Arran slapped his hands together and rubbed his palms so that they squeaked. "There, then, all is forgiven and forgotten. We are ourselves again. I suggest we ride out toward the north and take a look at things there."

"All is not forgotten," Struan told his brother. "I appreciate my son's pretty speech, but we will make things clear between us now. Max, you know that your mother and I have received the overtures of Countess Grabham on behalf of her niece, Lady Hermoine?"

Max leafed through a book, dropped it, and selected another.

"You *do* know this," the viscount said. "We have given them to believe that we look favorably upon a match between you."

"A man of my age may hope to make such decisions for himself," Max said.

"I'd prefer never to mention this, but you are not like most men of the standing you've come to regard as your due."

Max looked at him sharply. "Most gentlemen are not bastards from the gutters of London," he said. "Is that what you mean?"

"It is not what I mean," Struan replied. His lips were white and drawn tight. "I mean that we have done our best to bring you up as a gentleman and, in fact, that is what you are. But now it is of the essence that you have a suitable wife. A lady. Someone who will help you by opening doors that might otherwise be closed to you."

"I'm able to go wherever I choose," Max pointed out. "Why should I need to marry to continue to do what I already do?"

"Because we demand it," Struan said, visibly restraining himself. "Justine and I demand that you prove us right. We have spent all the years of your growing up defending our right to choose you as our son. Now we want to be certain there can be no more question."

"I didn't think you cared what people thought—"

"Not for ourselves! Think, Max, think. You will have children. They deserve the same chances Ella and Saber will give their children. And what of your younger brother and sister? They love and respect you. They think of you as their brother in every way. It would not be tenable for them to be forced to acknowledge you in the circles in which they will move if you insist upon being drawn to lower stations."

Max wanted to walk out. He wanted to take the very clothes from his back and toss them aside, saying he would keep nothing that had been granted him with a price attached. He wanted to punch his father for the snob he was, and for shattering the high regard in which Max had always held him.

"Max," Arran said, and Max glanced at him. "Time, boy, time. Give it time. Many things are said in the heat of emotion that would not otherwise be said. Or, if they were, they would be said differently."

"I asked the dowager a direct question," his father said. "I asked her if she had seen you during the night. She is a difficult woman, but an honest one. She said she had."

"True," Max told him.

"She is also far too attached to you and your sister," Father said. "I asked her where she had spoken to you, and she was evasive. But I had already been told, in a very discreet manner, of course, about Kirsty's presence here. The servants are talking, dammit. You were with Kirsty when the dowager came to you, weren't you?"

"I hardly think I have to account for my actions."

"Yes, of course you were with her. Thank you for admitting as much so easily. The question is, *where* were you with her? The hour was exceedingly late. The dowager should not have insisted upon going to you, but she will always have her own way. Where were you so late in the evening, my son?"

Arran opened Max's violin case and removed the instrument and the bow. As easily as most men raised a glass, he raised the violin and began to tune it.

"That diversion won't work, Arran," his brother said. "*Where*, Max? In bed?"

"Yes."

"Your own bed."

Max laughed. "What would constitute positive proof of what you evidently believe? The bed I slept in last night?"

"You may live to regret your lack of respect, my boy," his father said. "Answer my question. The sooner we clear the air, the sooner we can decide how to proceed."

Max met Arran's eyes. Arran nodded slightly.

"Very well," Max said. "I was in bed when Great-grandmama came. In the bedroom in the rosy rooms. I was with Kirsty Mercer. I'm glad I was with her."

"My God," Struan muttered. "And the staff all suspect as much. It will be all over the countryside in no time. What if she's with child?"

"He'll have to marry her," Arran said promptly, and with no hint of a smile.

"Kirsty isn't with child," Max said, seething at this inquisition. "A certain act would be necessary for that to be the case. I have lain in the same bed as Kirsty Mercer—and pray that I shall do so again—but I have not known her."

"You must think us weak-brained," Struan said.

Max approached until he stood toe-to-toe with the man he loved as he loved no other. "I think I would like to believe you are not calling me a liar. I have not copulated with Kirsty—although I'd be lying if I said I didn't want to."

"Praise be," Struan said. He punched Max's arm lightly. "I don't want you to think I am callous, my boy. I know how it is to love, and love deeply, and I wish it were sensible for me to encourage you in what I know you want. It isn't. But you are a man of finer feelings. You will be happier when you know your Kirsty is well taken care of."

Max said, "Meaning what?"

His father smiled, but not, Max noted, with any great assurance. "Why . . . Sometimes I forget you're not accustomed to all aspects of a gentleman's way. We must put family and family connections first. We'll get you married to Lady Hermoine. It'll do wonders for your stock, boy. And we'll find a suitable husband for Kirsty. Someone solid, who will respect and look after her. She'll soon be too busy as a wife and mother to remain in this position you've fabricated for her, and she'll leave. You may not believe it now, but there is some truth in the saying, 'out of sight, out of mind.' "

"Damn you!" Max lunged at his father.

Arran's unyielding arm wrapped around Max's body, bound his arms to his sides and stopped him from striking the man he loved most.

"You've got to come at once, son-in-law," Blanche Bastible said, her unfashionable blond ringlets bobbing. She held up her voluminous red, green, and gold tarlatan skirts and surveyed the mess in Max's library with distaste. "Her Grace sent me. Or rather I know she wanted me to come for you. What *is* the matter with you, Viscount Hunsingore? Are you feeling unwell?"

Arran filled his lungs and prayed for patience. "Everything is perfectly fine, mother-in-law," he said. "Why not return to the dowager and see what you can do to make her more comfortable. She undertakes journeys that are too strenuous for a woman of her age."

"Too strenuous? Hah, so you think. My dear lady will outlive us all, you see if she doesn't. And you have no need to think any of you will see a penny of her fortune. Oh, no, she won't be wasting her fortune on any of you."

Blanche's talent for switching topics never ceased to irritate Arran. "Well, since we'll all predecease the good lady, we need not concern ourselves with such matters. Please close the door as you leave."

"Oh, you don't understand. That dreadful female is here. She's with the dowager now, chattering and fussing. And she's demanding to see you." Blanche smiled adoringly at Max. "I'm sure it would be all right if the marquess went alone, though. There's no need for you or your father to be bothered with the nasty creature, my dear boy."

"Which nasty creature would that be?" Arran asked, smiling indulgently. Blanche was annoying but had proved her loyalty to the family on more than one occasion—and she was his beloved Grace's mother.

"She says she has information you won't want spread around. There is a *threat* in the way she talks, I tell you. Most distressing." Blanche fluffed her curls, tweaked the ribbons on her cap, and smoothed her bodice over very considerable curves. There was about her a youthfulness that belied her more than sixty years.

"I'll go down with you, Arran," Struan said.

"You'll do no such thing, young man," Blanche said, showing her ongoing disapproval of Struan, whom she considered to have supported Arran in keeping her from a suitably elevated position in local society. "I said she wants the marquess only. He is the one who stands to suffer if that creature doesn't get her way."

Arran looked from Max, to Struan. Struan frowned. His steady stare in his son's direction suggested they were far from done with their conversation. "What does she want?" Struan asked. "Whoever she is?"

"Satisfaction, she said." Blanche flapped her soft hands. "How should I know what that means? But she wants satisfaction because she hasn't *talked out of turn like some people*, she says. The dowager is obviously detaining the silly woman until Arran gets there."

At last Max turned from his father and gave his attention to Blanche. "What are you talking about, Mrs. Bastible?" His tone wasn't unkind. "Is Lady Hermoine here so early? I can't think why she would go to Great-grandmama."

"Lady Hermoine? Oh, no, not that charming, cultured creature—who, by the by, will make a most welcome addition to this household. This is a person of quite a different sort, apparently the daughter of an acquaintance of the countess's—undoubtedly someone of the lower classes. A Miss Dahlia, or so she calls herself. The countess, saint that she is, has undertaken the care of this Miss Dahlia and her two sisters."

"Thank you, mother-in-law," Arran said. "Most kind of you to put yourself out so early in the morning."

"It isn't good for my constitution to rise before noon," Blanche said, but she simpered. "However there is nothing that is too great a sacrifice for my dearest lady—or for any of you, and I must say that the girl, Mairi, has come along quite nicely. She accomplished my toilette in a remarkably efficient manner." Mairi would not see her thirty-fifth birthday again, yet she remained a "girl" to Blanche.

"I'd best go to the dowager at once," Arran said. "You two have considerable work to accomplish," he told Struan and Max, weighting his words with meaning.

"I shall accompany you, son-in-law," Blanche said, nimbly making her way through debris to the door. "The dear dowager will be quite exhausted by now."

"I'm right behind you," Arran said, and before closing the door told Struan and Max, "I shall expect to find you both here when I return. I don't anticipate a long interview with the fair Dahlia. Put your differences aside. Together we are a formidable power. We will not jeopardize that for the sake of misunderstanding and pride."

He didn't wait to see their reaction to his words, but followed Blanche's girlish tripping down flights of stairs to the entry hall, through a series of corridors, and up more flights in the Adam Tower to the rooms the dowager preferred to use on her visits. She awaited them in the Green Salon.

Seated beside her on a velvet divan, the woman Arran recognized as one of three sisters who lived at The Hallows sat with every appearance of one at war with her conscience. Her brightly rouged lips trembled, as did her hands, the fingers constantly winding the handle of the woven silver reticule in her lap. Large brown eyes shone with moisture, and she blinked repeatedly.

God, Arran thought, *please don't let the hussy start blubbering.* "Good day to you, miss," he said formally. "I understand you have requested an audience with me."

"Audacity," the dowager said. Still in her nightgown, robe, and cap, a large black shawl draped over all made her appear even smaller and more frail. "To push her way in here at such an hour, then to refuse to come out with what she thinks is so important. Audacity." She held her ebony cane before her and this she thumped on the floor—not, from Arran's experience, a happy sign for things to come.

"Oh, Your Lordship," the young woman said, rising, then sinking into a low and somewhat wobbly curtsy.

Arran said, "Yes, yes. Very well. What seems to be the trouble?"

Hair the color of carrots past their prime puffed out around Dahlia's face, and looped into many intricate braids. A jaunty chapeau in rose satin clashed badly with the ripe carrot. Her military-style Crispin mantle, trimmed with brown velvet braid, suggested that no expense was spared on Miss Dahlia's wardrobe.

Blanche Bastible fussed around the dowager, who continued to amaze Arran in her open affection for his mother-in-law.

"You see," the dowager said, pounding the floor with her cane again, "the foolish creature has come here and made a great many veiled threats and will *not* explain herself fully."

"I most certainly shall explain meself fully to the marquess," Miss Dahlia said in a tight, almost strangled accent that fascinated Arran to silence. "I 'ave hinformation of the greatest hinterest to you, me lord. I 'ave 'esitated to come to you because I don't want to risk bein' misunderstood. I wouldn't want you to think for one moment that I 'ave any personal motives for wantin' you to be aware of a most distressin' matter that 'as come to my attention."

Arran realized his chin had slowly jutted forward, and pulled it back. "You don't say."

"Oh, but I do, I hassure you. 'Owever, I believe we should speak of this alone."

No glance in the dowager's direction was necessary. "Whatever you can say to me, you can say to the Dowager Duchess of Franchot, a dear family friend, and to Mrs. Blanche Wren Bastible, who, in addition to being the dowager's companion, is my wife's mother."

A pleased warble issued from Blanche, and at least the dowager didn't pound her stick again.

Dahlia lowered her blackened lashes and her lips trembled again.

"Come along now," Arran said gently. "It can't be that bad."

"I've come 'ere at great personal risk," she said. "I wouldn't want you to think my motives self-servin', but, hafter all, a female who is dependent upon the kindness of strangers is always in a difficult position."

The baggage wanted money.

"Blackmail," the dowager snapped. "The lowest form of criminal behavior. Extorting gain from the real or perceived misfortunes of others. I say you tell the creature to leave at once, Arran."

Dahlia's black lashes rose, and they were gifted with a hard, dry-eyed stare. "Watch out who you call criminal. The pot calling the kettle black, that is. And I've got information to prove it."

Arran experienced an unpleasant tightening in his gut. "I think that's enough small talk, Miss Dahlia. If you have something to say, say it. I'm a busy man."

"Oh, of course you are. Too busy to spare time for the likes of me. After all, I'm nobody but a poor young thing forced to accept the kindness of my dearest mother's dearest friend."

"Yes," Arran said, his patience exhausted. "What is it you think would make you feel better about revealing whatever it is you have to reveal?"

"Well." Considerable batting of her impressive lashes followed. "Well, what do you think your family honor is worth?"

Dumbfounded, nevertheless Arran stood his ground and managed to maintain a calm expression.

The dowager's face showed no emotion at all. Blanche had been with her mistress long enough to pick up the cue and show nothing of what she might think or feel.

"Well," Dahlia said, with more than a hint of cockney creeping into her voice, "speak up, then. What's it worth to you?"

"I can't imagine what you're talking about," Arran said, "but I think it's time for you to leave."

"That's up to you." Dahlia rose. She smoothed her gloves and slipped the handle of her reticule over one wrist. "But I'll leave you with somethin' to think about. The journal's safe for now. It'll be safe for as long as I decide not to show it to anyone. If I do decide—and it's not you I'm showing it to—well then, it'll be very dangerous for the Rossmaras."

"Journal?" Arran said. "Which journal would that be?"

"Um." Dahlia frowned and swayed from the waist. "Well, it's a journal that's been hidden for a long time, only now I've found it."

"What's in this journal?" the dowager asked, underscoring her question with a single sharp tap of her cane on the carpet at her feet. "Speak up. No more shilly-shallying. What is it that you want? What is it that's in this journal that you think is worth blackmailing the Rossmaras for?"

"I want Mr. Max Rossmara to ask for my 'and in marriage instead of that self-satisfied cow Hermoine. She may have 'lady' in front of 'er name, but she's no lady, if you know what I mean. I'll be good for 'im and 'e'll be good for me. We'll 'ave plenty of fun." She winked, and her right eye remained shut a very long time.

Arran sat down.

Dahlia smiled as if hugely pleased with herself. "Surprised you, 'aven't I? Well, I know 'ow to make sure I get plenty, *and* 'old on to it. And I fancy 'im."

"She's mad," Blanche whispered. "I'll ring for Shanks to get rid of her."

"Tell me what's in the journal," Arran said.

"Well, now, I can't do that, can I? Not too much, anyway, until the preacher's done 'is business. When 'e 'as, you'll get the journal, and you can make sure it disappears. But I'll give you a taste. Some people may not be who they think they are. It could just be that there are some who think they've a right to grand titles and all that goes with 'em, when they really don't 'ave any right to any of it. And it could be that there's a record of just who should be king of the castle, so to speak."

Chapter Fifteen

Despite the hour—noon—when Kirsty opened the door to the Green Salon, the room was in near darkness. Heavy draperies had been closed over each of four floor-to-ceiling casements, and no lamps were alight. Even the fire had burned too low to cast more than a faint reddish glow on the hearth. Rather than the original arrangement—that she and Max should arrive here at ten—she'd received word to come alone two hours later.

"Shut the door," the Dowager Duchess of Franchot said, her tone autocratic. "Then come over here where I can see you."

Kirsty could see virtually nothing, but did as she was told and went forward, attempting to focus on the figure sitting in a large wing back chair to one side of the fireplace.

"That's better," the dowager said. "Now I see you well enough. Pretty thing, aren't you. I saw that when you were in bed with Max."

Kirsty blushed, and felt the heat of it to her very toes. She curtsied and said, "You wanted t'speak with me."

"I dislike restatement of the obvious," the dowager said. "Now, let's get down to business. We are in an extremely delicate situation, Kirsty Mercer. I find myself forced to interfere in the business of others—something I detest, and avoid whenever possible—but interfere I must, for the good of my dear friends, the Rossmaras. Our families are deeply intertwined, y'know, and the Rossmaras may be in trouble. That is a situation I cannot simply sit back and watch without giving them the benefit of my considerable life experience. I am an expert in human nature and behavior, and if ever I saw an occasion when human nature and behavior are at odds, well then I'm seeing it at present. I mean to ensure that right prevails. Will you help me, Kirsty Mercer?"

Mesmerized by the drone of the old lady's voice, Kirsty took a moment to fully understand the question. When she did, she said, "I would do anythin' t'be o' service t'the Rossmaras. My family has made their livin' on Rossmara lands for generations, ma'am."

"Yes, yes, so you say. Commendably forthright of you to mention it. But what I find myself confronted with is a situation that will require some diplomacy. Perhaps some covert diplomacy. Is my language too complicated for you?"

"I understand ye perfectly," Kirsty said. "Although, o'course, I've no idea what ye have in mind."

"I'm told that Max has retained you for some sort of position. Or so he's put it about."

Kirsty's eyes adjusted to the gloom, and she saw the old lady's face more clearly, an ancient, but well-preserved face. The eyes were bright and sharp, and didn't waver in their regard of Kirsty.

"When the tutor left to assist with the children in Cornwall she assumed you would be performing the duties she'd assigned for you to perform."

"True enough," Kirsty said.

"Sewing and so on. You are the tutor's maid, aren't you? Or some sort of nursery assistant under her direction?"

These elevated people often knew so little about the people who worked for them. "I was the tutor's assistant, Your Grace. I helped with the children's lessons."

"Really?" The dowager fussed with the gold chains around her neck until she located her lorgnette. She peered at Kirsty through this, starting with a long study of her face, then continuing to sweep every inch on the way to her subject's feet. "Of course you would have attended the village school, I suppose?"

"Yes, Your Grace."

"Scotland has reason to be proud of its educational record. No other country can boast to have taught its people to read and write as a due for more than a century."

"No, Your Grace."

"But such minimal accomplishments hardly qualify you to instruct the children of a *marquess*, young woman. Particularly as their needs grow demanding."

"Max taught me," Kirsty mumbled. "From when he came t'Kirkcaldy, he shared what he learned wi' me."

"Speak up!"

"I said—"

"I know what you said. I'm not deaf. You mean Max Rossmara spent time teaching a little girl, a tenant's child? Starting from when he would have been how old? Ten?"

"Thereabouts, madam."

"Why would a boy like that—full of spirit and with no time for such things—take the trouble to teach you anything?"

How did you explain something as special as she and Max had had to a lady such as this? "I canna tell ye. He was verra kind t'me. And there weren't any laddies his own age t'pass time with."

"So you expect me to believe he sought you out and insisted upon contributing to your education?"

"No, madam. I followed the poor lad around and pestered him somthin' terrible wi' my questions. And he was kind enough t'answer. We were friends. All through the years, we were friends."

The dowager raised her stick and pointed it at a chair. "Sit there."

Kirsty sat, and was grateful to do so.

"Are you an intelligent girl?"

The old lady's direct manner unsettled Kirsty. "I'm not unintelligent. Max always said I enjoyed lessons more than he did. He used to tell me that sharing his lessons with me helped him do his homework, but I doubt that's the case. He was just bein' kind."

"And I doubt that. Did you actually teach the marquess's children?"

Kirsty hesitated before saying, "Yes, Your Grace. It was the marquess himself who recommended me for the position. They were simple enough lessons at first, of course. I'm particularly fond of geography, so I took over that area of their instruction. And I shared a good deal of responsibility for their mathematics."

The dowager fell into a deep silence, staring into the embers of the fire and letting her chin rest on her chest.

"So it isn't outrageous to think of your being retained in some sort of administrative capacity for Max?"

The question was fired sharply at Kirsty, and she tensed. "I wouldn't think so," she said. "I've a great interest in farmin' and the business of managin' estates like this one. Not that I'm t'do more than deal wi' wages and keepin' books, and writin' correspondence, and the like. I'll find it a challenge, and I do well wi' a challenge. I've started studyin' what's been written on rotatin' crops . . ." She was saying too much. "I'll be happy to do whatever will make Max—Mr. Rossmara happy."

"Whatever will make Mr. Rossmara happy," the dowager said in her raspy voice. "*Whatever* will make Mr. Rossmara happy?"

Kirsty bowed her head. "I didna mean what ye're thinkin'."

"I know you didn't, but you're a quick-witted girl, and you understand me very well. Remember the scene I witnessed last night. We're in a pretty fix, Kirsty Mercer. I don't suppose you understand that as well as I do. You probably see the business as a simple one. It isn't. There are too many personalities involved now."

"I'd never want t'do anythin' t'hurt Max—Mr. Rossmara."

"Call him Max to me. It's natural to you. But be certain you don't call him by that name elsewhere. You love him, don't you?"

The stress of the night and the morning had stolen Kirsty's appetite. Now she felt weak. She put a hand to her cheek and tried to breathe deeply.

"Don't you?" the dowager persisted.

Kirsty whispered, "Aye. I've never loved another. I never will."

"Has he given you some reason to expect that you might have some future together—of an intimate, and a permanent nature?"

"Och, I canna bear t'talk o' it. I canna bear it, madam."

"Buck up, girl! Of course you can bear it. Answer my question."

Kirsty sank back in the chair. "When we were bairns— that is, until I was sixteen and he was twenty-two—we were close. More and more close as we got older. Not the way ye might think. Max is honorable. But we knew we loved each other. Not the way some do—not until right at the end, anyway—we didna do anythin' about it. My father and mother started t'worry, I know they did. I think my father spoke t'Max, told him he wasna right for me—or me for him, rather. But we made a promise t'each other before Max went t'Yorkshire that year."

"Promise?" The old lady leaned sharply forward. "What do you mean, a promise."

Despite an ache deep inside her, Kirsty laughed. "Dinna get yoursel' in a dither. We promised we'd always be friends, and that we'd be together again. And we made up a . . . och, just silly things young folks do an' say. But I'd be lyin' if I said I didna miss him somethin' fierce when he didna come back—or when he came back but kept his distance from me. I was young. It seemed as if my heart would break in little pieces. I hurt so just thinkin' about him up here and never comin' near me when we'd been so close. But I came to know he was bein' wise. It wouldna have done if we'd spent time together then."

"Interesting," the dowager said quietly. "You're thoughtful. It's a great pity you aren't of better breeding. You're a lady at heart. I've encountered such things before, but not quite like this, not quite like you."

Kirsty didn't answer. She recognized the compliment padded inside the insult and had no response to make.

"So you decided Max had made the right decision when he stayed away from you, yet, when he approached you a matter of days ago—with what must have seemed an extraordinary proposition—you accepted that proposition. Why would you do such a thing if you knew it was wrong?"

"I've told ye," Kirsty said, "I love him. I'm only human. He gave me the chance t'be near him, and I couldna turn that down. Besides, why is it wrong if I'm able t'do the work?"

"Does he love you now?"

"Och! Och, madam, I canna speak for Max on such a thing. He cares for me, I know that. He also knows his duty, and he'll put that duty above all else, so ye've nothin' t'fear."

The old lady's dry laugh chilled Kirsty. The laugh, followed by silence in the close room that smelled of dried rose petals, spent wax, and the sparking soot that clung to the chimney breast.

"I've been sitting here a long time today," the dowager said. "Sitting here and thinking about how I should manage this little *contretemps*. And manage it, I must, since I cannot trust men to manage such a thing without bringing another disaster upon our heads."

The temptation to ask what the other disaster might be was heavy upon Kirsty, but she resisted.

"I could bring pressure to bear to have you sent away from the castle," the dowager said. "They would defer to me if I insisted, but that would only cause more, rather than less trouble. Max might simply follow you. Your people . . . well, it wouldn't do. No, I have given all this a great deal of consideration and I know what must be done. But I shall require your cooperation. Did you . . . That is, did Max . . . Oh, of course he did."

"Madam?"

"Even I find this difficult. When Max, er, had his way with you last night, was there any attempt to avoid the possibility of a child?"

Kirsty's entire body flamed. "He didn't," she muttered.

"Oh, that foolish boy," the dowager said. "When will men learn some control?"

"I meant that he didn't have his way wi' me. We held each other, and we kissed. And he did touch me, but—"

"*Enough.* My goodness, I'm an old lady and not strong. I do not wish to know the minutiae." She coughed delicately. "But perhaps I should be strong and allow you to explain fully. Then I should know exactly what took place."

"Well, he didna risk getting me with child, Your Grace."

The Dowager Duchess of Franchot convulsed into spasms of coughing.

"I've lived around animals all my life, so I know full well how the wee animals come about, an' Max didna do that t'me with his Part, so there won't be a bairn."

"Well, we must be thankful for that."

"I do have t'tell ye that I think ye may have stopped it from happenin'. We'd neither o' us many clothes on t'speak of by the time ye arrived, and he did make me feel such feelings. I'd ha' done whatever he led me t'do. It was verra pleasant, but ye'll know that from your own experiences."

The dowager coughed so hard that Kirsty rose from her chair. "Can I get ye some water?"

"No," the old lady said between spasms. "I'm quite all right. We'd best get to the heart of what I have to say to you, before we're interrupted. You are aware that Max may marry Lady Hermoine Rashly?"

"I am."

"You must not have *very pleasant* interludes with Max again. At least, you mustn't have them just yet. Do you understand?"

"No," Kirsty said with honesty. "Either I must, or I mustn't. What d'ye mean, not just yet?"

"Oh, this is difficult. I'm asking you to be strong, to make certain there is no intimacy between the two of you—at least until after he's married and his wife has produced a child or two. Now, I know such restraint will require patience, but I will help you."

"Ye will?" Kirsty couldn't imagine how the dowager would go about such a thing.

"Trust me in this. But, and this is of the utmost importance, you must also continue in the position Max has given you. If you don't, you will only confirm all the gossip that's already flying around the countryside about you and Max. This is why I've decided you must remain here—to dispel rumors. I insist that you stay and work hard at being the very best assistant you can. I'm certain you will make an excellent job of it. After all, you're intelligent, interested, and willing to learn—and you're a woman. You're bound to be successful."

Confusion made Kirsty's head fuzzy. "I'm t'stay?"

"As Max's assistant. He needs an assistant and it might as well be you now that he's announced to the world that it's you he's chosen. We must just make sure that we squash any gossip suggesting that you are Max's mistress."

"I'm so worried about my family. How did ye say we make sure there'll no' be anymore gossip."

"By having you continue working for Max while we go ahead with preparations for his marriage. You must understand that my first duty is to my granddaughter—Lady Justine. She's a weakling, and if her ambitions for Max go awry, I fear she may slip into a decline."

"I care for Lady Justine," Kirsty said, feeling weak herself. "I'll have no part o' hurtin' her." Although, Kirsty thought, that lady had always seemed particularly strong.

"Good. You must exhibit great decorum. I understand a modiste is here to make you some gowns. I'll oversee that project myself. You will be demure and most serious about your work. And, especially in front of others, you will show distant deference to Max—and absolutely no personal interest. A little bob of a curtsy from time to time wouldn't go amiss. And you might hold your head on one side, with your eyes lowered, when he speaks to you. In fact, it would be better if you never initiated any conversation with him when others are present. Make sure you walk behind him a few paces. If you should ride out with him, do the same thing. Keep some distance, with yourself in the rear. Are you remembering all this?"

She nodded, and wondered how she would perform this drama without ruining the entire effect by laughing.

"Kirsty, I want to tell you a few things. I expect you think me a heartless old woman, don't you?"

"I think you a great lady who puts duty before all else. It canna always have been easy for ye."

"Of course it was easy," the dowager snapped. "When one is born to a certain station in life, the rigors of that station are second nature. Never mind me. I believe that young rake, Max, does love you. But I also believe he will do what he must do."

Every sweet word carried its own barb. Kirsty dried her moist palms on her skirts.

The dowager continued, "He will do what he must, but he will have his longings, and men are not as strong as women in these matters. It will be up to you to be strong for both of you."

Kirsty waited quietly, hoping she would soon be dismissed from this most terrible of interviews.

"However, there are certain ways in which a woman can assist a man to tolerate his disappointments. Do you understand?"

"No," Kirsty said. "D'ye mean he may try t'kiss me or somethin' even though he's married to Lady Hermoine? I dinna think he will. He's too principled."

"Hah! You may be highly intelligent, but you clearly know little about men who are accustomed to getting their way. If I have taken correct measure of the situation—and I am *never* wrong in these things—he will not only try to kiss you, he will try to do a great deal more. If you are not both strong, and practiced in the ways of reducing his sense of need, then disaster may occur regardless. You, my dear, can do a great service for Max, and the future of this great estate."

"I can?"

"You can. Do you comprehend the phrase, 'to pleasure?' "

Scrunching down as small as possible in the chair, Kirsty said, "I think I do."

The dowager grunted. "I doubt it. It means to give carnal satisfaction. With all the base sensations that go with it."

"Base sensations? Oh, I know Max would never want any part o' base sensations."

"Oh, *enjoyable* sensations, then."

"He'd like those, I'm sure," Kirsty said. "He seemed to last night."

The dowager was silent for so long that Kirsty shifted forward in her seat to peer at the old lady. "Are ye well?" she inquired.

"Perfectly well. Now, to pleasuring Max when necessary. We'll approach this in a cool, businesslike fashion. I imagine this will usually take place in his study."

Kirsty frowned, concentrating hard, and said, "In his study?"

"Yes, in his study. You will be able to tell the event is imminent by the manner in which he finds ways to be physically close to you. He may even touch you. Or attempt to kiss you."

Touching her mouth, Kirsty admitted to herself—with some chagrin—that she hoped Max would frequently try to kiss her.

"When this series of events occurs, the door should be locked to make certain there are no embarrassing intrusions."

"If someone tries to open the door, they'll wonder why it's locked."

"And you will always go immediately to Shanks—after an event of pleasuring—and inform him that you and Mr. Rossmara locked the door because the nature of your work required that you not be interrupted, but that the work is now complete."

This seemed remarkably complicated.

"Am I then t'let Max kiss me—after the door's locked."

"Oh, my dear girl." Deep sadness darkened the dowager's words. "If only I thought it could be that simple. No, no, you will be required to perform a selfless act which will ensure Max's satisfaction and be a great trial to yourself. Women have always been called upon to suffer so. But it will be over soon enough."

"Your Grace—"

"You're quick. You'll grasp the essence easily. It's what you call his *Part*. They've all got them. Did you know that?"

"I did assume as much."

"Well, you're correct. Each and every one of them owns a Part and is helpless to ignore its demands. When you feel them taking over his reason, lock the door, open his trousers, and take matters into your own hands. He won't argue."

Surely, Kirsty thought, surely she misunderstood.

"At least for the foreseeable future, follow my simple request and we'll get through. Later we may have to rethink matters. *Stimulation*. That will get the job done."

"Stimulation?"

"Yes, I'm afraid so. Stimulate the Part. Make sure you smile and appear delighted to do so, and he'll allow you to guide him almost immediately. And afterward he will be ridiculously grateful and, we hope, easily managed. There is only one unfortunate possibility, my dear. But you won't let it stop you, will you?"

"I shall do what you want me to do," Kirsty said, not at all sure she'd ever survive her first attempt.

"Good. But I wouldn't be fair if I didn't warn you that he may become almost, well, almost *addicted*. Or so it will seem. But if he starts coming to you first thing in the morning when you're expecting to get to your work, and he locks the door himself, you'll know what he wants, won't you?"

Max? Behaving so? The idea was bizarre, but she must give credence to the other woman's long experience with human behavior.

"I know you won't fail me. And if it should happen that he comes to you not just once, but several times during a day, well then, have courage. Just smile, close your eyes, and think of Kirkcaldy."

Chapter Sixteen

Max rotated his shoulder. The wound might be what Kirsty termed, "a scratch," but even though several days had passed since the attack, the injury was far from comfortable.

He'd left his father and Arran at the breakfast table—arguing as to which, if either, of them should be present at ceremonies to welcome Queen Victoria to Edinburgh in August.

Such issues bored Max—not that he'd been invited. He grinned wryly at the thought.

Of more interest, and far deeper concern to him, was what continued to be the unresolved mystery of who had invaded his rooms, and Kirsty's—and why.

There had been no further mysterious—or dangerous— incidents, but he had not had a night of sound sleep since the event. He awoke frequently, listening and peering into the darkness.

He smiled again, this time aware of quite a different feeling. No doubt if he had Kirsty in his bed at night, his slumbers would be a great deal deeper—if still frequently interrupted.

With breakfast over, there was a great deal to be accomplished today.

He'd decided that if he could train Kirsty not to leap up and lock the study door every time he approached her desk, their situation could be said to be almost perfect—in the professional sense. Yes, in fact, after a number of days working together things were settling down remarkably well.

He was far from satisfied with their personal relationship.

They had no personal relationship.

It was as if their night together had never taken place. Kirsty would not as much as walk beside him, choosing instead to remain some distance behind as she did at this very moment.

He mused about these things almost ceaselessly.

She had taken to curtsying frequently. Most annoying.

She never raised her eyes to meet his, although she did smile—constantly.

He should find her polite demeanor above reproach. It made his teeth ache with the longing to tell her to be herself.

Not a single conversation did she initiate.

And, most annoying of all, gowns produced by the modiste and her assistant—although of excellent cloth and not black—closely resembled the style worn by his great-grandmother.

He must try harder to put Kirsty at her ease, and speak to the modiste himself.

This afternoon he planned to join his father and uncle on a visit to several of the tenant farmers who worked land in the northernmost reaches of the estate. These hardy fellows enjoyed their independence but still liked visits from the lairds from time to time to discuss the state of things and deal with any needs.

Kirsty would accompany them. He had finally coaxed her onto a sweet-tempered little mare, and after four rides his pupil was already showing signs of becoming a competent, if timid, horsewoman. He had spoken with his uncle Arran and his father early the previous evening, and they'd decided to visit the Mercers early in the afternoon, before striking out north. Peace must be made between Kirsty and her family, and it had been agreed that if she was seen in the respected role she played at the castle, there might be hope of a truce between parents and daughter.

Max strode into his study—with Kirsty trailing behind—and halted. Lady Hermoine Rashly's presence there wasn't a happy surprise. She jumped up from her chair the instant Max and Kirsty entered.

"Be angry with me for intruding, Max," she said. "I deserve it. I left The Hallows before the household was fully awake. And I sneaked in here without being seen. But I simply couldn't stay away a moment longer. Hello, Kirsty, how lovely to see you again. I'm so glad you're here to make Max's burden lighter. I hope you try to make sure he doesn't work too hard."

Kirsty said, "I do my best, my lady. I'll leave ye alone."

"Remain please, Kirsty. We have a great deal to do. How are you?" Max asked Lady Hermoine, while he watched Kirsty settle in her chair and open a ledger.

"Better for seeing you, dearest." Lady Hermoine, a vision in pale purple, took tiny, hesitant steps toward him. "I haven't heard a word from you in days. Are you angry with me?"

"No." Not angry, *bloody furious.* She reminded him of what he wanted most to forget—his damnable social responsibilities.

"Dearest, you will come to the ball, won't you? It will be our first opportunity to be seen—really seen together in society. I wish it were not a whole week away."

Max evaded the question.

Kirsty turned a page but didn't seem to read anything she saw. She hadn't picked up a pen.

"Well, I know how busy you are, but we really do need to talk," Lady Hermoine said, her tone becoming higher, and less designed to charm. "About the arrangements for our wedding."

"Not until my mother returns to Scotland. And while my

sister is increasing, I shall find it difficult to concentrate on many things—except my duties."

Hermoine raised her bare shoulders and lowered her chin coyly. "I hope it won't be too long before you will be concentrating on another *increase*. One that will be of even more concern to you."

He stared at her for some moments before he realized she was alluding to being with child herself—with *his* child. He managed to disguise an involuntary shudder by brushing at his sleeves as if to remove dust. For once his eyes met Kirsty's. They looked at each other for longer than was necessary, and he was certain he read sadness and hopelessness in her expression. And he cursed convention.

"Is it true that Dahlia came to see you?" Lady Hermoine asked abruptly, all affected gentle nature discarded. "Well, I know that she did, because Zinnia told me so. I must warn you that those three, Zinnia, Dahlia, and Wisteria, are to be discouraged from thinking they are welcome visitors here. My poor aunt tolerates them out of reverence to the memory of a dear friend, their mother. Frankly I think the countess should send them packing. They are parasites, and meddlesome to boot."

"Hmm." Max tried to appear interested.

Lady Hermoine turned away and looked over her shoulder. "Sometimes I have an unpleasant notion that they are not even who and what they are supposed to be. Could that be possible?"

"Anything," Max said, "is possible, I suppose. But I understood they were the daughters of a friend of the countess. Surely—"

"Oh, don't mind me. I'm overprotective of the dear countess. What did you say Dahlia came here to discuss?"

"I didn't," Max told her. Kirsty had picked up a pen and bent her head over the ledger, but had yet to make a single stroke on the page. "I have never met Miss Dahlia. Or either of the Misses Zinnia and Wisteria, for that matter."

Lady Hermoine walked behind Kirsty and looked over her shoulder. "How very boring that looks, Kirsty, but someone must attend to these boring matters, I suppose."

Kirsty nodded, but kept her face hidden.

"If you didn't see Dahlia, who did?" Lady Hermoine looked up at Max.

Damn the woman. She had no right to question who came and went from this castle, not yet and possibly never. He would remain polite. "I am the estate commissioner here. I am not concerned with minor domestic matters, such as visits from neighbors."

Lady Hermoine laughed, suddenly, piercingly, and said, "Oh, you are *so* masterful, Max. A truly marvelous challenge. It's a wonder—and I shall be grateful until my dying day—a wonder that some strong woman has not persuaded you to let her take you into her hands by now."

Kirsty dropped her pen, and it rolled from the desk. Before she could leap to her feet, Max retrieved it and returned it to her. She made to take it, but he retained a hold until she was forced to look at him once more.

Some deep suffering hovered within her.

He smiled at her while he longed to take her in his arms.

He released the pen, and she lowered her eyes once more. His temper began to simmer.

With much swishing of her tiered and lace-edged skirts, Lady Hermoine came to his side and threaded both of her arms around one of his. She raised her face to his and favored him with an unsmiling gaze. She passed her tongue over her lips, then brought his hand to her mouth and kissed it slowly, keeping her eyes on his. That stare was laden with sexual invitation.

He glanced down. Her boned bodice thrust her enticing breasts high. The flesh trembled. She put herself between

Kirsty and Max, and this time it was to her bosom that she pressed his hand. "We have a great deal to discuss," she said. "You must feel that as much as I do." In case he was particularly dim-witted, she spread his fingers and maneuvered a nipple into his palm.

His rod sprang hard. He ought to send her packing, but if he was to be forced to take her as his wife, why not enjoy the one thing he was likely to enjoy about her—a willing and enticing body?

Using her considerable skirts to mask what she did, Lady Hermoine managed to touch him. He narrowed his eyes and shook his head sharply.

The lovely Hermoine smiled, and Max was reminded of a plump, white cat preparing for a tasty meal.

"Kirsty," Hermoine said, more evenly than Max would have imagined possible under the circumstances. "I'm sure you'll understand if Max and I ask you to give us a little time alone. After all, it's quite suitable since we are to be married."

Max opened his mouth to countermand her, but she had her strong fingers around the one part of his body that could become beyond his control.

Kirsty had set down her pen and risen from her chair. She went wordlessly toward the door, and now Max did not dare try to move away from Hermoine.

"Thank you," Hermoine said. "I told Max he had made an excellent choice in retaining you, and I was right. We'll send for you when we've finished our discussion."

With a rustle of drab green taffeta, Kirsty left.

Hermoine released Max and put a finger to her lips. "I shall laugh until I am sick," she whispered. "The poor thing hadn't a notion what we were doing."

"Don't ever—"

Her lips, sealed to his, cut off his words. She fastened her arms around his neck, flattened herself to him, and thrust her tongue deep into his mouth. Her hips ground against his, but then she shifted, lifted a knee between his thighs and rubbed his ballocks so hard he winced.

He'd never encountered a woman like her, not since a certain lady in Oxford some years earlier when he'd been too inexperienced to guess that her cries of passion were practiced frequently, and paid for just as frequently.

"Oh, this is wonderful," Hermoine breathed. "It's beyond all." She swung away from him and stood panting, her breasts rising and falling rapidly.

This, he supposed, was when he was supposed to throw her down somewhere or other and ravage her. Good Lord, but rather than rise even more willingly to the occasion, his rod withered at the thought.

Hermoine clapped her hands, and backed away from him. "You are to leave everything to me," she said, far too loudly. "I am naturally shy, but I'm more than ready to take matters into my own hands."

She locked the door.

A click sounded, and Kirsty knew the door to Max's study had been locked. If she could make her feet move, she would rush away. If Max and Lady Hermoine thought she didn't know what they were about, they were mistaken.

Lady Hermoine's raised voice had sounded excited. *I'm more than ready to take matters into my own hands,* she'd said.

Kirsty shrank back against the opposite wall. It was true that Max had not instigated what she was sure had been happening in that room, but neither had he stopped it.

Assuming their actions were hidden from her, they had been touching each other.

She could not abide it.

At last she could feel her legs again. Not caring that she passed the odious Fergus Wilkie, or that he leered at her, she caught up the cumbersome taffeta skirt and ran. She ran and ran until she reached the corridor leading to her rooms.

A person could only endure so much. To expect her to sit by while another woman made love to Max was more than this person could endure. She stumbled the final, short distance and found her door open. Inside, clearly visible as she turned the pages of the book Kirsty was reading, sat Blanche Bastible.

Not now. Surely she could be allowed to be alone for at least a little while.

Blanche glanced up and said, "There you are, Kirsty. Her Grace likes to spend the early-morning hours with some deep thoughts she isn't ready to share with me, so I decided to come and get to know you better today. I decided I'd sit here until you came back, no matter how long that was."

With heavy feet, and a heavier heart, Kirsty went inside.

"Close the door then, girl," Blanche said. "And do brighten up, for goodness sake. That sour face would pull clouds over the sun."

"I'm no' mysel', Mrs. Bastible," Kirsty said.

"You may call me Blanche. Now, I allow that privilege to very few, and only when I've a certain feeling about a person. I have that feeling about you. You're special."

Kirsty said, "Thank ye," and managed a smile.

"Don't forget I've known you since you were a little girl. I remember when your brother was born. A handsome child." She sighed, and sighed again, and her eyes took on a distant look. "I myself didn't have the good fortune to have a son. Had I done so, I know my life would have been very different. A son takes care of his mother. A son makes sure his mother never wants for anything. A daughter is *such* a burden. But I mustn't complain. It is a mother's lot to put her own needs aside and do the very best for whatever children God grants her. Of course, a daughter takes a mother's selflessness as her due and gives nothing in return, but, so be it."

Kirsty's spirits lifted a little. "I rather thought the marchioness went to great pains to be certain ye lived well. And ye've fine grandchildren to comfort ye in your old age."

Blanche raised her head and fluffed her ringlets. "I married my first husband—Grace's father—very young. I was a child bride, but he was a successful solicitor, and I was swept off my feet. My second husband, the Reverend Bastible, died very unexpectedly. I assure you I have many more vigorous years of my own before I consider doting on grandchildren." She considered. "Of course, my grandchildren are remarkable."

"They certainly are."

"But that's not why I'm here. I'm here to talk about you and to guide you. We must be certain we are not interrupted."

With resignation, Kirsty watched as yet another door was locked.

"I see you enjoy Mr. Dickens, too," Blanche said, placing the book she'd been reading on top of a low bookcase. "I haven't read *A Christmas Carol*. It seems it may be both moving and frightening."

"Yes," Kirsty said absently. "It's new. I'm very fond of Mr. Dickens's writings. Max gave it t'me. Ye may borrow it, if ye please."

"Max gave it to you." Blanche's puzzling powers of concentration had already sped away from Mr. Charles Dickens's latest masterpiece. "You must have him, you know."

Kirsty's mouth fell open.

"Men are foolish creatures. They rarely know what is best for them. And women, particularly the wrong kind of women, can influence them dreadfully. I am a most exceptional judge of character, you know. That is why Her Grace and I are so close. We both share certain special instincts. I am invaluable to her, and I hope you will not think me presumptuous if I say she is my dearest friend."

"How nice," Kirsty said, catching her breath again.

"Can I be certain that our conversation remains between us?"

"Yes, ye can." Who would ever believe such strange comments, anyway?

"Good." Blanche glowered at the door, grasped Kirsty by the wrist, and marched her into the bedchamber. "More private in here. I'm a little fatigued from rising so early, so I shall rest on your bed, if you've no objection. You can sit in that chair where I can see you."

Without waiting for a yea or nay from Kirsty, Blanche Bastible climbed atop the mattress, and propped her plump, much befrilled self against the pillows. "Ahh," she sighed. "Much better. I *think* so much better lying down. Now, let's get on with it. The matter in hand is securing Max Rossmara for you. How it shall be accomplished, and how we shall dispose of any obstacles in our path."

The chair Blanche had indicated, small and well upholstered, beckoned to Kirsty and she all but fell into it.

"Hmm," Blanche said. "A young gel like you shouldn't be exhausted. Not at this time of day."

"It's been an exceptionally tiring day already," Kirsty told her. "And I didn't sleep well last night."

"Or any other night recently, I'll wager," Blanche said, pursing her lips. "These rooms are all pink."

"Rose," Kirsty told her. "That's why they're called the rosy rooms. They used to be Lady Avenall's when she came to the castle."

"Another young woman with her head firmly on her shoulders. But never mind that. There's more afoot here that meets the eye." A huge wink made it impossible for Blanche to keep either eye open. "That Hermoine creature. Dreadful baggage. And all those females at The Hallows. I made a very gentle comment to my son-in-law suggesting he investigate them all. He, naturally, promptly told me to mind my own business. Not that I am ever surprised by his curtness. He is a most ungrateful cub. My Grace is far too good for him, and he knows it. He actually told me that there's nothing at all amiss at The Hallows, which means that there is much amiss and he knows it, but he doesn't want me to use my superior powers of deduction in the matter because I will show him up—as I have in the past. But I'll tell you all about that at another time."

Reason seeped slowly back into Kirsty. Why would Blanche Bastible choose to befriend her, of all people. It was well-known that Blanche was a social climber who only had time for people she considered capable of advancing her own social position.

"I take it I'm correct in assuming you have a *tendre* for Max Rossmara?"

Kirsty was growing tired of being asked the same question in only slightly different manners. "Why?"

"*Why?*" Blanche rose to her elbows. "Because everything depends on your feelings for him, that's why."

Emboldened, Kirsty said, "What o' his feelings for me?"

Blanche flapped a hand before her face. "He adores you. Plain as the nose on your face. He affects that masculine air of dominance and distance, but manages to look at you from a hundred different directions. He does so constantly. But you've stopped looking at him. Why is that?"

Oh, she was too tired for this subterfuge. "I was advised to be—*demure*."

"Demure? Well, I suppose demure is all well and good in its place, but managing to resemble a particularly obtuse mouse is singularly unattractive."

Obtuse mouse? "Max Rossmara is no' for me. He's a gentleman, and I'm a peasant who has the good fortune o' an education."

That direct piece of information garnered Kirsty another disgusted flap of Blanche's hand. "I've no time for that sort of stupidity. Listen and follow instructions."

More instructions.

"I know Her Grace spoke with you. She told me, and we are in absolute agreement except for one thing. You're aware that she feels you should groom yourself to become the man's mistress—when the time is right?"

Kirsty averted her face.

"Oh, do buck up! This shall be our secret—are we agreed?"

"Agreed," Kirsty said, wishing Blanche would go away.

"Very well. I believe you should become Max's wife, not his mistress."

Slowly Kirsty returned her attention to the older woman's face.

"And I believe that those people at The Hallows are all very dangerous. But I shall not be listened to, and when I'm proven right, there will be no mention that I foresaw disaster."

"Och, I'm sure ye're worryin' too much."

"I am not worrying too much. There is something very unwholesome about each and every one of them there. With the possible exception of that charming Mr. Horace Hubble. Now there's a man if ever I saw one." Blanche's gaze lost some of its focus. "Oh, yes, indeed. Not since the dear Reverend Bastible died have I seen quite such a magnetic specimen of the male variety."

To each, his own. "Could ye be more specific about why ye think Max and I belong together?"

Blanche yawned. "You have so much in common. You are both extremely intelligent—and enterprising. You are both from exceedingly humble beginnings and so determined to better yourselves."

Max was working at bettering himself as they spoke, Kirsty thought, stunned by the power of her misery.

"We'll all be going to the ball at The Hallows next week," Blanche said.

"Not me—er—Blanche. I'm just an employee. And ye told me we shouldna have anythin' t'do wi' any o' them there."

"A ball is a ball," Blanche snapped. "Lots of people. Everyone who *is* anyone from miles around. You shall attend at the dowager's insistence. In fact we have already agreed on the matter, so consider it arranged. And it will be a wonderful opportunity for you to annoy Lady Hermoine."

Not understanding Blanche's point, Kirsty sat forward in her chair.

"She will not want you there, of course," Blanche said. "She's afraid you could be a rival of serious proportions. And when she sees you there, she'll *know* you are."

"I'm no' going," Kirsty murmured.

"You certainly are."

"I couldna possibly. I know I shouldna be asked to dance, but if I were, I'd no' be able to because I never learned."

"We've a week. You'll dance in a week."

Kirsty clutched the arms of the chair. "I canna go. I've no gown suitable."

"That's about to be remedied. Fortunately Her Grace is leaving that to me. You're both fighters, you know, you and Max. He's a bastard. You're not, of course, but you've had no advantages."

Kirsty could not allow such a thing to be said. "I have the best of families. They're good, and true, and kind. I've always known I was loved."

"But you've always known you wanted more."

"No. No, that's no' true. If it weren't for Max, I'd probably have been happy wi' the life I'd have come by naturally. But I did meet him. And he opened the world for me. And he stole my heart." She wasn't controlling her tongue well enough.

"And you stole his," Blanche said, sounding inordinately pleased with herself. "So it is right for the two of you to be together. But you won't say I've interfered, will you?"

Kirsty studied Blanche. "I've promised I won't." There was something Blanche wasn't saying—something that would explain this unexpected and nearly desperate determination to bring Max and Kirsty together.

Blanche looked at the clock beside Kirsty's bed, and said, "Good. No need to mention that subject again." With remarkable agility, she sprang to the floor, shook out her skirts, and took a firm hold of Kirsty's hand. "Now it's time for you to come with me. I have a wonderful surprise for you."

"I'm supposed to be at work," Kirsty said weakly, aware that she'd be unable to return to the study until she was summoned.

"Work? Fiddle! A girl must have time to be a girl, and I shall make sure you have that time. I know you haven't seen my rooms. Exquisite, my dear. They have been kept for my exclusive use since I first brought Grace here to marry the marquess. It's in the East Wing. The *Serpent* Room." Blanche squealed like a girl and hurried Kirsty away.

The Serpent Room was a good distance from the Eve Tower and upon entering Kirsty contained a squeal of her own, but of horror, not glee. Drapes had been thrown open and she was confronted with what could only be described as a fearsome, reptilian creation.

"Isn't this just the most marvelous room?" Blanche demanded. "I have seen a great many wonderful things, but never, ever, the likes of this."

"No," Kirsty said. She did not add that her own experience was exceedingly limited, but that she found the place dreadful.

"The dear dowager has had a replica of this bed made for me at Franchot Castle. That's where the Franchots' seat is, in Cornwall, dear."

Many-headed gilt lizards swarmed over the posts of a massive bed topped, most strangely, with a quilt lovingly embroidered with clusters of spring flowers.

"There you are, Geneviève! Right on time, too," Blanche said.

The modiste Max had obtained hovered on the threshold, and several seconds passed before she masked her horror at the room before her.

"Come along in," Blanche said, smiling happily. "The box is on the table near the window. It arrived late yesterday. See what you think."

"I really should be in my room waiting to be summoned to work," Kirsty said with a sense that she might not care for what lay ahead.

"Fiddlededee. This is much more important. You know, my dear, you and Max are so very suited to each other."

How many times, Kirsty wondered, would the lady restate her theory, with all the discomfort it brought.

"Why your very presence here in this castle is proof that you're both of stern stuff. You have put your very humble beginnings behind you and are a bare step away from acceptance by anyone who *is* anyone."

Blanche, it seemed, put tremendous stock in "anyone who was anyone."

Max Rossmara did not need Kirsty to help him make his way. He had Lady Hermoine in his study at this very moment—taking matters into her own hands.

"The dowager and I are going to the ball, and we want you with us," Blanche said, swaying and smiling. "How nice that Mr. Hubble will be there, too." Her expression became momentarily distant.

"I'm sure ye'll have a time o' it," Kirsty said, quickly removing her hand from the painted red eyes of a dark wood dragon that draped the back of a chair. "Mayhap ye'll tell me all about it afterward."

"Now that," Blanche said, so sharply Kirsty flinched, "will be the last time you even suggest that you might not be in attendance. We will get down to what must be done immediately. Geneviève, what do you think of the material?"

"Magnifique." Small, dark, and swift of movement, the modiste carried an armload of shimmering silk moiré, light blue but shot through with other colors—lavender, magenta, a hint of gold, that shifted as the light caught different angles.

"Magnificent indeed," Blanche said, sighing. "Look at this, Kirsty. The dear dowager sent it in my care so that we may be certain it will be the perfect thing."

With something near nausea, Kirsty watched Blanche Bastible open an old, red-leather box. Inside, on a bed of slightly worn black velvet, rested the most fabulous necklace Kirsty had ever seen. She had never touched a necklace at all other than the fine gold cross her mother cherished, and which had been a gift from the marquess at the time of Niall's birth.

"Aquamarines and diamonds," Blanche said reverently. "Necklace and earbobs to match. Have you ever seen anything more beautiful?"

"Never," Kirsty said, with complete honesty. "Please thank Her Grace for lettin' me see them."

Blanche lifted the necklace and arranged it on top of the moiré. She pressed a hand to her breast and closed her eyes. "The perfection of it," she said. "You will be the envy of all."

"Me?"

The older woman's blue eyes popped open and settled crossly on Kirsty's. "Of course, you. Sometimes you are quite addlepated, or you choose to seem so. Your gown will be fashioned of this fabulous material, and you are to wear the dowager's aquamarines and diamonds."

"But—"

"And the dowager will brook no argument. And Max will also be delighted to have you there."

"He declined the invitation."

Blanche shook her head. "Such behavior. The dowager has informed the countess that the response was a mistake, and Max will definitely be in attendance."

Geneviève, who was already well acquainted with Kirsty's dimensions, produced several *Ackerman's* plates and spread them for Blanche to see.

"Oh!" Suddenly even more animated than usual, Blanche bobbed up and down. "This one. It simply must be this one. What do you think, Kirsty?"

Reluctantly, Kirsty went to look. The gown pictured all but defied description. A fantastic excess, from the feathered headdress, to the vastly full, many-flounced skirt. No exclamation could aptly express the sensation Kirsty experienced. So she said, "Oh."

"It steals the breath," Blanche said. "Oh, yes, this will do very well."

"You do not think it is a little, er, 'ow do you say, *sophistiqué* for one so, er—"

"You will make this for *me*," Blanche announced. "Of course it is too sophisticated for Kirsty, but I was simply surprised to see *exactly* what I had in mind for myself. Kindly see me about it this afternoon. Come, Kirsty, you will select your own gown."

"*There* you are." Max's ringing voice made Kirsty jump. "I've searched this bloody castle for you, girl."

"Kindly temper your language," Blanche said with hauteur. "And don't presume to enter a lady's chambers without invitation."

"Sorry," Max said, looking at no one but Kirsty. "I apologize for the unexpected interruption in our morning. Lady Hermoine has now left, and we have a great deal to do."

"We're in the middle of giving instructions for the gown Kirsty will wear to the ball at The Hallows."

"Kirsty?" Max glanced at Blanche.

Blanche folded her hands at her waist and simpered. "The dear dowager insists that Kirsty attend. We both enjoy her company, and we know you will not be opposed to seeing her there."

Kirsty felt overheated and longed to leave the room.

"I shall not attend the ball," Max said.

Blanche clapped her hands to her cheeks. "Not be there? Her Grace accepted for you—for all of us. Surely you would not disappoint her."

He pushed back his coat and planted his fists on his hips. His frown was magnificent. "Dash it all, when will I be able to speak for myself without my relatives interfering?"

"You know your dear great-grandmama has only your very best interests at heart," Blanche said, her blue eyes very round. "Why she does so want you to be happy. Of course, she is just a little selfish in that she enjoys your company. And she's very proud of you. So, naturally, she wants to show you off in public."

Max grunted something that sounded like "manipulation," then said, "Might I be allowed to see what you have in mind for Kirsty, Mrs. Bastible?"

"Oh, Blanche, you know you may call me Blanche, dear boy. Of course you may see."

He touched the material lightly, picked up the necklace and weighted it, then bent over the fashion plates. Blanche trotted forward to remove the one that she had selected. "This is for my gown," she said.

"And which of these is for Kirsty's?"

"She hasn't chosen yet," Blanche said.

Because I'm not going.

Max spread out the plates and studied each one with care. "This one," he told the woman, pointing out one Kirsty hadn't seen—she hadn't really concentrated on any of them. "Make sure it's ready for a fitting as soon as possible."

His rapid change of heart and show of interest took Kirsty by surprise. Surely he could not seriously mean that she should attend the ball.

The modiste curtsied to Max, and folded the material back into its box.

"That will do very well," Max said. "You should wear a great deal of blue, Kirsty, and that is most special. What are these?" He held out the necklace and did not appear pleased with it.

"It is the dowager's," Blanche informed him. "She hoped it might compliment the moiré."

"Great-grandmama's?" Max frowned and looked more closely at what he held. "Her aquamarines and diamonds. Yes, I see they are. And she wishes Kirsty to wear them?"

Blanche had turned a trifle pink. "The dowager has always been a woman of great generosity. Knowing that Kirsty does not own suitable jewels, she determined to offer some of her own."

"A woman of great generosity," Max repeated in a manner Kirsty found impossible to interpret. "Hm. I'm sure they will be much admired. They will certainly complement Kirsty's eyes."

She could scarcely believe he had made such a comment.

Blanche's expression became smug and knowing, and she said, "Geneviève, I've changed my mind. I should like you to accompany me now. I always do these things in the company of the dowager. She does enjoy making her little jokes about my taste although I know she admires it. I'm sure I can rely upon you to help Kirsty find her way back to the Eve Tower, Max?"

"I'm sure I shall manage," he said, placing the necklace

back in its box and giving it to her. "Tell Great-grandmama I think the jewels most suitable and that I shall thank her for her kindness in person."

"I shall do so," Blanche said. The modiste already awaited her in the corridor. "If you have matters to discuss with Kirsty, please feel free to use my room. I always consider it a tragedy that it isn't seen by more people."

Rather than answer Blanche, Max faced Kirsty and stared into her face.

But for the swish of her skirts, Blanche left silently, taking Geneviève with her.

"I do not love Lady Hermoine," Max said gruffly. "I did not invite her to visit this morning."

But, Kirsty thought, neither had he either sent her away or stopped her from . . . well, from doing what she had done with him.

"Are you angry with me?"

"No," she told him.

"You used to be almost painfully honest."

"I know my place."

"And does that mean you've decided you may not speak your mind—even when asked directly?" He narrowed his green eyes.

Kirsty crossed her arms. How should she explain what she felt? "My position is difficult. Ye've already told me your desires. And we have already discovered we enjoy each other far more than is good for an unmarried couple to enjoy each other." She should tell him the interlude had been wrong, that it wouldn't happen again, but she couldn't bear to consider that it might not.

"Evidently at least one member of my family doesn't frown on the idea of our being close."

"Who?" She turned from him and walked the room with measured steps.

"Great-grandmama. And this surprises me greatly. She

would not have assisted with your gown for the ball or lent you jewels if she were not encouraging our alliance. Contrary to Blanche Bastible's assertions, the dowager is *not* a generous woman by nature."

"She has been verra generous t'me. And kind. Always kind."

"How so."

"Oh"—Kirsty made airy gestures—"she tries t'advise me on how best t'deal wi' bein' a member o' a great household when I've no experience o' it."

"Is that a fact?" Max backed away, turned, and locked the door.

Kirsty swallowed and was certain she'd be unable to speak even if ordered to do so.

"You seem to prefer locked doors," he said, approaching her.

There was nowhere to go, no means of escaping him. Not that she wanted to. He came to her and grasped her shoulders. She must keep a clear head, but her limbs had lost all feeling, apparently because so much feeling had rushed to other places.

The way he looked at her was different, dark—angry. His fingers dug hard at the flesh on her shoulders.

He was going to kiss her.

At least she didn't have to find a way to go and lock the door.

"I want you," he said. "Not as it was that night. I really want you."

And she wanted him.

"All those wasted years . . . I should have come for you as I said I would."

She wetted her dry lips and said, "There wasna a promise, Max. I was only sixteen. Ye had your life ahead o' ye, and it had t'be different from mine."

"*Stop* making excuses for me. I can't wait for you any longer. Do you understand what I'm saying to you?"

Oh, she understood very well, and she knew what she must do.

Roughly he pulled her against him and kissed her. At first the kiss was also rough. He opened her mouth with his and drove his tongue deep inside. Releasing her shoulders, he anchored his fingers in her hair and moved her head to accommodate his assault on her mouth.

She held the sides of his jacket. Tears slid down her cheeks. She had not been instructed on how to deal with what she was supposed to do when what she wanted to do was quite different.

As abruptly as it had begun, the kiss ceased. High color slashed Max's cheekbones, and his eyes were overbright. "Forgive me," he said. "I never want to hurt you."

"Ye havena hurt me." Not quite true, but the hurt was bearable because it brought them close. "I wish I could take away the anger, though."

"Wishes." He laughed, not a joyous laugh. "What happened to our wishes?"

She had kept hers, and never saw a bubble but that it reminded her of a sunny day, and a serious young man—and the promises they'd made to each other. "We grew up," she told him. "And things changed."

"Then why are you crying? Because you're happy they changed?"

"I'm silly." She smiled, and closed her eyes. "Just a silly thing who cries at anythin'."

His lips met hers again, softly this time. This time his was the softest, the sweetest of kisses, and she knew he could wipe out her resolve with such a touch, with such a tender raid on her senses. The tip of his tongue found the tip of hers. He used his mouth as a caress, and she returned that caress.

With the backs of his fingers he gently rubbed the sides of her neck, then he held her face, and the kiss went on, and on.

Kirsty felt his warmth, and smelled the soap in his linen, and tasted salt on his skin.

When at last, oh, so slowly, he parted his lips from hers, it was so that he could see her face, place small, firm kisses where he pleased there, smile at her with his heart in his eyes, and in that smile.

He had said he didn't love Lady Hermoine.

But he would marry her, and she, Kirsty, would have what he could give her: stolen times.

She would share stolen moments of satisfaction with a married man.

The tears welled again, but she smiled, and closed her eyes, and reached for his trousers.

He said not a word. Not while she freed him, and not when she took him between her two hands.

She heard his great indrawn breath, but squeezed her eyes even more tightly shut, smiled even more widely. His hips moved.

His hands returned to her shoulders and once more his fingers hurt her.

What she had been told was true. He became like iron and swelled larger and larger, and grew hot. She felt the tracing of distended veins, and the smoothness of him, then the beginning of what she knew she was to expect. The essence of him escaping onto her skin meant it would soon be over.

She ached so deep inside. And she did not want to let him go.

The steady jutting of his hips ceased. "I cannot believe this," he murmured.

Kirsty considered another of the directions she'd been given, but feared she might lose control if she followed it now.

"Look at me," he said.

She couldn't.

"We must go somewhere else," he said. "This will not be enough."

Still she didn't answer him. Instead she increased the speed with which she stroked him.

"Stop." He gripped her hands. "Look at me."

Kirsty opened her eyes but kept them lowered. The sight of him made any thought impossible.

"My dear one. My Kirsty. What's going on in that head of yours? What are you thinking about?"

When she opened her mouth, her jaw ached. How could something so sweet, be so cruel? "Thinking?" She couldn't explain. Her eyes closed once more. "I'm thinking about Kirkcaldy."

Chapter Seventeen

"He went directly to her, I tell you," Hermoine told the countess and Horace. *Really, this was too, too embarrassing.* "She must be removed. I don't care how, but she must be removed."

"How can you be sure where he went?" Horace asked, extracting a pinch of snuff from a box he liked to say was a gift from a royal admirer. He "couldn't disclose the identity of the elevated personage." He sniffed the snuff delicately.

"Leave her alone, Horace," the countess said. "She's distressed, poor girl. Give her time to explain what went wrong."

"Nothing that was any fault of mine," Hermoine wailed, throwing herself down on a divan in the countess's parlor.

"He . . . He . . . Oh, it's too much. No, too, little. Oh, I hardly know how to contain myself at all."

Horace came to lean over the end of the divan where he studied her upside down. "Well then," he said, "don't contain yourself, love. I've always thought you were particularly sumptuous when not contained."

"Stop it," she told him petulantly. She wished he would go away—completely away again, and stay away this time.

"Let me remove your containers, my love. You are obviously weak from your exertions and should be cared for by one who really appreciates your talents."

She ignored him.

"Tell us what happened again," he said. "You thought he was mad for you, but . . . What exactly did happen then? You were vague."

"He's sick. He's obsessed with rutting the little peasant. *Assistant?* What kind of pathetic excuse for her presence can that be? He's acting out some sort of sick fantasy, I tell you. She's a poor, helpless child, and he's having his way with her."

"Sounds to me as if you should be sorry for her," Horace said. He'd removed his watch and began to trail the chain over the swell of Hermoine's breasts.

"Sorry?" she said. "I don't give a fig about her. You said we would get what we want and that your plan would work. We should be impossibly rich by now."

"We have to have the journal," the countess said, breaking her long, pensive silence. "Our friends are becoming restless. Too restless. I am receiving the kind of threats no lady should have to receive. I say it's time to make our move."

Horace held up a hand. "Not so quickly, dear Gertrude. Haste can ruin everything. Allow me to set the pace, if you please." With that he pressed his lips to Hermoine's brow, and whispered, "You and I must talk."

She drew back from pushing him away and looked up at him until her eyes crossed and she blinked. "What about?" she asked softly.

"A pie cut in two parts fills two stomachs so much more than a pie cut in three fills three stomachs, especially when one of those three stomachs expects to take a larger portion—much larger."

He wanted to cut the countess out. The idea both frightened and delighted Hermoine. The countess was capable of anything if she was crossed.

"Stop whispering," Countess Grabham demanded. "What are you whispering about?"

"Forgive us," Horace said, laughing and going to sit beside Hermoine. "Just a little love talk. She is a naughty girl, our Hermoine."

The countess huffed at that. "Kindly remember that *you* are not in charge here, Horace. In fact, you are supposed to be dead. Hermoine, explain exactly why your interview with Rossmara wasn't a success. You said the girl left."

"And as soon as she did he could think of nothing but her."

"How do you know that?"

"I *know*. He . . . He . . . ." She flapped a hand and squeezed out two tears.

"He *what*?" Horace asked. "Do stop teasing us, darling."

"I'm not teasing. I'm embarrassed. I had my hands on him. *On* him. I'd given him a feel or two and added the spice of him knowing the girl was behind me but couldn't see what I was doing—or what he was doing. So she goes away, and I've got his trousers undone and I'm down to my stays and drawers, and he . . . well, he . . . ."

The countess leaned forward.

Horace leaned forward.

Hermoine lowered her lashes. "One minute I held a steel

stake on the lookout for a deep hole to dig, the next a . . .
a . . . a limp snake with a fear of dark places."

Horace laughed. He clutched his paunchy sides and
howled, showing every tooth in his mouth. When he could
sputter a few words, he said, "Lost it, did he? Poor fella
wasn't up t'you, Hermoine. You frightened him. Oh, that's
rich, that is. That may come in useful, my dear. No man
wants a thing like that talked about."

"No woman wants it talked about, either," Hermoine
snapped. "Stop laughing at once."

"Then what happened?" The countess wasn't laughing.
"No more avoiding the truth, my girl. We've serious business at hand, and time has all but run out."

"Well, I got dressed, didn't I? What was I supposed to do?
He turned his back on me and straightened himself, then sat
at his desk and ignored me. I got dressed and sat at that creature's desk. He told me to leave, but I said if she could be his
assistant, so could I, and since he seems to like silly little
slaves better than real women, I supposed I better learn to be
a slave. An hour. More than an hour I sat there while he ignored me. Then he got up and left. Just like that. And he
went to her."

"You can't be sure of that," Horace said and, although she
fought him, he lifted her up and sat down with her on his lap.
"Kiss me. Kiss me as if I was him."

She shook her head. "I told you I have my sources. I
waited there, hoping he'd come back to me. But someone
came and told me he was with her, so I returned here." Tears
came easily enough, and she let them fall. A woman who
could cry prettily possessed a great gift.

Horace scratched her nipples through her dress until she
wiggled and began to want him. He smiled and bent to
tongue wet marks on the silk, and she wiggled some more.
"I think I've got a new plan forming, sweetness. Gertie, can

you stall our fat pigeons a few more days, d'you think? Until after the ball?"

"Possibly. Why then?"

"Wait and see. Hermoine dearest, you will allow me to guide you in the matter of your gown for the ball."

"You will do no such thing. Oooh!"

Horace lifted her again and set her down astride his thighs. "Yes, I will," he said, bringing his face close. "I'm going to make sure you hardly recognize yourself. And then—with Gert's help—we'll get what we want. *You* will be in a position to make sure we get the journal."

"I refuse to do anything unless I understand your plans," the countess said archly.

"So do I," Hermoine said. She looked at the fumbling bump that was Horace's hand beneath her skirts. "Oh, really. Don't you ever think of anything else?" she asked him.

"What can you be talking about? I am simply a man with a steel stake in search of a suitably deep hole."

Chapter Eighteen

Max avoided looking at Kirsty. He strode along beside her through the corridors leading to her rooms. She'd asked to be allowed to go alone, but he'd refused.

To say that this had been an extraordinary day would be to take understatement to ridiculous levels. First the humiliating debacle with the Rashly woman, then his gentle Kirsty behaving like a strumpet and babbling as if she were losing her mind.

He caught her elbow and pulled her to face him. "All I ask is that you explain yourself."

"I canna." Her chin came up defiantly, but her mouth trembled. "Ye're hurtin' me. And ye frighten me."

He released her arm. "You make me want to break something."

"Ye're badly behaved, Max Rossmara. Ye shame yoursel'."

"And you speak out of turn, girl. How dare you?"

She stood very straight. "I dare. I'll no' be afraid o' ye."

He planted his fists on his hips and put his face close to hers. "What was all that back there? In that awful room of Blanche's? Where would you learn such things?"

"I only sought t'please ye."

"And you did please me—until my mind cleared." He kept his voice low. "After all, I am only a man, and I have been sorely tried. Only tell me who educated you in the ways of the flesh, and I shall be satisfied."

She pursed her lips and shook her head.

"Do I know him?"

She shook her head, no, again.

"I do. That's why you won't tell me. But I'll find out, and he won't work these lands again."

"Och, ye're no' thinkin' Max. If I'd been wi' another man, would it be his sin, any more than mine?"

"You were an innocent."

"And a man canna be an innocent?"

"Not if he's able to instruct you in the finer points of, well, the finer points."

"It wasna a man." Her eyes filled with tears and she bowed her head.

Max worked his jaw. "Not a man? I don't think I understand."

"It was . . . a book," she said. "I read it in a book."

"What book?"

"Just a book I found in one o' the libraries here."

She was lying to him. "When I asked you what you were thinking about, you said *Kirkcaldy.*"

"I didna know what I was sayin'. It was the first thing that came t'me, I suppose." She glanced at him, and away again. "Ye didna seem t'mind me touchin' ye until then."

"Mind? What man would mind being touched so by you. Kirsty, please tell me the truth about it. I've no right to expect your faith, but I'd like to know how many men there have been."

"How like a man," she said, and swallowed. "What would ye say if I asked ye how many women there'd been for ye?"

"It's not the same." Blood pounded at his temples. The battle to remain calm rarely left him now.

"Why?"

He would not debate the issue with her. "It is different for a man. Let that be an end of it."

"Verra well. I agree. It's an end o' it. I can go alone from here. I know the way."

He struggled with his pride. "It doesn't matter," he said. "I want you. I can't help myself."

"And I love ye," she said, so quietly, he was drawn to bend over her. "I've loved ye since I was a lass."

Max backed her to the wall and braced a hand on either side of her head. "We're in a pretty fix, Kirsty Mercer. There's none who would approve of us being together."

She turned her face away.

The tender skin at the side of her neck was very white. He kissed her lightly there, and she leaned against him, held him as tightly as she could. "There has never been another man, Max Rossmara. Ye can believe me or not, but it's true."

Perhaps he didn't want to believe her, but he did. "I thought you'd accidentally told me what was on your mind. That you thought to better yourself at Kirkcaldy through an association with me. I'm a fool sometimes."

"That ye are," she said, still hanging on to him. "We've wasted the whole mornin'. Ye'll want your lunch soon enough, and we've no' done anythin' useful."

"We'll be riding out this afternoon. I'd best get you to your rooms so you can change."

"I'd rather not go."

"I want you reconciled with your parents."

Slowly she dropped her arms. "Every day I expect them t'send for me, but the message never comes."

Just as she uttered these words, they turned the corner toward his quarters, and hers, to discover Niall Mercer lounging in the doorway to Kirsty's sitting room. When he saw them, he straightened, and he stared at Max. There was none of the old friendliness in that stare.

"Niall!" Kirsty ran forward to hug her brother. "What are you doing here?"

"Mairi showed me where you're livin'. I told her ye'd no' mind if I waited for ye here."

"O' course I don't mind. Och, we've hardly been parted but I've missed ye. Let me look at ye." She stood back, smiling as Max hadn't seen her smile since she'd come to the castle with him. "I'd not realized what a fine man ye are, and that's not only because ye're my brother that I say it. Ye must be fightin' off the lassies all the time."

"I've no patience for that now. I'm too worried about ye and Father and Mother."

"Are your parents unwell?" Max asked moving forward and waving Niall into Kirsty's sitting room. "I plan to visit them this afternoon."

He noted how Kirsty went directly to the window seat and sat there quietly, as if removing herself from the men's conversation. This behavior in a woman like Kirsty surprised him.

"Your parents," he began again, addressing Niall.

"They're well enough. They keep t'themselves, and that's

mayhap for the better. There's a lot o' talk about ye and Kirsty and what it means, an' our mother and father dinna know what t'say. They love their daughter."

"Of course they do," Max said quickly. "When I come to see them I'm sure I'll be able to put some of their misgivings to rest."

"This afternoon?" Niall said.

"This afternoon. Within three hours or so. Will you tell them I'm coming?"

Niall considered, then said, "Aye, I'll tell them, and I'll be there, too. I'll warn ye, it'll not be easy. People are worried about their daughters. People all around. They're no' allowin' them far from home."

"Worried about their daughters? Good God, man, what can you be suggesting?"

"I'm tellin' ye the way o' it. They're afraid the lairds are takin' to pickin' out young girls to amuse themselves with the while."

Max felt sweat break out on his brow. His breathing grew shallower, and holding his tongue cost him a great deal.

"We're simple people." Niall eyed Kirsty. "We set great stock in lookin' after our own and each other."

"Damn!" Max lost his battle to remain calm. "Kirsty and I have been friends for many years. She is here to do a job. How dare the people who make their living on these lands presume to make some dark tale out of that. I've a good mind to raise their—" he stopped himself before he could say anything that would be too hard to take back. A crystal bowl rested near his left hand. He swept it up and threw it against the fireplace, where it smashed in pieces too small to be identifiable.

Kirsty let out a small cry.

"I didna say I shared the concern," Niall said quickly. "Ye can rely on me t'do my best t'back ye up. When I was a wee lad ye were like a brother t'me. And I know ye care about Kirsty. I regret causin' so much difficulty for ye."

"It's the small-minded peasants who have been sheltered from the ways of the world who are causing difficulties," Max ground out. "They deserve to be taught some lessons. The first should be that they have no place criticizing their masters. This family has clung to ways discarded by many because they would not allow the people they call their own to suffer, or to lose what they've worked for. Curse small minds. I shall speak to the marquess. We must consider making some changes."

"No, Max," Kirsty burst out. "Dinna punish them for bein' wary. They love ye—they love all the Rossmaras."

"They do," Niall said. "Ye dinna understand how it is when people who've lived the same for many generations have a change put on them. My mother and father know that ye and Kirsty were verra close. They know ye loved each other in the manner o' the young. But they also know there can be no way for ye to take Kirsty t'ye in an honorable way because ye're from different worlds, and ye'd never want a wife wi' naught but lowly beginnings."

Max felt the fight go out of him. How could he argue this point when he'd already asked Kirsty to be his mistress? "I'll speak with them this afternoon," he said with a sense of hopelessness.

"Aye," Niall agreed. He walked about the room, out of place in his rough woolen jerkin and trousers, and his dusty, laced boots. The wind that rarely left the hills had tossed his dark hair around but that only served to make him more striking. His face was fine-boned, but hard physical labor had honed his body, and strength emanated from him.

"It's a fancy place, Kirsty," he said, bending to look at porcelains and miniatures, and the many exquisite pieces that graced tables and chests. "I've never seen the like so close. D'ye not feel like ye're in a fairy story?"

"A little," she said softly. "But I'm here t'work, so I dinna spend much time admirin' it all."

"What d'ye call the game?" Niall asked. "It's the one ye taught her, Max, isn't it?"

"Parcheesi," Max told him promptly, then stared at the leather-covered board that had been Ella's and muttered, "I'm damned."

"It's back," Kirsty said. "How funny. Back just where it was. I'll ask Mairi if she knows anythin' about it."

Niall had already lost interest in the board and moved on, but Max bent to examine the unusually large pieces and looked at Kirsty. "Too bad we can't seem to keep everything together for long. Two pieces are gone. Never mind."

She frowned. "But they're made o'—"

"Never mind," he said quickly. Such discussions need not take place in front of Niall. "No doubt they needed repair."

Kirsty nodded and subsided into her shadowy nook.

"What are ye talkin' about?" Niall asked. "Has somethin' been stolen?"

Max sighed. There was little point in pretending. "This room was ransacked the other night and that Parcheesi board was one of the things that was missing. The pieces were left behind. Now—while Kirsty was elsewhere—the board has been returned but two of the silver pieces have been removed. All very troublesome."

"A thief," Niall said, his dark brows drawn together. "What if he came while our Kirsty was here? He'd like want t'make sure she couldn't tell who he was."

Max's mouth felt as if he'd eaten dust. "We won't speculate on that."

"That means we won't think about it, doesn't it? I'll think about it. I'll no' have a peaceful hour until I know my sister's no' likely t'be set upon by thieves."

"Then you can start feeling peaceful." Max clapped a hand on the younger man's shoulder. "I'll make sure

Kirsty's watched over, but I doubt there'll be a repeat. Whoever did this will be too afraid to try his luck again."

"And who'll do the watchin' over her?" Niall asked. "You?"

"Yes," Max said, meeting the other's eyes. "Yes, I'll be watching over her. She's my responsibility."

Kirsty's, "Oh, Max, ye shouldna say it," was faint. He didn't look at her.

"What d'ye intend then?" Niall asked.

What could he say? Max asked himself. He no longer knew the answer.

"T'use her?" Niall demanded. "Don't expect me t'believe ye've no interest but in her mind."

"I do expect you to believe it," Max said, grasping at the opportunity Niall had given him. "Yes, Kirsty is important to me because we've been friends a long time. But you should know that there can be nothing between us but a professional relationship." He took a deep breath. "Why, I'd return her to her family at once if I thought it would be for the best."

"It wouldna be for the best," Niall said. "Not now. Mayhap later when ye're married t'the lady from The Hallows and if ye can convince the people ye're no' a heartless debaucher."

"Niall!" Kirsty jumped to her feet. "Be silent, lad, before ye bring Max's anger on your head."

"Oh, aye, I must be careful o' his anger. It's well enough known throughout the estate that Max Rossmara's anger is a fearsome thing. Another thing we worry about. What if he turns his blackness on ye, Kirsty? Ye're a wee thing and no' used t'violence."

Max knew he must not retaliate or he would only fuel the rumors. "Today," he said quietly, "I will do my best to allay any fears in that direction."

With a troubled expression, Niall looked to his sister. "I'd wanted t'see ye was all. I miss ye, Kirsty."

"I miss ye, too. I didna want t'be told t'stay away from home. I never thought o' such a pass."

"No. I'll do my best to change things there. I'd best away now. D'ye have designs on her, Max Rossmara?"

The question was unexpected and Max felt the color drain from his face. "My design is for her to be the best she can be." He bent the truth, but he would not admit how his desire for Kirsty had made him into the different, the more driven man they spoke of as possessed of black humors.

"Have ye taken her, then?"

To look at Kirsty would be unbearable. "I have not," he said, grateful that in this, at least, he still told the truth.

"Then I remind ye that she's an innocent and deservin' o' your respect. There's a great deal o' talk. Ye're bein' blamed—called heartless. They say ye're a deflowerer o' innocent young girls."

"I'm not a young girl," Kirsty snapped. "I'm five-and-twenty and I'll thank ye t'stop speakin' as if I'm not here. Max has never tried t'force himself on me. I'm ashamed for ye that ye'd suggest such a thing."

She was protecting him! She was, in fact, lying for him. No, he hadn't gone as far with her as he might have, but he'd done more than he should.

Niall Mercer studied his boots. He changed his weight from one foot to the other, then regarded Max. "Verra well. I'll away now. And I'll be on your side when ye visit."

Max nodded. Would any of them know real peace again?

When Niall had left, Kirsty remained near the window and didn't speak. Max weighed the silver Parcheesi pieces and struggled with his conscience, his concern for her safety, and the knowledge that he knew what he should do. He should make sure her reputation was intact and be prepared to return her to her home, and, when the children returned from Cornwall, to her old job.

He heard the rustle of her skirts, then felt her at his elbow. "There's no goin' back for me now," she said. "Ye know that, don't ye?"

"I'm not sure. Perhaps—"

"People never forget. They decide somethin', and that's the way it stays. In time my position here will be accepted. There'll be hard times for a while, but I'm up t'them, and they'll no' affect ye."

"What affects you, affects me."

She laughed—a sad laugh. "No, no, we both know otherwise."

"You're still determined to carry on here with me?"

"It was your own idea, my bonnie friend. Ye were determined enough yoursel' when ye suggested it."

She made him feel so much less mature than she was. "I did. And I was. I'd like to teach you about the way we make the most of the land now. A great deal has changed." And he didn't want to let her go.

"Aye. I've seen it, although ye've chosen t'allow people like my father to go on as they were. I'm no' certain there's another estate in Scotland like this one."

"We are a wealthy estate. What we've done has served us well. We've moved with the times and preserved some of what made Kirkcaldy so successful. We're well pleased."

"And you want me t'be here with ye, Max."

He stroked her hair, he couldn't restrain himself. "You know I do. You'll have a good life here. And if you want to leave me later—if there's someone you think you'd like to make a life with, then I won't stand in your way."

"And you won't mind? You'd watch me go to another man and be happy for me?"

The pressure in his throat was as if a great hand had closed on his neck. "I'll mind, and I'll watch you go with murder in my heart. For him—whoever he may be." Please God he'd have the strength to keep that murderousness locked inside his heart.

"You'll never have to mind, Max. And if you've ever murder in your heart, it won't be because of any act o' mine."

She stood where he could see the silvery bloom on her skin, and the softness of her lips, the smooth moistness just inside, her small teeth, the way her tongue moved as she spoke.

Her breasts rose and fell gently.

Her eyes, when he looked into them, were waiting for him to concentrate on her, really on her. He smiled. "If I kissed you, would I be forcing myself on you?"

She shook her head, stood on tiptoe, and touched her mouth to his.

Max slipped an arm around her, supported her, and let the kiss be one of promise, of such sweetness that he ached. He was a man of the world, yet with her he was different. Just holding her stripped away the layers of cynicism. She made him new, new and open to the promise of what it would be like to allow her innocence to soften the toughness, the anger that so often colored the world a darker place.

She broke the kiss and rested her cheek on his chest.

"Oh, my dearest girl," Max said, a great sadness rushing in where the hope had blossomed. "How will I bear to look at you and want you? What am I going to do with you?"

She released herself from his grip and went to the fireplace, where she knelt and gathered the pieces of crystal he'd broken into a pile. "Ye'll make up your mind to become a different man. No more outbursts, or drownin' your sorrows in the drink."

"I don't like to be lectured to."

"What ye don't like would fill a large book. Ye're spoiled,

Max Rossmara. Spoiled and entirely too used t'gettin' your own way. It doesna make ye attractive, and it's t'stop."

Only Kirsty could speak to him so and not inflame him. "I don't drink a great deal," he told her, and it was true. "A man should feel free to take a glass of liquor when the mood takes him."

"The mood takes ye when ye're angry. That's no' the best time, Max, and ye know it. If ye can do this when ye're sober"—she indicated the rubble of the bowl—"well, then, I'd no want t'be near ye if ye weren't sober and ye felt like tossin' precious things around. Who'd know what ye'd choose t'break things on."

"The episode won't be repeated. There, see how you dictate my actions. I'm like a pet cat in your hands."

She smiled a little. "An awful big pet cat wi' a loud voice when he's no' pleased, but I'm glad t'hear it anyway."

He sobered. "But I'm desolate, Kirsty. Help me learn to bear not being able to have you."

"I'll help ye. Ye'll no' suffer."

How could a woman, and an inexperienced girl to boot, know the power of a man's desire? "I'll look forward to finding out how you'll manage that, miss."

"We'll manage it together. I'm goin' t'be your mistress."

Chapter Nineteen

"Yowill allow me to do the talking," Struan said. "After all, Max is my son and my responsibility."

"Am I wrong, or am I almost thirty-one?" Max raised his face to the sky as if considering. "Perhaps I've miscalculated and inadvertently added a great many years to my age. Yes, that's what must have happened. *No.* Oh, how could I be so foolish, I reversed the numbers, didn't I? I'm thirteen."

"I'll be the one to discuss the matter," Arran said, as if Max hadn't said a word. "In case you've forgotten, Struan, I am the elder, and I am the Laird of Kirkcaldy."

Struan snorted. "As if I'd ever be allowed to forget. You remind me constantly."

"No such thing," Arran said, spurring his mount to greater speed as they rode downhill, away from the castle. "You have always been difficult, Struan. You were a difficult child, and we will not discuss how difficult you were when you entered your twenties."

"Because I chose to go into the Church? That made me difficult?"

"You did so to place the entire burden of this estate on my shoulders. And we both know you could have brought disaster on our heads with your behavior."

"Can we save this discussion?" Max said, glancing back at Kirsty, who rode her little mare very slowly and carefully, even more so than usual. He still could not believe the declaration she'd made. "And could we go a little slower— under the circumstances?" He loaded his words with meaning, but evidently his father and uncle missed the nuance.

They rode ahead of him, their voices raised. "Do you intend to remind me that my years studying for the priesthood were brought to an unhappy end?" Struan asked. "Because if you do, I'll not ride in your company."

Arran chortled. "Hardly your fault if the flesh became weak, old chap."

"That's it." Struan wheeled about and rode beside Max. "It wasn't my flesh that was weak. It was all the fault of a scheming female who took advantage of my nubile body," he called to Arran.

Arran sputtered with laughter, and said, "*Nubile?* As you say. But I will speak to the Mercers. They trust me."

Max looked back and found Kirsty had fallen even farther behind. She had not wanted to accompany them on this visit, insisting that she should await a summons from her parents.

"The Mercers respect me as a man of God," Struan said. "And because they adore Justine, they will accept whatever I say."

"You think they respect Justine—whom we all respect, of course—more than they do Grace? Why Grace, they consider an angel. She is a frequent visitor in their home."

"I shall speak for myself," Max said.

"You can't trust the young these days," Struan said. "They make foolish, rash decisions with no consideration for the trouble they may cause. Then they expect their elders to clean up the mess they make."

"If you're speaking of me, I am not a child. I have not deliberately made any mess. And I don't want your assistance in this matter—other than to be present because the Mercers respect you both. But that was probably a mistaken notion on my part. In fact, why don't the two of you strike out for the north, and Kirsty and I will follow you when—"

"These whippersnappers never accept the blame for their own foolish actions." Arran rode a little harder. He was a very large, very powerful man who rode a huge black animal that most men would have avoided at all costs. He liked to gallop across his lands at a great pace. "Imagine. The foolhardy boy literally abducted Robert and Gael's girl and bore her away to the castle, and then thought they wouldn't be nervous about such a thing."

"She already worked at the castle," Max called after Arran. "She simply has another job and lives there, rather than tramping back and forth every day. Most of the staff live there. And you knew my intention. I believed you approved."

"As if it weren't bad enough," Struan shouted to his brother, "he installed her in rooms where he is the closest breathing creature during the night hours. And I suppose he thought such a thing wouldn't be noted by others, who would then talk about it. A young, single girl of fine character and a disreputable rake whose record of questionable morals is the talk of the land."

"Good God!" Max pounded after his father. "Where do you get such propaganda? Questionable morals? What time have I had to develop questionable morals? I've worked for the two of you since I left Oxford, and apart from journeys to overseas on estate business, I've barely had time for myself."

"This marriage will cool him down," Struan said. "Don't you agree, Arran?"

Arran was too far ahead to hear. He galloped downhill toward the cluster of buildings at the bottom of the hill.

"Infuriating," Max said, to no one in particular. "And deliberate. I'm supposed to hear every word and mend my ways, but I'm not given a chance to defend myself."

Kirsty had fallen so far back that he feared she would decide to return to the castle. He went to meet her. "Come, Kirsty. You can do much better than this."

"I dinna want t'go."

"So you have told me on a number of occasions today. It's important for your family to see that you are all in one piece and, in fact, doing well."

"They'll think I'm showin' off. Ridin' a fine horse."

"You're riding a little mare who is very suited to your nature. It would be impossible for you to perform all the duties I have in mind for you if you didn't ride."

She gave the mare's neck a tentative stroke. "She's a sweet, wee thing. Could I no' wait here for ye? I know the three o' ye will say the right things. I'd be so verra happy if my mother and father sent word that they'd like me to come t'them."

When she spoke so persuasively his resolve wavered. "I think it's best this way," he said. "You are quiet people, I know, and thoughtful. You like to work things out alone and in your own way, but sometimes a lot of time can pass that way, a lot of unhappy time when it doesn't have to be so."

A movement on the high horizon caught Max's attention. He'd heard talk of a lone rider, now he thought he saw him.

"That one alone," Kirsty said. "No one knows who he is."

Max shielded his eyes from the light. "He's watching us, damn his nerve. On our land. If I'd the time, I'd track him down and demand an explanation."

As if the stranger heard, he raised an arm in a wave, then dropped from sight on the other side of the hill.

"No matter," Max said, smiling at Kirsty. "I want you to be happy."

She surprised him by leaning to pat the nose of his own mount. "Soft," she said, "like velvet. I'll do what ye think is best. You're going to be my guide, Max. In a great many things—and until ye don't want t'be that guide anymore."

He caught her hand, brought his horse closer, and raised Kirsty's fingers to his mouth. "I'd like us to guide each other—always."

A shout went up. A shout, and an animal's snorting whinny. Max wheeled about.

"It's the marquess," Kirsty said, urging her mare forward. "Och, he's fallin', Max. Be quick!"

"*Arran,*" Max yelled, surging forward. "You stay where you are, Kirsty."

He'd turned just in time to see Arran hit the rough ground while his horse's hind legs plunged into a hole.

Struan had already leaped from his mount and dashed to his brother.

With terror in his breast, Max spurred his own horse headlong downhill, drawing up as he came level with a gash in the earth that had claimed the stride of Arran's horse. The creature had all but cleared the place when his back legs must have caught the rim of the hole.

"The horse," Arran cried. "See to the horse."

His uncle's voice was the sweetest sound to Max's ears. Fearing the worst, he did as Arran instructed and dismounted. Spewing lather, Arran's great black beast writhed, but as Max grabbed for his reins he felt it gain some balance. Scrambling, it made an ungainly way to level ground, and would have made it away had Max not clung to its bridle and driven his bootheels into loose scree.

Kirsty trotted beside him and slipped to the ground. "I'm needed," she said. "I must tend the marquess." With that she dropped the mare's reins. The little creature moved a safe distance from Arran's snorting animal and waited patiently.

Leading his own, and Arran's horses, Max swiftly followed Kirsty. At the sight of blood streaking his uncle's face, his pulse quickened. With Struan's arm around his shoulders, Arran sat up, his forearms on his knees, and Max praised the Lord that the man was as strong as an ox— stronger, some said.

"What happened?" Max asked. "Didn't you see the hole?"

Arran raised slightly dazed eyes. Rather than answer the question, he looked at his horse, and said, "He's not hurt?"

"Only his temper," Max said, laughing—as much from relief as humor. "But he's a bad-tempered beast, and I wouldn't want him for my own."

"You aren't getting him for your own," Struan said gruffly, kneeling beside Arran now. "So don't ask for him."

Max shook his head, but said nothing. There were times when he wished he'd had a brother with whom he shared the kind of closeness these two had been blessed to share.

"Your head, Your Lordship," Kirsty said, tentatively

touching Arran's brow. "It needs cleanin' properly. I'll tend it for ye. Ye've other pain?"

"There's nothing wrong with me," Arran said, and attempted to get up. He winced and wrapped an arm around his chest. "I must speak with your parents. I'll take my horse, Max."

"Ye'll sit where ye are the while," Kirsty said. With no concern for her fine wine-colored riding habit, she scooted on her knees until she could open Arran's coat and ease his arm away. She pressed the place he'd favored, and air hissed in through his teeth. "It's the bones in your chest. Ye'll no' want t'use the arm this side till they're healed."

"Rubbish," Arran said, making it to his feet. But when he took another breath, he grimaced and bent over. *"Damn. How could I have ridden right into that?"*

Max's question exactly, but he didn't respond.

A babble of voices reached them. Struan looked past Arran. "Help on the way," he said with false cheer. "Why aren't I surprised to see Robert Mercer in the lead?"

"Fuss over nothing," Arran said. "I'll have a word and get back to Kirkcaldy."

"Ye'll gi' yoursel' time t'be quiet," Kirsty told the man who had fostered both respect and affection in his tenants.

The party of men and boys arrived, and Robert Mercer went to Arran direct. "Your horse threw ye. I didna think any horse would dare t'do such a thing t'ye."

Arran chuckled, and immediately coughed and sank to the ground again.

"He shouldn't ride back," Struan said. "I'll go and—"

"We'll take His Lordship in a cart," Robert said. "If ye've no objection, that is."

Several men had already started downhill again.

"I'm all right," Arran grumbled.

"He's broken bones in his chest," Kirsty said, speaking

for the first time since her father had arrived. "Mother has some strips of cloth we could use to ease the pain."

Father and daughter stared at each other while the other men looked on. Robert broke the silence. "Verra well. My house is closer, Your Lordship. Will ye allow us t'take ye there and make ye more comfortable? After all, ye were comin' t'speak o' somethin' anyways, were ye not?"

"We'll do that," Struan said quickly. "And you have our thanks."

Kirsty braced Arran's arm across his chest and held it there as if her strength was enough to make a difference.

Max glanced at the faces of those men who had remained and, one by one, they avoided his eyes. Damn them. They had judged him, judged Kirsty, yet they were guilty of nothing—yet. Deliberately formal, he said, "You have experience with such injuries, Miss Mercer?"

She nodded, "Aye. Niall took a tumble when we were small, and he suffered the while. Several weeks. But the bones healed well enough because he did as he was told." She loaded her words with significance, and Arran glowered at her.

Niall. Max searched around but saw no sign of Niall Mercer, he who had promised to be present for the discussion with Kirsty's parents. Max frowned, but was diverted by more shouts from below as the returning men urged on a nag pulling a cart without sides. The sorry vehicle arrived soon enough. Blankets had been spread on the rough wood, and Arran managed a good-natured smile when the gathered band lifted him on top and propped him against sacks of grain.

"Turn toward the pain," Kirsty ordered. "It helps. I remember that."

Arran did as he was told and nodded, but soon hissed some more as the conveyance bore him over bumpy ground toward Robert Mercer's house. Struan rode beside, drawing

Arran's horse with him, and was oblivious to anything but his brother.

"I'll go t'help my mother," Kirsty said. "She's never been a strong woman, y'know. And she loves the marquess. She'll be beside herself worryin' about him."

"I know," Max said, but his thoughts were on other things. "Go to her. I'll be along shortly."

She looked troubled, but didn't question his reason for remaining behind.

Max waited until she'd set off, leading the mare rather than riding, then he swung back into his saddle and returned to the place where Arran had been thrown. He walked his horse around the area, studying the hole. Not so much a hole as an area where the earth was soft and fallen away.

He dismounted and went to his knees. Where Arran's mount had lost its footing, grooves scarred the churned ground. At the bottom of the grooves water mixed with rocks and soil in a muddy mire.

How long had it taken to do this? And it had been deliberately done. Very recently someone—someone strong—had dug away the earth, replaced the softer surface dirt in the bottom of the hole, added rocks and poured water on top, then replaced some of the harder earth from beneath. Any heavy animal hitting such a spot would be bound to come to grief—and its rider with him.

There hadn't been any prior mention to anyone else that Arran and Struan might come today, and certainly not of Kirsty's presence that Max could remember.

A man's shadow rolled out over the ground.

Max remained on his knees, but raised his face and looked into Niall Mercer's eyes. Niall returned the stare, but his sun- and wind-tanned face flushed.

"You thought I would come alone," Max said.

Niall kicked a clump of hard earth. His clothes were filthy. "Ye said ye would."

"That's true, I suppose. At least, I didn't say anyone was coming with me."

"Why didn't ye tell me?"

"Because I didn't think to."

"Ye always ride like a wild one," Niall said. "Straight downhill with never a bit o' fear. We all know it."

Max pointed to the ground. "Someone worked fast to make this. They hadn't much time to get it finished. I expect that's why they didn't dig it wide enough. It was all a matter of luck, or the lack of it. Just the right stride and the horse plunges in, just the wrong stride and he clears it."

Niall hung his head, and Max was reminded that although the other man was physically mature with the heavy muscles of one who had worked hard all his life, he was just twenty, not much more than a boy.

"Clever idea," Max said. "Easy enough to cover up the truth afterward."

Spreading his hands, Niall made no attempt to keep the frustration from his expression. "I'll make no fuss when they come for me."

"Have you arrested? What would that accomplish? Other than to deal your parents and Kirsty another blow."

Niall frowned. "I could have killed someone."

"You wanted to."

"No' the marquess." The pain in Niall's voice might have touched Max if he didn't know what the intent had been. "And no' ye, either. I was desperate, and I didna know what t'do."

With Niall on his side, matters would go a great deal more easily with the Mercers. "I'd better keep that appointment with your parents. Will you come with me?"

Niall fidgeted. He shook his head in disbelief. "Ye'll no' tell them what I did?"

"No. You have my word as a gentleman that this will remain between the two of us—unless the marquess is more severely injured than he appears to be."

Relief brought pathetic gratitude to Niall's face. He said, "Thank ye. I'll come with ye t'my parents' house."

"And then you'll make sure this track is safe again?"

"I'll do that, and gladly."

"Let's go then." Max started forward. He would never be able to trust this young man again.

They walked with Struan's horse between them. After a few yards, Niall caught at the horse and stopped him.

"What?" Max asked. "What is it?"

"Promise ye'll no' tell Kirsty. Never."

"I hadn't planned to." Max had tired of playing games. "We'll put the entire affair behind us."

"I meant, if I tell ye somethin', will ye keep it from Kirsty?"

"If it would be best."

"It would be best for me. She'd never speak t'me again if she knew what I'm going t'tell ye."

Max disliked the idea of keeping a secret with Niall—to the exclusion of Kirsty—but he said, "Very well."

"I lied t'ye. With every shovel o' dirt I lifted back there, I hoped ye'd break your neck and die. Ye've given your word ye'll no' tell anyone what I did. Now I'll give you my word. I promise ye that if ye can't give my sister back her good name, I will find a way t'kill ye."

Chapter Twenty

Kirsty bound the marquess's left arm against his chest. She had to tie many strips of cloth together to make the bandaging thick and firm enough for the task. She worked, and tried not to hear the voices around her. She'd already cleaned the wound on his head and found it not as deep as she'd feared.

"A good year," the marquess said. "The turnips pleased us all."

"Aye," Kirsty's father responded.

The viscount said, "Let's pray we never see another potato year like '37."

"Aye."

This cool courtesy was her fault. The lairds were doing their best to make peace because of her, and her family's poor, but deep pride was wounded because of her. She offered up silent thanks that the other men who had come to help had dispersed to go about their business.

"We could do again what was done in '37," Max said. "We'd be helping the less fortunate. Crop rotation has changed Scottish farming forever—and for the best—but we're still in a more enviable position than most."

He seemed a stranger to her in these surroundings, in her parents' home, where they'd once been friends and free to come and go at will. Then he'd been a boy, a familiar boy who made her laugh and took pleasure in telling terrible tales.

The strangeness she felt between them now bewildered

her. For love of him, she had accepted what he had proposed and gone to work for him. And now she had accepted his other—*the* other offer, because she could not bear to let him go.

He spoke as if she didn't exist.

So did her family.

"I'm sorry to put you out like this, Gael," the marquess told her mother.

"Ye couldna do anythin' to put us out, Your Lordship." Mother spoke softly and with a quiver in her voice. "We're always honored to have ye under our roof."

But they weren't honored to have Kirsty under their roof anymore. Neither of her parents had spoken a word to her since she'd been told to come and help with the marquess.

Max coughed. From the corner of her eye she saw him spread his boots a little wider. "I'm finding Kirsty very useful in her new position with me, Mr. and Mrs. Mercer."

Seconds passed without response.

"She learns quickly. And she reads a great deal. Very soon she'll be as knowledgeable about the problems of estates like this one as I am."

Kirsty bowed her head farther and tore a length of the cloth in half. She tied a knot to stop threads from fraying and secured the bandage in place.

"Already she's taken over my correspondence," Max continued with forced cheer. "And she's a wonderful head for numbers. A great deal better than mine. You should both be very proud of her."

The silence that followed this statement appalled Kirsty. She looked at the marquess, who frowned, and shook his head slightly. "A patched man, am I then, Kirsty?" he asked, and when she nodded, he took her hand in his free one and squeezed lightly. "You're a gem, my girl. Always have been. Always will be."

Kirsty got up and retreated to a wall. Not a single glance did her parents send in her direction.

They had decided to protect themselves by wiping her out of their lives. She wanted to cry out to them. To plead for them to understand that she loved them so, but that she also loved Max Rossmara and she wanted to have them all.

"We intended to stop and see you this afternoon," the viscount said, the awkwardness making him even more formal. "We were on our way here when my brother fell. Our plan was to ride north afterward, but we'll put that off now, at least until tomorrow."

"No such thing," the marquess said. "I don't need two arms to ride a horse."

"We shall return to the castle from here," the viscount said. "And you will go there in the cart we've sent for. You won't be able to ride until those bones knit. Mr. and Mrs. Mercer, we had hoped to put your minds at rest about Kirsty's position with my son at the castle."

Kirsty glanced at her father, and quickly away. He had closed himself off. She had never seen him so, and the sight frightened and sorrowed her.

Max said, "You're well aware that Kirsty is an exceptional woman. She is educated far beyond her station."

Before Kirsty's stomach had finished turning, her father said, "For some of us our station is good enough and we've no wish t'move beyond it."

"I didn't put myself well," Max said. "I meant that she had unusual abilities—and that they would be unusual regardless of who she was. And if there's an opportunity for her to better herself, surely you would not wish to stand in the way of that progress."

Mother moved to the open fire that burned in readiness for preparing supper. Kirsty slipped along the walls to reach her. "Mother," she whispered. "I love ye."

Her mother poked the fire and said nothing.

"That'll never change, no matter what happens. Please dinna turn me away. Ye'll break my heart if ye do."

"Robert doesna want me t'speak t'ye. Ye know our ways."

Kirsty looked at the three Rossmara men, two standing and one seated. Their clothes were fine. They were fine, and strong—and different from her kind. Her father, a slight man with thinning fair hair, wore his years working land in all weathers on his face, in the deep lines there. His shirt was of clean, but coarse stuff, his boots hefty and worn. A laboring man, glad to labor and with no ambition to do otherwise.

"Why do our ways have t'mean we canna choose to go another way? Why are ye so angry because I've decided t'use the mind God gave me?"

"It doesna matter t'ye what we think. If it had, ye'd no' ha' left as ye did."

"I'm five-and-twenty. Ye treated me like a bairn still, and I'm no' a bairn."

Her mother looked sideways at her, looked from her face, to the lovely dark red riding habit Max had instructed the modiste to make for her. "No," mother said, "no, ye're no' a bairn. And ye're no' the Kirsty I knew."

"I *am* the Kirsty ye knew. I havna changed except for the job I do. I thought ye'd come t'be proud o' me."

Her mother set aside the poker. "D'ye think we're daft? D'ye think we don't know all about what's goin' on? Ye've lost the respect o' your own people. By turning from them and wanting to be part o' that." She indicated the big men behind her. "And now ye've made your bed, and ye'll have t'lie on it. Ye'll never be part o' them, either. Ye know that. Ye'll never be thought of as other than what ye are by them."

"What I *am*?"

"A peasant, and a girl willing t'be no better than she ought because there's things she wants that she'd never have here."

Kirsty squeezed her eyes shut and fought with tears.

"Ye've judged me wi'out givin' me a chance to speak for myself."

"Ye dinna need t'talk. The evidence is in front o' us. Look at ye. Keepin' company wi' important men. D'ye think they want ye for your wonderful mind? Och, Kirsty, ye're ruined. And we've to accept the pity o' our friends and neighbors because o' it."

"Mother—"

"Those clothes. What were ye thinkin' of, comin' here dressed like that? A year's money comin' into this house wouldna pay for that. And a horse. A *horse*. Ye came t'flaunt all they've given ye."

Anger grew apace in Kirsty's breast. "I came because I hoped ye'd say ye still love me, that I'll always be your daughter, and ye're glad o' it. I've waited every day for word from ye, but ye're too stubborn t'set aside old prejudices and see that the world has changed. We have to change *with* the world, Mother, or we'll be left behind. It won't always be the way we've known it. Have ye thought that perhaps for me I've taken the best path?"

Gael Mercer rubbed the back of a hand over her brow, and Kirsty noted, for the first time, how her mother's thin shoulders were permanently stooped. "For us what we have is all we could want," she said. "Ye've shown that ye dinna think us good enough for ye—that's what your father thinks."

"And ye?" Kirsty whispered urgently. "What about ye, Mother? What d'ye think?"

"I know my place. I think what your father thinks. He's always done his best for me, just as he's done his best for ye. Ye've brought us even more shame today. Don't ye think they're all talkin' about ye, and how ye look, and how ye came, and wi' who?"

Kirsty made to touch her mother, but she jerked away.

Niall came into the house, and said, "There's a cart arrivin' from the castle t'take the marquess."

"Mother, will ye help us t'mend our differences, please?" Kirsty asked.

Her mother's reply was to turn her back on her daughter.

Hoofbeats and the grinding of cart wheels sounded. The men helped the marquess to his feet and, bent over, he walked outside.

She knew what she had to do. "Ask me t'stay wi' ye, Mother. Tell me ye want me."

Max came back and looked from Kirsty to her mother. "I'm sorry. I'm interrupting."

"No such thing," Gael Mercer said. "How can ye interrupt what's yours t'command?"

Kirsty couldn't feel her hands or feet. Her mouth tingled, and her skin was cold all over. "Mother?" she said.

The viscount appeared in the doorway. Silently he surveyed the scene, and his frown was terrible to see. "We'll speak later," he said to Max. "I'll send for you. When I do, don't keep me waiting."

"Thank you for your hospitality, Mrs. Mercer," Max said with a formality that pained Kirsty. "I hope you'll allow me to visit you again shortly. Perhaps you can persuade Kirsty to bring me with her."

"Good day t'ye, Mr. Rossmara," Mother said with a quick curtsy. "And t'ye, Your Lordship. We'll hope t'hear good news o' the marquess. He's a strong man. He'll soon be well enough."

"Good day, Mrs. Mercer," both men said, and the viscount walked out.

Max stared into Kirsty's eyes. "Should you like to spend some time here with your parents? You could return to the castle a little later."

Wiping her hands on her apron, Mother went outside, and when Kirsty followed, passing Max on the way, her parents stood side by side, their eyes similarly lowered.

"Perhaps there's something I could do t'help ye," Kirsty

said, aware that Niall stood a small distance away, his hands in his pockets. The cart was already being drawn away, with the viscount riding beside.

"Good day to you all, then," Max said, walking to his own mount. As soon as he'd swung himself into the saddle, Kirsty's parents walked toward their house.

Kirsty made to follow, but her father swung around, his face pale and rigid to his very lips. "We wish ye well in your new life. Good-bye t'ye."

The rosy rooms no longer felt exciting. All the expensive furnishings and the collection of porcelains, the silver toiletry pieces on the dressing table and the exquisite ormolu clock on the mantel—they had lost their charm.

Her parents would never welcome her again.

When they'd turned their backs on her, Max gave her a few moments to compose herself, then he dismounted and helped her onto the horse she thought was sweet, but which she hated to ride. Niall and Max had exchanged a long look she hadn't understood, and now didn't want to think about.

The ride back to the castle had seemed so long. At first Max spoke of estate matters as if he hadn't witnessed her being banished by her family. Then, when she'd failed to respond, he'd grown silent, and she'd felt his anger settle heavy around him. If she'd been able, she'd have tried to ease that anger, but she hadn't been able.

He'd left her in the stable yard.

Self-pity would change nothing, but she pitied herself anyway.

She had changed from the riding habit into one of the plain dresses the dowager had approved for her. Kirsty thought it ugly and heavy, but then, she no longer made any of her own decisions.

In the silence of the sitting room her own laugh unnerved her. The great adventure she'd been so determined to embark upon, her chance for a wider, more free life, had robbed her of even what she'd had at home—the power to wish and to believe a wish could come true. From now on this would be her lot. A lonely lot consisting of work, and waiting for a man she loved but whom she would never have a right to call her own.

Darkness pressed against the casements.

She smiled a little. From her earliest moments she'd liked darkness, had found it comforting because it meant it was time to be closed safely away with her family.

Well, she could still wish, couldn't she? She'd wish for love to overcome prejudice, and for a message from her father and mother asking her to come to them.

What she would not do was dwell on the vision of soap bubbles in the sunshine, or Max's narrowed green eyes when he smiled at her, or silly childish notions of clubs for two.

Soft tapping came at the door. She'd been too preoccupied to hear approaching footsteps.

The next knock was louder. "Kirsty?" Max said. The handle turned, but she'd locked the door out of habit.

When he'd left her in the stable yard, it had been without a word, either of comfort or for the sake of civility. Not a word, or a glance. Now he was ready to speak to her—or whatever.

A trembling overtook her. So violently did she shake that she locked her knees. The shaking jarred her whole body, and she sat down.

"Kirsty! Kirsty, open this door, *now*."

He had the right to do as he pleased here.

He had the right to do as he pleased with her.

She pushed herself to the back of the chair and held its arms tightly. If she asked for her old position back, would they allow it? And could she go home again, then?

No, no, no.

"Ye've made your bed," her mother had said.

"Kirsty, open this door." Max hammered the wood so hard the door rattled in its frame, and she knew he used a fist now. "Damn you, open the door."

He'd been drinking. She could hear it in his voice.

"Damn all women. Open up, I tell you, or I'll break this down and you'll wish you had opened it."

She couldn't move. Her heart beat so hard and so loud she clutched her chest. Violence had never been any part of her experience. Nor harsh words.

"I know you're in there. Let me in."

With a great effort she said, "Go away, please."

"What? What did you say? Open up."

"I said, go away, please," she told him, much louder. "I'm tired."

"We need to talk."

"Ye've been drinkin'. Ye frighten me."

"Frighten you?" His laughter made her jump. *"Frighten* you? You're alone. I'm the best friend you've got. I'm *all* you've got. What happens to you is my affair now, so we'd best find a way to be very good to each other."

He was angry, angry with her for not doing as he told her at once, and angry because he'd wanted her on his terms, not because she'd nowhere else to go, not because no other living soul wanted her.

"Did I imagine it," he said, his voice thick, "or did you tell me you wanted to be my mistress? Didn't you tell me that?"

She covered her face.

"Well, Mistress Kirsty, I've come to give you what you want."

"Go away." Dropping her hands, she stood up. "Go back t'your rooms, ye bad man, ye. Threatenin' someone ye know is weaker. *Go away.*" He would not find her a limp girl ready to be wrongly used by him.

"I'm no' your belongin'. How dare ye say as much? Ye canna own another."

Clapping her hands over her ears, she rocked to and fro, humming as she'd hummed when she was a child and she'd been trying not to hear other children argue.

She didn't know how long she rocked, and hummed, but when the clamoring inside her cooled, and she was quiet, and she dropped her hands, no voice shouted at her.

Very carefully, she tiptoed to the door and listened. Not a sound reached her. She'd told him to go away, and finally he'd gone.

The room was chilly now. Chilly and still. He'd told her she was alone, that he was all she had now.

He would never hurt her, or force himself on her, not Max. No, not Max. And he wouldn't want her to suffer as she suffered now.

She needed him so.

Fumbling, her fingers responding clumsily, she turned the key and wrenched the door open. "Max!"

He wasn't there.

She turned toward his rooms but only took a few steps before she stopped again. Max stood in the doorway to his library, looking at her.

"I'm sorry," she cried. "I want t'talk t'ye."

For an instant she thought he'd carry on and leave her. He ran his fingers through his hair and hesitated, but then he retraced his steps. His walk was uneven, and as he drew close she saw how disheveled he was. He wore no cravat, and his shirt was unbuttoned at the neck.

He stumbled, regained his balance, and reached her. He reached her, looked at her as if he'd never seen her before, and went into her rooms.

A wise woman might choose to escape—if she'd anywhere to go.

"Cold in here," he said when she followed him. "What's

happened to the bloody fire?" He dropped into a chair, stretched out his legs, and rested his head on the back.

Kirsty was no stranger to lighting fires. She went to her knees and lighted one now, moving as quickly as she could, and as quietly. Perhaps he'd fall asleep. She prayed he would, and that he'd awaken as her gentle Max again.

"Boots," he muttered.

Flames sprang to life and she stood.

"Boots," Max repeated, more loudly.

Kirsty stood before him. "Ye have your boots on, Max."

"Hah!" He jerked forward and peered at her. "Think I don't know that? Take them off."

She'd helped her father with his boots often enough, and willingly enough. Her father had never been drunk and demanding.

"Hurry, damn you!"

Ye've made your bed . . .

Max's boots weren't as easy to remove as her father's. Made to fit his legs as gloves might be to fit the hands of the rich, she had to work each one, pulling first on the heel, then on the toe, over and over again until she all but fell over when they came off.

He murmured, "Ah," when she'd finished, and closed his eyes.

Moving as quietly as she could, Kirsty sat in the chair opposite his, laced her fingers together in her lap, and watched him. He wasn't still for long. Soon he turned his head from side to side and grimaced. No doubt feeling the effects of the liquor—and dreaming nasty dreams, perhaps.

"God, to be free," he said suddenly, opening his eyes and glaring toward the fire. "Hasn't a man the right to be free?"

She knew he wasn't speaking to her.

He pulled himself upright in the chair. For a long time he was silent, his attention still on the flames. When he spoke again he didn't sound as drunk, but neither did he sound himself. "You think you're the only one suffering. You pity yourself and have no pity left over for me. It's your fault that I will never know how it feels to awaken with peace in my heart."

Her fault? What could he mean?

"I'm damned. Forever damned. And I cannot turn back without hurting those who gave me everything I have. I might have been dead now if not for them."

"I'm sorry. Can I—"

"*Silence.*" His chest rose and fell hugely with each breath. Then he stared around. He grabbed up a porcelain lady from the table beside his chair and threw her at the wall. Even before the broken pieces had finished falling, he hurled another, and another.

Instinctively Kirsty shielded her face. Like explosions, the small treasures burst on impact.

He didn't stop until the table was bare. He doubled over and his breath came in sobs.

Kirsty wrapped her arms around herself and held her bottom lip between her teeth.

Once more he became quiet and still.

If she moved, he might start again. She wouldn't move. The urge came to rock and hum, but she quelled it and pressed her limbs tight together.

He suffered greatly. From within him welled a vast torment she thought she might actually touch if she reached out a hand.

"My father conducted his interview," he said at last. "I was summoned as he used to summon me when I was a child, and I went."

The expression on his face, the haunted, drawn lines, struck horror to Kirsty's heart. She held herself even more tightly lest she give in to intuition and try to comfort him.

His mouth twisted. "He told me I'm a fool, a romantic fool." Glancing at her quickly, he narrowed his eyes to glittering slits. "Because I had been unable to put my feelings for you behind me and replace them with ambition. Given my early childhood, I should have been able to do that. That's what he told me. I should have learned that softness is useless in this world."

She tried to speak, but at first her mouth was too dry. Instead she coughed and swallowed. Then she asked timidly, "Your early childhood, Max? What of it?"

His attention returned to the fire. "I never told you, did I? No, I didn't. I have trusted you with more than I have trusted any other human being, except my sister. And my sister and I lived through those days—we had the same things in common. Well, it will do no good to tell you now. Don't mention it again."

From a pocket inside his jacket he withdrew a thin silver flask. He unscrewed the cap and swigged thirstily at its contents. Then he sat with the flask open against his belly, a slight smile on his beautiful mouth. He blinked slowly while the bleak shapes and shadows settled around his features once more. Kirsty felt she saw ghosts in his eyes. His long-fingered hands curled around the flask in a grip so tight it turned his knuckles white.

"Father is angry with me." His voice was distant. "Disappointed. I have lacked judgment. He insists I should return you to your old position in this household. And that you should live with your family again."

"They willna have me," she said, barely above a whisper. "I asked Mother if that's what they'd like, but they don't want me. I've shamed them, they say."

His sneer wasn't a pretty thing. "So we are both in the same predicament, you and I. Both a disappointment to the people we have sought to please. How ironic. Yet we have done nothing wrong—not really wrong. I told Father as much. He believed me that you could not go back, but not, I think, that I have not bedded you in the real sense."

He drank again.

Kirsty moved forward in her chair and extended a hand.

Without looking at her, he said, "Hold your tongue, woman. Hold your tongue, or I will bear no responsibilities for my actions."

They needed each other, but he wouldn't open himself and allow her in as he always had in years gone by, years she would never forget.

"I hate myself," he said, slouching deeper in the chair. "I hate what I have become because of you."

She could not bear that he blamed her when she'd had no choice but to love him, yet she'd made no move to do anything about that love until he'd come to her.

He leaned forward to work off his jacket, then fell back again, and fell into a silent brooding. The lamps burned lower, but Kirsty hadn't the will to tend them.

Alone. Oh, yes, he was right, she was alone. He would only have to take her into his arms and hold her, to share his warmth and strength with her, and she could laugh at the cruelty of men. But between outbursts he hardly seemed to know she was there.

He'd said he was come to give her what *she* wanted, and he'd meant that he'd come to take her as his mistress. She was no unlicked puppy. She knew what he meant. There might have been a time, a wonderful time, when to join with him would have crowned her life. No more. Now he would only take her in anger.

He was devilish handsome in his white linen, the red lights in his wild dark hair glinting, a growth of dark red beard upon his cheeks and jaw.

And he had such substance.

And he had such a familiarity for her.

She needed his strength, to feel his arms around her so tight they squeezed out her breath.

There was no going back. Her position here was untenable but she could make a success of her work for him, and . . . and she could learn to ignore the sly looks of the servants, and the pity of his family. No doubt that pity would turn to contempt as time went by, but there was no choice.

Max's eyes had closed, and he'd left the flask upon his belly. His hands were relaxed, and the tension had seeped from his face. He slept.

Kirsty eased herself from her chair and slipped into the bedroom. There she took out her best nightgown, a poor enough thing of white cotton. Her mother had embroidered tiny roses around the neck. Lengths of the same fabric had been fashioned into ties there, above an opening to make the neck large enough to go over her head. The garment was voluminous, with many little tucks where the body of it joined a plain yoke. The only richness was in the narrow lace at the edge of the yoke and around the cuffs. That lace had come from the bottom of a chest her mother kept by her bed—the bed she shared with her husband.

The heavy dress Kirsty wore wasn't easily removed, but she accomplished the task and stripped to the skin, then pulled on the nightgown. Before the mirror, she undid her braids and brushed her hair until it sprang out around her shoulders in shiny waves. Her face was pale, but she wasn't practiced in the art of paint and didn't think she ever would be.

Her feet were bare. She possessed none of the soft little house shoes of the rich.

She looked at the bed. If she went there, he might simply sleep until morning, then leave when he awoke with the headache he was bound to have.

But she needed him. He was all she had and her love of him had only grown. Her desolation cried out for his comfort. Perhaps she could persuade him to lie in her bed again as he had before. To sleep until morning when she would tend him until he felt well enough to tend himself.

With dread in her heart, and in her belly, she went quietly back into the sitting room.

Max wasn't asleep anymore.

Kirsty hesitated and almost turned back. She'd not be a ninny. "May I help you?" she asked. "Ye're troubled, and ye need your rest."

Idly, he waggled the flask to and fro. He set his head on one side and regarded her from head to toe until she burned all over.

She could entice him.

The thought made her weak. There had been opportunities to observe how females went about such things, but she wasn't sure she wouldn't appear foolish if she copied them.

She smiled and approached him until she stood, almost touching his knee. And she extended a hand. "Come, let me lead ye. Ye can get out of those clothes and lie down. I've clean water and soap. I'll wash ye if ye like. Ye'll sleep like a babe soon enough."

His brows rose. "Why, Kirsty, I didn't know you had the seductress in you. Even in your little-girl gown and bare feet." He jerked forward and raised her gown far enough to reveal her ankles and feet. "Very nice bare feet, too."

She couldn't move.

He raised the gown a few more inches. "And beautiful limbs. Strong. Just what we need when you wrap them around me."

Flustered, she clamped her hands on her thighs lest he decided to explore much farther.

He laughed at that and dropped the gown in favor of taking another drink. When he was done he rested his head back and studied her. "You've beautiful hair, Kirsty Mercer. And the face of an angel. All blond innocence."

"I'm no' so innocent."

That seemed to fuel his humor even more. He laughed

aloud, and drank again, then looked at the flask in disgust as he must have found it empty. He tossed it aside.

"It's been a terrible day," she said. "A day of revelations and losses."

"You might say that. And I, so my father says, will marry the Rashly woman and like it. He tells me I am an ungrateful cub who has behaved irresponsibly. Now I am to cover for that irresponsibility." She saw his eyes close and open slowly. He appeared momentarily confused. "Irresponsibility, that's what I was talking about. He tells me I am to fulfil my duties to you because it is my fault that you are in such a predicament. Those responsibilities apparently mean that I must be exceptionally rigorous in my training of you for the job in which you will be seen publicly."

"I see."

"Do you, Little Miss Goldenhair? I doubt it."

"I am more than capable of being your right hand in business matters."

"I believe you are. And in the other? Do you think you can help me to train you as a fine, discreet mistress?"

She thought she must be suffering punishment for some indiscretion she'd forgotten. "I'll do my best."

"You will, will you?" He smiled, and shot out a hand to take her by the arm and place her before the fire. The smile faded instantly. "Light and shadow. Such beautiful light and shadow."

He did want her. He would be glad to hold her, and he'd hold her through this dreadful night and chase away the demons of desolation.

She shook back her hair. "Should you like to lie with me?"

His silence was terrible. He looked at her face, and she felt as if he could see inside her head. "Why would I want to do that, Kirsty? Perhaps you should make me want to."

Was it the thing the dowager had taught her that he asked for? She didn't think she could do that again, not just yet.

Max liked her body. She'd seen it in his eyes, felt it when he'd touched her. Her breasts tingled now at the thought of his touching them again. And the place between her legs . . .

Crossing her arms in front of her, she grasped handfuls of the modest gown and pulled it over her head until she stood, naked, before him. With as much nonchalance as she could accomplish, she tossed the gown aside and settled her weight on one leg.

The look in his eyes turned hot.

Kirsty put her hands on her hips and took a deep breath, thrusting her breasts high. Her hair parted at her shoulders, and some of it slid forward again, but she left it where it settled, some of it all but covering one of her breasts.

"Will ye come wi' me, Max?" she said, extending a hand. "Will ye let me take ye to my bed and comfort ye?"

He leaned forward and took her hand, but when she made to pull him to his feet, he drew her between his knees instead. All expression left his face—except for his eyes, and she could not tell what he was thinking.

With his hands spanning her waist, he pressed his face against her belly. She felt his mouth open, and the dampness of his tongue in her navel. Slowly he slid his hands downward and inward. He parted her already moist folds with his thumbs and darted his tongue between.

Horror weakened her knees. Horror, and pleasure—and shame.

She held his shoulders but he released her long enough to knock her hands away before returning to his task. Back and forth his tongue moved.

"No, Max. No, please. Not like this."

He continued, speeding the strokes. When he paused for breath, he looked up at her and reached to pinch her nipples, to cover her breasts, to pull on them as if they were fruit to be picked from a tree. With a hand behind her neck he drew her down until he could suck each nipple, and play the end of his tongue over it.

She grabbed for his shoulders again. Again he shrugged her off.

Such sweetly exquisite sensations, but made tawdry because he was only causing them to put her in her place, to remind her that he could control her at his will—and control himself.

"Please, Max," she breathed. "I need the comfort o' ye."

He let a nipple pop loudly from his mouth. "And this is not comfort?"

"I need to feel ye, really *feel* ye with me."

"Ah. Forgive me. I was diverted for a moment." He sank to his knees and returned at once to pleasuring her most private place, but he kept his hands on her breasts, squeezing and pinching. His breath came in gusts.

Tension mounted for Kirsty.

He moved suddenly, and she would have fallen if he hadn't caught her. She clutched for a hold and found his thick hair while he hooked her knees over his shoulders, held her bottom, and buried his face deeply.

She was open to him, and helpless to resist. His was not love play, but domination. He was making certain she knew he could do as he wished with her.

A dart of sensation drove into her. It drove, and spread, and grew hotter and hotter. Her hips rose and fell of their own volition, and her body forced itself ever closer to him.

He drove her to the edge and it all broke wide, like ripples in the water when a stone has fallen. She cried out.

He set her on her feet so abruptly she flung out her arms for balance.

Max laughed, but she was helpless to do anything but sink to her knees before him. And for seconds the sensations washed over her, making her jerk, jerk and throw her head back.

The uncontrolled magnificence of it weakened, faded away, but not Max's laughter.

Bathed in sweat and pulsing from deep within, she opened her eyes to find him standing in front of her.

"You are passionate," he told her. "Passionate and a willing pupil. Quite a combination."

"Please hold me," she asked.

He looked down into her face, but didn't answer. His cool assessment of her brought deep humiliation.

"Max," she said, "will you come to my bed and lie with me?"

"My little mistress," he said, stepping away from her. "Ready to perform her duties."

"*Max*. Please."

"Well," he said, catching up his coat, retrieving his boots and going to the door, "it's pleasant to know you'll be here when I want you. But not tonight, thank you."

And he left her.

Chapter Twenty-one

"This household is beyond all," the dowager said. "I have summoned you two men because I need, no, I *demand* your support. I simply cannot tolerate another interview such as the one I had with that other strumpet *unless* I have your presence from the outset."

"Hush, now," Blanche Bastible said, fussing around the old lady. "You are not to upset yourself like this. I've told you that I will be more than glad to dispose of—what was the name given for this one?"

The dowager duchess pounded her cane, and Struan mentally prepared himself for an even more difficult encounter than he'd anticipated. "Miss *Wisteria*," she said, grunting as Blanche tucked pillows behind her thin body on the green chaise in her boudoir. "Have you ever heard such nonsense. Zinnia, Dahlia, and Wisteria. Why, any parent who would give such names to her daughters must be weak in the head, or evil-minded. Having met both Miss Dahlia and Miss Zinnia, I tend to think the former is the case."

"I didn't know you'd met Zinnia," Arran said. Wearing a somewhat threadbare silk dressing gown over his heavily strapped chest and a bandage on his head, he sat in a large armchair. "It was Dahlia who came here with the innuendos I told you about, Struan. Something about a journal that could prove Rossmara indiscretions, and that someone or other wasn't who they thought they were. Oh, and if she married Max, she'd keep it all quiet." He chuckled.

"Miss Zinnia also made a visit," the dowager said, setting her bony little frame more comfortably. "While you were all out gallivantin' and maiming yourselves yesterday. When you came back, with all that commotion, I decided to wait to share what she had to say. Her announcement was that there was a book or some such thing, and that it contained information about a club of some sort. The League of Jolly Gentlemen, if you ever heard anything so foolish. Something to do with the late King George IV when he was Prince Regent. He named names in the book. And disgraceful liaisons between these so-called jolly gentlemen and women who were no better than they ought to be. She implied that a member of this family had belonged to the league although she didn't seem to know who. *And* she suggested that the league hasn't been disbanded but that there may yet be a Rossmara performing some sort of sexual rituals."

Blanche squealed and fanned herself. "I've said it before,

and I'll say it again, it's something to do with the stranger on horseback. Perhaps he's a Rossmara no one knows about, and *he's* doing, well, whatever's being done."

"Pah!" The dowager flapped at the back of her companion's hand with a lacy handkerchief before continuing. "There is no such person, and there is no other Rossmara. Kindly keep tighter control on your imagination.

"Zinnia went on to say Max shouldn't marry Lady Hermoine because she intended to use the book in some way to bring disgrace upon the family, but she, Zinnia, would find a way to save the day. After Max married her. Seems he has quite a gaggle of admirers—awful though they may be. Anyway, it's all rubbish. I note there has been no further mention of a journal that might reveal some horrible family secret that would prove the Rossmaras aren't the Rossmaras or whatever. Really, such wild tales. At the very least the silly creatures might try to tell the same story about their wretched book, or journal, or whatever."

"We're a wild lot," Arran said, but he didn't look concerned. "I admit I should like to know the identity of that fella that's riding about on land he's got no right to ride about on."

"Bound to move on soon enough," Struan said, although he didn't like the idea of the man spying on the castle, either. "I agree with you, Grandmother. It's all rubbish. These girls are trumping up pieces of nonsense with a view to turning them into cold cash."

Arran laughed. "And a warm-blooded husband. The little hussies want your Max as a husband, don't forget. Jealous of Lady Hermoine, that's obvious. Did you tell Max?"

Struan hadn't told Arran about the conversation he'd had with Max the previous evening. The ill feeling between himself and the man he would always consider his eldest son troubled him deeply. "I didn't tell Max," he said to Arran. "He's enough on his mind at present."

"He has indeed," Arran said, shifting a little in the chair, and wincing.

Blanche rushed to him and stroked back his hair, failing to make her customary mention of its being too long, and the tail unfashionable. "My poor boy," she crooned. "Thank goodness our dear Grace didn't witness that terrible fall. She hasn't a strong mind, and it might have quite unhinged her."

"Grace has a steel mind," Arran said shortly, jerking his head from his mother-in-law's ministrations, and wincing at the pain he caused himself. "Your daughter is the most sensible woman I ever met." He smiled at Blanche. "She is also the most sensual creature on the face of the earth, thank God. And I shall always be grateful that she's mine."

"Well," Blanche said huffily. "*Sensual?* Oh, really."

"Perhaps we should deal with this Wisteria person," Struan said. He wanted to talk to Max, to make things right between them, not that one inch could be given on the question of Kirsty Mercer. Max, however, had made himself scarce since last evening.

Blanche rushed to pull the bell. "My lady must not become excited," she said, positively bobbing on her toes. "Son-in-law, do tell her that all will be well."

"Ah, the trials one bears for the women one loves," Arran said. "Don't worry, mother-in-law. Like your daughter, the dowager duchess has a steel mind, and a steel will. She will do well enough, I'm sure."

Just then Shanks appeared and was told to bring up their visitor. He returned and showed in a plump female indistinguishable from her pretty, if vacuous sisters, except that rather than black or red, her hair was white-blond. However, it billowed out around her face in exactly the same manner as her sisters' hair. With a rush of tiny steps she gained the center of the boudoir and stood winding her fingers together, holding her lower lip in her teeth, and batting heavily painted lashes.

Only by exercise of extreme will did Arran suppress a groan.

"Very well," the dowager said. "There is no need for any introductions. We know who you are. The only question is, what do you want?"

The creature swayed, and smiled coyly, and dimpled, and made little crooning noises.

"I feel a serious headache descending," Arran said.

The dowager said, "Be quick, girl. Can't you see we are not at our best today?"

"You're the marquess." Wisteria pointed at Arran and dipped a curtsy. "And you're the viscount." Struan got a dip. "The Dowager Duchess of Franchot. Oh, I'm so honored to meet you, m'lady." Yet another dip.

Blanche got no acknowledgment.

"I'm Miss Wisteria. My mother was Countess Grabham's dearest friend and when my mother died the countess *insisted* that she take me to live with her. Of course, I wouldn't hear of being separated from my sisters, so the countess took them, too. She's done her best with them, she really has, but you can't make a sow's purse out of a silk ear, can you?"

Struan realized his mouth was open and closed it.

"I couldn't agree with you more," Blanche Bastible said.

"You," the dowager told Blanche, "will be silent. Now, girl, why are you here?"

"It pains me," Wisteria said, lowering her heavy lashes. "I'd much rather not 'ave to do this, but a girl's got to do what a girl's got to do. I've no means but those the countess is good enough to give me, so I need to find my own way, don't I?"

Struan assessed Wisteria's expensive fringed, glacé silk shawl. The garment was exquisitely embroidered and of the same pale yellow as her gown. Of silk, the latter creation frothed with rows of exquisite lace. The same lace peeked from beneath the brim of her bonnet.

Poor Wisteria. "The kindness of strangers can be hard to bear," he said.

She pointed at him rudely. "You understand perfectly. Anyway, I think it would be better if I talked to the old lady on my own—being that Max is her grandson."

An awful silence followed.

Wisteria opened her blue eyes wide. "Did I say something out of place?"

"We will all be remaining," Arran told her. "Mr. Max Rossmara is Her Ladyship's *great* grandson, her grand-daughter's son."

"Ooh," Wisteria said, peering at the dowager. "You are really old, aren't you."

The sound of the dowager's dry chuckle made Struan start. "Amazing," she said. "Truly amazing. Tell your tale, please, Miss Wisteria."

"In front of all of them?" She hooked a thumb over her shoulder.

"Yes."

"But it's about you, dowager."

"Really?" the dowager said. "Then I hope it's interesting. It's been a *very* long time since there was anything interesting to be said about me."

"Suit yourself." Wisteria shrugged her rounded shoulders. "There's a certain book. A journal thing."

Struan looked at the ceiling.

"It's been hidden, see, but now it's come to light, and someone's got it. And I know who that someone is, and I can get it."

"A journal?" the dowager said.

Blanche fanned faster.

"Damning, is it?" Arran asked.

Wisteria nodded emphatically. "Oh, yes, very damning. Are you sure I should talk in front of them?" she asked the dowager.

"Quite sure."

"Well, it's about how you were a live one when you wasn't so old."

Struan shook his head, met his brother's eyes, and suppressed a laugh when he saw how Arran struggled with the same problem. One wondered why the daughter of the countess's closest friend spoke in such a manner—and possessed no social grace.

"You was quite the one in London back then."

"Was I?"

"You know you was. I'm afraid to come out and say it. It's so awful."

"Oh, good," Struan remarked.

"You shouldn't make fun of an old lady," Wisteria admonished him. "Especially when she's being told how her reputation's going to be ruined if she doesn't do as she's told."

"Well, I never," Blanche exploded. "I'm calling Shanks to have her thrown out at once."

"Hush," the dowager said. "This is most entertainin'. Let Wisteria finish."

Wisteria affected wounded sensibilities and even managed a tear or two. "I wouldn't do this if I didn't 'ave to. You 'ad an affair with the king. There, 'ow about that? That should be worth something to all of you to keep me quiet."

"Which king was that?" the dowager asked, and the rest of the company—with the exception of clearly confused Wisteria—burst into laughter.

Wisteria's confusion turned her face red. When the laughter subsided, she said, " 'Ow many kings did you 'ave it on with, then?"

"Answer the question," Struan told her. "And be quick about it. You've already overstayed your welcome—you had when you arrived."

"Well, it was King George III, of course. The mad one.

Long before my time, of course, but I was told 'ow they used to meet at Windsor Castle and use the King's own bedchamber, the one he shared with his wife. And quite often 'is wife was with them. Isn't that one that'll rock the *ton*."

"Oh, rock it, rock it," Arran said, and hummed. He tapped a rhythm on the arm of his chair with his free hand. "Rock it, rock it. There could be some form of primitive verse there. Perhaps I could write a tune to go with it."

"Anyway," Wisteria said, her lips thinned, "I'm prepared to bargain."

"Blackmail, you mean," the dowager said. "Your terms?"

"A girl like me 'as to look after herself. I need something permanent. Now, Lady Hermoine wouldn't be any good at all for Max Rossmara. I want you to make sure he marries me instead."

Max returned to the castle soaked, from a rainfall in the early hours of the morning, from dew later, and from his own sweat once the sun came up and he'd become too heated by his efforts.

He'd walked the moors all night since leaving Kirsty, and come daylight he'd climbed to a high vantage point on Kirkcaldy to think and wait for a vicious headache to pass. He'd decided that he had no driving need to drink, and in future he would not do so except in moderate quantities. And he would control this habit of venting his temper. After all, before he became so desperate about the situation with Kirsty he had neither drunk to excess, nor lost his temper unnecessarily. But now he returned with no more idea of how to proceed with Kirsty than he'd had when he left. Her soft voice whispered over and over, *Ye bad man, ye. Threatenin' someone ye know is weaker.* Words spoken through a door. And, *Max, please,* as, naked and so lovely, she'd offered herself to him, and he'd denied her.

At that moment he'd felt crushed by his inability to comfort her as she deserved to be comforted. His own confusion had disgusted him. He was unfit to breathe the same air as that poor, dear girl and he must find a way to beg her forgiveness.

When he passed her rooms, he crept, ensuring he made no sound. No doubt she remained there, hiding, too embarrassed to show her face.

He reached his own door and stopped. He could not face going in yet. Not to be shut away alone with the knowledge of what he had done to her. And knowing that she was so close yet there was nothing he could think of to ease the humiliation he'd heaped upon her sweet head.

Like Kirsty, he was without choices that were possible to make. She'd left her family thinking they would never turn their backs on her. She'd been wrong. If he denied his parents wishes now, he was certain he would be severed from their love. After all, his real parents had found it simple enough to turn their backs on him. He didn't even have a blood relationship with the Rossmaras.

He hadn't eaten since the previous day.

Retracing his steps, he made his way belowstairs to the kitchens. Mrs. Moggach didn't like intrusions from "themselves," and still regarded Max as an interloper anyway— what she termed, an upstarty laddie—but she now made sure she didn't openly offend him.

Mrs. Moggach wasn't in the kitchens.

Much giggling greeted Max as he entered and some moments passed before a group of maids, a groom, and a male servant he didn't recognize became aware of him. They'd been huddled together around one maid who sat in a chair near the great fireplace. When they looked up, the seated maid stuffed a small book into her apron pocket and leaped to her feet.

Max nodded in response to their chorus of greeting. He made no comment about the groom's presence, nor did he comment on their rowdy behavior. "Coffee?" he asked. "And some of the apple pie from yesterday, if there's any left."

The maid with the book, a tall, pretty, dark-haired girl, put herself forward and said, "There's no' any pie, Mr. Rossmara, but we've a fresh lemon tart if ye'd care t'try it."

"That will do very well, thank you. Make it a large piece, and I'll take two cups of coffee and plenty of cream."

The slightest giggle was quickly snuffed out, but he didn't miss the knowing glances that passed between the servants. There must already be talk about his relationship with Kirsty. Let them think what they might. He must make certain she didn't suffer more than she had already.

"Where will ye be takin' it then, sir?" the maid asked, suppressing a smile. "It'll be along very shortly."

"I'll carry it with me, thank you." He smelled the coffee bubbling on the hob. "If that's not *too* much trouble?"

While a tray was assembled, Max wandered around the kitchen, and stopped before the closed door to the butler's pantry. Curtains were drawn across windows that overlooked the kitchen. Almost drawn. Through a narrow gap in the curtains he saw Shanks and Moggach seated close together and reading from the same book, a small book. From time to time they slapped their own, or each other's thigh, winked, and snuggled close.

Max frowned, unable to believe what he saw. He was actually witnessing some sort of romantic encounter. Between *Shanks and Moggach*. And what the devil was this reading craze that had overtaken the staff?

"Mr. Rossmara? It's ready if ye please. Are ye sure ye—"

"Quite sure, thank you." He picked up the tray and carried it to the main floor, then crossed to the Eve Tower and climbed to the corridor leading to the rosy rooms.

He balanced the tray in one arm and knocked. When there was no response he put his face to the very door and said,

"Kirsty. It's Max. May I come in, please." A quiet and rational approach would be best.

After several attempts to get an answer from her, he tried the door and was surprised to find it unlocked. Inside, the sitting room was entirely neat. Not a sign of his childish breaking spree remained except for the bare tabletop near the chair where he'd sat.

She'd cleaned up after him and gone to bed—and been unable to make herself get up again.

On the balls of his feet, he went toward the bedroom where the door stood open. "Kirsty, it's Max. I've come to beg you to forgive me. I'm a fool. I don't deserve you. I never have. I should be horsewhipped for the way I treated you last night."

Of course she didn't answer him. She must be exhausted from crying and sleeplessness.

With the tray in both hands, he went cautiously into her bedroom and looked at the bed.

Not a wrinkle showed in the counterpane. The bedroom was as immaculate as the sitting room. And Kirsty wasn't in either room.

For an instant he thought she might have left. Gone to beg her parents to take her back, perhaps, or if he was truly unlucky, simply taken off with no idea where she was going.

But he soon discovered that her clothes were still in the wardrobe and her cheap, worn Bible with its cardboard covers was in its place beside the bed. The nightgown she'd worn the previous evening was carefully folded in the top drawer of a chest where her pathetically few personal possessions had been put.

He picked up the tray from the chest under the window and sat on the same chest with the tray on his lap.

Where was she?

Had she made the room neat so that no one would think there was anything amiss, then gone to do something awful?

Would she take her own life?

Max didn't know where to start looking for her. He picked up a cup of coffee and drank it to the dregs in two mouthfuls. The tart he ate by breaking off pieces with his fingers. He finished the huge piece, barely noticing its taste, and topped it off by drinking the second cup of coffee.

She could be out there somewhere, wandering, desperate and looking for a way to end it all, and he sat eating lemon tart and drinking coffee.

Leaving the tray behind, he made a dash for the stairs and didn't as much as hesitate until he reached the hall. Shanks strutted into view and gave Max a decidedly sheepish look.

"May I help you, sir?" he asked, and Max had no doubt other members of the staff had mentioned that he had been observed peering through a gap in the curtains in the butler's pantry window.

"Sir?" Shanks prompted.

"Hm? Oh, no, I don't think so. Unless—have you see Miss Mercer this morning?"

Shanks wrinkled his brow. "Some time ago, sir. I think she went into your study."

"Thank you." With no attempt at decorum, Max raced away and all but ran past his study. Skidding to a halt, he flung open the door and rushed inside.

Kirsty looked up from the book in which the record of staff wages was kept.

"I've been out of my mind with worry about you," Max said, slamming the door shut with the heel of his boot. "I thought you'd be in your rooms. Then I thought you must have tried to go home again."

"Dinna shout if ye please."

He gulped air.

"If this isna done, there'll be folk without their wages."

Dressed in another grandmotherly creation, this one puce

with a line of jet beads from high neck to waist, Kirsty sat behind her desk, her back straight as a poker.

"How long have you been here? Did you hear me pass your rooms earlier?"

"I've been here since six this morning, and, no, I didna hear ye pass."

"Oh." He looked at his boots, and back at her face. "You don't appear to be well."

"I'm verra well, thank ye."

"No you aren't. Don't lie to me. Your eyes look as if they've ghosts inside them."

"How nice. Thank ye."

"You've never worn your hair like that before. All scraped back, and harsh, and old-maidish."

"I am an old maid," she said calmly. "I'm quite sure I can continue to manage here if ye'd care t'attend t'your ablutions."

He narrowed his eyes. "I beg your pardon."

"I said I'm quite sure I—"

"I heard what you said. What do you mean by criticizing my appearance—and you are not an old maid."

"An old maid is a woman who hasna married. We'll no' discuss it. And since ye're still wearin' what ye wore last night, an' ye've no' shaved or washed, or combed your hair, I thought ye might like—"

"Kindly come with me, Miss Mercer."

"I'm otherwise occupied."

"Come with me."

She stood up and came around her desk. "Come with ye where? I've work t'do."

"You are employed by me. Kindly remember that. And remember that you will do what I tell you to do."

Kirsty lowered her eyes, and he realized with something close to horror that she was clinging to dignity but with such difficulty. Her face was devoid of color, and dark marks underscored her eyes.

"Forgive me," he said. "I had a bad night."

When her eyes met his again, her expression was incredulous. "A bad night? Why, I'm sorry t'hear that. It's hard when ye don't sleep well."

"I'd appreciate it if you'd finish what you feel must be done, then come to my rooms."

"Your rooms?"

"My rooms." He left before she could question him further, or decline to obey.

Two could play the game of worrying the one who cared most about them—and he knew she cared for him deeply. Rather than go directly to his rooms, he climbed to the floor above his own and wandered toward a window at the end of a corridor. The view of Kirkcaldy's forested lands was particularly impressive from there. He would pass at least some of the time there until Kirsty might come to him.

He was within feet of the window when he heard rustling, and groaning, and a woman's keening moan. The noises came from a room to his left.

None of these rooms was occupied—or supposed to be occupied.

Bracing himself for attack, he threw open the door and said, "Don't move!"

He was rewarded with a female, "Oh, Lordy," and the interesting sight of the said female's naked bottom in the air. She balanced on the back of her head and her shoulders atop the bed, with Wilkie, dressed in only his shirt, astride the back of her thighs.

Wilkie pushed his hair from his reddened face but didn't appear to consider removing himself from what was evidently an involved copulation position. He patted the woman's derriere rhythmically and said, "There, there, Ada, don't ye worry, you just leave this t'me."

Max did not find the scene arousing.

Ada, whom he didn't recognize from this particular angle, whimpered and made a futile attempt to cover her breasts with her hands.

"This," Wilkie announced, straightening his spine with the inevitable result that Ada uttered another loud, "Oh!" "This is my intended. I'm sure ye understand how hard it is when a man and his intended are tired o' waitin' t'be wi' each other."

Ada's next "oh," had quite a different note. This time she sounded delighted.

"My congratulations to you," Max said with a private smile. He'd become a matchmaker without having intended to do so. "And my best wishes to you for a long and fruitful marriage."

He turned to leave, and saw that a small book lay open on the bed where Wilkie was able to see it. Unable to contain his curiosity, Max took a careful step closer so that he could see the volume.

A picture of two people in a similar position to the one that must be cutting off all circulation to Ada's head by now—and a text beside the picture that might be instructions, perhaps.

He shook his head and left the room. What was going on in this household? Where were these books coming from?

Chapter Twenty-two

Tread carefully, Struan told himself, *tread very carefully.* He'd expected to find Max in his rooms, possibly sleeping. That his son had left the castle last night and not returned until the early hours of the morning was a fact both he and Arran knew well. They'd kept watch. And while they'd watched, Arran had made no attempt to temper his comments. He believed Struan would come to rue his opposition to Max's affection for Kirsty Mercer.

Max wasn't in his rooms.

Enlisting the unlikely help of Blanche Bastible had gained him the intelligence that Kirsty Mercer was at work in the study—alone.

Struan sat at Max's writing table in his library. How did you tell a son who was now a man that you understood the choices he wished to make, but that there were choices he must make. And that in making the choices he must, he must also be certain to cause no harm to anyone.

"Father?"

He hadn't been aware of Max's approach.

"You're a disgrace, my son. A damnable disgrace." Of all the greetings, why had he chosen such a one?

"Thank you. So I've already been told."

"By whom?"

Max came in and threw himself into a worn and favorite chair. "No one whose opinion matters to you."

Kirsty Mercer.

"Was there something of particular importance, Father? If

not, I hope you won't consider me disrespectful if I suggest we postpone any social exchange."

"Kirsty Mercer's opinion matters to me." There, now he had said it, and the statement raised Max's chin, and hovered between them, as solid as any rock edifice might be.

Max's green eyes could be so cold. They were cold now.

"I love you, my son." Good God, his brain spilled directly to his mouth without consulting caution on the way.

The coldness in those eyes turned to something else instantly. Confusion? *Hope?* Why, hope? Max's throat—beneath its growth of red stubble—jerked.

"If you allow that fungus to grow on your face a day or so more, you'll look more Scot than any Scotsman."

"It takes more than a red beard to make a man a Scot. But then, I've been many things, made so many changes that it must be becoming difficult to recall exactly what I am, hm, Father?"

"Only two days to the ball at The Hallows."

"Yes, I'm attending under duress, but it isn't like you to avoid answering a simple question."

Struan pushed back from the table. "That was no simple question. It was a cry from inside you, Max. It tells me you still are not sure of yourself. After all our efforts, your mother's and my own, still you suffer inside because of the one thing we can do nothing about: where you came from."

"You do not even know where I came from."

This had to happen, this confusion about himself. The wonder was that it had been so long in coming. "I know you were born in London. And that you and Ella had the same mother. And I know you are exceptional in every way. You have become a right hand to your uncle and to me. You are my son. Nothing else matters."

"Your son, but not your possession."

How like Max not to give an inch. "No, not my possession. But you owe me respect. I should not have to mention the high esteem in which you are held because of your relationship to me."

"I am not your son."

Struan felt the words like a blow. "Yes," he murmured. "Yes, you are my son. I made you so."

"You could not do the impossible. It was not your seed that made me."

"Would that it had been," Struan said, looking at Max direct. He raised his voice. "And *damn* you for the suffering you bring me with your harsh words. I have given you all I could give in love and possessions. I have made no distinction between you and Ella, and the children of my own loins. What more will it take to convince you how much you mean to me?"

Max got up and turned to the nearest bookcase. Clearly he saw nothing before him. His shoulders hunched.

"I have requested nothing of you that I did not consider best for your own well-being."

"I have no real place as your son."

"Yes, you do. You are adopted, Max."

"Edward is your rightful heir." Max remained with his back turned but held up a hand. "Please, know that I do not crave my younger brother's place as your legitimate heir. I merely state the truth. There is a difference between Edward's position and my own. You and Mother have done your utmost to make me feel that no difference exists, but we know it does."

What could he say? He could not deny the truth. "You are doing so well. Your future is assured. You are indispensable to Arran and me."

"I know. And I'm grateful. But I pay a great price."

Struan stood and leaned on the table. "What the *hell* do you mean? A great price?"

"I am not a free man."

"Not . . . Damn you, you ungrateful cub. Of course you're

a free man. You have a fat bank account. You have a fortune to call your own. What would make you suggest you are not a free man?"

"I am not free. My love for you ensures that I can never be truly free."

Struan fell into the chair again and gripped its arms.

"You are more than a father to me. I should have told you so a long time ago, but a man must swallow his emotions, isn't that what we're taught?"

"Not by me," Struan said softly. "I am an emotional man."

"You have never encouraged me to demonstrate my feelings. But, again, I do not criticize you for that. You have done your best for me, and more. But for you I should almost certainly be dead by now, or rotting in a debtors' prison. And my dearest sister, my Ella, would have been sold as little more than a child to be some rich man's plaything—until she grew older and he no longer wanted her. Then only the Lord can know what might have become of her."

"History," Struan snapped. "Let us put history behind us. Your sister is happily married and a mother. She has a husband who adores her. And you will have a wife who adores you."

"No." Max shook his head. "Ella married a man of wealth and position, but he is the man she loved, the only man she ever wanted. The woman I am told I must marry means nothing to me."

"You will come to care for her. She is of fine stock."

"A broodmare." Max sneered at him and Struan felt the cut deeply. "A broodmare and one more attempt to make a gentleman out of me by marrying me to a lady—despite the fact that not even that can gain me a title."

"It will gain you a good deal, my boy. It will gain you social status, and for that, if marriage to her is a sacrifice, then the sacrifice is worthwhile."

Max faced his father. "I understand. There is no need to discuss the issue further."

"Do you doubt our love for you? Your mother's, and mine?"

"No. No, absolutely not. I never have."

"Then do you understand our reason for wanting to ensure that you make an advantageous match?"

"I understand. That doesn't mean I have to enjoy the prospect. I don't find Lady Hermoine appealing."

Struan frowned. He had intended for this to be a conciliatory interview. "She is beautiful."

"Oh, yes, if you like that sort of obvious beauty."

"And she has a title."

"Indeed—we all know this."

"And she has been well schooled."

"So we're told."

Irritation began to shorten Struan's temper. "Have you any reason to doubt that the lady is educated?"

"I have no reason to doubt or believe. We have never had a conversation that would prove her wit one way or the other."

"Then that must be remedied. As soon as the rest of the family returns from Cornwall we shall want to proceed with the folderol and get the two of you married."

"Most men choose their own wives."

This direction in their discussion had been inevitable. "Most men of our class," he said, keeping his voice even, "are not in the position of having to help wipe out all memory of what they once were. Let us not shilly-shally, Max. *You* are in that position. And for your own future good, and the good of our position as a family, it's important that you do nothing to draw attention to your—unusual background."

"No attention to my being a bastard from the streets of

London, you mean?" Max said, adopting the annoyingly bland tone he usually employed when being particularly bloody. "After all, there could be some who would as soon not take a man such as me seriously. That would be inconvenient for you and Arran, wouldn't it?"

"*Damned* inconvenient," Struan exploded. "And it's not going to happen because you're going to do as you are told. Do I make myself clear?"

"Abundantly," Max said. He stripped off his coat and began to remove his shirt. "The point you are making is that the woman I want, I may not have."

"Not *at all.*" Struan felt his temper slip away entirely. "The point I'm making is that you must think of these things as any gentleman would think of them. You can have it all. You can marry Lady Hermoine and solidify your social position. And you can take almost any mistress you bloody well please, and no one will think a thing about it."

Max tore his shirt the rest of the way off, ignoring the scatter of buttons. His sheer physical size silenced Struan. The puny boy became a youth with the promise of a fine physique. That youth had turned into an incredible specimen of mature manhood, not that Max was presently concerned with his appearance—which was every bit as disgraceful as Struan had first remarked.

This might not be a son of his own body, but, damn, Struan was proud of him. He glanced away, away and through a window. On the crest of a nearby hill stood a lone rider astride a massive black horse, a figure in a large hat and wearing a cloak.

"Our watcher is with us again," Struan remarked. "I'd give a good deal to know who he is and what he wants."

"Just a man who crosses the land on his way to and from somewhere else," Max commented. "He does no harm."

"No harm that we know. I don't like it. Neither does Arran. We just can't seem to intercept him."

"I need to wash," Max said, stating the obvious, and changing the subject. "And change my clothes."

"It's time you took on a permanent valet," Struan told him, reluctantly taking his attention from the rider. "This fending for yourself was all well and good when you were younger. Now it's become an affectation."

"Now it's become an absolute necessity. Damn, I want a drink."

"Then have one," Struan said. "What will it be?"

"Nothing. Kirsty doesn't like me drinking when I'm angry, she—"

Struan sighed. "And now we put a name to the true cause of our disagreement."

"Disagreement?" Max gave a short, harsh laugh. "You call such a thing merely a *disagreement*. What lies between us is a disaster of monumental proportions. I am struggling with decisions no man should have to struggle with. And unless there is some miracle, Kirsty's life is already ruined as far as her family is concerned."

Struan rose again. "What do you mean?" He went around the desk. "Speak up. What are you talking about?"

"They've turned her out." Max walked into the bedchamber. "Told her they don't want anything to do with her. Told her she's shamed them. How many more ways do I need to explain that Kirsty Mercer has already been wounded to the heart because *I* must be put first at all costs."

"Arran and I were aware of the awkwardness there."

"Her parents walked away from her, I tell you. They told her that in coming here to work for me she had made her choice, and it meant she no longer had any place with them. They accused her of being no better than she ought to be—even though that is not true."

"They had no right," Struan said, furious that no matter how hard they tried there were some things they could not do for the simple people who were so aware of a chasm between themselves and those who supplied them with their living.

Max poured water into a bowl, took soap, and washed himself. He lathered his beard area and shaved it quickly and efficiently. He rinsed himself and ran his hands over his face. "They had no right—*yet.*"

Struan swept up a towel. "You'll keep your hands off that girl."

With water dripping from his hair, his face, and his torso, Max turned on Struan. "What did you say?"

"I said, you will keep your hands off Kirsty Mercer."

Max took the towel and began drying himself. "Didn't you just tell me that as long as I marry the *right* woman, I may find what I want and need to find elsewhere?"

"Not with Kirsty Mercer."

"That is not your decision to make."

"Arran would *kill* you if you compromised that girl. I would kill you."

"I would be twice dead."

"Do not joke about such a matter. Her family are of great importance to this family."

"They are peasant tenants. Below notice. Unworthy."

"*Stop* it. What has come over you? You brought that girl into this house because you said it was a waste of a good brain for her not to have a chance to better herself."

Max dried beneath his arms and tossed aside the towel. "You know as well as Uncle Arran does—as well as I do— that I brought Kirsty into this house because I want her— and not only as an assistant. In fact, I don't give a damn about her being my assistant. *I want her.*"

"But you said—"

"I lied. I want her the way you want Mother. I am driven to have her, the way you were driven to have Mother."

"Don't bring your mother into this."

"Why? Because Mother is a *lady* and above being mentioned in a conversation dealing with desire. With *carnal* desire, as well as love."

Struan readied himself for the biggest struggle he had ever had with Max. "You do love her, then?"

"You know I do. You've warned me away from her many times."

"And you defied me by waiting until I left for Cornwall this year and installing her in this very house."

"Yes, I did."

Of course he did. And of course he would fight for what he wanted. He, Struan, had encouraged him to pursue what he considered important and he considered this girl more important than anything else. "Max, listen to me."

"Do I have a choice?"

"No. You don't just want to bed the Mercer girl, you want to marry her, don't you?"

By the stubborn set of Max's mouth, Struan doubted he would get any useful answers, but he pressed on. "You are determined to have her at any cost."

"I am, and I will. I am now all she has. She is as much my responsibility as you have considered Ella and me yours."

"Not so, dammit!"

Max took a fresh shirt from his wardrobe. "Yes, her future is in my hands."

"You will not turn that lovely girl into your ladybird."

Max was silent as he put on his shirt and buttoned it.

"You will do nothing to hurt her. Do I make myself clear?"

"Indeed you do. I am touched by your sense of honor toward one so lowly."

"How *dare* you taunt me so? That you would accuse me of caring less for a man or woman because they did not have the fortune of a high birth is outrageous. You know better of me."

Max tucked in his shirt and slicked back his soaked hair.

"This weekend," Struan said. "Only two days from today the ball takes place at The Hallows. You will be attentive to Lady Hermoine. By the end of the evening I want no doubt as to where your affections lie. Do I make myself clear?"

"Very clear."

Struan was tempted to hurl something, but contained himself. "There is a way out of all this misery. Help us to find Kirsty a suitable husband. A man of breeding and education, but one who does not have designs on a high place in the land."

"And I do?"

"Yes, you do. Your uncle and I hope to see you in politics one day. You are what this country needs. But more of that later. Will you help us find a good husband for Kirsty? Someone who will love and appreciate her for who and what she is? Someone who will have no interest in her parentage or growing years, but who will give her the chances she needs? A parson's son, perhaps? Or a parson. I've asked that the new man from the village—Pottinger his name is—be invited to the ball. He hasn't a wife, and he ought to have one. Very suitable."

He didn't care for Max's stare.

"Will you help?"

Max tossed his towel beside the bowl. "I shall do my best to see Kirsty as happy as she deserves to be."

Feeling guilty for eavesdropping, Kirsty hovered by the outer door to Max's rooms. She'd arrived in time to learn that they intended to find her a husband. The new pastor from the village was the prime candidate. Kirsty had seen him once. An earnest young man, he was also a boor and very interested in himself.

Max had made his decision. He didn't want her, not even as his mistress.

She wanted to flee. But where could she go? The same

answer came—as it had so many times since the previous day: she had nowhere to go anymore. This castle had become her home until she was passed along like a trunk, or an old chair, to someone else who needed such an item.

She'd best make her presence known. "Hello," she called. "Mr. Rossmara? It's Kirsty Mercer. Ye sent for me."

Rather than Max, it was the viscount who came to the partly open door to his son's rooms and ushered her inside. "Come in, come in. Max didn't mention that he'd summoned you." He sent a significant and displeased glance in the direction of Max's bedchamber. "He'll be out shortly."

"Thank ye," Kirsty said.

"Yes, well—" Evidently the viscount quickly forgot what he'd been about to say because he folded his hands behind his back and looked thoughtful.

Max came from the bedchamber. His cravat was clumsily knotted and he shrugged hastily into a jacket. His hair was still wet but his growth of red beard had disappeared.

"I'm sure you'll understand, Father, if I choose not to help—" He saw Kirsty and stopped talking.

"Absolutely," the viscount said, and his laughter was uncharacteristically hearty. "Time to get Kirsty to the dowager and Mrs. Bastible for that dance instruction I'm told has been arranged. You have quite the champion in the dowager duchess. She is determined to broaden your experience."

Surprised, Kirsty took a backward step.

"Come, come now, child," the viscount said kindly. "I understand you've let it be known that you haven't learned to dance. We can't have that with you going to a ball on Saturday. The most important ball to be held in these parts for many a moon."

"The *only* dance in many a moon," Max said, sounding gruff.

"I came t'see Max," Kirsty said. "He asked me to do so."

"Because he wanted to take you along for your dance

lessons no doubt," the viscount said. "We shall all help out. A girl ought to dance well enough to have a good time at a ball. Especially a girl as pretty as you. You're bound to be sought after. Dance card will be filled in no time."

Panic welled in Kirsty's chest. "I'm only going t'watch t'people."

"Rubbish! You'll dance the night away like all the other young girls. Max here will have his betrothed on his arm. But there will be other, less fortunate gentlemen present."

"I am not yet betrothed," Max said.

Struan put a hand beneath Kirsty's elbow. "Let us lead the way to the music room. Come along. You, too, Max. You'll be needed for this exercise."

She heard Max follow but would not let herself look back at him.

They proceeded toward Revelation, the tower in which the marquess and his family lived.

"I'm sure I shouldn't be able to learn nearly enough to accept an invitation to dance within two days, and I'd no' like t'look the fool."

"You couldn't look the fool," Max said at once, from behind her.

"That reminds me," the viscount said. "You'd better go to your great-grandmother and see if she's ready, Max. Then accompany her and Mrs. Bastible to the music room."

"But surely—"

"Do as I ask, there's a good chap," the viscount said, and Max left without another word.

They seemed to travel a vast distance through the castle, and Kirsty wondered if the dowager would be able to walk so far at all. "This part of the castle is older than the rest, isn't it?" she asked.

"Yes," the viscount told her. "The marquess has always preferred it here. So does his wife. Did you know she's a painter—she paints what she calls *representational* art.

Shapes representative of people without clothes, so I understand."

Kirsty gasped. "Wi'out clothes? I don't suppose ye've been allowed t'see them, or ye'd know if they were people."

"Oh, I've seen them. It's just that I don't always see the people in them. But no matter, they are becoming quite famous. Not, of course, that anyone knows they're painted by a woman. The marquess will be delighted to see us. At least he can order us about, even if he cannot play. He'll have great pleasure in criticizing my own poor efforts."

They climbed a spiral staircase of wafer-thin stone steps and entered a great room at the top. "Have you been to the marquess's music room before?" the viscount asked.

Kirsty whispered, "No," and walked into the most beautiful room she'd ever seen. Dark blue silk carpets graced glistening wood floors. Beautiful old tapestries hung on towering, paneled walls. In the center of the room stood a piano, and a second piano all but filled a curved casement where red velvet draperies were pulled aside. The marquess sat at this second piano picking out a tune with his good right hand.

Kirsty looked upward and made a slow revolution. The ceiling was all arches and garlands of leaves and musical instruments made of plaster and painted soft colors that were picked out with gold. She pressed her hands together. Chairs covered with more tapestry stood around a lovely table with patterns in the wood. A bright fire burned in a white-marble fireplace. On couches everywhere stood cases for instruments. Kirsty recognized fiddles, very grand fiddles, but not some of the others.

"Kirsty," the marquess said when he saw her. "Welcome. What a fine surprise—"

"Here we are," the viscount cried in a very loud voice. "Come for Kirsty's dancing lessons. Max has gone to make sure the dowager and Blanche are on their way. Then we must all concentrate on getting this young woman ready for her first ball."

The marquess closed his mouth and nodded.

"You choose suitable pieces, Arran. You'll have to tolerate my poor efforts at the keyboard, but we shall manage well enough."

"We're going to teach Kirsty to dance," the marquess said as if he was trying the idea out rather than making a statement. "She dances very well, you know."

"She does?" the viscount said.

"Never saw a better reel."

"I doubt they dance our sort of reels at a ball, my lord," Kirsty said, growing deeply anxious. "And as I've told ye, I certainly couldn't learn enough not to embarrass everyone—not in only two days."

"Certainly you can," the marquess said. "We shall teach you several dances. You will accept invitations to dance those, but plead that you are already taken for others—dances you don't know. And when they come along, you should pop off for refreshments."

"Very good," the viscount said. "I doubt the Reverend Pottinger engages in a great deal of dancing, but you should accept any invitation he makes, then tell him you are thirsty if you don't know the dance."

"Pottinger?" the marquess said.

"New chap in the village. Bound to be invited. Very suitable for Kirsty, don't you think?"

Kirsty could not believe the manner in which the viscount was attempting to manipulate the lives of herself and his son. "Have ye met Mr. Pottinger?" she ventured.

The viscount stared at her. "Met him? Well, not exactly, but I'll make a point of introducing myself to him and then introducing him to you. You'll sweep him off his feet."

She was of a mind to ask if Mr. Pottinger was likely to sweep her off her feet, but at that moment the door burst open and Max entered, *carrying* the dowager duchess. He took her to a couch and set her down with extreme care. She patted Max's arm and appeared extremely pleased with events. Mrs. Bastible puffed in behind her and sank into the nearest chair.

"Mrs. Bastible wasn't aware that there were to be dancing lessons today," Max said to his father. "In fact, she seemed very surprised."

"Blanche is forgetful," the dowager said in a firm voice. "*I* was aware of the lessons. Now, let us begin."

"We won't need you after all, Max," the viscount said. He seated himself at the piano in the center of the room. "Arran is more than capable of guiding Kirsty around. You must have work to do."

"Not a bit of it," Max said. "Arran isn't up to dancing, are you, Arran?"

"Well—"

"Never mind," the dowager said. "Blanche plays very well, don't you, Blanche?"

Mrs. Bastible said, "It's been so long since I played."

"You are entirely too humble. You shall play. Arran will point out your mistakes. I shall give directions for the dance. Struan shall partner Kirsty. And you, Max, shall go about your own business. Good afternoon to you."

Max made his way very slowly from Revelation to Eve. He had been summarily dismissed because his father was terrified he might fail to manipulate Max into a marriage he didn't want.

In his study Max went not to his own desk, but to Kirsty's, where he sat in her chair. Idly, he pulled open drawers. Each was neat, everything placed squarely with those things that would be most frequently used being the easiest to reach.

He stretched his feet beneath her desk, and kicked something aside. Leaning down, he discovered Ella's old

Parcheesi board, and a piece of cloth wrapped around something. He lifted both and set them on top of the desk. Upon unrolling the cloth he found a silver game piece, a lady, in two pieces. Her head screwed off. He peered inside but found nothing but a piece of very old satin. On closer inspection he decided this was one of the pieces that had disappeared, then reappeared. Each of the pieces was unique in that they wore gowns from different eras. This was an Elizabethan lady.

He turned his attention to the game board, lifted it, and turned it over several times. An odd board, thick enough to be a box rather than a board, very light.

He remembered the board as being heavy.

Max examined each side with great care.

A box.

It *was* a box.

Covered with dyed leather, the sides of the board were actually the sides of a box with an extremely tight-fitting lid. Taking up a sharp paper knife, he made a space for his nails, and pried off the lid.

The box was empty.

It could be that the game pieces were intended to be stored inside the board. They would certainly make it heavy. He put the one he held into the box. There wouldn't be room for all the silver ladies in their ornate gowns.

He gazed straight ahead, thinking. But of course, both the game pieces, and the so-called board, were hiding places for other things. Or they had been.

The board had been one of the few possessions Ella had when the viscount rescued her from that nightmare in London's Whitechapel. As soon as he could, he would get a message to his sister—who could not be far short of confinement—and ask if she'd been aware of anything hidden inside her Parcheesi set.

Oh, it was probably nothing at all. And the so-called missing pieces could have rolled beneath furniture and been retrieved by a maid during cleaning.

Max set the board and piece under the desk where Kirsty had left them.

There was a conspiracy afoot, not a subtle conspiracy, to make sure he and Kirsty Mercer spent very little time together until they could both be safely and irrevocably entangled with the mates that had been chosen for them.

The Grabham ball was in two days. Max had a decision to make, and very little time in which to make that decision.

Chapter Twenty-three

Mairi jiggled on her toes, waiting for the modiste to declare that she was finally satisfied.

"*Voilà,*" the woman said at last, standing back, her head to one side and her hands clasped before her.

"Does she mean she's finished, then?" Mairi asked Kirsty, who managed to remember enough of the French words Max had taught her to thank the modiste, and to dismiss her.

"At last," Mairi said, when the woman had left. "Now let's get ye out o' it so we can do your hair and put on a little o' that paint Mrs. Bastible brought."

"Och," Kirsty said, "my hair always looks t'same. Why not leave the dress on—indecent as it is, and I'll no' be wearin' any paint, thank ye."

Ignoring her entirely, Mairi commenced to undo the back of the gossamer blue gown. Its low-cut bodice folded into many tiny tucks that crossed over Kirsty's breasts to form a deep V. "It's a tiny waist ye've got," Mairi said. "Ye dinna need these stays at all, ye lucky thing. Kirsty Mercer, this is a dress for a kelpie. We're t'use the headdress, and for that we'll need t'do your hair."

Kirsty felt mutinous. "I'm no' a fairy and I dinna want my hair any different."

"The dowager duchess hersel' gave me instructions," Mairi said, peeling the dress down and waiting for Kirsty to step out of it. "And Mrs. Bastible, bless her sweet heart. There's many who dinna like that lady, but I do. She's always kind t'me."

Kirsty stood shivering in her chemise, stays, and petticoats. Mairi proceeded to remove several layers of the latter. Then she went to pat the stool before the dressing table. "Come along then, fairy princess. I remember when I helped the marchioness. She wasna the marchioness when she first came here. A tiny thing wi' pale hair. She looked as if a wind off t'moor would blow her away, but she's a will stronger than any man."

"She's lovely," Kirsty said, remembering her own early recollections of the Marchioness of Stonehaven, whom she'd met the night Niall was born.

"Sit here," Mairi said, and kept beckoning until Kirsty gave in and seated herself before the mirror. "Then there was Ella. Lady Avenall now. Dark-haired, and with skin like ye never saw. Golden. And her eyes as dark as her hair. A beauty."

"I know. I've seen her for myself, remember. Any sister of Max Rossmara's would ha' t'be a beauty."

Mairi giggled, and Kirsty realized what she'd said. "I meant that they're good-looking people, nothin' more."

"O'course ye didna mean anythin' more," Mairi said, taking down Kirsty's hair and brushing it with long, sweeping motions. "I'm glad Ella—Lady Avenall—got her Saber. Now there's a handsome man and only more handsome because of those scars he hid from her so long."

"We do silly things to ourselves," Kirsty said. "With no' thinkin' we're worthy o' this or that for some foolish reason."

"Aye," Mairi said, catching and holding Kirsty's gaze in the mirror. "We do that, don't we?"

Kirsty was the first to look away. "Max never has told me the whole story o' what happened after Ella married Viscount Avenall. D'ye know why there was talk of it no' being a marriage at all?"

"Devlin North," Mairi said, and sighed. "Another beautiful man. He fell in love wi' Ella—like so many did—and tried t'take her from the viscount. His love for her drove him t'do terrible things. He injured Viscount Avenall and locked him away. Accused him o' all sorts o' crimes against Ella. But she fought for her husband, and everythin' came out all right."

As Kirsty watched, Mairi fashioned natural curls into ringlets and pinned them on either side of Kirsty's head. Across the crown she secured a narrow piece of the material used to make the dress. This had been stiffened and white rosebuds sewed at each end. The roses nestled among Kirsty's ringlets.

"There," Mairi said. "Ye're a beautiful girl yoursel'."

Self-conscious, Kirsty began to poke at the roses.

"Now then," Mairi said sternly. "Ye'll no' do that, miss. Here." She applied the tiniest amount of light rouge to Kirsty's lips.

Rather than protest, Kirsty looked at herself and felt too surprised to do other than say, "It looks nice."

Mairi laughed. "O'course it looks nice. Now, the jewels."

"I'd as soon put on the dress now," Kirsty told her. "The jewels make me nervous."

Once more she climbed into the petticoats and stood still while Mairi maneuvered the dress into place and fastened the back. A sash was attached at the back of the waist, then draped gracefully forward and down the length of the skirt. At the ends of the sash were more roses.

Standing before a long mirror, Kirsty held Mairi's shoulder and put her feet into slippers covered with the same fabric as the dress. With every move she made, colors shot through the gown. She thought of her mother, and wished she could be here—here and happy to see her daughter dressed so.

Her mother wouldn't be happy. Neither would her father. They'd both think she was shaming them by taking such finery from strangers. "I feel foolish," Kirsty said. "As if I'm doin' somethin' I know I shouldn't, and everyone will know."

"Well, ye're not," Mairi said, and frowned when a knock came at the door to the sitting room. "Who is it?" she called.

"Max Rossmara," came the low reply.

Kirsty's hands went to her throat.

Mairi left her side at once and went into the sitting room. "No," Kirsty said urgently. "Mairi, dinna let him in." She looked at herself again, at the expanse of her skin that showed over her shoulders and the tops of her breasts. And she looked at the rouge on her lips. Mother would say she was a painted lady.

"Come in, sir," she heard Mairi say.

It was too late to change, or to plead being indisposed, either.

She saw Max enter. In evening dress he was a splendid sight.

"Come along then, Kirsty," he said. "Great-grandmama asked me to accompany you to The Hallows."

Mairi giggled, and Kirsty closed her eyes for a moment, praying she could be composed. She walked into the sitting room.

The smile on Max's face faded. His hands dropped to his

sides and he stared at her. From head to foot, he stared at her, coming back to look into her eyes.

"Och," Mairi said suddenly. "We've almost forgotten the jewels."

"She doesn't need them," Max said. "She's more beautiful than any jewels. But I've brought what she'll wear."

Flustered, Kirsty looked about until she found the fan the dowager had sent for her. She laughed lightly and flipped it open. "Another speedy lesson. I'm afraid I dinna know how t'say anythin' wi' the thing, but at least I can use it to make mysel' cooler."

Still Max didn't smile. His dress was severe. He did wear a white waistcoat but it was made of a heavy, plain fabric rather than satin. His cravat was simply tied and secured with a smooth gold pin devoid of any gems.

From his right coat pocket he pulled a handful of glittering stones. "I decided I should like to see you entirely in diamonds. Aquamarines are pretty enough, but not pretty enough for you. May I put these on for you?"

She hadn't even the wit to argue. At a loss for words, she stood and allowed him to fasten a necklace formed like a collar made from a web of diamonds. A matching bracelet soon adorned her left wrist, and he carefully put a single large diamond on each ear.

Kirsty drew in a shaky breath, lifted her wrist so that the bracelet threw prisms of light in all directions, and said, "Max Rossmara, ye foolish man. Ye know it's no' seemly for me t'be seen in such finery. Take it off now. What would people say?"

He laughed aloud, and with such delight that she caught his hand and shook him to try to get his attention. "It's no' seemly for ye t'have me wear these."

Max kept on laughing until Mairi joined him.

"Och," Kirsty said. "Look at the two o' ye. Daft, ye are. Laughin' at nothin' but foolishness."

When she tried to unfasten the bracelet, Max stopped laughing and his large hand descended on hers. "Oh, no, dear one. I went to some lengths to obtain those, and you will wear them."

Mairi withdrew discreetly to the bedroom and closed the door.

"What'll everyone think?" Kirsty asked when she was alone with Max.

"Let them think what they please."

"And what will the dowager say when I dinna arrive in her—"

"Tell her quietly that I insisted you wear these. She is a tyrant, but she reacts appropriately to such things."

Kirsty decided not to pursue that topic. "I'm no' goin'. I'm no' meant t'be at such things."

"The carriage is at the door, Kirsty," Max said. "And I am going to take the most beautiful guest of all to the ball."

Max took the light shawl and arranged it over her shoulders, and held out her reticule.

"We appear to be ready," Max said, offering his arm.

Kirsty looked at it.

Max waited, then said, "What is it? What are you thinking?"

She placed her hand on his arm and glanced up at him. "I'm thinkin' o' moors in summer. An' bare feet. An' the smell o' flowers in the sun." She had to stop and swallow. "An' I'm thinkin o' pretty bubbles shinin' in the air."

"And wishes?" he asked.

She nodded. "Aye, and wishes."

"I won't lose you, Kirsty. I can't."

Her breaths grew shallow. She parted her lips and felt her color rise.

"You do know that, don't you?"

"I know there are plenty who intend t'make sure we canna be together. An' they're powerful, Max."

He brushed the backs of his fingers over her cheek. "When I look at you there is no man more powerful than I am. I could slay dragons for you, and I will if I have to. And I'm no longer prepared to make do with compromises. Do you understand what I'm telling you?"

She could only frown at him.

"Do you understand?" he persisted. He raised her left wrist where the diamonds he'd placed there shimmered with white brilliance. "I have purchased something else to go with this, and one day you shall wear it. There are matters I must attend to first, but you will wear it, Kirsty."

He spoke of marriage. Kirsty's heart plunged. He was big and strong, and at this minute, in this place, alone with her, he was sure of himself and determined. But when his family stood, shoulder-to-shoulder, they persuaded him that he had certain duties, and he could not go against them. Then what? She had agreed to be his mistress, and then she'd offered herself. She had stood naked before him, and he'd denied her. Did that mean he would not have her on those terms?

Max pulled her into his arms so unexpectedly she cried out. His mouth on hers made certain that if she made another sound it wouldn't be heard. He kissed her gently enough, but left her in no doubt that she had, indeed, been kissed.

"We must go," he told her softly. "I should prefer to remain here with you, but I would bring my father's wrath upon our heads, and I don't intend to do that. From time to time my uncle and Father have suggested I should make a fine politician. I think I shall show them that they may be right. Persuading them of the wisdom of leaving me to make my own decisions regarding my personal life would certainly be an excellent example of my potential as a statesman."

Kirsty smiled at him and went with him downstairs and outside to the carriage, expecting to see other members of his family present.

The carriage was empty.

As if he heard what she was thinking, Max said, "There are too many of us for one carriage," and helped her inside.

The coachman put up the steps, and they were off, swaying and trundling over the ground. Kirsty didn't know for sure where The Hallows lay, but she knew it was some miles distant.

Max sat opposite. Light from the swinging coachlamps spread precious little illumination inside. Kirsty's voluminous skirts spread over Max's knees, and she attempted to move the material aside.

Without warning, Max reached down and clasped her ankles. He lifted them onto his thighs, and before she could protest, he said, "Don't begrudge a man a small pleasure. A chaste touch of his beloved's feet beneath the drape of her skirts. What harm can there be in that?"

"It isn't seemly," Kirsty said, proud of her firm voice. "And we both know how these things have a way of leading to other things."

"Oh, no such thing," he told her, managing to sound vaguely outraged at the suggestion. "A man such as myself, above reproach in all things? You think I would take advantage of the fact that you are a great deal smaller than I, and that I have your ankles in my grip so that if you try to escape me, I can have you tumbled and completely at my mercy with the minimum of effort?"

"You, Max Rossmara, were a bad laddie, and ye're a bad man."

His grip on her ankles tightened until it hurt.

"Max!"

"Don't call me that again."

"Ye change so swiftly. What did I say t'make ye angry now?"

The last thing she expected was for him to go to his knees

on the floor—between her legs. And she didn't expect him to put his head in her lap.

"Get up," she told him urgently. "Quickly. What if we have t'stop for somethin'?"

"We won't have to stop for anything. Comfort me, Kirsty. I need your comfort. I need *you*."

Bewildered by the sudden change in him, she rested a hand on his hair. "I'll always gi' ye comfort. Ye know that."

"Hold me."

Kirsty bent over him. She ran her fingers beneath his stiff collar, combed her fingers through his hair, stroked his back. "What is it, Max? Tell me."

"I hate the world. I hate the way it takes and twists things. Good things. I hate the way it doesn't treasure what's good, and how it rewards evil and avarice."

"And you do your best to be fair," she told him. "You do your part to make the world better. But we've only one tiny bit o' the world. Think o' that and dinna try to deal wi' the rest."

"Wise Kirsty," he said.

He ran his hands up the backs of her legs to the tender places behind her knees.

The effect shocked Kirsty deliciously. She jumped and pressed against the squabs, turning her head aside. "Ye shouldna, Max. It's no' seemly."

"It's no' seemly," he mimicked, his voice oddly rough. "But it feels so good, my love. And I yearn for what feels good—as long as it's with you."

So easily he switched his attention to the tops of her thighs above the garters that held her stockings in place. "This is such arousing flesh. Did you know that?"

"No," she told him very firmly. "How should I know such a thing . . . except, I admit . . . it does feel verra good when ye touch it."

He raised his head and reached up, seeking her mouth,

and she kissed him back with all the passion she felt for him. The tickling of his fingertips in her groin made her nipples tingle, and she squirmed. Max chuckled and darted his tongue into her mouth. For an instant his fingers left their quest, but only long enough to separate her drawers and find a way inside. He tugged lightly on the hair there, kissing her all the time.

She grew impossibly hot and managed to shrug out of her shawl. Max used the opportunity to lick the tops of her breasts, and to thrust his tongue beneath her neckline to tease a nipple.

"Oh, Max," she said, sighing. "Oh, Max." She blinked and tried to focus on what was outside. Very little was to be seen. "Please stop. I dinna know how much more I can take an' still manage to look mysel' when we get there."

"You will never be who you were again, my love. I claim you for my own. Remember those words," he said against her breasts. "You are mine."

The heat in her body was wonderful, wonderfully sweet. In the distance she saw lights. "Max, I think we're almost there."

"Then I must not be so leisurely, must I," he said. With one finger he found that most private opening into her body and moved inside the slightest way.

"Max!"

"Hush, sweet. It's all right. I'll do nothing to hurt you."

He moved the finger, and while he did so, he flipped his thumb back and forth on the smooth place that swelled at his attention. Everything he touched swelled, and grew damp. Kirsty slid her bottom forward on the seat. She shouldn't, but she couldn't help herself.

"My love," Max whispered, moving his finger and thumb faster. "Relax and let this happen to you."

Kirsty already knew what to expect, and she yearned for

it, strained from her inner self to reach it. "What about you?" she asked him. "I want to do this for you."

"And I want you to do it for me. And you shall. And you will also tell me whose idea it was for you to initiate that little shock you used to all but bring me to my knees the other day."

"Oh," she gasped. It was happening, the darting, burning feeling that joined breast and belly, and the places beneath his fingers, in exquisite sensation. Her hips rose from the carriage seat, and rose again. She could do nothing to control the movements of her body.

"Who told you to do that to me?"

"The . . . dowager."

He paused for an instant before continuing. "Your mind is addled."

"That little shock almost brought you to . . . Oh, Max. To your knees. You're on your knees now. Oh, Max!"

With mouth and tongue he moved one side of her bodice beneath her breast and fastened his teeth on the nipple. Each firm suckling echoed a contraction within her womb and her womanly passage.

He released her nipple, and said, "The dowager told you how to fondle a man until he loses control of himself?"

"Yes." She couldn't think anymore. "To make sure there would be no babies until you and your wife have your own babies, I think she said. She said a mistress must be practiced in such arts."

"That woman will always have the power to amaze me." Making what sounded like a growling noise, Max tossed her skirts over his head and used his tongue to finish what he'd started.

Chapter Twenty-four

Gertrude hadn't struggled against abject adversity throughout her early years without developing enough courage to deal with the likes of the man who glared down at her tonight. She had spent years grooming herself, making enough of herself eventually to entice a doddering old count to bed her, then marry her when he was too drunk to know what he was doing.

The old fool had had money, too, and he left it all to her when he died. He just hadn't had enough money to keep Gertrude as she intended to be kept forever. The opportunity to make sure she never wanted for another thing in her life had finally presented itself, and she would not allow it to slip through her fingers.

She stood in her parlor, ready to go down to the ball. Why had this impressive man chosen this, of all nights, to arrive with his demands?

"You will never speak my name, is that understood?" he said, stopping his pacing for a moment to fix her with a stare that might wither most people. "I know a certain other gentleman came to see you on this matter. He reported back to me, and I had expected the offending material in my hands some time ago. Where is it?"

The countess checked the fastening on her diamond and jet bracelet. "I think you may have forgotten the terms of our agreement, my lord."

"I never forget anything," he told her, bowing his large head slightly. "*You* may have forgotten that I am the man who has brought thousands to their knees on the field of battle. I shall not be intimidated by one greedy woman. Harriette Wilson's nonsense memoirs were one thing. Damn courtesan past her prime. Commonplace enough affairs, so to speak. Publish and be damned was what I told her of her foolishness when she asked for money to keep me out of them. This is another matter. *This* I will not have made public. I demand that you present what you have at once."

"Not possible," she said haughtily, ignoring his reference to the famous courtesan's exposé. "It is locked away and will not change hands until each person mentioned has complied with the terms of the agreement *I* have set forth."

"Damnable luck," the man spat. "He became even more foolish later. When he was king. His affair with Coneyham was evidence of that. But when he was regent, he was bored, and a man like that does poorly if not entertained at all times. If only his letter hadn't become lost among his solicitor's papers. Intended to be presented on the occasion of his death—not years afterward. Damnable inefficiency."

"The letter explaining how he'd kept the Journal of the League of Jolly Gentlemen, you mean?" Gertrude said, enjoying the power she felt. "And how you should continue with the league in his name? So many well-known gentlemen, too. He liked his joke, didn't he? Wanted you all to have to get together and hear your exploits read aloud. My, my. Speaking of needing to be entertained. You certainly like to be entertained, don't you?"

"I'll thank you to keep your speculations to yourself."

"Speculations? You seem to forget. I've seen the journal. Most interesting diagrams. Your Prinny was quite the artist."

Her uninvited guest grew red. "I'm prepared to pay whatever you want."

Gertrude's heart beat faster. Those were the words she wanted to hear. Now, if only that fool Hermoine could get her part of the bargain completed. "Very soon I shall contact you," she told the man. "And we'll arrange an exchange."

"Why not now—tonight?"

"I've already told you. There are others involved. I shall want you all together when the transaction is completed."

"All together, you say? Absolutely not. Never."

"Well, we'll have to see." Gertrude knew when to be less officious.

"Damn Prinny. I had no idea he was keeping his wretched journal. Fool. He always had to play his silly games. And then to allow the thing to be stolen by some street urchin and carted off like that."

"Yes." Gertrude attempted a sympathetic note. "But thanks to myself, you no longer have to worry. It's in a safe place again." She had considered approaching Max Rossmara directly and offering him money for the journal, but had soon changed her mind. He wasn't the kind of man to take part in any scheme designed to extort money from others. And he was unlikely to be amused when he found out that she knew he'd been a pickpocket—and journal thief— in Covent Garden before Viscount Hunsingore came along. And above all she never wanted him to realize she had been the girl who slept with the master of the pickpocket gang. How angry that common man became when he learned Max had been taken away by Viscount Hunsingore. No, she must not arouse any suspicions that she had known Max as a small boy. She must simply pray Hermoine would find a way to get her hands on the journal. Tonight, perhaps. She'd told Hermoine that tonight she was to seduce Max, or suffer consequences she wouldn't like.

"A ball tonight, is it?" her visitor inquired.

"Yes." A delicious thought came to Gertrude. "Please be my guest. A most superior kind of person inhabits this part of Scotland. Do you know the Rossmaras? Or the Dowager Duchess of Franchot, perhaps?"

"I know of them," was the dubious response.

"Then do join us, please."

"I shall consider it," he said. "In any case, I cannot leave until morning. Kindly put suitable quarters at my disposal."

"Why, of course, my lord. And every possible comfort. Do you prefer brunette, redhead, or blonde?"

The man frowned for an instant, then chuckled. "You have audacity, I'll give you that. Arrange for my quarters at once if you please. As to the other, well, we'll see if I encounter a specimen who happens to take my fancy—of any of the varieties you describe."

Chapter Twenty-five

They were announced as Mr. Max Rossmara and Miss Kirsty Mercer. Instantly hundreds of curious eyes turned in their direction and Max didn't fail to note that as many male eyes were fastened on Kirsty as female eyes took stock of him. He'd been successfully fending off the marriageable females from miles around for years and thought little of it. He did not like the way men looked at Kirsty.

What any of them was thinking—male or female—he would prefer not to know.

With Kirsty's hand on his arm, he descended the staircase to the moderate-sized ballroom at The Hallows. By inclining his head to Kirsty and keeping up a stream of near-nonsensical conversation, he made it unnecessary to greet any of the other guests. His plan was to dance every dance with the girl on his arm and to hell with the opinions of others.

"There you are, my boy." His great-grandmother's voice reached him. With its dry quality there was a tone that seemed to echo across the best part of the century the woman had lived. "Max, over here at once. Where have you been? We got here *ages* ago."

He met Blanche's eye, and she winked hugely. Blanche Bastible had improved vastly in the years he'd known her.

"Evening, Great-grandmama," Max said. "You know how the carriages line up for these affairs. You can only wait your turn. You look ravishing. Doesn't she look ravishing, Kirsty?"

Kirsty dropped a graceful curtsy. "Ye're a picture, my lady. Gray suits ye. I've never seen ye wear it before. Your eyes are gray. It's a pretty thing, ye are."

The dowager flipped open her fan and flapped it. "Oh, stop with your flattery both of you. I'm too old to look anything but old in anything I wear. And I don't give a fig about it."

"Ye're a strong-minded woman," Kirsty said. Her comfort with the dowager always surprised Max.

"I certainly am," the old lady said. "You think the color of my gown complements my eyes?"

"Och, I do indeed."

"Hmm. Perhaps I shall have something else made in the same color. Your father has been borne away to talk business somewhere, Max."

"He invariably is." And Max would be amazed to avoid a similar fate for long.

"That son-in-law of mine is very glad of his wounds tonight," Blanche said good-naturedly. "You know how he detests events such as this."

"Especially without Aunt Grace to cheer him," Max remarked. He bent to whisper to the dowager, explaining why Kirsty wasn't wearing the aquamarines. Great-grandmama's expression became inscrutable, but she nodded.

"Oooooh, there you are, Max." Positively rushing through the throng, showing no consideration for those she thrust aside, Lady Hermoine Rashly made a path straight for Max and threw her arms around his neck. "Oh, I cannot tell you how glad I am to see you. I absolutely hate all the fuss of these affairs, but with you at my side I shall bear it. Let me look at you."

He detested her.

The revelation shocked Max. He managed to smile, but felt sickened. She was a strumpet. She wore surprisingly demure clothing and was almost devoid of jewels, yet she was a strumpet nevertheless.

"You are divine, Max, darling. I am the envy of every female present. Don't you agree with me, my lady?"

The dowager grunted.

"I'm sure you do, Kirsty," Hermoine said, and there was a sly meanness in her tone. "You must feel as if you were in a fairy story, Oh, my, where *did* you find that frock. Perhaps I should send for my maid and have her try to find something more suitable among my things."

Silence followed, and Hermoine had the sensibility to color slightly. "Of course," she said hurriedly, "what you're wearing does at least fit relatively well. I shall ask my cousin Horace to dance with you. What do you say to that?"

Kirsty made no attempt to say anything.

Lady Hermoine shook her head until her hair bobbled back and forth. "No, you shall not thank me. I insist upon making sure you have a lovely evening. After all, it's only likely to happen once that you'll be at a ball like this."

Max took solace from the pitying expression on Kirsty's face. She remained silent.

And Lady Hermoine bobbed and bubbled girlishly in a high-necked gown of pale green. Her sleeves were long, with puffs at the elbows, and she wore a single long strand of pearls at her neck.

The woman was a virginal parody.

Max couldn't help but admire a very clever move, but even a nun's habit wouldn't disguise the true nature of Lady Hermoine Rashly.

The odious Horace approached and bowed low to the dowager and to Blanche. Blanche, resplendent in pink, with pink roses decorating every inch that could be decorated, simpered in response to Horace's greeting and appeared ready to swoon when he kissed her hand. Horace immediately asked Blanche to dance. For a moment Max looked at Arran's mother-in-law and saw that she was still a very attractive woman for her age, but a whispered comment from Horace to Hermoine in passing swept away any thought that Horace might find Blanche appealing. Horace said, "You shall owe me for this annoyance, my love," to Hermoine. "I'll expect to collect later. You were wise to take my advice with that gown. Now try to act the innocent—if you can."

Hermoine sniffed and turned her head aside.

"There you are!" Countess Grabham bustled up, her black gown particularly sumptuous this evening, and her jet offset with diamonds. Even the veil she wore was dotted with diamonds. "You are the only people who matter. We are delighted you're here. And little Kirsty from the valley. How charming a gesture to bring her. Enjoy yourself, my dear."

"Thank you, my lady," Kirsty said.

A waltz struck up, and Max turned to Kirsty. "One of the dances you know, I believe," he murmured. Without giving her a chance to refuse, he fastened an arm around her waist and propelled her to the dance floor. There he swept her into his arms and began to dance. At first she tripped over his feet, but soon enough she settled down and her natural grace took over. They circled the floor without speaking. He held her sedately, correctly, and swirled her around and around, delighting in the color that came to her cheeks, and the sparkle in her eyes.

"I am the envy of every man in the room," he said, training his gaze over her head. "Every one of them wishes he could be the one to hold you."

"Hush, Max Rossmara," she told him. "Ye were wrong t'do this. Your great-grandmother won't be pleased."

"I doubt she will." He saw a familiar figure winding a path between revelers, a glass in each hand. "Any more than my handsome devil of a father will be. Aha, he sees us."

"Och, dearie me," Kirsty said, stumbling again. "Ye should take me back and dance with the Lady Hermoine."

Max met his father's eyes briefly before turning with the dance. But that look was long enough for the son to see sympathy in the father's eyes. Struan Rossmara, Viscount Hunsingore, knew what it was to love a woman beyond all reason, and he knew his son loved Kirsty Mercer.

"Max," Kirsty whispered fiercely. "Ye should dance wi' your betrothed."

"What do you think of her dress?" Max said, drawing his darling girl closer.

"It's . . . well, I'm sure it pleases her. Max, please, everyone will look at us."

"Yes, they will. We make a grand couple."

"You're holding me too close."

"I intend to hold you much closer before long."

Her face flamed. "People are watching us," she hissed.

Max pulled her even nearer until he could smell her subtle, summer flower scent and see the glints in her pale hair.

"Max."

"I dinna care," he said, copying her accent. "Ye're a bonnie lassie, and I'll ha' ye for my own, or die."

That silenced her. He saw how she took a great breath and let go of her inhibitions. They whirled and swirled, her gorgeous skirts swinging. Her lips parted, showing the edges of her teeth. The dewy texture of her skin glistened.

When the piece finished he wasn't ready to stop, but did so, holding both of her hands and looking into her eyes.

A smattering of applause startled him, and he looked about. A space had cleared around them, and brilliantly dressed men and women had stood aside to watch. Now they clapped. Max bowed and grinned, and led Kirsty from the floor.

Expecting a tirade from his father and great-grandmother, he guided Kirsty to a chair beside Blanche. "I'll go for some drinks. What will you have, Kirsty?"

She looked at her hands in her lap and shook her head.

This was too much for her. His fault, but what choice had there been? He'd needed a forum for a grand gesture, and this was the best he was likely to get.

"Lemonade it shall be then. Does anyone else need something?"

"Here," the dowager said, pushing a glass into Kirsty's hands. "My granddaughter's husband brought me lemonade, and I can't abide the stuff. Evidently he thinks ancient ladies shouldn't take strong liquor."

That brought a little chuckle from Kirsty.

At last Max could no longer avoid turning to the countess and Lady Hermoine. Both returned his regard with fixed expressions. He smiled. They didn't.

Max glanced about. "Has that cousin of yours absconded with Mrs. Bastible, Hermoine?"

"I think he took her for refreshments," Lady Hermoine said, sending a venomous look in Kirsty's direction. "The next dance is ours, isn't it, Max?"

He frowned deeply, as if trying to remember. "Is it? No, no, it's not, my lady. May I see your card, Kirsty?" When she handed it to him, he opened it and said, "I thought as much. Kirsty must put up with me again."

The orchestra struck up another waltz and he offered Kirsty his hand. She took it, but he didn't miss the misery on her face.

"I shall want to speak to you, Max," his father said, as Max passed him. "The Reverend Pottinger is to be a little late—duties keep him—but when he arrives I shall want to introduce him to Kirsty."

"We do not always achieve what we want to achieve," Max told him before taking Kirsty away.

"Ye are . . ." She blinked rapidly. "I'll say it, if it's right, and it is. Ye are a bad man, Max Rossmara. Ye were the one who told me there was none who would approve of ye and me, yet ye do this in front o' all the important people for miles around."

"I'm dancing with the only person in this room who is important to me. I love you. There's nothing I can do about that, nothing I want to do about it."

"Max, dinna say it."

"You don't love me?"

"Ye know I do. But we've no future but a future o' pain. They'll no' allow us t'be together. Ye've an important place in the world for your family. Important wi' society. I canna be what ye need. We were wrong t'start what we've started. I'll go away, Max. I must go away."

Anger gnawed at him. "You will not leave me. Do you understand?"

"Ye canna make me stay."

"Can't I? We shall see. Where would you go anyway?"

"Ye'll help me. Find me a place in another house where I'm no' known."

"No."

"Please, Max."

"Well, I'm . . . I'm afraid we may be heading for trouble of another nature. Your brother has somehow managed to gain entrance here. How I can't imagine, but I may have to rescue him. He's behind one of the palms near the statue of—I don't know who it is. The one missing an arm."

Kirsty looked wildly about until she sighted Niall. He tried to appear to be tending the palm Max spoke of. Already several guests stared at him, and looked at each other askance.

"What would possess him t'do such a wild thing?" she whispered. "He'll get in terrible trouble."

"We'd best dance in his direction," Max said. "Try to draw as little attention as possible. He's only making sure you're all right, and he can see that you are. I see his smile. What young man who loves his sister could fail to be delighted at seeing her happy. You'd best smile."

"Och, ye're a sly one," she said, but she smiled nevertheless, and tipped back her head when he spun her about. "He'll tell Father and Mother. I canna guess what they'll think. Probably that my soul is claimed for the devil himself."

"I disagree. I think they'll know I choose to show you off in public and that they'll guess the depth of my sincere feelings for you."

The orchestra swelled its efforts, and the dancing became more spirited. More and more dancers took the floor, and Max lost sight of Niall Mercer. When he glimpsed the statue again, the young man was gone. Just as well.

He must brace himself for what would follow when his father took him aside, but he must also brace himself to tell his father how it would be in future. Looking at Kirsty now, he felt only elation, elation and adoration. They had been friends for a long time, and in love a long time. What could be wrong with his wanting her for his wife?

"Kirsty," he said in her ear, "I should like to ask you something."

She clung to him, clearly a little giddy, and looked expectantly into his face.

The music stopped.

Max frowned. The piece wasn't finished.

A drumroll sounded and, amid laughter and whispered conversation, the assembly turned toward the dais.

Countess Grabham stood there, visibly very comfortable and composed before her guests. She clapped her hands, then took a glass of champagne from a tray offered by a servant. "Champagne for all of my friends," she ordered. "This is such a happy night for me."

Max saw Blanche Bastible and Horace Hubble. They were trading sips from the same glass of champagne, and Blanche was giggling. Apparently she had already drunk too much, and the thought made Max furious with Hubble.

"Hurry please," the countess cried. "Champagne for everyone. We're going to drink a very special toast. As you know, I've only been in these parts a year, yet I cannot tell you how much I treasure the kindness you have all shown to me and my wards. And to my niece and my nephew, of course." Holding her glass aloft in both hands, she smiled around.

Nearby Max saw one of the wards the countess mentioned. He didn't know her name, but she was a redhead in a red dress and she gazed adoringly into the rheumy eyes of an elderly, white-haired gentleman in military regalia who swayed at her side and seemed intent on peering down the front of her gown.

"Very well," the countess cried. "Come here, my dearest Hermoine. Come along, come along. Here she comes. Isn't she an angel? Such a lovely, innocent creature, but I cannot keep her for myself forever, so tonight I must be happy to announce her engagement to Max Rossmara, whom you all know and love. Max, I see you there. Come along and let us all raise a glass in a toast to our two lovebirds. Will you also join us Viscount Hunsingore?"

"We're getting out of here," Max whispered. He feared for the countess's health if he remained another moment.

"Go up there," Kirsty said, and she would not move. "Go and allow the people t'drink your health."

"I cannot."

"Do it. Do it, or you'll be the fool in front of everyone. And your family will suffer, too. Go, Max."

"I tell you, I cannot."

"If ye don't, I'll never speak t'ye again."

He saw how pale she was, how the light had gone out of her. She really believed he would accept Lady Hermoine as his wife.

A hand slipped into his, twined fingers with fingers, and he found that he stood beside the very woman he wished he might never encounter again. "Isn't this exciting?" Hermoine said. "The countess has always had a flair for the dramatic. I had no idea she'd planned such an announcement. Smile, darling. Smile so everyone will know how delighted you are."

"Smile," Kirsty murmured. "I'm smiling, and I'll raise a glass. It's for the best, Max. Please."

An excited hush had fallen, but gradually people started to whisper. Kirsty stood a little apart from him, her eyes downcast. Because of him, she was being humiliated. He must get her away from here.

A woman's scream shocked the company to utter silence. Another scream followed, and a man's shout of, "Stop him!"

From the corner of his eye he saw a movement. Kirsty saw it, too. Niall Mercer, his face stark, made his way toward them, and against his thigh he held a knife.

More screams rose, and a swelling buzz of other voices.

Max made to put Kirsty behind him, but she evaded his grasp and all but ran to her brother. She reached him and put her arms around him, and spoke close to his ear. Niall shook his head violently, but Kirsty continued to talk, and Max saw when the young man got his rage under control.

With marked caution, several men began to close in. Max

cried, "Leave them be." Kirsty would never forgive him if he did anything to hurt her brother.

Holding his sister's hand, Niall bowed his head and let her lead him from the room.

"Let them go," Max ordered loudly. "I'll deal with him outside." He made a motion to follow, but the company had quickly lost interest in a peasant intruder and closed in about him and Lady Hermoine.

While the drums rolled again, they stood together, Hermoine gripping his hand so hard his fingers hurt. He strained to see Kirsty and Niall, but they must already have left the ballroom.

"You will not come to me, so I must come to you," the countess shrieked, breaking from the crowd into the space that had formed around Max and Hermoine. Max's father arrived at almost the same time, and there was nothing but concern in Viscount Hunsingore's eyes. The countess loudly announced, "Let us drink to the health of the future Mr. Max Rossmara and Lady Hermoine Rossmara."

Chapter Twenty-six

"Niall, stop! Stop, now. Where are we going?"

The instant they had fled the ballroom, with its loud buzz of excited conversation, it had been Niall who assumed the lead, rushing Kirsty down the front steps of The Hallows and around to the side of the house, to a stand of pines. They hurried into the cover of the trees, and she recognized the small mare Max had given her to ride.

She saw at once that the animal wore a bridle, but no saddle. "Niall, will ye speak t'me, please. This is no' the answer t'anythin'."

"It's the answer t'gettin' ye away from that villain. He'll pay. I'll make sure he pays for the terrible thing he did t'ye in there. Makin' ye a spectacle so they all watched ye dance. Then lettin' ye be set aside."

"He didn't do anythin'. Circumstances couldna be controlled."

"He's a voice. An' legs. He could ha' turned away from them all. But he's one o' them, and they cling t'their own."

"He was as confused as I was. As confused as ye are. And now ye've made the bigger fool o' me. I should ha' stood my ground wi' my head high. Now they all think I'm pinin' and runnin' away."

Niall gripped her waist, and she struggled. "We canna ride like this, w'out a saddle." He ignored her and with no concern for her beautiful gown, plunked her on the horse's bare back. He scrambled up behind her, and Kirsty was certain his boots must drag the ground. He breathed in rasping sobs, and she felt how shudders passed through him.

"On wi' ye, foolish creature," he told the mare, jerking and flailing his feet. "On wi' ye, I say."

The animal trotted forward and Kirsty could see Niall's feet flying high and driving back against its flanks. As far as she knew, he'd never ridden before; he'd certainly not had the benefit of careful instruction from Max.

She would not cry.

How could she ever have imagined that the end of their tale would be any different? Now was the time to go onward and make the best of whatever came her way.

In the trees, darkness was almost absolute. When they emerged to open ground there was but a little more light. The moon hid behind layers of cloud and gradually grew more dim. Kirsty smelled an approaching storm.

"Damn them all," Niall railed. "I'll kill them, for this."

His boots rose and fell, and despite the weight of the inexperienced riders on her back, the mare made a valiant attempt at more speed.

Fear gripped Kirsty's throat. Her young brother wasn't himself. His impotent anger had overcome his reason.

She could tell they headed north. "Niall, will ye listen t'me, please?"

"I'll no' listen to a foolish wench wi' no sense. Moonin' after a man who wants ye for nothin' but a boon t'his lust. I'll kill him for it, I tell ye."

"Ye're no' yoursel'," she told him, grappling to wrench the reins from him. "Let me, Niall, before ye murder the horse and kill the two o' us."

He was too strong for her. "I'm takin' ye where he'll no' find ye."

"Where's that?" she asked, her heart pounding.

"I'm takin' ye there, then I'm away back t'kill him."

For the first time since they'd left The Hallows, Kirsty felt mortally afraid. "If ye kill him, ye'll kill me," she told him.

"Ye'll get over him," Niall said. He coughed, and coughed, and fought to catch his breath. "Ye'll meet one o' your own and forget Rossmara. Please God, help me do what I must do."

Riding sidesaddle—minus the saddle—Kirsty squirmed within her brother's arms. "I want ye t'let me down, Niall. Ye're frightenin' me."

He took a hand off the reins and forced her back into position.

Dutifully doing what her rider seemed to want, the mare veered to the right. Niall cursed and gained his full grip on the reins again.

"*Where* are we going?" Kirsty cried, clutching Niall's sleeves. "Please tell me, Niall."

"I canna."

"Why?"

"Because ye'd fight me the harder if I did."

There was only one place they'd go, Max thought, home to their parents.

"Come back," Struan said, striding behind him past stalls in the Kirkcaldy stables. Horses shifted and nickered on both sides of them. "You've insulted the countess and Lady Hermoine. We should go back and beg forgiveness—plead a case of the nerves. Anything." They'd returned to the castle in the same carriage. All the way Max had listened to his father's pleas for "common sense."

"The countess was warned not to announce a betrothal to which I had not agreed. She thought that if she announced it in a public forum, I would bend. She was wrong."

"The countess is a foolish woman. But the fault is as much yours."

"How so?" Max entered the tack room and hefted down his saddle.

His father reached for another saddle. "You flaunted your feelings for Kirsty Mercer in front of everyone. You danced like a man possessed and drew the attention of everyone in the room."

"You don't need a saddle," Max said. "You'd best go back to the lodge and get some rest. I expect we'll be besieged with visitors from The Hallows come morning. We shall all need our wits about us."

"I'm coming with you. Regardless of the decisions I'd rather see you make, you are my son, and I stand with you."

Max faced his father. "No. No, you are not coming with me. Thank you, but I know what I have to do, and I'll do it alone. It cannot be done in any other manner."

"I should like to be at your side."

His father meant what he said, Max would never question that. "Knowing that you want the best for me will give me strength. But if you were in my shoes, you would not do this differently."

Struan, Viscount Hunsingore, replaced the saddle and faced Max, his almost black eyes inscrutable. "You're right. I would not do it differently. I would have fought dragons for your mother—and I would have accepted no man's help. But I ask you one last time to reconsider."

Max carried his tack to his horse and saddled him.

"Max?"

"No. And if you could be honest, you would admit that you wouldn't respect me if I did reconsider."

His father laughed, a hollow sound. He said, "You have me there. I fear for you, but I applaud you. Even if I could turn my back on you, your mother would never forgive me. I assure you I have no intention of risking such an unspeakable fate."

Max mounted and turned the Thoroughbred toward the yard. "Trust me to do what is right."

Looking up at Max, his father told him, "God go with you, my son."

Clouds finally snuffed out the moon completely, and within minutes the first large raindrops fell.

"Where are we going?" Kirsty asked yet again. Niall had been silent for a long time while the mare made slower and slower progress in a northerly direction. "Please answer me. It grows so late, and I dinna know where we are. I'm scared, Niall. Please listen t'me."

He urged the horse onward.

Soon the raindrops fell faster and thicker. A wind picked up and drove the rain sideways to cut through the flimsy stuff of Kirsty's bodice. Her voluminous skirts began to sag and cling to her limbs. They'd traveled perhaps two hours, but Kirsty didn't think they'd covered much ground.

"I will kill him," Niall muttered.

Kirsty shook her head and wiped rain from her face. "Ye aren't yoursel'. And ye are wrong-headed. Max hasna done anythin' t'hurt me. I've made my own decisions. He's no' forced me at all."

"If he hadn't spread his enticin' promises before ye like gold before a beggar, ye'd be at home wi' all o' us yet."

"Where are we going?" Kirsty came close to screaming at Niall. "Ye must know."

He pulled the horse to a halt.

Kirsty tried to see something familiar. There was nothing. She was drenched now, and chilled. "Niall—"

"I dinna know, I tell ye," he said, his voice breaking. "I dinna know where we are, or where we're goin' except t'the north and the sea, where I've always heard it said a man can earn his way fishin'. All I know for certain is that we've got to be away from this place. We've got t'be where I can do for ye what he wouldna. I'll work and make a place for ye, and ye'll never know want or shame again. And I'll find a way t'let our parents know we're all right."

With a heart that swelled with sadness, Kirsty caught her brother's dripping hands and brought them to her cheek. From when he was a wee laddie he'd talked about fishing in the north. She kissed his big knuckles, and said, "Ye're the best brother a girl ever had. Please God we can get us safely out of this place." Then she'd concern herself with trying to put things right for both of them.

A sound reached Kirsty, a sound that terrified her much more than not knowing where they were.

"Someone's coming," she cried to Niall. "Following us. How can that be?"

Hoofbeats, at first distant but rapidly growing closer, warned that a rider approached at high speed.

Niall drove his heels into the mare's sides. She whinnied, but didn't move.

"Hold still," Niall said into Kirsty's ear. "Mayhap he's just passin' this way and he'll no' see us."

"The lone horseman, d'ye think?" Kirsty asked, her heart thudding so hard she opened her mouth to breathe and try to quiet herself.

The man on the other horse wasn't just passing this way, or if he was, he'd sighted them. Kirsty strained to see around Niall as a big beast bore down on them, its rider bent over its neck.

"Kirsty? Kirsty, is that you?"

"Go back, Max," she shouted the instant she heard his voice. "Turn about. I don't need your help!" Then, more quietly to her brother, she used a calming voice. "It's all right, Niall. I've told him t'go, see. We'll no' worry about what he's in his mind. We'll just wait for him t'leave again. Don't say anythin' or do anythin'." She knew she babbled but couldn't stop the tumble of words.

Niall's response was to leap from the mare's back and stand close to her head. "Ye're the one t'say nothin'," he said to Kirsty. "Leave it all t'me."

The night became a frantic blur of rain and flying mud, of angry voices and the spatter of lather from the powerful beast Max rode. Kirsty put her hands over her ears and fought down the panic that gripped her stomach and pummeled her temples. Niall was no match for Max. He had his knife, but Max might well have armed himself with a pistol.

"Ye had t'follow," Niall said in as close a thing to a sneer as Kirsty had ever heard from him. "Ye couldna just let her go, even though ye've torn her good name apart in front o' the whole countryside."

"I want you to be silent, cub," Max said, jumping to the ground. "And be grateful if I don't thrash you for bringing Kirsty out in this. If she sickens, God help you."

"How did ye find us?" Niall said, his voice different, distant. "Ye couldn't know we'd made it away, so how did ye come here?"

"I owe you no explanation. But you weren't at your parents' home, and Robert told me you'd always spoken of the north and making money fishing. Then I discovered the mare was gone. The rest was luck, luck that I chose the right path, in this direction first, and luck that the mare couldn't possibly carry two people far."

He pushed Niall aside and reached to take Kirsty from the animal.

"Ye'll no' touch her again," Niall shouted. "Take your filthy hands off her now."

Max's fingers closed about her waist and he lifted her into his arms.

Niall seemed to dance before them. He spread his arms and bellowed his rage and his disbelief.

With fury a silent force that Kirsty felt in his hard body, Max carried her, and set her upon his own mount. "Your parents are beside themselves with worry over both of you," he said, and Kirsty's heart soared. "I had to stop Robert from coming with me. They want to know you're safe." He flung the reins across the horse's neck and put a boot in the stirrup.

"What the blazes?" He flailed and swayed backward as Niall grabbed him. "Damn you, Mercer, for the fool you are. Let go, d'you hear me? *Let go.*"

Laughter, Niall's hysterical, scaling laughter, caused Kirsty to come close to vomiting. She gulped air and began to slide from the horse. Despite her efforts to steady herself, she failed and landed on her hands and knees in rock-strewn mud.

Cries rent the soaked night. Niall's broken yells that verged on screams, and Max's shouts for his assailant to come to his senses. The two hit the ground together.

"Stop it!" Kirsty drew up her skirts and circled the

squirming mass of arms and legs. "Stop it, I tell you. Get up. Please, get up."

"I'm going to kill you," Niall promised Max.

The flash Kirsty saw fulfilled her nightmare. Niall had managed to draw his knife. Max grabbed for Niall's wrist and held the knife hand above his head. Niall was strong, stronger than Kirsty had known, and with the righteous anger that drove him, he was stronger yet.

The two men rolled over, and over again. Niall rose on top. With his left hand he found Max's throat and squeezed while he struggled to wrest his right wrist free.

Max made a gurgling sound.

"Let him go," Kirsty screamed. "Niall, let him go." She made a dash at her brother, but even in the madness he saw her coming, and kicked at her. He kicked her hip and sent her sprawling, the wind knocked from her. Pain burst from the blow.

"Niall—"

Again they rolled over, and Niall lost his hold on Max's throat. Slowly, but surely, Max forced his foe's knife hand toward his body. Kirsty saw when the point of the blade turned toward her brother's chest, saw when it inched down, down, and came to rest there.

She could do nothing. She could not even cry out. With rain beating into her face, she stood with her arms hanging at her sides. Feeling receded from her limbs, and from her brain.

"Drop it," Max said, loudly, but evenly. "You have no cause to make trouble with me, Niall Mercer. I have always been your friend, your family's friend. Drop the knife."

Kirsty took a shaky breath, and said, "Do as he says, Niall. Quickly." Except for the glint of his eyes, she couldn't see her brother's face. "Do it!"

"Drop it," Max repeated, shaking the other's wrist.

"Aye," Niall said quietly. "Aye. All right. I give up."

Relief brought Kirsty to her knees and she knelt, hearing the squelch of mud, feeling it seep through her skirts, but caring for nothing but that the horror would be over. She murmured, "Thank God ye see reason."

Max got to his feet and offered Niall a hand. He refused it and stood up alone—and rushed Max, the knife held high and poised to strike.

They struggled, each grappling to gain a hold on the other. Once more Max took Niall's wrist in his strong hand and shook, and shook, trying to knock the knife loose.

Desolate, Kirsty hunched over, not caring that she was drenched and covered with slimy earth.

Max's cry brought her head up. He was wounded, but she didn't know where, or how badly until he forced Niall closer to her and she saw a gash that had opened his jaw. Blood poured from the wound.

"Die!" Niall shrieked. "How many times do I have to cut ye t'kill ye?"

"Like you cut me in my rooms at the castle, you mean." Max's words came in gasps.

"I should have waited for ye to sleep. I'd have had ye then."

Locked in mortal combat, they swung around, and Kirsty saw the moment when Max tore the knife from her brother's hand. "What were you searching for in my rooms?" Max asked.

"Nothin'," Niall said. "I didna touch ye're rooms. Ye've nothin' I'd want except what ye've no right to—my sister. I saw the other one, the one who threw the books down."

Max's blood soaked the front of his linen. He'd soon grow weak.

"Please, Niall, if ye love me, let him go," Kirsty pleaded.

"So that he can stab me."

"He'd no' do that." Not as Niall had done.

But Niall didn't let go. Instead he continued to fight, until the inevitable occurred and Max's superior strength won out. Niall stumbled, and Max cut him. It was a deliberate cut to the arm, not meant to kill, but to wound and incapacitate.

Instantly Niall clamped the opposite hand over the torn flesh and bowed his head. For moments he just stood there, bleeding through his fingers.

"It's over," Kirsty said, desperately casting about for how she should get them back and cared for. "I'll dress your wounds." She hauled up her skirts and began to strip lengths from her petticoats.

Max's next yell was the most desperate he'd made and her head jerked up to see him flying backward, arms and legs outstretched, directly under the hooves of his horse. Niall was bent over, his shoulder lowered as he must have used it to thrust Max at the Thoroughbred.

Kirsty ran at the horse. If she could grab its reins and drag it away, Max would be safe. Even as she ran, she knew she would never be in time.

Max hit the ground and the beast skittered sideways, dancing nervously. One powerful leg rose and in that second she saw the hoof aimed at Max's head.

She closed her eyes and covered her face.

"Away wi' ye," she heard Niall cry. "Dinna interfere where it's no' your affair."

Kirsty dared to look and was in time to see another horse and rider that had arrived unnoticed amid the noise and flurry. The man had caught the reins of Max's horse in time to drag it away, in time to make that deadly hoof barely miss Max's skull.

Niall made another rush at Max, but this time he didn't go far. The stranger leaned down to catch his collar and knock him off-balance. Pulled backward by the newly arrived and powerful horse, Niall staggered and almost fell before he was thrown against the mare.

"On with you," a very cultured voice said. "Mount her

now and make your way from here as fast as you can. If you want to be alive in the morning."

"I'll no' leave my sister," Niall said, but the fight was gone from his voice.

"I will not tell you a second time," the newcomer said. "Your sister shall come to no harm. You have my word as a gentleman."

Niall opened his mouth to protest, but caught sight of Max's slitted eyes as he advanced down on him, and pulled himself onto the mare's back instead. Momentarily confused, he turned in all directions before heading off, not north, but south and toward home.

Shaking, beyond attempting to control her limbs, Kirsty collapsed on the ground and bowed her head.

"You'd best tend to your lady," the stranger said. "And yourself. I'll bid you good night."

"Don't go," Max said. "I know you, don't I?"

"I must leave you now."

"Who are you?" Max cried. "Tell me your name and where you live, so that I may come and thank you formally for your aid."

"It was nothing."

"It was everything. Had you not arrived, I might be dead beneath my horse's hooves by now."

"Get yourself and your lady home," was the reply. "I only did what had to be done." With that he wheeled his mount and urged him into a gallop. He made a generally northward progress but was soon enveloped in rain and mist and no longer visible.

Kirsty hadn't the strength to care for Max's wound as she knew she should.

"Darling girl," he murmured, crouching beside her. "My coat isn't dry, but it will shield you from the wind." He took off his coat and wrapped it around her.

"Ye've lost a deal o' blood," she told him. "We must get

ye t'help. Your father would want t'look over your care, so it's t'the lodge we'll go."

He laughed, but without his usual abandon. "Always in charge, even when you can scarcely move. Oh, my love, my love, I think I could happily lie here with you in my arms and wait for someone to find us. I'm so tired."

"And what if we're dead when they find us?"

He pushed back the heavy wet strands of hair that streaked her face and kissed her brow. "At least we'd be together," he murmured.

"Och, ye've been readin' Mr. Shakespeare again."

He drew back to study her face. "You amaze me, amaze me wonderfully. We are at a pretty pass yet you do not break."

"I'm broken, Max, but it's where ye canna see."

A great blast of wind tore at them. Lightning tore through the heavens. "You don't have to be broken anymore," Max told her, "unless you don't think you could stand a man who will doubtless have an ugly scar forever."

"Lady Avenall's husband has terrible scars from fightin' in those foreign wars. She loves him. Maybe more than if he wasna scarred at all. A woman in love doesna care about such things."

"And you're a woman in love?" he said softly.

She nodded. "Oh, yes, I'm a woman verra much in love. I always will be. Ye took my heart when ye were a gangly, redheaded laddie, and ye never gave it back t'me."

He gathered her in his arms. "Well, I'd never have confessed as much then, but it was at just about that time that I decided you weren't as silly as other females. I saw from the start that you had promise."

She said, "Hah. Well, that's good o' ye. I want t'get that face tended before all your blood seeps away into the mud."

"It's slowing down already. Concentrate on this important conversation we're having."

Oh, she was concentrating. Bittersweet words she would never forget.

"You're a woman in love," Max said softly, and kissed her lips with lingering passion. "And I'm a man in love. I love you more than my life, Kirsty Mercer."

"Do ye?"

"If I didn't, I wouldn't have followed you and Niall, knowing he blames me for destroying the family he so loves. He blames and hates me. It won't be easy to overcome that, but we'll manage."

She was cold and the cold struck inward. "Ye need your coat yoursel'." When she made to take it off, he stopped her.

"You do want to spend your life with me, don't you, Kirsty? I'm not being presumptuous to think that?"

"You're no' bein' presumptuous."

"It would make you happy to be my wife and to have my children?"

Her heart seemed to stop. "Please don't. I canna bear it."

"It would make you happy?" he pressed.

"Happier than I know how t'say."

"I want to see you holding our babies. I've never particularly cared about such things, but I do now."

"It comes to all men of position. Ye all need your heirs."

"No . . ." He broke off and raised her chin. His mouth descended on hers. He held the collar of his coat close around her neck and kissed her deeply. When he broke the contact, he barely parted his lips from hers and whispered, "Be mine, Kirsty. Forever. Say you'll be my wife."

The cold in her body intensified. Her hands and feet had lost all feeling—not so her heart, or her head.

"Is it a question that requires you to think long and hard?" He sounded playful. "I'd hoped for a speedy answer."

She looked into his eyes, into their glittering depths. He was all she could ever hope for, all she could ever want. She would never want another.

"Kirsty, I'm on my knees." He held both of her hands. "Will you do me the honor of becoming my wife?"

Finally the thunder rolled in the distance, grumbled among the clouds until it clapped hard and angry.

"Kirsty?"

"Max—" She smiled at him. "Thank ye. I'm honored, but, no. No, I can never be your wife."

Chapter Twenty-seven

The marquess poked his head into the breakfast room and said, "How are we this morning?"

"I'm much better than I was yesterday morning, thank ye, my lord," Kirsty said. "I'm rested now." Not true, but she mustn't show how exhausted and troubled she was. After she'd refused Max's offer of marriage in the early hours of the previous morning, they'd returned to the castle and parted in silence. She hadn't seen him again since then.

The marquess came into the room and poured himself coffee. This he brought to the table. Then he returned to the sideboard and lifted several covers to examine the contents of the dishes. "Kippers," he said, and placed two on a plate. "Never could resist a good kipper." To the fish was added eggs Kirsty knew to be cold. She also knew the marquess had already breakfasted. Wilkie had been clearing his master's dishes when Kirsty arrived.

Arran joined her at the table, smiling more than she'd ever seen him smile. Each time she glanced at him he smiled. "You were somewhat the worse for wear yesterday?" he said finally. The kippers and cold eggs began to disappear as if they were delicious.

"I'd had a difficult night," she said, referring to the ball and all that followed. "I'm grateful to bear no lasting ill from being so cold and wet."

"Too bad young Max bears a lasting ill—from whatever."

She raised her eyes to his.

The marquess looked away.

"Sad," he said, "very sad."

Kirsty waited.

"I expect my brother has spoken to you about it all."

"I've no' seen the viscount. What's wrong wi' Max—wi' Mr. Rossmara? Did he take a chill? Is there some new problem with the wound?"

The marquess sighed. "No, no. The wound will heal well enough. It'll probably make him an even more handsome devil in the eyes of some females. And he shows no sign of a chill. Strong as they come, Max. No, but he's pining. He hasn't had a word to say to a soul since the night of the ball and that mysterious—whatever—that happened to the two of you."

"Not a word?" Kirsty asked, frowning.

"Not one."

"Even when he's spoken to?"

"Especially then. He gets violent if anyone tries to converse with him."

She knitted her brows. When he'd returned her to the castle, he'd turned about at once and left without a word, but he'd gone in the direction of the lodge where his parents made their home.

"He shouldn't drink."

Kirsty looked sharply at the marquess. "Drink?"

"Drink."

"Strong liquor?"

"The strongest."

She struggled with the desire to say what she thought of men who turned to strong liquor in moments of frustration because they couldn't have their own way. "He'll come t'bless me for it," she muttered.

"What did you say?" the Marquess of Stonehaven asked loudly.

She regarded him squarely. "I said he'll come t'bless me for it." Best be direct. Her parents had taught her that.

"Bless you for refusing to be his wife, you mean?"

Kirsty's mouth fell open. The only way he could have known such a thing was because he'd heard it from Max's own lips.

"There you are, Struan." The marquess greeted his brother with cheer so great that Kirsty guessed he was not pleased with his own efforts at nonchalant questioning. "Kirsty and I were just talking about that son of yours and how poorly he's doing. Won't get out of his bed. Refuses to eat. Won't even speak now. And he got so drunk yesterday, he all but died from the sickness he caused."

"Is that what you were talking about?" Struan said, pouring coffee and piling a plate with a mountain of toast. "I hope you haven't said anything to worry her. After all, I suppose it's not her concern whether he lives or dies."

Kirsty didn't know whether to be afraid—or furious. "Is there word of my brother, my lord?"

"Yes," Struan said, appearing puzzled. "Your parents sent word. I almost forgot."

"You did forget," Arran pointed out mildly.

"All right, I did forget. I'm sorry. I've a good deal on my mind. Max downing enough brandy for an army and getting delirious. Only name on his lips was yours, Kirsty."

"You did forget about her brother," the marquess said. "You know. Word from her parents."

"What?" The viscount blinked, then nodded. "Niall's well. That was the message, not that I knew he'd been ill—

not like Max. I thought he'd poison himself with the drink. It can be an illness you know. The drinking."

"I do know," Kirsty said, not amused. "He promised me he had no reason to drink and that he wouldn't anymore."

The pile of toast before the viscount diminished steadily. He said, "I imagine that was before you turned him down." Kirsty had been told that both of these men had already breakfasted—together.

"Is Mr. Rossmara drunk now?"

"Oh, no!" Struan shook his head emphatically. "Not a bit of it. And if he thought he had something to live for, I doubt he'd touch another drop. He told me he believes it's like poison to him and that he doesn't think of the stuff unless he's desperate and convinced his life is over."

"Did he ask ye t'tell me this?"

"No!" the marquess and the viscount exclaimed together.

Showing no sign of embarrassment, Struan said, "He'd never forgive us for coming to you. You won't tell him we did, though. I know we can trust you on that. But I also know it would be a great boon to him if you could find it in your heart to go to the lodge and tell him you care for him— even the smallest amount."

She folded her hands in her lap and sat very straight. "I love him more than my own life. I freely admit that to ye. But I'll no' be tellin' it to Mr. Rossmara. We've t'put any such feelings behind us."

Struan frowned and seemed uncomfortable. "Please go and have a few words with him. Congratulate him on the birth of his sister and brother-in-law's second son, perhaps. They've a daughter and two sons now, y'know."

She hadn't known Ella had been delivered of her latest child. "I'm verra glad for them, and I look forward t'seein' the new bairn." The twist deep inside her was something she must ignore. Wanting to bear Max's children was a futile longing that could never be fulfilled. "No doubt Mr. Ross-mara's pleased, too."

"No doubt," said Arran, "not that he's said a word one way or the other, and you know how much he adores Ella."

"She's coming home as soon as she's strong enough," Struan told Kirsty. "Ella doesn't believe in long lying-in periods, you know. Says she's too strong and too anxious to be about her business for that." His smile was smug, but quickly disappeared. "Please go to Max."

"How can ye beg me t'do it?" she said. "Y'know as well as I do that there's no' a future for us."

"You are so rational," Arran said. "Perhaps too rational. You understand exactly what our problems are, but for now we must put Max's welfare first. He needs to see you. By the by, I don't know how I should manage without you as long as Max decides to hide himself away. I understand you were even at your desk yesterday afternoon."

"There's work t'be done," she told him, but she was distracted. "That doesn't stop for anyone's personal dilemmas. Mr. Rossmara should no' be so selfish that he neglects his duties, either. What exactly are your problems, my lord? The ones I understand?"

"Why," Struan said, grimacing over his cold coffee, "you've just explained them very well, really. Although we understand how it is to be in love, there are times when one must put duty first."

Kirsty wasn't sure what he meant, or what he was asking of her.

"We want you to go to him," Arran said. "Go to him and tell him you won't leave. He seems to think you will go away."

"I won't." She never could.

"Exactly what Struan and I have told him. But he needs to hear it from you, just as he needs to hear from you the reason you turned down his proposal."

She felt her cheeks turn red.

The viscount leaned toward her. "Why did you turn him down, Kirsty?"

With a heavy heart she said, "Because I fear that in the end I'd no' be the wife he needs. I couldna bear it if he came t'hate me one day."

Struan's gaze became piercing and the lines around his mouth deepened. "Hate you?" he said. "He'd never hate you. But I don't know the answer to our dilemma, do you?"

Kirsty had no idea how she was expected to answer such a question.

"Do we press him to do what will be best for family standing?" asked Struan. "Or do we toss that to the wind and support whatever decision he makes?"

"I think," Arran said quietly, "that we pray Max's decision is the right one—for everyone concerned."

His father had insisted that the latest wisdom about turning a man off drink was to make him feel sick at the sight of the stuff. Well, Max thought, he already felt sick at the sight of it. The row of brandy bottles glowing in the sunlight that hit the mantel in his old room was an excessive punishment to his stomach—and to his head.

He hadn't slept here in years. The bed was big enough because he'd grown tall when he was quite young and his parents had installed a large four-poster. The foolish playthings of his youth were in the adjoining room, thank God. At least he didn't have to look at them all and possibly sink into some maudlin depression over his lost childhood. In his present frame of mind, that would be quite likely.

Please, if only he could sleep, and die in that sleep, he need never again face the fact that Kirsty had refused to be his wife.

Lying flat upon the bed, he closed his eyes and willed that endless sleep to come.

The drink was responsible. Once he started drinking, he didn't want to stop. If he paused in pouring the liquor into himself, the fading of the blessed numbness reminded him to remedy the matter.

He should never drink.

With Kirsty at his side, he could conquer the urge. She'd help him, just as father was determined to help him. They'd all help him.

But she wasn't at his side and never would be.

"May I come in, Max dearest?"

For a delightful instant he was able to convince himself that he'd only imagined Lady Hermoine's voice, but then she loomed over him and settled a gloved hand on his brow.

"How the hell—" He closed his mouth without finishing the sentence. What did he care if she was too self-involved to remember to remove her glove before ascertaining if he was fevered.

"I know you don't want me here," she said in very sub-dued tones. "I accept that you do not care even the smallest amount for me, but I beg you to allow me to care for you."

This was his punishment for the excess of liquor.

"I ask your forgiveness, Max. I have been selfish, and too concerned with myself. I have not taken the time to note that you are a deeply troubled man who needs a woman to wait on his every whim. Oh, how I regret my shortcomings."

She must go away.

She must stay away.

She must never return.

"If you would speak just one kind word to me, I should hug it to my bosom for the rest of my life. And I shall need it in the nunnery."

The corners of his mouth twitched, but he managed not to laugh.

"I have decided upon a contemplative order," she said. "I shall be locked away from the world and condemned never to speak again. But I shall have the satisfaction of giving my prayers to the world. And all of my prayers, every single one for as long as I live, shall be for you, dear Max."

"I thought you just said you were going to give your prayers to the world."

Confusion clouded her golden eyes. "Did I?"

"Yes."

"Well, I meant that by praying for you, I should be praying for the world because you are a boon to the world, and with my prayers you will be even more of a boon."

"Kind of you," he said, closing his eyes.

"You rest. I'll just sit here and watch over you."

"Very useful," he muttered, then added, "I'm going to sleep, and I prefer to sleep alone." The latter part of the statement was a misfortune, but he could hope she wouldn't notice.

"Oh, I don't think that's quite true," she said, her voice turning plummy with innuendo.

She'd noticed.

Max kept his eyes shut and affected even breathing.

Minutes passed.

Not a sound.

He raised his eyelids the merest fraction and peered through his lowered lashes.

Lady Hermoine watched him intently. She watched, her own eyes narrowed, her mouth pinched, and when she seemed convinced he was asleep, she turned and left the room on tiptoe. Max smiled to himself, but the smile faded soon enough. Subdued sounds came from the other room.

He opened his eyes and listened. Small scrapings and rattlings, as if items were being moved around while whoever moved them attempted not to be heard.

With the deepest gratitude for the excellent structure of his bed, Max eased his feet from beneath the covers, and to the floor. Wearing a nightshirt he'd never seen before and had no recollection of putting on, he crept to the door and peered through a crack into what had at first been his playroom, then his schoolroom.

Lady Hermoine had discarded her gloves for the task presently in progress. And she'd pushed up her sleeves, and hiked up her skirts to tie them in a large, clumsy knot that left her very nice ankles free of encumbrance.

She was about the business of going through his old books. One by one she took them from the shelves, flipped them open, and returned them. From his side view of her he could see that her face was flushed and angry. She turned from the books to a large chest containing toys and squinted to see into it, angling her head first one way, then another— evidently afraid to touch the contents for fear of awakening the man she would spend the rest of her life praying for.

"Can I help you find something, my lady?" he asked mildly.

She jumped and clasped both hands over her heart. "Don't creep up on me like that," she snapped, gasping for breath. Then she said, "Oh, oh, dear, you shocked me, dear Max. I thought you were asleep."

"Evidently."

"I was looking at the things of your childhood, dearest."

"So I noticed."

She waved a hand toward the chest. "Such a poignant thing—putting one's hand on the very toys your little hands touched." She closed her hand and appeared deeply pained. "Ah, well, forgive me for disturbing you, my sweet. Go back to bed. I must leave now."

"Good-bye."

"Yes. Such a sweet sorry—to part."

He noted the unfortunate play upon verse but chose not to mention it. "There is much that is sorry, I find."

"Indeed." She backed from the room. "I shall hope to see

you very soon, my love. Meanwhile, take comfort in know-ing I shall be praying for you."

And he would be praying for her—to be very far away from him.

To remain in bed any longer was pure self-indulgence. He could lie there until he turned to stone—lie and try to will Kirsty to come to him—and accomplish nothing at all.

Morning had turned to afternoon. He'd refused lunch—brought by Mairi, who had undoubtedly been summoned to the lodge by his father, and sent to Max as a trustworthy spy upon his physical condition, and his frame of mind.

A rapping at the door startled him, but not as much as the sight of Horace Hubble's florid, plump-lipped face preced-ing that gentleman by inches into the bedchamber. "All right if I come in, old chap?" he asked.

To feign sleep now would be pointless, since their eyes had already met. "Briefly," Max said. "I'm exceedingly tired."

"'Course you are. Understand you had quite a scare." He jutted his chin and lowered his head to look at the gash on Max's jaw. "I say, ugly thing, that. Little bit lower and you'd have been able to smile with your throat, don't you know. Dead as a doornail, you'd have been. Bled like a calf for veal. I say, very nasty."

"Thank you for your evaluation," Max said. He had seen his wound and couldn't summon enough interest to care how bad it looked. "Lady Hermoine didn't seem to notice I'd almost had my face cut off."

"Oh, I say." Horace delicately touched a handkerchief to the corners of his mouth. "Let's not overdo, old chap. Sick-enin' and all that."

"I expect you had a reason for coming—other than to as-sure yourself of my good health. I'm very healthy, by the way. I'm simply resting."

"Quite so. I came about my poor cousin, Hermoine."

Max waited for what might come next.

"Word spreads, y'know," Horace said, raising his pale brows. "It's all over the country by now—England as well. Ireland, too, I shouldn't be surprised."

"Word spreads," Max repeated slowly. "That's true."

"I'm glad you agree," Horace said rapidly. "So I suggest we get down to it, man to man. Settle a price on things and be done with it."

"Settle a price?"

"On my dear, innocent little cousin's humiliation before the world."

"Ah," Max said. "I thought we were only speaking of Scotland, England, and Ireland."

"And Wales, of course," Horace said. "She'll need to be very well set up if she's to attract a man who can keep us— keep her as she should be kept, but who won't care about the gossip."

"If she's that well set up, surely she won't need to worry about any particular man."

Horace took a backward step. "What are you suggestin'? Hermoine wants to be married, to have children, to raise a happy family. She wishes to dedicate herself to that family. But unfortunately, and you know this to be true, a girl cannot attract the *right* kind of man unless she is well set up. I know you will want to make sure that she *is* well set up—to make amends for the shameful way in which you have disappointed her—*publicly*."

"Well." Max frowned so deeply he was forced to blink or cease to see at all. "I should certainly have wished to do exactly what you suggest, but Lady Hermoine, bless her dear, pious heart, has already visited me."

"What?" Horace looked around the room as if expecting to see his cousin hiding behind a piece of furniture. "That hussy beat me—I mean, she was already here?"

"Oh, yes." Max folded his hands one on top of the other on the sheet over his chest. "Didn't she inform you of her plans?"

Horace studied him with deepest suspicion. "What plans?"

"Why, to withdraw from the world of sinful men, of course. To enter a nunnery, where she will spend the rest of her life praying for me."

The man stood there, staring, for so long that Max rose to his elbows for a closer look, unsure that Horace hadn't died of shock but failed to fall over in the process.

Then, without so much as a farewell, he walked out.

Max fell back on his pillows and grinned at the canopy over his bed. Miserable he might be, but he could still take pleasure in watching a useless popinjay foiled.

Kirsty was bound to come soon. Mairi had checked on him again and had been unable to resist telling him, "Miss Kirsty's a sad one, sir. She's grievin' over ye."

Something scraped in the other room.

Max rose to his elbows again and listened.

Soft, sliding sounds, as if someone searched very carefully out there, trying to make no sound.

Gritting his teeth, wincing at the soreness along his jaw, and in a great many other places, Max left his bed and went to a spot where he could see through a crack at the doorway.

With his knees slightly bent as if ready for flight, Horace Hubble slowly examined volumes from the bookshelves. From time to time he reached behind a row of books and felt around, then withdrew his hand and executed a noiseless tantrum in which he waved his arms and shook his mane of blond curls.

"Lost something?" Max asked pleasantly. "Can I help you look?"

The shriek Horace emitted caused Max to clap his hands over his ears and shudder.

"You have all but shocked me to death," Horace cried, clutching his chest. "Shocked me to death." He rushed away.

The very obvious question was: what did he have that so many people wanted?

Not that he cared. Another hour had passed since Horace left and still Kirsty hadn't come to him. Of course, he could go to her, but Mairi had told him Kirsty was well and going about the castle, whereas he was recovering from a vicious attack that might well have left him dead.

And he'd asked her to marry him.

And she'd turned him down.

He wanted her to come to him.

He could send a note. Keep the tone cool, somewhat distant. A simple, polite inquiry about her own health, perhaps?

She would come to him, she wouldn't be able to stop herself eventually.

"Mr. Rossmara," a female voice sang out from the other room. "Are you receiving?"

Max closed his eyes and willed the visitor away. If he spoke at all, she'd know he was awake and to refuse to see her, whoever she was, would be damnably rude. No, he must not speak. His one chance lay in pretending to sleep.

"Oh, my poor, dear, Mr. Rossmara."

He felt a flurry in the room, heard the rustle of fine fabrics, smelled . . . mothballs?

"Oh my goodness, what a horrible sight. No wonder you are unable to make sensible decisions, you poor, dear boy. They have beaten you to a pulp. Disfigured you. It's as well that you sleep."

Max had the greatest difficulty remaining still and keeping his eyes closed.

"We must give you time to come to your senses. If Hermoine had explained your condition, I should have understood your inappropriate response to her at once."

He opened his eyes in time to feel Countess Grabham's veil brush his cheek. She peered closely at the wound on his jaw. Her lip curled. Her nostrils pinched tight. She swallowed loudly.

"One wonders," she said as if he were not present at all, "if there are other, more *affecting* injuries elsewhere. Why, perhaps you turned poor, dear Hermoine away because you fear you will never again be able to, well, *never be able to.*" She wafted a hand in the air.

Without noticing that he looked at her, she took the edges of the covers where they rested on his chest between finger and thumb, and lifted them and peered beneath. The countess peered, in fact, at Max's supine body.

"What in God's name do you think you are doing?" he said, slapping the back of her hand and pulling the covers up to his chin. "*Molesting* me?"

The countess staggered backward. "How could you suggest . . . But I forgot. You are not yourself, you poor, dear, boy. I was simply ascertaining the full extent of your injuries."

"Extensive," Max snapped.

"Yes, yes," his visitor agreed. "So I see. You have my deepest sympathy."

"I am injured, not dead."

She clasped her hands, and said, "True, but sometimes, when pain is particularly great, one might wish for death. No matter. I came to ask you to think things through, and to tell you that in light of your injuries, we will, of course, give you more time to finalize the arrangements."

"Arrangements?"

"For your marriage to Lady Hermoine. I know you will come to your senses. If she were older and wiser, she would also know, but she came to me directly after leaving you and she was beside herself. She was convinced you do not love her."

Perceptive woman.

"May I ask a favor of you, Mr. Rossmara?"

He let his eyelids lower slowly, parted his lips slightly, and contrived to produce a snore.

"I knew you'd agree," the countess said softly. "Hermoine shall come and care for you so that she may feel useful. She does adore you entirely, you know."

Max continued to snore gently, and waited for the odious woman to leave the bedchamber. As soon as she did so, he held very still and strained to hear any sounds that might come from the old schoolroom.

Within moments there came subtle scratchings, and shiftings, and the sibilant sliding of pages being turned.

Max groaned and pulled the covers over his head.

Chapter Twenty-eight

Kirsty set the Parcheesi board and the two returned pieces on the chest beneath the window in her sitting room. She'd worked hard all day, not even stopping for lunch, all the while trying to blot out thoughts of Max, and all the while listening, and hoping to hear his approach.

Daylight took a long, long time to fade at this time of year. She welcomed the purple of late evening pressing in upon the casement. Soon it would be fully dark and she could justify going to bed—her one hiding place.

Only by accident had she discovered that the heads of the large Parcheesi pieces unscrewed. She'd intended to show them to Max, but there hadn't been an opportunity. How strange that someone had stuffed cloth inside the ladies. And how odd that the board was really a box. Surely it had contained some treasure.

She fetched the rest of the pieces and placed them on the board. Then she selected the figurine of a woman dressed for court in the reign of King Henry VIII. Kirsty took hold of the head in its padded hood and back veil and began to twist. Like its companion, the piece was beautifully made and detailed, even to voluminous fur sleeves and a pomander case on a long chain belt.

With a slight squeak, the body began to move, and soon the silver lady was beheaded. Faded red satin peeped from inside her body. Kirsty pulled and found it did not come out easily, but she persevered until she discovered why. This time the satin wasn't empty, but contained a small, exquisite earbob of some deep green stone set in very yellow gold.

Kirsty rested it on her palm. A clever hiding place for a treasured possession. Surely Lady Avenall wouldn't forget such a valuable piece.

A lady wearing a loose gown with sleeves that puffed at the shoulder, grew tight as they descended the arm, and with pleated ruffs at her wrists was, Kirsty thought, modeled after the fashion of Queen Mary's time. Max had taught Kirsty a great deal when she was still little more than a child, and taught her well. How grateful she was to him for the gift.

Queen Mary's lady lost her head and offered up a scrap of blue chiffon wrapped around three pearls. Whether or not the pearls were of great value, Kirsty could not guess.

One after another, the pieces yielded baubles. A small gold brooch set with a blood red stone, a gold chain, a cloudy white stone that burned red at its center when Kirsty turned it in her palm.

Every lady contained something interesting, and, Kirsty decided, probably valuable.

Then there were the two pieces that had disappeared, then reappeared—empty.

Max had said that no one would think she'd stolen the missing pieces, but what would he say now that all the others were revealed as treasure boxes? She grew hot. If she said nothing, perhaps no one would ever find out about the jewels. But someone had taken two of the pieces and brought them back minus their contents. Kirsty was certain that, just like all the others, they must have contained something.

She could be accused of stealing. From Max's sister.

Well, she had never stolen a single thing in her entire life; in fact the possibility of stealing had never entered her mind.

Boldly, she pulled the bell cord beside the fireplace, then sat down to pen a swift note. That done, she placed it in an envelope, sealed it, and bent to the task of replacing the contents of the Parcheesi pieces. She set the board aside and stared at it.

"Kirsty? Or am I supposed to call ye *Miss Mercer* now ye're so important?"

She jumped, and looked up into Fergus Wilkie's insolent face. She didn't answer his question, but said, "Thank ye for comin'. Would ye be kind enough t'take this letter t'the lodge."

He glanced at the window. "*Now?*"

"Aye, it's of great importance." Great importance if she hoped to get any sleep at all this night. "I'm sure there'd be no objection t'ye takin' the cart they usually use t'get there."

Wilkie sniffed. "I'll be faster afoot." He sidled closer, took the envelope and rudely read the name written there. "Writin' t'your master. What's up wi' ye? A lovers' tiff?"

Kirsty had never been good at argument. "I will be grateful t'ye, Fergus."

"Oh, I'm Fergus now ye want somethin' am I? Well, I'll take it for ye, but then I'll expect payment o' my choice—when I choose t'collect it."

After he left, with his sly manner of studying her, and his almost silent way of moving, Kirsty settled in to wait.

For the first hour she leafed through a copy of the magazine, *Punch*, that she'd brought up from the study. It had been published for the first time the previous year. This edition was from December and showed a great many very disrespectful drawings of important people with their worst features presented to make them even more frightful. Kirsty couldn't help smiling at some of them.

It was some distance to the lodge—a hunting lodge before the viscount took it over to be his and Lady Justine's home—but Wilkie might have made it there and back by now.

She went into the corridor and walked toward the stairs, planning to look down at the hall below.

As she turned from the corridor, she encountered Lady Hermoine Rashly, puffing, apparently having hurried upstairs. Her face was pink from being outside.

"Oh, Kirsty," she said, and her golden eyes filled with tears. "Oh, forgive me for being so silly as to cry, but I saw you, and suddenly I feel I can't cope anymore. It's all too much. Please say you'll help me. I'm so worried about Max."

Kirsty held her breath and waited for Lady Hermoine to continue.

"I've been with him, you know," the lady said. "At least, I've *tried* to be with him. He doesn't really want me there." She turned her face from Kirsty, who saw a tear slide down the other's cheek.

"My lady," she said tentatively, "what has happened? How can I help ye?"

"I understand you've been helping the marquess while Max is ill."

Ill? Perhaps that was the story being put about to cover the fact that Max was in his cups. "Aye, I've been working with His Lordship."

"Max said he was grateful for you and the marquess because he doesn't have to worry about estate matters, and he doesn't feel he could at the moment."

"I see," Kirsty said. "I'm glad if I'm helpin' him." Could he be really ill?

"Yes, but . . . b-but . . ." Lady Hermoine broke into loud sobs. Her shoulders heaved, and Kirsty was moved to sympathy by the sight. She would have patted the lady's back but knew better than to touch someone of high rank.

"Oooh," Lady Hermoine moaned. "I do love him, you know. But he doesn't love me. But because I love him, I've come to ask you to go to him. You mean a great deal to him. He's so ill. Would you go to him now and see if you can bring him some comfort? Perhaps there is infection. I don't know, and he refuses medical assistance."

Kirsty listened to Lady Hermoine with mounting horror. "You think there's infection, my lady?"

"I don't know. It pains me so to come to you when I wish he wanted me, but I cannot be so selfish as to stand between him and the one who may be able to bring him some solace." She looked at Kirsty, caught her hands, and squeezed them. "Go to him, my dear. Go now before it is too late."

Kirsty pulled her hands free. "I will," she said. "I'll go at once, and bless ye for the unselfish woman ye are. I've misjudged ye. God love ye, my lady."

Without taking time to return to her room for bonnet and mantle, Kirsty sped down the flights of stairs to the hall and outside into a cool night. She noticed the chill air, but paid it no mind.

She would follow Fergus Wilkie's lead and go to the lodge on foot. At least she wore relatively sturdy half boots and could negotiate the rough path well enough as long as she was careful of ruts and rocks along the way.

Now she wished the day were even longer. The last traces

of evening purple had fled the sky, and there was only the hint of the moon's glow. She stumbled frequently, but steadied herself each time and pressed on. The way to the lodge was better now than it had once been but it was still no path to take in the darkness.

She wasn't prepared to hear the approach of a horse and stood to one side of the path, squinting in all directions.

The animal and its rider were upon her almost immediately. There was no chance to get out of the way. Kirsty pressed her back into the hedgerow and cried out at the piercing of thorns into the skin of her neck and arms, at the snagging of her hair.

Against the black sky, the even darker form of the horse reared up at her side, its rider cloaked and hooded—as good as invisible. Kirsty's heart beat so hard she thought she might choke. She would have turned to run, but there was no avenue to take, and the rider slid quickly from his mount and took her by the arms. With never a word, he spun her around and tied her wrists together. She thought she cried out, but couldn't be certain, so abject was her fear.

"Who are you?" Surely this was the same man who had come to Max's aid. "Let me go or you'll be sorry." He bound her wrists tightly. "Someone's coming this way to meet me. He'll be here at any moment, and he'll be carrying a pistol."

His laughter chilled her.

The cloth he pushed into her mouth and knotted at the back of her head silenced her.

Another cloth, this one thick and secured over her eyes, stole what sight she'd had in the night.

He moved so rapidly. Bundled and pushed, lifted and tossed, very quickly she was slung, facedown, over the horse's neck, with the man in the saddle behind her. They rode full tilt, the horse's gait jouncing her until she was sure no bone remained whole. Her body must be bruised over every inch.

He was going to kill her.

Kirsty's scream died in her throat. She felt she might choke on the wad of stuff the man had forced into her mouth.

So far he took her. Kirsty rolled toward the saddle, and knew they rode uphill, then the rider held her to stop her from sliding forward, and she felt they were going downhill again.

The horse's hooves scrunched on gravel. There were shouting voices, then a single command from the rider, "Silence!" And there was silence but for running feet, and slamming doors, and the occasional incomprehensible whisper.

Inside a house. Yes, she was carried up some steps and into a house.

Then he hoisted her over his shoulder, wrapped an arm around her legs, and climbed flight after flight of stairs while someone ran behind him.

There couldn't be so many flights of stairs in a house.

The smells grew musty. Her abductor reached a door and threw it open. He bundled her inside and set her on her feet. Then, to her amazement, he untied her hands and removed the blindfold and gag.

With the hood pulled low over his face, he stood just out of her reach. Whoever had been behind him fled, his or her feet clattering on bare steps. "Here is food," he said, his voice muffled. He pushed a tray forward with his toe. "If you wish to relieve yourself, you'll find a place and a way."

Kirsty surged toward him, but he fended her off with a single outstretched arm.

"Let me go," she cried. "Please, who are ye? What have I done to ye? How long are ye goin' t'keep me here?"

He snickered. "That will depend."

"Depend upon what?"

"Whether or not we get what we want."

"But why are you doing this to me?"

"Because you get in the way."

"Who are you? I know you're the lone horseman, but who are you? What do you want from me?"

"So many questions," he said, and backed quickly from the room.

Kirsty looked about her with horror. She was in an attic, of that she was certain. An attic filled with old trunks, dusty pictures, furniture losing its stuffing.

"No!" she yelled. "No, don't leave me here. Please don't leave me here."

She threw herself at the door and grabbed the handle— and heard the key turn in the lock.

Chapter Twenty-nine

Into every man's life came a time when he must put pride aside. At least it did if by putting pride aside the general good would be served.

Or even a substantial part of what was good.

He should not, Max thought, feel quite as first-rate as he did this morning. Striding the way from the lodge to the castle should at least have caused his headache to return. Or made him weak. Encouraged renewed bleeding from beneath the plaster strips the sawbones had applied to the wound on his jaw perhaps.

In fact he felt quite marvelous.

If the tossing away of a man's pride could do good for even a single soul, then toss it, he most certainly should.

And he would.

For that one deserving soul Kirsty Mercer, he would not only toss away his pride, but he would *grind* it into the dust beneath his feet!

Max scuffed at the said dust with the toe of a boot, checked in all directions, and made a sideways leap into the air. He executed the feat of clapping his boots together before landing, and caught sight of a gardener who had paused his work to observe the spectacle.

The gardener doffed his cap.

Max grinned and gave the man a mock salute and a cheerful, "Good day to you."

Oh, why not simply admit that his generosity of spirit was for his own good as well as Kirsty's? And knowing that she was at least twice as generous as he was, he could only be assured that she would melt at his contrition and admit that she had merely been affecting nobility when she'd refused him.

He entered the building by the main door beneath its clock tower and castellated balcony and strode toward Eve. At the foot of the stairs to his apartments—and Kirsty's—he hesitated. The hour of ten was past. His father had informed him that she was working side by side with Arran to keep estate affairs running smoothly.

She would be in his study.

Fergus Wilkie emerged from belowstairs, reading as he walked. He was too engrossed to notice Max, who said, "Good book, Wilkie?" and smiled when the other man jumped.

"Aye, sir," Wilkie said, tucking the small volume into the pocket of his livery. He attempted to slide away again.

No doubt Wilkie was studying for his next amorous encounter. "I'd been meaning to inquire about your nuptials to . . . Ada, is it? Fine figure of a woman, that."

Wilkie had the grace to turn bright red. He cleared his throat and nodded, and mumbled, "Thank you, sir. You know how it is. Sometimes it takes time to arrange these things. We can't inconvenience the household, after all, can we."

Max stared at him and wondered if Ada would be well served by marrying the man. He decided she would, even if only to give her the married status that would bring her suitable respect within the household staff.

"We'll have to see what we can do to work things out," Max said, and strode on toward his study where he found the door shut tight.

A rumble of masculine voices came from within.

Grinning, Max threw open the door and marched into the room. His father and Arran stood facing each other. Each man wore a deep frown.

And Kirsty was not at her desk, dash it all.

"Max!" Father said, and advanced rapidly to take him by the arm. "Wonderful to see you looking yourself, my boy. But don't overdo things too soon. Come and take a chair."

"Yes," Arran agreed. "Take a chair."

"I'm feeling better than ever," Max informed them. "If you'll excuse me, I just remembered what I intended to do before coming in here." He would go to the rosy rooms. No doubt Kirsty had finally fallen into a decline for the want of him and could no longer pretend herself capable of continuing to work.

"We need to talk to you," Father said.

"I—"

"Now," Arran told him. "We've a dilemma on our hands."

"I'm back now," Max said, and he could not contain his wretched grin. "No need for either of you to worry yourselves about matters here anymore. Kirsty and I will take care of everything."

His father and uncle looked at each other before Struan turned his back on both of them and went to the window.

"Sit down," Arran repeated. "We've got a bit of a pickle

on our hands. We were deciding how to proceed when you arrived."

Impatient to be off, Max still declined to sit. He asked, "What's the problem?" and tried to appear interested.

"We think Kirsty's missing," his father said without turning around.

"Good God, Struan," Arran bellowed. "Why don't you learn not to be so subtle when announcing these things?"

"I wasn't subtle."

"Exactly. You have the subtlety of a team of oxen. Damn it, man, after all these years you'd think you'd learn to think before—"

"What are you talking about?" Max asked. He felt suddenly quite cold. And perhaps he was weak after all. "Kirsty? Missing? How can she be missing?"

"She's not with her family," Arran said. "I went down there myself to see, and they haven't had a word from her. They're worried, but I tried to ease them. I told them we would inform them when she returns."

Max looked from one man to the other, backed away, turned, and fled the room. He took the stairs several at a time, ignoring the throb in his jaw, and strode to Kirsty's rooms.

Not a sign of her.

The bed was smoothed with not so much as a wrinkle in the counterpane. Absolute order wherever he looked. He opened a drawer in the dresser. Empty. And the next. And the next. All empty. And the wardrobe? Empty—but for the new clothing she hadn't wanted. He looked to the table beside the bed. The Bible was gone.

He returned to the sitting room and sat on the chest near the window, his mind whirling, yet blank of inspiration. Where would she go? She *had* nowhere to go.

"Sir?" Fergus Wilkie, a hesitant expression on his thin face, hovered on the threshold. "May I come in, sir?"

Max stared at him, then remembered himself, and said, "Yes, yes. Come in. What is it?"

Wilkie closed the door carefully behind him and approached. "I'm no' sure I should ha' come t'ye, but I know Kirsty Mercer is by way of bein' important t'ye." Hastily he added, "Because of how she's good with numbers and so on."

Max watched him narrowly and decided there was definitely something he did not care for about Fergus Wilkie. "We would all appreciate any help you can give us," he said, as impersonally as possible under the circumstances.

With his gaze fixed firmly on the carpet, Wilkie said, "I was passing this way verra late last night."

"Really? Why would you be passing this way? You have no reason to come here unless summoned, do you?"

That brought Wilkie's eyes to meet Max's briefly. He gave a one-sided, "man-to-man" leer that Max disliked intensely. "If ye recall, sir, Ada and—"

"Yes," Max said quickly. "Quite so. You were passing this way. And?"

"Kirsty was sitting where you are."

Max gripped his knees and leaned forward, and said, *"And?"*

"I dinna like t'say it."

"Say it."

"I'm sure there's a good explanation for it, sir."

Now he no longer felt weak. He did feel angry. "Speak plainly, Wilkie. I've no time for foolishness. Spit it out, man. *Now"*

"Aye. Well, she had those." He turned and pointed to Ella's Parcheesi set. "The pieces."

When Wilkie didn't immediately continue Max had to stop himself from taking hold of the man and shaking him. "Was there something unusual about that?"

"She'd the heads off all the silver ladies, and she'd made

a pile o' things she was putting in a little bag. Sir, they were precious, I could see that, and that they must have come from inside the ladies. Jewels they were. Brooches and such. Glittered, they did."

Bewildered, Max frowned and looked at the board. The pieces appeared to be all there and not one was without her head. "When did this . . . when did this supposedly happen?"

"Midnight or so, I'm thinkin'."

"I see." In other words Wilkie was suggesting Kirsty was a thief. "Is that all? If so—"

"No, sir. There's somethin' else. Verra early this mornin'. Before six. Ada saw it from the window." He snickered and thrust his hands in his pockets. "I was dozin', but she woke me. Unfortunately I was too late t'see it, but Ada's good eyes."

"Nice for her."

"Aye. She said she could hardly believe them, though, Kirsty bein' such a quiet one and all. But then, it's often the quiet ones who—"

"Keep to the facts. What did Ada see?"

"The horseman. He came from the hills yonder." Wilkie pointed west. "And Kirsty went t'meet him. She carried a big bundle wi' her, and he took her and what she carried onto the horse wi' him. And away they went."

Max stood up. "She was abducted! You knew Kirsty was abducted early this morning and waited until now to report what was seen?"

"Not abducted, sir," Wilkie said, wringing his hands. "I'd ha' come t'ye at once if she had been. No, sir, she went willingly. Ada said it was a meeting. Kirsty went the way none of us goes because there's nothin' there. And when the horseman approached, Kirsty hastened t'meet him. She didna run from him. She *went* t'him, and away with him."

* * *

The house, whatever house it might be, was utterly still and silent. Once the attic door had closed the previous night, Kirsty had been left in absolute darkness. She'd not slept for hours, but had crawled to find a wall against which she could lean and think. Using the furniture had been out of the question. It reeked of mildew and dust.

Her thought had been that if the only way out was the door, then she must find a way to open that door.

But she had slept eventually, and had awakened because she'd been wrong in thinking there were no windows in the room. In fact there was a skylight and with morning the determined sun had forced a dimmed ray through the grime-encrusted pane.

Three times she had piled trunks one on top of the other and attempted to reach the skylight.

Three times she had tumbled from her rickety plinth. She hurt wherever she touched herself. But she was considering her next move. The base of the platform must be built more sturdily and she must go slowly and carefully, both with the construction, and when she made her precarious climb. To reach her goal she had to move slowly upward, then lift more items and pile them higher.

Above all, she must keep trying to get out and she must not give in to the fear she could not expect to avoid.

At least she'd discovered a chamber pot!

A hastily penned letter was dispatched to Ella at once. Max congratulated her upon the birth of Nigel, Ella and Saber's second son, then, as delicately as possible, asked about the Parcheesi board and pieces. A post rider, half of a very handsome purse in hand, the other half to be paid upon his return, had ridden out with instructions to attempt to break all records for speed on the journey.

Max, with his father and Arran flanking him, waited in

the dowager's sitting room. They had been summoned to see her on "urgent" business.

At the sound of her entrance all three men turned to greet her.

"And well you may look grim," she said, smacking the tip of her cane on the floor with each step. "If you didn't insist upon treating those who are older and wiser than you will ever become as if they were dolts, we would never have lost so much time."

Max rubbed his eyes and willed tiredness away. Far too long languishing in his bed had left him with little energy— at least after he'd discovered Kirsty's disappearance.

"Hurry up, Blanche, do," the dowager said irritably. "Get me settled so that we may commence to get the rest of this mess *settled*. Ooh, I am beside myself at such careless inefficiency."

"Yes, my lady," Blanche said, and Max noted that her eyes were puffy as if she'd been crying, and crying long and hard. "Settle against the cushions. How are your knees?"

"Do *not* mention such things in mixed company."

Max hid a smile and didn't dare glance at either his father or his uncle.

"Now," the dowager said, waving Blanche away, "let's get on with this before there is absolutely no hope of coming up with a useful plan." She pointed the cane at her three visitors. "First I want to be certain the three of you can restrain yourselves from any outbursts. There will be no raised voices. Do you all understand?"

They murmured assent, and Max muttered, "Except yours."

"If you ever become as old as I am, Max Rossmara, you may raise your voice when you please."

His father and uncle chuckled, and Arran said, "Not that you'll be able to hear as the dowager hears, even if you do reach her age."

"Stop wasting time on prattle," the lady ordered. "It's unfortunate that we had to learn what's been going on from a servant rather than from our own kin."

"We didn't want to—"

"Worry me," the dowager finished for Max's father. "Ridiculous. Blanche, kindly repeat what you've already told me."

Blanche's face immediately crumpled and she began to cry.

"Oh, do stop that," the dowager duchess said. "Come and sit beside me. Bring those things with you. I've told you this isn't your fault—it's just a happenstance and one you will learn from. Now, let's get on with this."

Carrying a reticule and sniffing mightily, Blanche did as she was told and sank to the couch beside the dowager. She opened the reticule and fumbled inside before bringing out what appeared to be two of the pieces from Ella's Parcheesi game.

Max went closer to look. Blanche set one piece in her lap and held the other out. "I'm dashed," Max said. "The ones that disappeared, then reappeared. What d'you know about them, Mrs. Bastible?"

Her sniffing instantly became full-blown wails. She didn't bother to search out a handkerchief, choosing instead to haul up part of her peach-colored skirts to cover her face.

"Now look what you've done," the dowager said to Max. "Why will none of you men allow yourselves to be led by me? There, there, Blanche. It's all right. You have repented, and that's all that matters."

"Ah," Arran murmured. "I do believe we've had a return of the magpie syndrome."

His uncle and his father did not, Max recalled, know the full story of what had happened with the board and pieces.

The dowager patted Mrs. Bastible's back, and said, "Just tell them what you told me. I'll take care of the rest."

Gradually Blanche's back stopped heaving, and she raised her reddened face. "It started the day I waited for Kirsty in her rooms," she said. "I was interested in these ladies so I examined them—and discovered the heads came off. Well . . . Oh, it's too awful. And you know, son-in-law that I used to have a little problem, but that I overcame it."

"Stealing to support a gambling habit, you mean," Arran said, so bluntly that even Max winced.

Blanche Bastible collapsed into a fresh gale of weeping and could not be consoled for some minutes.

His great-grandmother eased her distraught companion's head onto her lap, a sight Max found extraordinary. Then the old lady took the two silver ladies and screwed off their heads. From inside each one she produced a very white diamond, each very obviously of several carats in weight.

"Now," she said, "if you three could contain any comments, I will explain what these are about, why Blanche has them, why and when she replaced them, and the story of the Parcheesi board as my darling Ella explained it to me years ago."

"You know about it?" Max said, starting forward.

The dowager looked heavenward, and Max's father put a restraining hand on his arm. "Please go on, madam," said Father.

"As you know, Max, Ella brought the board from that dreadful house in London where Struan found and rescued her. A gift from the, er, ladies who lived there and who wished her well. From their own, er, acquisitions, they donated trinkets of some value for Ella to sell if she ever needed money. That's the story of the jewelry. Ella never needed money, and preferred to keep the pieces as they were."

"She never told me about it," Struan said, sounding irritated.

The dowager smiled, and said, "There are things one

shares with some, and things one shares with others. Ella has shared *everything* with me. When Blanche took these it was no more than a momentary lapse. She no longer has any interest in low pursuits such as gambling, but she has a keen fascination for beautiful things—as do I. So I quite understand that she wished to spend more time examining the diamonds, although she does admit that she should have mentioned her intention."

"Have you ever considered taking up the law, madam," Arran asked. "I should think you might make an admirable barrister."

"Women do not become barristers, you foolish boy. Blanche returned the diamonds this morning, after she assumed Kirsty Mercer had gone down to your study, Max. She went into Kirsty's sitting room, put the diamonds in the appropriate pieces, and left."

"What time was that, Mrs. Bastible?" Max asked, breathing through his mouth and praying he could remain calm.

With much sniffling, Blanche said, "S-seven. When I was . . . well, I didn't want her to know what I'd done, did I? And she goes to breakfast by then."

"Is this helping us?" Arran asked.

The ebony cane hit the carpet once more. "Of course it is, if you will just stop interrupting! According to the report I was given, Kirsty was seen meeting some mythical horseman just before six this morning. With all of her possessions. When Blanche went to the rosy rooms at seven—to replace the diamonds—a number of items belonging to the girl were there. A shawl on a chair. Her Bible on the table beside that chair.

"The manner in which the room had been left caused Blanche to wonder if Kirsty might have taken to her bed. She checked the bedchamber and although there were a number of possessions scattered, Kirsty wasn't there. So, it simply cannot be that she left the house before six this morning, carrying all of her things with her, and leaving the rosy rooms immaculate, can it? Yet they were immaculate when you went to them, weren't they, Max? I put it to you that Kirsty Mercer may be in dire trouble."

Max bowed his head, and said, "Heaven help us. Where do I start looking for her?"

"I'd suggest inviting that obvious criminal, Fergus Wilkie, to help you search for her," the dowager said. "He'll either slip up on his own story all by himself, or you'll have to get the truth out of him some other way, won't you?"

"Thank you," Max said, retreating. Arran and Struan followed.

"Blanche," the dowager said. "Please bring me Ella's Parcheesi board."

Max turned back and said, "Why?"

"Simple curiosity," Max's great-grandmother said airily. "She never would allow me to look at the little books that were stored inside it. It's a box really, you see. She said I wouldn't care for them, that they were *racy*. Some sort of instructional texts—apparently quite rare—that had also belonged to the, er, ladies at Lushbottam's. That was the name of that place where she used to live.

"Really, one would think me of an age to read *anything* I please, wouldn't one?"

Chapter Thirty

Wiping grime and sweat from her eyes, Kirsty stared at the exposed beams of the ceiling high above her where her only hope of escaping undetected grew steadily more difficult to see.

Darkness would soon be upon her.

Five falls. Now they amounted to five.

She'd made herself eat the biscuits that had been left for her, and the wedge of dry, white cheese. The ale she'd sipped, making it last without particular difficulty since the taste was foul.

All attempts to force the door had failed.

But now, in the center of the attic room, beneath the skylight, stood a veritable mountain of unwanted debris. The base she had constructed with great care, but as soon as the pile grew too high, she could only toss things up, catch those that fell, and toss them again. When she climbed, she would have to finish her ladder to freedom as she went—just as she'd already attempted. *Five times.*

She took another tiny taste of the ale—just to moisten her lips and tongue, put the last, hard and slippery morsel of cheese in her mouth, and began to climb.

Her progress was so slow, but she knew it must be or she would come crashing down yet again. So far she had been fortunate enough not to break any bones, but even the prospect of more bruises was unbearable.

Trunk by trunk by box stuffed with old clothes, by valise similarly stuffed to make it stable, she climbed, leaning against the pile, leaning inward to make herself as much part of her mountain as possible. Her progress was so slow, each hand- and foothold painful to secure. And the higher she went, the less sturdy her mountain became, until she reached the place where the things she'd thrown were very precarious, and she had to stop and attempt to shore them up.

Now she moved inch by inch. She had nothing more to make the heap higher. Her only hope was to manage to balance herself atop it all and make a grab for the skylight.

A black leather case fell, and crashed open when it hit the

attic floor. It was filled with instruments Kirsty had never seen before. They bounced and skittered, and she waited, holding her breath, expecting someone to come.

No one came.

This place must be very high above everything.

A toehold, and another, and she could ease over the top and lie there, panting, until she had the strength to stand.

She should have taken off her dress. Now she was forced to pull up her skirts, bunch them above her knees, and make the final move.

Wobbling, Kirsty crouched atop her miraculous mountain, her fearsome mountain, and waited to feel it crumble beneath her again.

It remained sturdy.

Very slowly, very cautiously she began to stand, straightening up a little at a time, pausing between, until she was upright. Then she raised her arms over her head.

She couldn't reach it.

Oh, please, please, let her reach the skylight.

Her fingers caught the wooden frame and found a firm hold. She felt around, searching for the handle to open the window.

It was there.

Morning had become afternoon, and afternoon, evening, and they were no closer to finding Kirsty than they had been at the beginning of the day. Arran had assumed control, exerting his position as Laird of Kirkcaldy. They had gathered all the castle staff together, then word had spread to the village, and to the tenants, and they'd all come. First a few marched up the hill, then larger numbers who said little but showed themselves ready to do whatever they must do.

When the tenants came their faces were set in a manner that told of how they were rallying behind one of their own. And in their midst were Robert Mercer and his son, Niall.

This great company came and went according to the in-structions they received and no man or woman searched harder than Robert Mercer—unless it was Max Rossmara.

"If she's dead, it will be because of me," he said to his fa-ther. They had gone out together to scour the village, and the church, to make sure Kirsty hadn't sought refuge there be-cause she had become frightened to return to the castle. "I should never have wavered from my promise to her."

His father didn't answer, but his face bore anguish that needed no explanation.

"Damn Fergus Wilkie," Max said through his teeth. "Damn him for the traitor he is."

"Wherever he is," Struan muttered. "We might have known he planned to take off. At least we have proof that our suspicions about the man were right. But I cannot be-lieve he worked alone. Why should he? If theft was his aim, and he intended to escape afterward, there was no need to stay and give you that story about Kirsty."

"No," Max agreed. "I pray that we find out what was be-hind that, and find Kirsty alive. I must go out again. Forgive me, but I will go alone this time. I'm not fit company for any man."

"Go then," his father said. "I'll take the opposite route."

Max took off once more. He went by the westerly path that Wilkie had spoken of and quickly entered dense forest. He'd ridden the same way several times that day but no longer knew where to go that would be fresh.

Another's horse galloped behind him and he groaned, longing to be alone. If he could not be with Kirsty, he pre-ferred the company of no man or woman.

"Hold up there, Rossmara," came a man's voice. "Hold up, I say. It's me. Horace Hubble."

Max pulled up his mount, cursing his misfortune to have to greet such a man.

"Sympathies, old chap," Horace said, drawing near.

"Why wasn't word sent to us so that we could do what we could to help? Terrible thing. Absolutely terrible. Poor little maid, where can she be? You look absolutely done for, Rossmara. I insist you allow me to accompany you."

Max slumped in his saddle, and confessed, "To be honest, Hubble, I don't know where I'm going anymore."

"Then let me lead you. Just give it up and allow me to make the decisions, just this once. I know it's contrary to your nature, but you'll do the girl no good if you're aimless. Come. We'll cut downhill, then to the east a way, just to look for anything that may have been missed."

This new, helpful Hubble made Max more than mildly suspicious. Unless he was a very poor judge of character he'd swear the fellow never did anything not almost guaranteed to benefit him.

"Come along, man," Hubble said. "At least allow me to try to be useful."

"Why not?" Max said, and followed the other. The terrain leading down was sheer, and he had to concentrate on working with his horse. Then the land flattened out somewhat, but they entered trees again.

They rode a goodly way, each taking a side of the track and peering for some sign, any sign that Kirsty had been here.

Hopeless.

Max was surprised when he emerged from the trees and saw that they had ridden all the way to The Hallows. The house lay only a short distance away now.

"We'd best turn back," Max said. "Or I must. Thank you, Horace. You've done your best."

"At least come in and take some refreshment," Horace said.

"I can't. I must get on."

"Oh, but you can," Horace insisted. "Of course you can. And you must."

At the jab into his back of what was almost undoubtedly a pistol, Max dropped his head back. "What in God's name are you about, Hubble?"

"Making sure you accept my invitation to rest and take some refreshment," Hubble said pleasantly. "Then we'll have to see."

The ride to The Hallows was indeed short and when they arrived it was the three sisters who ran out, twittering among themselves, and took charge of the horses, while Horace kept his weapon pressed to Max's back. He kept it there and forced him inside the house.

He was "ushered" into a large, garish drawing room, where the countess and Hermoine waited.

Horace put the pistol to Max's temple. "Sit there. In the red chair."

"All the chairs are red," Max pointed out.

"Don't attempt to annoy me," Horace said, "or you won't see the morning."

"Just get on with it," the countess said. She paced, throwing her skirts behind her at every turn, and staring at Max each time she approached him. "We want the journal. The one you stole from the Prince Regent—when he was the Prince Regent, that is."

Max stared at her, and sat on the nearest chair.

She came close, drew herself up, and smacked his face. "There. I've longed to do that from the moment I set eyes on your face. I remember you when you were no more than a nasty little pickpocket in Quick's band. Not that it matters now."

Quick's band? Covent Garden. The dirty basement where the boys and girls returned with their night's pickings and presented them to Gaston. Gaston took what they stole, fenced it, and gave them a pittance that wasn't enough to keep them fed.

"Do you hear what I say?" the countess said. "The journal you stole the night you got away? Where is it? You obviously took it with you because you knew it was valuable. I want it. And I want it now."

"Are they really coming tonight?" Hermoine asked. She actually appeared scared. "Would they come so late?"

"Hold your tongue," the countess snapped. "Foolish creature. You failed at everything you were told to do. You paid that incompetent Wilkie. For what? What good did he do that we couldn't have accomplished without him? And now he's made off with perfectly good baubles, by the sound of it. Those could have been ours, too."

So, Max thought, *Wilkie has been Hermoine's paid informant and helper. The countess is probably right about the fate of the jewelry.*

"And you couldn't even get a common pickpocket to marry you," the countess continued, scowling at Max, who assumed he was the common pickpocket in question. "So much for the legendary charms."

"Very legendary," Horace said, and chuckled. "Of course they'll come this late, my love. Not one of them wants to be seen here in daylight."

"What journal?" Max asked, too bewildered to concentrate fully. "How do you know about Covent Garden?"

The countess threw back her veil, and said, "Now do you know?"

He peered at her. "No." He didn't recall having seen her before.

"I was Gaston's girl then."

Max peered more closely and said, "That was a long time ago," and earned himself another sound slap.

Hermoine tittered. "Not so young as you used to be, Gertrude. You're so old he doesn't recognize you."

"Gertie?" Max said. "Dirty Gertie?"

"Oh!" The woman flounced away. "That's quite enough.

Tell us where the journal is hidden, or you'll die right where you sit."

A cool, calm sensation settled at his center. He was dealing with inept bunglers. He must take control. "Where is Kirsty?"

"Oh, he's still worrying about that peasant," Hermoine said. "You could have had me, you fool, and I'd have found a way to make sure you did very well out of the entire business."

"How would you have done that, my love?" Horace asked. He amused himself by poking the barrel of his pistol into various parts of Max's head and neck.

"Well, if we'd married, I'd have looked after him. I'd have shared what I got. After all, he's very . . . well, he is quite the man, isn't he."

Horace very deliberately delivered a blow to the wound on Max's jaw. Pain made Max light-headed, but he managed to stop his eyes from closing.

"You never were the faithful kind, were you, love," Horace said. "When would you have told Mr. Quite-a-man that you were already married."

Hermoine tossed her head. "Oh, that was ages ago, and I thought I was a widow when we started this, remember."

"Well I'm not dead," Horace said, "and therefore you aren't a widow. Be grateful I saved you from bigamy."

Hermoine was married to Horace? Of course, she was. Naturally. What would he discover next on this night from hell? Probably nothing that caused him less disappointment. "Where is Kirsty?" he repeated.

"Locked in the attic," Dirty Gertie said. "And if you don't give us what we want, she'll die in that attic, and so will you. Actually, you'll die here and be put in the attic with her."

"Charming," Max said, automatically looking upward. If they were telling him the truth, he must get to Kirsty.

"I hear a carriage," Hermoine cried, running to the window. "Oh, my gawd, it's Wellington again. He won't go away empty-handed this time. He's getting out. Beaufort's with him."

Max made no attempt to close his mouth.

"They're all in the journal, you see," Hermoine said avidly. "All rich and powerful, and they're going to pay us to get rid of it rather than having it published. Only they won't pay until they see the evidence, so you've got to give it to us."

"But—" Max stopped himself from saying he didn't know anything about a journal. If he didn't find a way to play this out to his own ends, he would indeed be delivered to Kirsty like an animal carcass.

He saw Wellington pass beneath a lamp outside the windows. And Beaufort.

Another coach ground to a halt and shortly, another.

"Lord Bessborough," Hermoine said, clasping her hands together. "And *Palmerston*. Oh, my. And Viscount Melbourne. How did he stand being married to that Charlotte Lamb even as long as he did? I'll never understand it."

"Apparently she drove Byron to near madness," Horace said. "Too bad he's dead. I should like to have heard his opinion of the woman firsthand. And he's mentioned in the journal, of course—bound to be. There's *Cavendish*. That man's pockets reach his boots. Give it up, Rossmara. We *will* have the journal before the night's out."

"Oh, *that* journal," Max said, madly casting about for some way out of this disaster. "That one. Yes, yes, I feel it coming to me. The journal. Where did I put the journal? Kirsty knows part of it, part of where it is. We took it in turns to memorize the steps to the hiding place. Kirsty! Kirsty, where are you? I need you, Kirsty!"

"Make him be quiet," Dirty Gertie said. "Hit him with the pistol again, Horace."

"Don't knock him unconscious," Hermoine cried. "If he's unconscious, he can't tell us where it is, can he?"

"Kirsty," Max yelled as loud as he could. "Come to me, Kirsty."

"The fella's gone off the deep end," Horace said. "Gone mad from the strain of it all, I should think."

Max shot his feet out in front of him and stiffened his legs. He rolled his eyes back and managed to drool.

"Oh, gawd," Hermoine wailed. "He's having a turn."

"I want Kirsty," Max moaned. "Kirsty, Kirsty, Kirsty." The back of his head and his rear were the only parts of him touching the chair and he slid slowly down until he was stretched out on the floor where he twitched, and jerked up his knees, and rolled from side to side.

These thespian performances used to come so easily when he'd been a great deal younger and less inhibited. At Eton he'd become quite the celebrity because of his entertaining "interludes." Necessity would just have to pull him through tonight.

"We'd better do as he asks," Hermoine said. "Get that little peasant—if she hasn't suffocated up there."

So she was, indeed, hidden in this house. Max threw himself to his back and scooted along the floor in the manner of a worm: stomach up, feet pulled, stomach down, head pushed. "It's coming to me," he said dreamily. "Under. The first clue is *under*. Kirsty! Kirsty, the second clue, if you please."

"Get her," the countess ordered. "You put her there, Horace. You bring her down."

"I'll do no such—"

"*Get* her." The countess aimed her own, very small pistol at Horace, who seemed to have forgotten he was also armed. He hurried from the room at once.

Max went limp and stared at the ceiling—and waited. He must consider how he would fight his way out of here.

"All the gentlemen are in the Puce Salon," a female voice, one of the sisters, announced from behind him. "And they're getting very cross. And two other people have arrived. They say they're barristers or something, and they want everyone together for whatever's going to happen."

"Gawd," Hermoine said. "They've brought law with them."

"Calm yourself," the countess told her. "Posturing is all it is. Just posturing. Have the barristers wait in the small study, Zinnia. Tell them we'll be there shortly. Where is Horace? What's taking him so long? Oh, there you are. Good heavens, what *has* happened to you, girl?"

Max flipped to his stomach, raised his head to see Kirsty—a very dirty, bedraggled, but apparently healthy, Kirsty—and began to laugh and pound the floor with his fists. He also began to pray his childhood friend hadn't forgotten his penchant for theatrics.

"He wants the next clue," the countess said. "Shut the door, Horace. Use your head. The next clue, girl. To finding wherever the journal is. He said, 'under,' now you have to give the next bit."

Max fell silent and waited.

"Deep," Kirsty said.

"Long ago," Max cried at once, overwhelmed with gratitude that Kirsty had risen to the occasion. "All so long ago I won't remember. I just know I won't remember. We hid it so long ago. *Under.*"

"*Deep,*" Kirsty said.

"*Under.*"

"*Deep!*"

"Gawd," Hermoine muttered.

Zinnia came in again, her face flushed. "You've got to come now. At least come and say something to keep them quiet. They say they're coming to find you."

"Give Zinnia your pistol, Horace," the countess said.

"You and Hermoine come with me. Zinnia, you're a capable girl. Keep these two here until we come back."

Left alone with Zinnia and Kirsty, Max remained still. This was likely to be their best, if not their only chance for escape.

Zinnia's frantic, pained "Ouch!" rang out, followed by another "Ouch," and another and another. Horace's pistol shot across the floor and Max trapped it before leaping to his feet to watch Zinnia fleeing Kirsty, who was much more fleet, and the large pair of metal pincers she chased her with. She chased, and repeatedly caught up—and repeatedly clamped the evil-looking device shut on whatever part of Zinnia's anatomy could be reached.

With the pistol in one hand, Max captured Zinnia with the other.

Kirsty held her pincers aloft, and said, "Meant for pullin' out teeth, I think. They were from a case filled wi' nasty-lookin' things. I almost made it away up there, but the handle was old and it broke off. Just as well it did, or it's a pretty fix ye'd likely still be in."

Max decided he would wait for an interpretation and bundled wailing Zinnia into a convenient cupboard with no means of being opened from the inside.

Listening to Zinnia's muffled shouts, he and Kirsty looked at each other. He went to her, touched her face. "I thought I'd lost you. You're hurt." Her unbound hair had hidden a bright purple bruise on her cheekbone.

She caught his hand and kissed his fingers, and said, "I'm hurt all over. I'm no' the best climber, and I've taken a few wee falls today."

Max wanted only to hold her, to carry her away to safety. He couldn't do either unless they got out of here. "They're in a room on the other side of the vestibule," he told Kirsty. "With some luck we can slide out of the house without being seen and make it away."

"What journal are they blatherin' about?" Kirsty asked.

He shook his head and shrugged. "I don't know. But I'm supposed to have stolen it from the Prince Regent when I was a boy in Covent Garden."

Kirsty's eyes grew very round. "The fat one who came t'Scotland when I was a bairn? My father spoke o' him."

"The same," Max said. "We have to get away from here."

"Where's that garden place the countess talked about, then? Ye stole things there, Max?" She looked part incredulous, part amused.

"Later," he said. "I'll tell you all of it later."

A covert check of the vestibule revealed it as empty, although a considerable noise came from the salon, where a great many of England's most famous men were gathered—and a few from other parts.

Holding Kirsty's hand, Max slipped from the drawing room—just in time to see Dahlia and Wisteria heading for the front door with large valises in their hands.

Kirsty and Max managed to hide behind the staircase that rose from the center of the vestibule. They nodded at each other, knowing they had best wait until the two "sisters" had left.

"We were solicitors to the late King George IV," a deep voice announced in the salon, where the rumble of angry voices had faded. "We traveled from England at the request of one of you—who shall remain nameless for his own protection—one of you who is aware of the contents of this letter."

"Who?" someone shouted. "Show yourself."

Max made to leave their hiding place, but Kirsty held him back. She pressed a finger to her mouth and shook her head. She wanted to listen, the minx. He grinned at her. He wanted to listen, too.

Squeals sounded at the front door, squeals that were quickly cut off. Max took a speedy look and hid himself again. He hid and drew Kirsty into his arms. "McCrackit. And several men from the village. They've got Wisteria and Dahlia and they're keeping them quiet."

"Hush," was all Kirsty said.

"I have," droned the deep voice, "to read this in its entirety, but since it's very short, it should not overtax your patience, gentlemen."

"Nothing of a personal nature, one hopes," a man shouted.

"Pass the thing around," said another. "We'll read it for ourselves."

"*My friends,*" said the first man, with no note of uncertainty. "That is how the letter begins. '*My friends, my old and dear friends, members of The League of Jolly Gentlemen: We were jolly indeed, weren't we? My, what extraordinary entertainments we shared. We shall all miss them although I have faith in each of you that you are carrying on our noble pursuits.*'" The reader cleared his throat. "His Highness continued, '*I am aware that you were told about a certain journal, and how I explained the manner in which it was lost to me. No doubt you have all suffered considerably as you wondered when and where this journal would reappear, and who would learn of our escapades.*'"

"Don't read details aloud," someone said inside the salon.

He was ignored. "There is very little more. He finishes thus, '*Fear no more, dear friends. There is no journal. There never was a journal. Just my little joke. A jolly good joke for some jolly good gentlemen, what?*' He signs himself 'HRH, etc.'"

Chapter Thirty-one

Amid the confusion of stories told, and retold, to those who had searched, then waited out the night at Kirkcaldy, Max gradually pulled Kirsty from the chattering throng that included pompous Constable McCrackit. While he held forth about the manner in which he'd been retained by "a famous London gentleman and two barristers from that town," she followed Max through the castle and out into the early sunshine of a perfect high summer's morning.

"I'm sure you're too tired to take a walk with me," he said. "You must want to wash and sleep."

"I'm too tired not t'walk first," she replied. "Are ye too tired?"

He looked at her and smiled, and she had to smile back. Tears prickled in her eyes, but they were tears of gladness. Whatever happened now, she thought they would always be friends—and they were safe, and in the place they loved the best.

"I'd like to go over the hill and down to the valley," Max said. "Then through the trees to the river. You used to like that very much."

Kirsty said, "I still do, or I will wi' ye. I have no' been quite that way since—well no' for some time."

"Neither have I." He held out his hand, broad palm and long fingers flat. "Not since I went with you."

She placed her hand on his, laced her fingers into his, and laughed. "The same for me. But I was a very clean girl then. I'm a disgrace today."

Max wrinkled his nose, and his green eyes held the old impishness she so relished. He said, "You're perfect to me."

Swinging their joined hands, they climbed the hill. At the top they paused a while and squinted toward the valley, and the trees. The sun rose higher, and climbing had made Kirsty hot. "Some would say we're mad," she said, "out here when we've no' had a decent sleep in days."

"And they'd probably be right," Max told her. "But they'd also be jealous. I'm not tired anymore."

"Neither am I. I'll race ye t'the bottom of the hill." She shaded her eyes and watched his face. When she ran from him and down the hill, it was as much to give her time to deal with all the feelings she had as to race. He'd win anyway.

The smile had left his mouth back there. He'd watched her as if he wanted to hear her very thoughts, and for her to hear his. He watched her like a man with shadows inside him, shadows of questions unanswered. She wanted those questions to be there, but she wanted them to be the right ones.

Rather than overtake her and turn back to yell his victory, as he would have when they were children, Max satisfied himself with catching up and loping along beside her, casting sideways glances, and finally holding her hand again.

The grass was knee-deep in the valley, and scattered with wildflowers. Pink, and white, and mauve, and blue, they waved with the grass that swayed this way and that before a busy breeze.

"Smell it," Kirsty said. "Warm grass and warm flowers, and a breeze that's stroked the heather. There's no better place than right here, and right now. I couldna wish for more."

"Ye couldna?"

She shaded her eyes to see him again. "Ye like t'make fun

o' me," she said, but without reproach. "I'll never be a lady. That's the way o' it."

"You are more of a lady than any I ever met, Kirsty Mercer. And there's no better time and place than this for me, either, but I could wish for more." He turned to face her and began to run backward. "Now. Through the trees and the last one to the river is slave for . . . slave forever."

He turned away and ran, and Kirsty ran, too, calling after him, "It used t'be slave for the day, Max Rossmara. Ye're a greedy one."

Through the trees they dodged. She would see him, dash to the spot, and he would be gone. "Ye teaser," she cried. "Ye know ye're the faster one, but ye taunt me."

She paused, peering in all directions. Sun pierced the trees, dappling lush turf and last year's fallen leaves. "Where are ye? Don't ye *dare* jump out at me. Ye know I canna bear that." There was no sign of him.

"Verra well, if it's a mean game ye're playin', I'll say ye cheated and no' be yer slave." Laughing and gasping, she made her way in as straight a line as possible through the trees, pulling her already tattered skirts away from thorny bushes, and not stopping until she broke into full sunlight and the final downward sweep to the willows that lined the river. He would be there, behind the trunk of a willow, ready to pop out and grab her.

At the river's edge she stopped, panting, and swung around. And she dropped her arms to her sides and felt the tears again, and a lump in her throat.

Max came toward her slowly through the willows, his hands in his pockets, and whistling. She'd never heard him whistle before, and she thought she'd advise him not to make a habit of it.

Raising a hand as he drew near, he said, "You win. One slave reporting for duty, oh fleet one."

"Ye cheated," she said. "Ye didna try t'win."

"Oh, and that's cheating, miss? I think not. I felt a trifle tired and came as quickly as I could. It wasn't quick enough to beat you. That's that. What would you have me do first?"

Kirsty considered him from head to foot. "Just let me look at ye. Ye're safe, and I'm safe." She spread her arms and turned her face up to the sky. "And it's warm and the bad people didn't win. All's right in the Lord's great world."

"Is it?"

She looked at him sharply. "Isn't it?"

"Perhaps. Time will tell."

She couldn't look into his eyes a moment longer. Dropping to sit on the riverbank, she slipped off her ruined shoes and rolled down what was left of her stockings. Remembering herself, and that she was in the presence of a man, even if they had known each other from childhood, she made sure her skirts were well down before taking her stockings all the way off.

Max came to sit beside her and proceeded to work off his boots.

Gingerly, Kirsty put her feet into clear water tinted the same color as the pale blue blossoms of the tufted forget-me-nots that grew in clumps along the river. "It's verra cold," she cried, gasping at first. "But it soon warms, and I'll ha' the cleanest feet in the land."

Hissing, Max pushed his feet beneath the surface, too. "Ow," he muttered. "Ow, ow. Ooh, good."

Little swirls of sandy mud rose to cloud the water, but settled quickly.

"Give me your bidding," Max said, grinning again. "I could wash your feet."

"Ye'll do no such thing," she told him, horrified.

"Am I released for a while, then?"

"Released?"

"From slave duty?"

"O'course ye are, ye daft man."

How soon she regretted her generosity. Before her eyes Max shed his coat, then undid his shirt and threw it down— his cravat had disappeared hours earlier.

"What are ye about?" she asked him.

"I'm going to take a bath."

Kirsty frowned. "In the river?"

"Of course, in the river. We used to swim here, didn't we?"

"Och," she said in a low voice. "Ye promised ye'd never speak o'that. And it was only a time or two when it was so hot."

"I promised not to speak to anyone but you about it. And I haven't, and I'm not now."

He had such shoulders, such a chest, such a flat stomach and the strongest-looking arms. "Ye're verra appealin'," she said.

"Am I now?" He began to unfasten his trousers. "Do you think you ought to say such a thing to me?"

"Only if it's true, and it is."

"Appealing is a rather weak word. Lacks *passion*."

She rolled her lips in to contain a smile.

"You're laughing at me now?" he asked.

Kirsty sighed, and said, "Ye're too well made for your own good. And lookin' at ye brings me a great deal more pleasure than it ought. Mayhap it brings me passion. Ye steal my breath and make me . . . och, such feelings, Max."

He considered that, a smug expression on his face. "I don't think you can use the word passion like that. You could say that looking at me makes you feel passionate."

She looked down at her hands in her lap. "Lookin' at ye makes me feel passionate."

"And a little frightened, perhaps?" he asked softly.

"Perhaps."

"You never have to be frightened of anything you feel

with me—and you don't have to hide anything you feel, either."

From the corner of her eye she saw his trousers and his smallclothes land on top of his shirt. Dull heat throbbed in her face. She turned her head away.

A giant splash, followed by whoops and howls followed. "Kirsty," he called. "Kirsty, I'm drowning, look."

She looked at once, rising to her feet in the shallows at the same time. He'd always been a strong swimmer, and he'd struck out some distance from the bank until he could stand on the bottom with only his head and shoulders out of the water.

"Get back here, Max," she said. "Ye'll freeze."

"It's wonderful." With that he dived, flipping his naked nether regions into full view before disappearing.

Kirsty's heart thumped harder than it had ever thumped. And she felt one of those feelings inside, in the womanly parts of her.

He surfaced again, slicking back his hair and squinting at her across the sun-scattered ripples of the water. "Paddle a little, at least, my love. It'll refresh you."

"Ye're naked, Max Rossmara."

"That I am," he agreed. "Wonderful." He swam closer and stood again, with the water only reaching his hips.

This time she didn't look away. She wanted to join him. How long had it been since she'd swum? And she would be clean again. "Look away," she told him.

"Why?"

"Because I'm going to take off my dress. Ye make me jealous, and I want t'swim, too."

"Naked?"

"No such thing, sir. I'll keep on my smalls."

Assuming a most serious expression, he turned his back. Kirsty shed her filthy dress, and the heavy petticoats. Down to her stays, chemise, and drawers, she considered. The stays were foolish, uncomfortable things and they weren't made for swimming. She took them off and immediately struck out until she swam past Max—sucking air through her teeth at the chill of it—and out to the middle of the river. Deliberately keeping her eyes averted from him, she dunked her head and rubbed at her hair. It wouldn't make it properly clean, but it would be better than before.

With water streaming down her face, she tossed back her sodden locks and squeezed them. They squeaked so they must be clean enough.

A hand behind her neck shocked her into a silent scream, and her eyes flew open.

Max's face was so close she could see the black flecks in his green eyes. With his free hand he cupped water and set to scrubbing her face and neck.

"What d'ye think you're doin'?" she protested, batting at him without stopping him for an instant.

"Being your slave. Slaves wash their masters."

"I'm no' your master."

"I respectfully suggest that you remain silent before you get yourself into trouble with that pretty mouth of yours. I imagine you're in need of a wash all over."

"No such thing," she told him at once, but a great many parts of her had those feelings, and she wished she didn't have to protest the idea.

"You know I'm a bastard, don't you?" he said, concentrating on her shoulders where the chemise had slipped down. "And that Viscount Hunsingore and his wife adopted Ella and me."

"I only know the rumors. They were never very clear. And ye didna speak o' it, and I always thought ye'd tell me your story one day—if ye wanted to."

"What Countess Grabham talked about was true. As a boy I was with a gang of pickpockets in Covent Garden—that's a district in London. There are theaters there. But no matter.

I came from nothing but the humblest of beginnings. I never had a mother and father I knew as you know yours."

His hands at her waist supported her. "Ye're well loved by all," she told him. "Considered the gentleman ye are by all. And the viscount and Lady Justine love ye."

"All true. But you and I are not different. We are both survivors who have had good fortune. And the greatest part of that good fortune is that we found each other. Would you like your slave to kiss you?"

It wouldn't stop with a kiss, but she said, "Yes," and parted her lips, and raised her chin, and slid her arms around his neck. She felt his Part, hard and insistent against her belly, and sucked in a sharp breath. But she kissed him nevertheless, she kissed him the harder, and he framed her head and rocked their faces together.

They kissed for a long time, the sun growing hotter on their heads.

Max bobbed her high out of the water and gazed up at her, the laugh lines crinkled around his eyes and mouth. Kirsty covered his hands at her waist and dared to look down at herself. If she were naked, she'd be less embarrassed than she was by the sight of transparent cotton layered over her breasts. Her nipples showed pink, and stiff. It was true that there was not so very much of her, but what there was he could not fail to see.

"So pretty," Max said, and touched the tip of his tongue to a nipple. "So very pretty." He drew the other into his mouth and the burning darts went their speedy way to her womb, and to the throbbing place between her thighs.

"Can you still float?" he asked, no doubt trying to sound nonchalant, but failing. "We used to float."

Keeping an arm around her shoulders, he brought up his legs and stretched out on his back.

"Oh, Max," Kirsty said, but try as she might, she couldn't look away. That Part of him was long and large and most interesting. "Oh, Max." She floated up onto her own back. "What are we t'do, then?"

"You think we have to do something?"

"Yes, I do."

"What would it be?"

"I canna lead t'way. And I canna say it."

"Then don't say anything, love. If you want it, I want to make love to you, right here in this river. It's clean, and we're clean, and it seems so right to me." He put a finger on her mouth, and said, "Our new beginning for the rest of our lives. Exactly what we wished for when you were sixteen. To stay as we are, and not allow the precious moments to be stolen from us. Just nod if you agree."

Her heart hammered so that she could hear it in her head and feel it pulse just beneath her skin.

She nodded.

Max closed his eyes and spun them both upright, upright and pressed close together. He took his time kissing her again, and again, and again. He kissed the hollows above her collarbones, and the shallow cleavage between her breasts, and stripped down the chemise until she could free her arms, and kissed her breasts in tantalizing circles that drew ever closer to her nipples.

Desire blossomed. It buzzed inside her, and demanded, and clamored.

But he was teaching her the ways of leisurely lovemaking. He made no sudden or rapid moves as he gradually took off her drawers and rubbed their bodies together.

His face grew strained and the veins in his neck distended, his teeth ground together and his lips drew back. Kirsty watched each tiny change in him with fascination and a deep awareness of her own growing need.

"D'ye like bairns?" she asked him, never having intended to ask any such thing.

His eyes opened and slowly focused. "Very much. I want lots of them myself."

"Lots?" She frowned. "Hmm. D'ye think a person o' very lowly birth could be a good wife to a man who's learned t'be the gentleman he was intended t'be?"

"I wonder," Max said, his smile so gentle it tore at her heart. He took hold of her legs and wrapped them around his waist. "I think such a person could, don't you. I think they'd make a team like no other team."

She felt suddenly quiet inside. "Ye drink too much, Max."

"Sometimes."

"It's no' an easy thing to stop."

"Not alone and angry. But with someone at your side who means everything to you, not so difficult. Have you seen me in a black humor when I've been with you, and I've been almost certain I could stay with you?"

"Ye've a terrible temper, Max Rossmara. I'll no' put up wi' a bad-tempered person. Not ever."

He kissed her mouth again. The Part of him that wanted to be inside her pressed into the folds where her thighs joined. She was beginning to open to him, and she hadn't the will or the desire to stop herself.

She must be herself, impetuous as that frequently might be. "I'm goin' t'be verra forward, and I'm goin' t'do it now. Ye may not want me then, but I'm goin' t'do it."

His breathing grew heavier and heavier and his eyes took on a glazed quality. He buried his face in her neck. Very deliberately he played the tips of his thumbs along her groin until she jumped, and brought his hardness pushing insistently against her.

"Max, I want ye t'listen t'me so we'll both know where we stand."

He groaned against her throat, and bowed to draw a nipple into his mouth again.

She could scarcely think at all.

His long fingers surrounded her bottom and ran down the cleft and beneath her. He took hold of himself and rubbed it against her until her need screamed in her and she writhed.

With his very tip he stroked the hot little place that rendered her helpless in his arms. Harder and harder he stroked until the burning explosion of sensation flowered and made her a limp thing at his mercy. She felt open wide to him and was glad.

He didn't come into her.

Kirsty shook her head and looked at him. "It's amazing," she said, and he smiled a little. "I want to do it for ye. To make ye feel as ye've made me feel. If I've t'catch up and keep accounts straight between us, I'd best get started."

Max laughed, and was transformed back to the very young man she'd known. "You will get started soon enough. Ask your forward question before I expire from the want of you."

She summoned her courage and said, "Ye asked me if I'd go away wi' ye. Ye spoke o' marriage, but I said I wouldna do it."

"I did ask. And, yes, you refused me."

"Now I'm askin ye." She must say it quickly or lose her nerve and the opportunity might never return. "Would ye consider comin' away wi' me and marryin' me? I'll understand if ye canna say yes, but I wanted t'ask because I love ye, Max Rossmara. I'll always love ye."

His eyes closed. He wrapped her tightly in his arms. So tightly she dug her fingertips into the hard muscles in his shoulders.

And he drove into her.

Kirsty cried out. It wasn't a terrible pain, just an unexpected one.

"Hush," he said against her lips. "Hush, hush, my love. It will fade soon enough."

He told the truth, except that when he started to move

within her she felt her passage stretching, but she also felt triumph. She had never wanted another man.

Faster and faster he moved, and he raised his face to the sky, and bellowed, and all strain drained from his face. She felt warmth fill her and it soothed the sore skin. And she knew it was his seed entering her body. She reveled in the knowledge.

Shudders racked him, and when they faded he turned onto his back again and pulled her on top of him. Holding her with one arm, he kept them afloat with the other.

"That does it," Max said. "No choice now."

"What d'ye mean?" she asked, kissing his wet chest, then reaching to cover his lips with her own.

"I'll come away with you," Max said. "And marry you."

She raised her face and looked at him. "Out o' duty?"

"Because we've proven the heart knows best. So much better than any conventions we think we should follow. And because I love you. I've loved you for so long, and I'm going to love you forever."

Epilogue

"Dashed high-handed if you ask me," Struan said, shading his eyes against the sun to scan the hills in all directions. The breeze whipped his hair across his brow. "Gone almost two weeks without so much as a by-your-leave, then instructions to await his pleasure as if he was sendin' out invitations to a ball. Needs taking down a peg or two."

"Fiddle," his wife, Lady Justine, said, standing almost as tall as her husband. Her hair was wavy and held similar red highlights to those in the hair of her brother Calum, Duke of Franchot.

"Fiddle?" Struan said. "Surely I misheard you."

The company that had descended the hillside from the castle chuckled, and Struan was too good-natured not to join in. "Nevertheless, his behavior just isn't on, and I intend to tell him so." He flapped open a note and looked around at his audience: Calum and his dark-haired wife, Pippa, Arran with tiny, fair-haired Grace at his side, the dowager and Blanche and, of course, the absolutely beautiful, doe-eyed, golden skinned Ella, her youngest babe in her arms and warmly swaddled against the morning chill. Ella's handsome devil of a husband was at her side. Saber, Viscount Avenall, bore vicious battle scars, but was still so handsome no woman could ever keep her eyes off him.

The family looked back at Struan and movement, a number of movements, caught his eye from above, in the direction from which they'd come. "Drat," he muttered. "Have you no control over your household, Arran?"

His brother glanced over his shoulder, and grinned. "And have you no control over yours? Or, more precisely, have you no control over your tongue? Possibly if you hadn't ranted all the way from the lodge to the castle when you got that note from Max, the staff wouldn't know there was to be an unfolding drama on this hill this morning. And they wouldn't be attempting to catch a glimpse of the proceedings. You can hardly blame them for their curiosity."

"Damnable circus," Struan said, glowering at the straggle of household staff that could be seen hovering in the distance.

"Language," came the expected chorus from his male relatives.

"You should probably have been harder on Max when he was a child," Calum said, wincing when Pippa's elbow met his ribs. "What d'you say, Arran?"

"He'd best not say anything," Grace announced. "We have a most loyal staff, and they are hoping to witness a happy reunion."

"I never thought I'd see a daughter of mine married to a man who would allow her to henpeck him," Blanche Bastible announced. She was especially magnificent in a pink-and-white-striped silk dress. "Stand up to her, son-in-law, do."

"Mind your own business, Blanche," the dowager said shortly. She had refused to remain in the carriage in which she and Blanche had been brought from the castle.

"Quite," Blanche agreed with no sign of ill feeling. "But I am concerned for your health, Your Grace. It is far too early for *any* of us to be abroad, and quite chill, I might add. Why, I shouldn't be surprised if you became ill."

Leaning her slight weight on her cane, the dowager stood her ground. "I have an excellent constitution, thank you, and no time for becoming ill from a little fresh morning air. If you feel a swoon coming upon you do return to the carriage. Are you sure you have the right day, Struan? The right morning?"

"This is the appointed morning," Struan said, although he began to feel anxious. He longed to see Max's face, and to hear his voice. Dammit but the boy had come to mean so much to him.

"He'll come," Justine told him softly. "Have faith in our son, my love."

Struan stared into her eyes and drew her into his arms. "I have faith in him," he said, kissing her cheek. "How could I not when you have so much faith in him?"

Ella held her baby on her shoulder and grinned. When she grinned one saw the familial resemblance to her brother. Saber looked upon her with open adoration, just as he had ever since he'd given in and accepted that she loved him with or without scars on his face.

Max's almost curt summons had arrived a week previous—with no return address—requesting that his family meet him today, "beneath the skies where Kirsty and I are most comfortable." Struan had been inclined to keep the reunion intimate, but the dowager insisted that all adult members of the family be present. She had alluded to some premonition "in ancient and wise bones that herald a moment that should be suitably marked." Accordingly the children of each union had been left in reliable care while the parents traveled to Scotland.

The smile on Ella's lips wavered. With the slightest inclination of her head she indicated for Struan to turn around. He did so, and saw three figures climbing the hill. Apart from a brief and difficult exchange with Robert and Gael Mercer, he had not spoken with them since the absence of Max and Kirsty had been discovered.

Robert Mercer held his red-haired wife's hand and approached with a firm step. Niall strode at his mother's other side, his face serious but not so serious it extinguished hope from his eyes. This was, Struan thought, a wild one, but a brother who adored his sister.

"Mr. and Mrs. Mercer," the dowager said in ringing tones when they arrived. "You are to remember that your daughter is by no means at fault here. Max is some years older and very persuasive. I'm certain poor Kirsty was defenseless against his sweet words. She is a wonderful girl, a girl I respect and count among those I would trust. And *that*, my dear people, is a *very* small number. That rascal Max simply swept her off her feet. But we must put all that behind us and get them married as soon as possible."

Robert frowned. "If ye say so, my lady. But Gael and mysel' ha' somethin' that needs sayin'. We've been wrong. Wrong to our daughter, and wrong t'Max. In the name o' old notions about the rich and the poor and how they canna exist together as the poor exist wi' the poor, or the rich wi' the rich, we made our girl suffer. And we insulted Max Ross-mara, one o' the finest men I know, and a man I had the honor o' watchin' grow from a braw boy into that fine man. I'll be grateful to be able t'tell him as much."

Amid much clearing of throats and sniffs from all sides, Struan tried to compose himself. Now a line of men and women made their way uphill from the valley. He recognized every face. There were those who worked the land, and those who were villagers. "How does word spread so," he said through his teeth. "Look at them all."

"Happiness pulls them," Justine said, "the promise of happiness. There's enough of the other readily to hand. Let them all come."

"Indeed," the dowager agreed. "Let them all come, and you and I shall put our heads together, Mrs. Mercer, to make sure there is enough merriment to cheer all."

"Aye," Gael Mercer said with one of her shy smiles, "we could do that all right. If those two ever come."

"They aren't late, Gael," Robert said, and Niall put an arm around his mother's shoulders.

Justine's sharp elbow applied to his ribs stole Struan's breath, and he looked into her face, perplexed.

"Say somethin'," she whispered. "Robert has grace and diplomacy. Have you any less?"

"Oh," he said. "Oh, yes. Robert and Gael. Whatever your sin in what was almost a disaster, mine was far greater. I tried to foist a dreadful woman on my son because I thought family pride required it. And I didn't make sure she was who she said she was. Your daughter will be a greater asset to us all than any other could have been, and I thank you for your patience, and your kindness and generosity in dealing with us."

"Oh, no," Gael said. "It was far more our—"

"You were all noddy polls," the dowager said bluntly. "Now save your apologies for your children. Of course, as the matriarch here, I graciously accept all of your apologies."

A titter passed through the swelling crowd, a titter instantly quelled by the old lady's sweeping and haughty glance. She surveyed the half circle, then raised her face to the horizon above. "Our horseman," she said, and they all turned to see the big man on the big horse, a dark presence against a pale blue sky touched by a soft sun.

"He saved us," Niall said in strangled tones.

"So we understand," Struan said. "But then, if rumor is to be believed, he kidnapped Kirsty. We'd best hunt the bas— hunt him down, Arran, Calum."

"Later," Calum said. "He presents no threat as long as we are all gathered together here."

"But—"

"It will wait," Arran said, placing a restraining hand on Struan's arm. "I do believe you would do almost anything to be away from here. But you won't be able to evade what must be accomplished with your son. Healing."

Struan scowled at him, but didn't argue.

"We dinna think that's your kidnapper," Robert said. "But we'd not press our opinions, o'course."

"We do thank ye all for your kind words about our Kirsty," Gael said. "We'd want to have a feast in the couple's honor. Isn't that right, Robert?"

"Right," he said with the look of a man who longed simply to fly away.

"This is what Max's damnably rude letter says," Struan announced. " 'Kirsty and I felt it necessary to get away after our very trying times recently. We are both feeling well rested and are ready to return to Kirkcaldy. I am anxious to take up my duties again. If Arran will still have me.' "

" 'Course I'll have him," Arran said. "Damn place is falling apart without him."

"Hush," Grace said. "Don't interrupt."

"Henpecked," Blanche murmured.

Struan rattled the paper. " 'We expect to arrive on the morning of the twenty-seventh, quite early—say around ten—and should like to meet with as many members of the family as can be present on the hill we all know, the one we take between the castle and the valley, beneath the skies where Kirsty and I are most comfortable. We long for those skies and those hills. Your respectful son, Max.' " Struan folded the note. "*Respectful.* Sneaking away while we were all too exhausted to notice. *And* taking an innocent girl with him even though he knew he put her reputation in grave jeopardy."

"Max wouldn't take advantage of Kirsty," Ella said. "He loves her."

"Hmph," the dowager said. "Mrs. Mercer, we would very much like to have a celebration of the nuptials at the castle. Isn't that right, Struan and Arran?"

"Quite true," Arran said. "But I'm sure the Mercers will want to do what we all like to do for our daughters. And we'll be delighted to take part in your celebrations."

"The first thing is the license," Struan said. "Not a problem, though. I'll give a significant donation to the Bishop in Edinburgh, and he'll make sure we get it at once. With the right incentives he'll be more than happy to perform the ceremony, too."

"Lovely," Grace said. "Justine should see to the decorations. She's so good at them."

"Oh, yes," Pippa agreed, her beautiful dark blue eyes softly joyful. Struan always thought that she was the most perfect duchess he'd ever seen. She continued, "Justine should also sew the dress. If you'd like to, that is."

"You know I would," Justine said. "I have few talents, but that is one of them."

"Very few talents," the dowager said of her granddaughter, producing another joint family chuckle which rendered her silent and pinched. The Dowager Duchess of Franchot had always been convinced that Justine was a weakling, to be protected from almost everything. Certainly no extra burden should be placed upon her.

"And I shall paint them a wedding portrait," Grace said.

Arran pulled her to him. "I'm sure they'll be honored to own one of your pieces, dear." He met his brother's eyes with a look that clearly said he dreaded a wedding portrait in Grace's representational style complete with no clothes— or should that be, incomplete with no clothes?

"All the invitations have already been made out and are ready for dispatch," the dowager announced. "Dear Blanche did that—with Mrs. Mercer's assistance on the list of course," she said, and Struan promised himself he would kiss the old lady later for being so diplomatic.

Pippa, Duchess of Franchot, pointed, and said, "I see them coming."

At that the company fell silent.

Rather than on horseback, Max and Kirsty came across the grassy slope on foot. As they drew closer Struan was aware of a restrained murmur in the assembled crowd and he studied them, turning to see first one, then another group, and he knew that such a gathering had never been seen here before. People from every walk of life standing together beneath the sky Max and Kirsty so loved and standing with no sign of the separations of rank and privilege. Even those from the lodge and the castle had gradually moved downward to join the others.

"They're such a handsome couple," Ella said, jiggling her baby. "Aren't they, Saber?"

"Yes," he said. "And so in love. They would do anything to be together, and that's how it has to be if marriage is to survive and flourish."

"Aye," Gael said quietly. "They'll do anything for that. We should never ha' stood in their way."

"No," Robert said.

"And they'll make their own wishes known where a weddin's concerned," Gael continued. "Although I'm sure the chapel would be verra nice if that's what they want."

"Well," the dowager began, but subsided beneath Arran's hard stare.

Grace clapped her hands, and said, "They're here. Oh, I can hardly wait to tell them our plans."

Ella said, "I can hardly wait to embrace them."

Max and Kirsty arrived, side by side. Max wore his customary somber suit of dark cloth and, as usual, his hair was whipped into unruly curls. His arresting companion's simple, white muslin dress had narrow lace at the neck, the cuffs and the edges of the tiered skirt. As they arrived before their parents, she grew visibly more shy and held Max's hand in both of hers. Somewhere along the way she must have stopped to pick wildflowers and tuck them into her hair, which was caught up into a big, softly braided chignon.

Ella rushed to place baby Nigel in her brother's arms.

"Beautiful," Max said, kissing the tiny face. "Of course he's beautiful. But what are you doing here so soon after his birth?"

"I'm as healthy as a horse," Ella said. "And I wouldn't miss your homecoming after we've all been so worried about you. And Kirsty, dear Kirsty. Where have you been? Where were you last night?"

"At the inn in the village," Max said. "We've walked a long time this morning. Thinking, and planning."

Struan considered and instantly discarded the idea of chastising his son for disappearing as he had and taking a young woman to whom he was not married—or even officially engaged—with him. The atmosphere was positively convivial, no point in dampening that. "Welcome home, son," he said.

Max surprised him by enveloping him in a bear hug, and

saying, "Bless you, Father. I've wanted your approval, and you've always given it to me. Hello, Mother, and all of you. Quite the gathering of the clans."

"This family clan always gathers for important occasions, my boy. You know that."

"We're going to have a celebration here and invite the entire neighborhood," the dowager said. "Aren't we, Grace?"

"If that's what Max and Kirsty want."

"Quite so," the dowager agreed, somewhat testily. "And Mr. and Mrs. Mercer insist they want to have a, er, wedding feast, also."

"Such fun," Blanche cried, clapping her hands. "Let's set the date and make it soon or I shall die of anticipation."

Kirsty's attention was on her family. She took a hesitant step toward them, and her mother held out her arms. While everyone else pretended to be engrossed in other things, the little Mercer family reunited with quietly poignant emotion.

"You were kidnapped, Kirsty," Ella said, concern in her eyes. Ella had endured her share of violence against her person. "By someone known as the lone horseman. He's up there on the top of the hill, watching."

Kirsty frowned. She looked toward the rider and waved. And he waved back. "Not him. It was Horace pretending to be him. He told me."

Ella looked blank, and said, "Oh."

"He just sits up there," Niall said, his voice sounding rusty from his long silence. "As if he needs to see all's well. He did us all a service, didn't he, Max?"

Struan didn't fail to notice the conciliatory note in the young man's voice.

Max looked steadily at Niall, and said, "He most certainly did. I think he saved both of our lives, don't you?"

Niall kept his gaze steady, and said, "Yes. My father encountered him and thanked him. He said he didna want thanks. He was payin' back a debt to Viscount Avenall and his wife."

"Ella and Saber?" Pippa said.

Saber rested a hand on Ella's neck. "I think I know who that would be, dearest."

She looked up at him. "I didn't think he would ever return to these parts."

"He's Devlin North," Robert Mercer said. "The gentleman who caused so much trouble to Miss Ella—Viscountess Avenall, that is. But he'll be away again soon."

Struan didn't fail to note the sad expression in Ella's eyes, or Saber's faraway look, but those days were behind them.

"We thought the castle chapel," Justine said. "I would do the decorations. Also your dress, Kirsty, if that would please you."

Kirsty smiled but made no comment. She looked to her parents, and they exchanged more shy smiles. There was a deal of building to do there, but they'd made a start.

"And we rather like the idea of a really grand affair," Grace said. "The marriage, then the wedding breakfast, games in the afternoon, a ball in the evening. And Arran's going to arrange for the Bishop to come from Edinburgh to perform the ceremony. I took the liberty of sending him a little note myself, since we have a long acquaintance."

If Arran was irritated at the interference, he covered it well.

"Actually," the dowager said. "I also took the liberty of setting the date. Only because the bishop is such a busy man of course. Next Friday. The fourth. Pure coincidence, of course, but it also happens to be my birthday."

"And how old will you be?" came the chorus.

The old lady smiled her secret smile, and said, "Very old."

Struan saw Kirsty nudge Max, saw their eyes meet, and how they became lost in each other. "Yes," Max said abruptly. "You are all so kind, and so well meaning. But we have decided that this is an occasion for building. It's an occasion for putting aside old ways, old separations. We had intended to marry in Edinburgh, but Kirsty—" here he paused and smiled at her "—she believes that we can be a sign of building a bridge over the separation between laird and those who work for him. We can respectfully acknowledge the pattern of things. Each of us takes his or her part for the good of the whole—the good of all. But none of this means the lines can't be crossed."

Silence fell and seemed to last a very long time. The scent of flowers floated on the wind and the sun grew a little warmer. Rattling uphill came a small, black carriage pulled by a pair, but no one seemed inclined to take more than passing interest in the vehicle.

"These changes aren't easily made," Max said. "Kirsty and I know this. But this estate has prospered because of, not despite, the respect we hold for each other here."

Arran nodded. "You will hear no argument from me on that subject."

"We owe you an apology, Max," Struan began.

"Not *now* noddy poll," the dowager said, her small face severe. "Later you shall give all the many necessary apologies—as will the Mercers, no doubt, and anyone else guilty of poor judgment. For now, could we get on with the matter in hand?"

Max put his arms around Kirsty and smiled broadly. "We'll do that. But I'll be looking forward to the apologies."

Struan couldn't contain his own grin, and he said, "Insolent cur."

Toiling up from the carriage came the Reverend Pottinger, and behind him a small boy in a white surplice who carried a large Bible. Last to join the group was the village greengrocer's son, pipes in hand. He wore a kilt and sporran, a dark green velvet jacket, and a great deal of cascading white lace. A bright feather adorned his bonnet.

"What's this?" Struan asked.

"I suggest you hold your tongue," Justine said. "Just enjoy whatever comes."

Puffing, red-faced, Pottinger confronted the congregation. He produced a stole and draped it about his neck before spreading his arms. In a sonorous voice he announced, "It is with happy hearts that we are gathered here to witness the joining of this man to this woman."

Several gleeful cheers went up, but were quickly stifled.

"Wait!" Gathering daisies and small orange poppies, yellow tansy and purple speedwell as she went, Mairi arrived beside Kirsty and thrust the bouquet into her hands. Then she stood aside, the self-appointed attendant.

The vows were clearly spoken, declarations of the love of two people, a love that had grown from childhood, and promised to continue throughout their shared lives.

Closer and closer together drew the assembly until peasant and laird intermingled. When they prayed the prayers common to them all, the only difference was in the manner of their speech.

At last the couple faced their people and the Reverend Pottinger said, "I present to you, Mr. and Mrs. Max Rossmara. They want you to know that they have everything they ever wished for."

The pipes soared over the sound of clapping, and Gael Mercer's sweet, high voice sang, "*Wherever ye go, I shall go. Wherever ye dwell, there shall I dwell. Your people shall be my people . . .*" The pipes all but drowned out her voice before she sang, "*And our love will be the love of our lives.*"

My Dear Readers:

When you read one of my books, we—you and I—hang out together for a while. We become companions watching a story unfold, and my hope is always that you will care as much about my people as I do.

I want to share a few of the inside elements of storytelling that I take for granted if I don't stop and think about them. I want to share the thrill I get when I feel a story begin, the excitement that comes with treading the ground where the story takes place, and something of how these elements come together, how they came together for THE WISH CLUB (and the rest of the Rossmara stories) and for my next historical romance, MORE AND MORE.

I want to take you with me to Scotland, and then to London!

Max Rossmara and Kirsty Mercer met when Max was ten and Kirsty a little bit of a thing in pinafores.

Max was the newly adopted son of Struan, Viscount Rossmara and his wife, Lady Justine (who appear in my novel, BRIDE). Young Max was destined to enjoy good fortune to which he had not been born. Kirsty, the only daughter of tenant farmers Robert and Gael Mercer, was born in poverty and expected to live in poverty—but the happiness she found with her family was so great that she couldn't imagine needing more.

Max and Kirsty waited for me to take you on our dream flight to Scotland. They were the reason for it all. The idea for their story came to me during a trip to the twin towns of Dunkeld and Birnam.

I stayed in Birnam with my son and the younger of our two daughters, and they went patiently with me as I wandered the banks of the River Tay, and tramped through Birnam Wood of Shakespeare's *Macbeth* fame. Somewhere along the way I met Arran Rossmara, Marquis of Stonehaven (who first appeared in FASCINATION), and his friend Calum (from CHARMED), and looked to the hills, to the place where Kirkcaldy Castle stood in the mists of imagination.

Scotland is a magnificent country, bold of line, windswept across its crags and heaths, yet coyly soft in its gentle valleys, and with beauty enough along its grass-fringed rivers to clog the throat and film the eye with tears. Too much. Sometimes so much is too much. When the smooth, emerald green River Tay reflected scudding clouds and bending sycamores in its polished surface, I could scarce breathe for love of so much mystery.

A conspiracy, I thought. That place conspired to snare and keep me, and I was a ready captive. My children were captives despite themselves. Although their recollections are not always mine, they smile at the mention of those days in Scotland. My task and my pleasure were to take you there also, and that's why I wrote about the Rossmaras, about Max's sister, Ella (from my novel BELOVED), and eventually about Max and Kirsty in THE WISH CLUB.

I built Castle Kirkcaldy. A tower here, a salon there, a kitchen garden, a stable, a wheel staircase, a hunting lodge, studies and libraries, and boudoirs and music rooms, a great hall, a porter's room, a butler's pantry, and on, and on. I swiped bits and pieces of great old castles and houses and designed Kirkcaldy and its lands.

I went to lovely Dalmeny House, where a Rothschild daughter brought her fabulous inheritance of furnishings that had once belonged to the Dauphins, and to Napoleon and his Josephine. From that house I borrowed a wealth of sets fit for the finest of theatre stages. Oh, there may have been some pieces from English Athelhampton House and Wilton House—and I'm certain a little of Hidcote Gardens in the Cotswolds transplanted roots to those northern hills, but for you and me, Kirkcaldy is all Scottish.

I almost forgot. Despite the assurances of a woman in the Edinburgh bus station—"Och, Dalmeny's a wee bus ride out of Edinburgh. The driver will tell ye when ye're there. Ye canna miss it"—

Dalmeny House isn't easy to find. The bus driver set us down on a deserted corner at the crossroads of four seemingly endless hedge-lined roads. A cattle grill across one road suggested that in that direction there was something to be kept in. Then, behind pretty rose trellises, we saw a gate house. We didn't see a living soul, but we were brave and set off along the way. After all, if we walked so long that darkness began to fall, we would simply retrace our steps and hope . . . well, we'd hope, that's all.

After two miles, a herd of cows, and a field of sheep from the crossroads, we came to an opening in tall, clipped laurel, and found Dalmeny. Once inside I forgot my fear of cows! I would walk those uncertain miles again and again to catch a glimpse of that deep blue Sèvres china and a bed that had once belonged to Napoleon. My children are more fond of the memory of fruity Dundee cake and cups of milky tea taken on a terrace where cheeky peacocks wandered, eyeing succulent crumbs.

THE WISH CLUB is the book I never intended to write, the fifth story in what was to have been, and was dubbed, THE ROSSMARA QUARTET! But THE WISH CLUB *had* to be written. Although each book is a complete story to be enjoyed without needing to read the others, I couldn't countenance not knowing all about Max and Kirsty. And I couldn't bear thinking that you might wonder in vain about them, too.

Now I'm getting ready to share some new friends with you.

The story of MORE AND MORE was one of

those surprises that are the very best, the kind you don't realize has happened until *after* they have. Then you frown a little. Then you shake your head. And, finally, you grin and get one of those "Aha" feelings.

I was passing through London on my way to the West Country, where I was born. Rather than travel on directly as I had planned, I decided to spend a few days in London just walking through some areas that used to be very familiar to me when I lived there. I called my friends Sue and Bar at Beehive Manor in Maidenhead and arranged to stay in one of their lovely old rooms, then set off on my first stolen day to rediscover Mayfair.

The best way to see any city is on foot, and London is a gem where there are areas filled with unexpected twists and turns that would be missed if you drove. Mayfair is one of those areas, and I wandered from the wider streets into small groves and terraces where tall, narrow houses jostle companionably side by side.

And then I found Mayfair Square.

On four sides elegant houses faced a central garden where tulips and daffodils were in bloom and nannies sat talking together while their small charges played on the grass.

I set off for a quick walk around the square before going in search of a pub lunch—until I saw that Number Seven, a gracious, four-story house built of white stone, the brass knocker gleaming on its shiny black door, displayed a discreet sign declaring it "Open to the Public on Monday." My instant thought was that it wasn't Monday, but as I stood at the bottom of the smooth marble steps, the door opened and an old gentleman studied me. He didn't smile. In fact he drew his impressive white brows together with a ferocious snap and said, "Come in or go away. Don't just stand there."

I've tried to recall what I said, but I can't. In fact I'm almost certain I didn't say anything at all before he added, "You saw the sign. Only open on Monday. It won't do you any good to come back tomorrow."

So I went in.

What a house. What an absolutely fabulous house. Its proportions were perfect, the ceilings high, the rooms beautifully furnished in a manner that would have caught the eye of even that Rothschild heiress at Dalmeny. The windows were tall, too, with fringed velvet draperies caught back from diaphanous panels that shut out prying eyes, but not all of the light.

"More," the old man said from behind me.

"Oh," I said. I'd forgotten he was there. "I'm sorry?"

"More," he repeated, his hands behind his back.

Confused, I opened my bag and took out my wallet. "Actually, I haven't paid at all," I told him.

He shook his head. "No, no, no. More was the name of the people who lived here for a while. Finch and Latimer More. Brother and sister. He was an importer. The eastern pieces were left by them."

"When was that?"

7

He shrugged. "I'm getting too old for this sort of thing. If I didn't feel a responsibility to watch over things, I'd . . . I'd rest on my laurels."

What was I supposed to say to a comment like that? I just nodded and smiled politely.

"They only had this floor," the man continued and sniffed. "Imagine the place being *rented* to *lodgers*." He shuddered.

I gave another polite smile.

"Broken up into *flats*. The Mores were on this floor. Sibyl and Meg Smiles lived up a flight, and Adam Chillworth was above them. Come on, come on. I don't have all day."

I followed him back into the generous hall to the base of a staircase I shall never forget. Wide, rising from the center of the hall, the oak balusters and curving banisters were encrusted with intricate carvings of people and animals, of birds and fish, and flowers and leaves. I had never seen such a staircase before, nor have I seen another since.

"Hurry up," my guide snapped.

Looking up at him as he climbed the stairs, I realized how very bent he was and that his clothing was of fine quality but old-fashioned. Caught by a strap beneath the insteps of his shoes, his trousers clung tight to his spindly legs, and he wore both a high winged collar and a tailed coat. I decided he must be dressed as a butler to act as guide to tour groups.

"The Smiles sisters were orphans," he said, showing me through another floor of lovely rooms. "Genteel, of course, or they would never have been allowed to stay at all. But they did earn a living teaching young ladies . . . well, that's neither here nor there."

"When was this?" I ventured.

His hair was splendid. Snow white, but thick and brushed back in deep waves from a finely boned face. "Let me see," he said. "Must have been in the twenties. Perhaps the early thirties. Even the best of memories—and mine is extraordinary—even the best of memories will eliminate unimportant details."

I didn't press the subject but I did find the courage to inquire, "Would you mind telling me your name?"

"Why?" He was on his way up another flight of stairs toward the third floor and stopped abruptly. "Why do you want to know?"

"I'm sorry." The apology was automatic.

"Spivey," he said. "Septimus Spivey."

"Well, Mr. Spivey," I said, "thank you so much for showing me around. This is an unexpected treat."

"Sir Septimus," he said.

"I beg your pardon?"

"I am Sir Septimus Spivey."

"Are you?" I said, and it was hard not to grin. "I'm honored to meet you."

He didn't ask my name. "Quite You would be honored. Just make sure you get it all straight."

"Get it straight?"

"It's late," he said, although it wasn't. "Never overstay your welcome."

I looked significantly upward.

"You'll have to use your imagination for the rest," he said, following my gaze. "That's why I chose you."

There was no opportunity to question him anymore. With spry steps he passed me and went down to the hall. I had no choice but to follow. He went directly to the front door and held it open.

Without another word, "Sir Septimus" showed me out.

The sound of conversation made me turn toward the street. A couple got out of a black Bentley and started up the steps. Then the woman saw me and stopped. The man with her sensed his companion's hesitation and also looked at me. "Good morning," he said. "Can we help you?"

For the first time in my life I felt like a trespasser caught in the act. But I remembered the sign and relaxed. "Monday," I said, tucking my purse under my arm. "Open day. Beautiful house."

The man was tall with dark hair and eyes. Handsome. The woman was also tall. Her red hair curved smoothly to her shoulders. They suited each other, and they suited Mayfair Square.

"I'm afraid I don't understand," the man said.

"Open . . ." I looked behind me at the front of the house. The sign was no longer there and I felt foolish. "Sir Septimus Spivey showed me." He'd probably taken the sign in.

The couple glanced at each other. "I'm Hugh Lloyd," the man said pleasantly. "This is my wife,

Nancy. We live here. This is Number Seven. I expect you've got the wrong address."

Embarrassment overwhelmed me. I rushed down the steps, mumbling apologies, my face glowing hot. "Sorry," I said before fleeing behind the Bentley and taking refuge in the park.

Seated on a bench with beds of waving flowers and iron railings separating me from the house I'd evidently had no right to enter, I took out my notebook and pen and made notes while my heart gradually slowed to a normal rate.

Sir Septimus Spivey I wrote, determined to go to a library as quickly as possible and find out if there was such a man. After all, titled people could always be traced.

"I was right." A voice, a thin, crackly voice said those words to me. I looked around but saw only the nannies and the children.

A gust of wind whipped gravel from the surface of the path and whirled it in eddies. "I was right." The voice spoke again, seeming to move about my head with another burst of wind.

I couldn't move. My legs felt numb, my hands glued to the pages of my notebook. "What do you mean?" I whispered.

A sigh? Or was that the wind again. No, I heard a long, long sigh before was I told, "This is how you will begin."

Once more I searched around, but I was alone.

"It's about Finch More, and Ross, Viscount Kilrood. He lived at Number Eight."

The house to the right of Number Seven was larger.

"But most important of all, you will begin by writing: 'I used to think I needed a body.' "

It's taken me longer than I planned to continue this letter. Remembering that morning and what followed unsettles me even now, even after the story is told. It's been an adventure I wouldn't have missed.

But I promised to take you with me and so I will, in MORE AND MORE.

May we always be dream travelers!

Stella Cameron